Deemed 'the father of the scienti
**Austin Freeman** had a long and d
a writer of detective fiction. He was born in London, the son of a
tailor who went on to train as a pharmacist. After graduating as
a surgeon at the Middlesex Hospital Medical College, Freeman
taught for a while and joined the colonial service, offering his skills
as an assistant surgeon along the Gold Coast of Africa. He became
embroiled in a diplomatic mission when a British expeditionary
party was sent to investigate the activities of the French. Through
his tact and formidable intelligence, a massacre was narrowly
avoided. His future was assured in the colonial service. However,
after becoming ill with blackwater fever, Freeman was sent back to
England to recover and, finding his finances precarious, embarked
on a career as acting physician in Holloway Prison. In desperation,
he turned to writing and went on to dominate the world of
British detective fiction, taking pride in testing different criminal
techniques. So keen were his powers as a writer that part of one of
his best novels was written in a bomb shelter.

# Dr Thorndyke Intervenes

R Austin Freeman

This edition published in 2001 by House of Stratus, an imprint of
Stratus Books Ltd., 21 Beeching Park, Kelly Bray,
Cornwall, PL17 8QS, UK.

www.houseofstratus.com

Typeset, printed and bound by House of Stratus.

A catalogue record for this book is available from the British Library
and the Library of Congress.

ISBN 0-7551-0351-3

# CONTENTS

# CHAPTER ONE

## Of a Strange Treasure Trove and a Double Life

The attendant at the cloakroom at Fenchurch Street Station glanced at the ticket which had just been handed to him by a tall, hawk-faced and rather anxious-looking man, and ran an inquiring eye over the assemblage of trunks, bags and other objects that crowded the floor of the room.

"Wooden, iron-bound case, you said?" he remarked.

"Yes. Name of Dobson on the label. That looks like the one," he added, craning over the barrier and watching eagerly as the attendant threaded his way among the litter of packages.

"Dobson it is," the man confirmed, stooping over the case, and, with an obviously puzzled expression, comparing the ticket that had been pasted on it with the counterfoil which he held in his hand. "Rum affair, though," he added. "It seems to be your case but it has got the wrong number on it. Will you come in and have a look at it and see that it is all right?"

The presumptive owner offered no objection. On the contrary, he raised the bar of the barrier with the greatest alacrity and took the shortest route among the trunks and portmanteaux until he arrived at the place where the case was standing. And then his expression became even more puzzled than that of the attendant.

"This is very extraordinary," he exclaimed.

"What is?" demanded the attendant.

"Why!"the other explained,"it is the right name and the same sort of case; but this is not the label that I wrote and I don't believe that it is the same case."

The attendant regarded him with a surprised grin and again remarked that "it was a rum affair," adding, after a reflective pause: "It rather looks as if there had been some mistake, as there easily might be with two cases exactly alike and the same name on both. Were the contents of your case of any particular value?"

"They were, indeed!"the owner exclaimed in an agitated tone. "That case contained property worth several thousand pounds."

The attendant whistled and apparently began to see things in a new light, for he asked a little anxiously:

"When do you say you deposited the case?"

"Late on Saturday evening."

"Yes, I thought I remembered," said the attendant. "Then the muddle, if there has been one, must have happened yesterday. I wasn't here then. It was my Sunday off. But are you quite sure that this is really not your case?"

"It certainly is not the label that I wrote," was the reply. "But I won't swear that it is a different case; though I don't think that it is the right one. But you see, as the name on the label is my name and the address is my address, it can't be a matter of a simple mistake. It looks like a case of deliberate substitution. And that seems to be borne out by the fact that the change must have been made on a Sunday when the regular attendant was not here."

"Yes," the other agreed, "there's no denying that it does look a bit fishy. But look here, sir; if your name and address is on the label, you are entitled to assume that this is your case. As you say, it is either yours or it is a deliberate substitute, and, in either case, you have the right to open it and see if your property is inside. That will settle the question right away. I can lend you a screwdriver."

The presumptive owner caught eagerly at the suggestion, and began forthwith to untie the thick cord which surrounded the case. The screwdriver was produced, and, while the official turned away to attend to two other clients, it was plied vigorously on the eight long screws by which the lid of the case was secured.

The two newcomers, of whom one appeared to be an American and the other an Englishman, had come to claim a number of trunks and travelling-bags; and as some of these, especially those belonging to the American gentleman, were of imposing dimensions, the attendant prudently admitted them that they might identify their packages and so save unnecessary hauling about. While they were carrying out their search he returned to Mr Dobson and watched him as he extracted the last of the screws.

"Now we shall see whether there has been any jiggery pokery," he remarked, when the screw had been laid down with the others; and Mr Dobson prepared to raise the lid. And in fact they did see; and a very singular effect the sight had on them both. Mr Dobson sprang back with a gasp of horror and the attendant uttered the single word "Golly!"

After staring into the case incredulously for a couple of amazed seconds, Dobson slammed down the lid and demanded, breathlessly, "Where can I find a policeman?"

"You'll find one somewhere near the barrier or else just outside the station. Or you could get on the phone and – "

Mr Dobson did not wait to hear the conclusion of the sentence but darted out towards the barrier and disappeared in the direction of the main entrance. Meanwhile, the two strangers, who had apparently overheard Mr Dobson's question, abandoned for the time being the inspection of their luggage and approached the case, on which the attendant's eyes were still riveted.

"Anything amiss?" the Englishman asked.

The attendant made no reply but silently lifted the lid of the case, held it up for a moment or two and then let it drop.

"Good Lord!" exclaimed the Englishman, "it looks like a man's head!"

"It *is* a man's head," the attendant confirmed. And, in fact, there was no doubt about it, though only a hairy crown was visible, through a packing of clothes or rags.

"Who is the chappie who has just bolted out?" the Englishman enquired. "He seemed mightily taken aback."

"So would you have been," the attendant retorted, "if you had come to claim a package and found this in its place." He followed up this remark with a brief summary of the circumstances.

"Well!" observed the American, "I have heard it said that exchange is no robbery, but I guess that the party who made this exchange got the best of the deal."

The Englishman grinned. "You are right there, Mr Pippet," said he. "I've heard of a good many artful dodges for disposing of a superfluous corpse, but I have never heard of a murderer swapping it for a case of jewellery or bullion."

The three men stood silently looking at the case and occasionally glancing round in the direction of the entrance. Presently the American enquired:

"Is there any particular scarcity of policemen in this city?"

The attendant looked round again anxiously towards the entrance.

"He *is* a long time finding that policeman," said he in reply to the implied comment.

"Yes," rejoined Mr Pippet; "and I guess that policeman will be a long time finding him."

The attendant turned on him with a distinctly startled expression.

"You don't think he has done a bunk, do you?" he asked uneasily.

"Well," replied Pippet, "he didn't waste any time in getting outside, and he doesn't seem to have had much luck in what he went for. I reckon one of us had better have a try. You know the place better than I do, Buffham."

"Yes, sir, if you would," urged the attendant. "I can't leave the place myself. But I think we ought to have a constable as soon as possible, and it does rather look as if that gent had mizzled."

On this, Mr Buffham turned and rapidly made his way through the litter of trunks and packages and strode away towards the entrance, through which he vanished, while the attendant reluctantly tore himself away from the mysterious case to hand out one or two rugs and suitcases, and Mr Pippet resumed his salvage operations on his trunks and portmanteaux. In less than three minutes Mr Buffham was seen returning with a constable, and the attendant raised the barrier to admit them. Apparently, Mr Buffham had given the officer a general sketch of the circumstances as they had come along, for the latter remarked, as he eyed the case:

"So this is the box of mystery, is it? And you say that there is a person's head inside it?"

"You can see for yourself," said the attendant; and with this he raised the lid, and, having peered in, he looked at the constable, who, after an impassive and judicial survey, admitted that it did look like a man's head, and produced from his pocket a portentous, black note-book.

"The first question," said he, "is about this man who has absconded. Can you give me a description of him?"

The three men consulted and between them evolved a description which might have been illuminating to anyone who was intimately acquainted with the absent stranger, but furnished indifferent material for the identification of an unknown individual. They agreed, however, that he was somewhat tall and dark, with a thin face, a torpedo beard and moustache, and a rather prominent nose; that he was dressed in dark-coloured clothing and wore a soft felt hat. Mr Pippet further expressed the opinion that the man's hair and beard were dyed.

"Yes," said the constable, closing his note-book, "he seems to have been a good deal like other people. They usually are. That's the worst of it. If people who commit crimes would only be a bit more striking in their appearance and show a little originality in the way they dress, it would make things so much more simple for us. But it's a queer affair. The puzzle is what he came here for, and why, having come, he proceeded to do a bolt. He couldn't have known what was in the case, or he wouldn't have come. And, if the case wasn't his, I don't see why he should have hopped it and put himself under suspicion. I had better take your names and addresses, gentlemen, as you saw him, though you don't seem to have much to tell. Then I think I will get on the phone to headquarters."

He re-opened the note-book and, having taken down the names and addresses of the two gentlemen, went out in search of the telephone.

As he departed, Mr Pippet, apparently dismissing the mysterious case from his mind as an affair finished and done with, reverted to the practical business of sorting out his luggage, in which occupation he was presently joined by Mr Buffham.

"I am going to get a taxi," said the former, "to take me to my hotel – the Pendennis in Great Russell Street. Can I put you down anywhere? I see you're travelling pretty light."

Mr Buffham cast a deprecating eye on the modest portmanteau which contained his entire outfit and a questioning eye on the imposing array of trunks and bags which appertained to his companion, and reflected for a moment.

"The taxi-man will jib at your lot," said he, "without adding mine to it."

"Yes," agreed Pippet, "I shall have to get two taxis in any case, so one of them can't complain of an extra package. Where are you putting up?"

"I am staying for a few days at a boarding-house in Woburn Place; not so very far from you. But I was thinking that, when we have disposed of our traps, you might come and have some dinner with me at a restaurant that I know of. What do you say?"

"Why, the fact is," said Pippet, "that I was just about to make the very same proposal, only I was going to suggest that we dine together at my hotel. And, if you don't mind, I think it will be the better plan, as I have got a suite of rooms that we can retire to after dinner for a quiet yarn. Do you mind?"

Mr Buffham did not mind. On the contrary, he accepted with something approaching eagerness. For his own reasons, he had resolved to cultivate the not very intimate acquaintanceship which had been established during the voyage from New York to Tilbury, and he was better pleased to do so at Mr Pippet's expense than at his own; and the mention of the suite of rooms had strongly confirmed him in his resolution. A man who chartered a suite of rooms at a London hotel must be something more than substantial. But Mr Pippet's next observation gave him less satisfaction.

"You are wondering, I suppose, what a solitary male like me can want with a suite of rooms all to himself. The explanation is that I am not all by myself. I am expecting my daughter and sister over from Paris tomorrow, and I can't have them hanging about in the public rooms with no corner to call their own. But, until they arrive, I am what they call *en garçon* over there."

Having thus made clear his position, Mr Pippet went forth and shortly returned accompanied by two taxi-men of dour aspect and taciturn habit, who silently collected the baggage and bore it out to their respective vehicles, which, in due course, set forth upon their journey.

Before following them, we may linger awhile to note the results of the constable's mission. They were not very sensational. In the course of a few minutes, an inspector arrived, and, having made a brief confirmatory inspection, called for the screws and the screwdriver and proceeded in an impassive but workmanlike manner to replace the former in their holes and drive them home. Then he, in his turn, sent out for a taxi-man, by whom the case with its gruesome contents was borne out unsuspectingly to the waiting vehicle and spirited away to an unknown destination.

When Mr Buffham's solitary portmanteau had been dumped down in the hall of a somewhat seedy house in Woburn Place, the two taxis moved on to the portals of the quiet but select hotel in Great Russell Street, where the mountainous pile of baggage was handed over to the hotel porter with brief directions as to its disposal. Then the two men, after the necessary ablutions, made their way to the dining-room and selected a table in a comparatively retired corner, where Mr Buffham waited in some anxiety as to the quality of the entertainment. His experience of middle-aged American men had given him the impression that they were not, as a class, enthusiastic feeders, and it was with sensible relief that he discovered in his host the capacity to take a reasonable interest in his food. In fact, the gastronomic arrangements were so much to his satisfaction that, for a time, they engaged his entire attention; for, if the whole truth must be told, this dinner was not an entirely unforeseen contingency, and, as he had providently modified his diet with that possibility in view, he was now in a condition to do complete justice to the excellent fare provided. Presently, however, when the razor-edge had been taken off his appetite, his attention reverted to larger interests and he began cautiously to throw out feelers. Not that an extreme amount of caution was really necessary, for Mr Pippet was a simple, straightforward, open-minded man; shrewd enough in the ordinary business of life and gifted with a massive common sense. But he was quite devoid of cunning, and trustful of his fellow-creatures to an extent that is somewhat unusual in citizens of the United States. He was, in fact, the exact opposite in mental and moral type of the man who faced him across the table.

"Well!" said Buffham, raising his newly-refilled glass, "here's to a successful beano. I suppose you contemplate laying a delicate wash of carmine over the British landscape. Or is it to be a full tint of ver-milion?"

"Now you are talking in tropes and metaphors," said Pippet, with an indulgent smile, "but, as I interpret the idiom, you think we are going to make things hum."

"I assume that you are over here to have a good time."

"We always like to have a good time if we can manage it, wherever we may be," said Pippet, "and I hope to pass the time pleasantly while I am in the Old Country. But I have come over with a more definite purpose than that; and, if I should tell you what that purpose is, I should make you smile."

"And a very pleasant result, too," said Buffham. "I like to be made to smile. But, of course, I don't want to pry into your private affairs, even for the sake of a smile."

"My private affairs will probably soon be public affairs," said Pippet, "so I need not maintain any particular reticence about them; and, in any case, there's nothing to be ashamed or secret about. If it interests you to know, my visit to England is connected with a claim to an English title and the estates that go with it."

Buffham was thunderstruck. But he did not smile. The affair was much too serious for that. Instead, he demanded in a hushed voice: "Do you mean that you are making a claim on your own behalf?"

Mr Pippet chuckled. "Sounds incredible, doesn't it? But that is the cold-drawn fact. I am setting up a claim to the Earldom of Winsborough and to the lands and other property that appertain to it, all of which I understand to be at present vacant and calling aloud for an owner."

Mr Buffham pulled himself together. This looked like a good deal bigger affair than he had anticipated. Indeed, he had not anticipated anything in particular. His professional habits – if we may so designate them – led him to cultivate the society of rich men of all kinds, and by preference that of wealthy Americans making a European tour. Not that the globe-trotting American is a peculiarly simple and trustful soul. But he is in a holiday mood; he is in unaccustomed surroundings and usually has money to spend and a strong inclination to spend it. Mr Buffham's rôle was to foster that inclination, and, as far as possible, to collaborate in the associated activities. He had proposed to fasten upon Mr Pippet, if he could, in a Micawber-like hope that something profitable might turn up. But the prospect opened up by Mr Pippet's announcement was beyond his wildest dreams.

"I suppose," Mr Pippet continued after a brief pause, "you are wondering what in creation a middle-aged American in comfortable circumstances wants with an English title and estates?"

"I am not wondering anything of the kind," replied Buffham. "The position of a great English nobleman is one that might well tempt the ambition of an American if he were twenty times a millionaire. Think of the august dignity of that position! Of the universal deference that it commands! Think of the grand old mansions and the parks planted with immemorial trees, the great town house and the seat in the House of Lords, and – and – "

"Yes, I know," chuckled Pippet, "I've had all that rubbed into me, and, to tell the bald truth, I wouldn't give a damn for the whole boiling if I had only myself to consider. I don't want to have people calling me 'My Lord' and making me feel like a fool; and I've no use for baronial mansions or ancestral halls. A good comfortable hotel where they know how to cook answers all my requirements. But I've got to go in for this business whether I like it or not. My womenfolk have got me fairly in tow, especially my sister. She's just mad to be Lady Arminella – in fact, if I hadn't put my foot down she'd have settled the matter in advance and taken the title on account, so to speak."

"I suppose," said Buffham, "you have got your claim pretty well cut and dried? Got all your evidence, I mean, and arranged with your lawyer as to the plan of campaign?"

"Well, no!" replied Pippet, "at present things are rather in the air. But, if we have finished, perhaps we might take our coffee up in my sitting-room. We can talk more freely there. But don't let me bore you. After all, it isn't your funeral."

"My dear sir!" exclaimed Buffham, with genuine sincerity, "you are not boring me. I assure you that I am profoundly interested. If you won't consider me inquisitive, I should like to hear the whole story in as much detail as you care to give."

Mr Pippet nodded and smiled. "Good!" said he, as they ascended the stairs to the private suite, "you shall have all the detail you want. I shall enjoy giving it to you, as it will help to get the affair into my own head a trifle more clearly. It's a queer story and I must admit that it does not sound any too convincing. The whole claim rests upon a tradition that I heard from my father."

Mr Buffham was a little disappointed; but only a little. As his host had said, it – the claim – was not his funeral. A wild-cat claim might answer his purpose as well as any other; perhaps even better. Nevertheless, he remarked with an assumption of anxiety: "I hope there is something to go on besides the tradition. You'll have to deal with a court of law, you know."

"Yes, I realise that," replied Pippet, "and I may say that there is some corroborative matter. I'll tell you about that presently. But there's this much about the tradition; that it admits of being put to the test, as you'll see when I give you the story. And I will do that right away.

"The tradition, then, as I had it from my father from time to time, in rather disjointed fragments, was that *his* father was a very remarkable character; in fact, he was two characters rolled into one, for he led a double life. As my father and mother knew him, he was Mr Josiah Pippet, the landlord of a house of call in the City of London known as the 'Fox and Grapes.' But a persistent tradition had it that the name of Josiah Pippet was an assumed name and that he was really the Earl of Winsborough. It is known that he was in the habit of absenting himself from his London premises from time to time and that when he did so he disappeared completely, leaving no hint of his where-abouts. Now, it seems that the Earl, who was a bachelor, was a somewhat eccentric gentleman of similar habits. *He* also was accustomed periodically to absent himself from the Castle, and he also used to disappear, leaving no clue to his whereabouts. And rumour had it that these disappearances were, as the scientists would say, correlated; like the little figures in those old-fashioned toy houses that foretold the weather. When the old man came out, the old woman went in, and *vice versa*. So it was said that when Josiah disappeared from the 'Fox and Grapes,' his lordship made his appearance at Winsborough Castle; and when his lordship disappeared from the Castle, Joseph popped up at the 'Fox and Grapes.'"

"Is there any record of the movements of the two men? "Buffham asked.

"Well, there is a diary, along with a lot of letters and other stuff. I have just glanced at some of it but I can't say of my own observation that there is a definite record. However, my sister has gone through the whole lot and she says that it is all as plain as a pike-staff."

Buffham nodded with an air of satisfaction that was by no means assumed. He began to see splendid possibilities in his host's case.

"Yes," said he. "This is much more hopeful. If you can show that these disappearances coincided in time, that will be a very striking piece of evidence. You have got these documents with you?"

"Yes, I have got them in a deed box in my bedroom. I have been intending to make a serious attack on them and go right through them."

"What would be much more to the point," said Buffham, "would be to hand the box to your lawyer and let him go through them. He will be accustomed to examining documents, and he will see the significance – the legal significance, I mean – of little, inconspicuous facts that might easily escape a non-professional eye. I think you said you had a lawyer?"

"No. That's a matter that I shall have to attend to at once; and I don't quite know how to go about it. I understand that they don't advertise in this country."

"No," said Buffham, "certainly not. But I see your difficulty. You naturally want to get a suitable man, and it is most important. You want to secure the services of a solicitor whose position and character would command the respect and confidence of the court, and who has had experience of cases of a similar kind. That is absolutely vital. I recall a case which illustrates the danger of employing a lawyer of an unsuitable kind. It was, like yours, a case of disputed succession. There were two claimants whom we may call 'A' and 'B.' Now Mr 'A' had undoubtedly the better case. But unfortunately for him, he employed a solicitor whose sole experience was concerned with commercial law. He was an excellent man, but he knew practically nothing of the intricacies of succession to landed property. Mr 'B,' on the other hand, had the good fortune to secure a lawyer whose practice had been very largely concerned with these very cases. He knew all the ropes, you see; and the result was that the case was decided in Mr 'B''s favour. But it ought not to have been. I had it, in confidence, from his lawyer (whom I happened to know rather well) that if he had been acting for Mr 'A,' instead of for Mr 'B,' the decision would certainly have gone the other way. 'A' had the better claim, but his lawyer had not realised it and had failed to put it before the court in a sufficiently convincing manner."

Having given this striking instance, Buffham looked anxiously at his host, and was a trifle disappointed at its effect. Still more so was he with that gentleman's comment.

"Seems to me," the latter remarked, "that that court wasn't particularly on the spot if they let your lawyer friend bluff them into giving Mr 'B' the property that properly belonged to Mr 'A.' And I shouldn't have thought that your friend would have found it a satisfactory deal. At any rate, I am not wanting any lawyer to grab property for me that belongs to somebody else. As long as I believe in this claim myself, I'm going for it for all I am worth. But I am not going to drop my egg into somebody else's rightful nest, like your Mr 'B.'"

"Of course you are not!" Buffham hastened to reply, considerably disconcerted by his host's unexpected attitude; so difficult is it for a radically dishonest man to realise that his is not the usual and normal state of mind. "But neither do you want to find yourself in the position of Mr 'A.'"

"No," Pippet admitted, "I don't. I just want a square deal, and I always understood that you could get it in an English court."

"So you can," said Buffham. "But you must realise that a court can only decide on the facts and arguments put before it. It is the business of the lawyers to supply those facts and arguments. And I think you are hardly just to my lawyer friend – his name, by the way, is Gimbler – a most honourable and conscientious man. I must point out that a lawyer's duty is to present his client's case in the most forcible and convincing way that he can. He is not concerned with the other man's case. He assumes – and so does the court – that the opposing lawyer will do the same for his client; and then the court will have both cases completely presented. It is the client's business to employ a lawyer who is competent to put his case properly to the court."

Mr Pippet nodded. "Yes," he said, reflectively, "I see the idea. But the difficulty in the case of a stranger like myself is to find the particular kind of lawyer who has the special knowledge and experience that is required. Now, as to this friend of yours, Gimbler; you say that he specialises in disputed claims to property."

"I didn't say that he specialised in them, but I know that he has had considerable experience of them."

"Well, now, do you suppose that he would be willing to take up this claim of mine?"

Mr Buffham did not suppose at all. He knew. Nevertheless he replied warily:

"It depends. He wouldn't want to embark on a case that was going to result in a fiasco. He would want to hear all about the claim and what evidence there is to support it. And especially he would want to go very carefully through those documents of yours."

"Yes," said Pippet, "that seems to be the correct line, and that is what I should want him to do. I'd like to have an expert opinion on the whole affair before I begin to get busy. I am not out to exploit a mare's nest and make a public fool of myself. But we didn't finish the story. We only got to the Box and Cox business of Josiah and the Earl. It seems that this went on for a number of years, and nothing appears to have been thought of it at the time. But when Josiah's wife died and his son – my father – was settled, he appears to have wearied of the complications of his double life and made up his mind to put an end to them. And the simplest and most conclusive way to write Finis on the affair seemed to him to be to die and get buried. And that is what he did. According to the story, he faked a last illness and engineered a sham death. I don't know how he managed it. Looks to me pretty difficult. But the rumour had it that he managed to get people to believe that he had died, and he had a funeral with a dummy coffin, properly weighted with lumps of lead, and that this was successfully planted in the family vault. I am bound to admit that this part of the story does sound a trifle thin. But it seems to have been firmly believed in the family."

It would have been a relief to Mr Buffham to snigger aloud. But sniggering was not his rôle. Still, he felt called on to make some kind of criticism. Accordingly, he remarked judicially:

"There do certainly seem to be difficulties; the death certificate, for instance. You would hardly expect a doctor to mistake a live, healthy man for a corpse – unless Josiah made it worth his while. It would be simple enough then."

"I understand," said Mr Pippet, "that doctors often used to give a certificate without viewing the body. But the lawyer will know that.

At any rate, it is obvious that someone must have been in the know; and that is probably how the rumour got started."

"And when did the Earl die?"

"That I can't tell you, off-hand. But it was some years after Josiah's funeral."

"And who holds the title and estate now?"

"Nobody; at least, so I understand. The last – or present – Earl went away to Africa or some other uncivilised place, big-game shooting, and never came back. As there was never any announcement of the Earl's death, things seem to have drifted on as if he were alive. I have never heard of any claimant."

"There couldn't be until the Earl's death was either proved or presumed by the permission of the court. So the first thing that you will have to do will be to take proceedings to have the death of the Earl presumed."

"Not the first thing," said Pippet. "There is one question that will have to be settled before we definitely make the claim. The tradition says that Josiah's death was a fake and that his coffin was a dummy weighted with lead. Now, that is a statement of fact that admits of proof or disproof. The first thing that we have got to do is to get that coffin open. If we find Josiah inside, that will settle the whole business, and I shan't care a hoot whether the Earl is alive or dead."

Once again Mr Buffham was sensible of a slight feeling of disappointment. In a man who was prepared to consider seriously such a manifestly preposterous cock-and-bull story as this, he had not looked for so reasonable a state of mind. Of course, Pippet was quite right from his own idiotic point of view. The opening of the coffin was the *experimentum crucis*. And when it was opened, there, of course, would be the body, and the bubble would be most effectively burst. But Mr Buffham did not want the bubble burst. The plan which was shaping itself vaguely in his mind was concerned with keeping that bubble in a healthy state of inflation. And again, his crooked mind found it hard to understand Pippet's simple, honest, straightforward outlook. If he had been the claimant, his strongest efforts would have been devoted to seeing that nobody meddled with that coffin. And he had a feeling that his friend Gimbler would take the same view.

"Of course," he conceded, "you are perfectly correct; but there may be difficulties that you don't quite realise. I don't know how it is in America, but in this country you can't just dig up a coffin and open it if you want to know who is inside. There are all sorts of formalities before you can get permission; and I doubt whether a faculty would be granted until you had made out some sort of a case in the courts. So the moral is that you must get as impressive a body of evidence together as you can. Have you got any other facts besides what you have told me? For instance, do you know what these two men – Josiah and the Earl – were like? Do they appear to have resembled each other?"

Mr Pippet grinned. "If Josiah and the Earl," said he, "were one and the same person, they would naturally be a good deal alike. I understand that they were. That is one of the strong points of the story. Both of them were a bit out-size; well over six feet in height. Both were fair, blue-eyed men with a shaved upper lip and long sandy side-whiskers."

"You can prove that, can you?"

"I can swear that I had information to that effect from my father, who knew one and had seen the other. And there is one other point; only a small one, but every little bit of corroboration helps. My father told me on several occasions that his father – Josiah – had often told him that he was born in Winsborough Castle."

"Ha!" exclaimed Buffham, "that's better. That establishes a definite connection. It's a pity, though, that he was not more explicit. And now, with regard to these documents that you spoke of; what is the nature of them?"

"To tell you the truth," replied Pippet, "I don't know much about them. I've been used to an active life and I'm not a great reader, so I've not done much more than glance over them. But, as I mentioned, my sister has gone through them carefully and she reckons that they as good as prove that Josiah and the Earl were one and the same person. Would you like to have a look at them?"

A mere affirmative would have been inadequate to express Mr Buffham's ravenous desire to see whether there was or was not the making of a possible legal case. Nevertheless, he replied in a tone of studied indifference:

"My opinion is not much to the point, but I should certainly like to see what sort of material you will be able to give your lawyer."

Thereupon Mr Pippet retired to the bedroom, from which he presently emerged carrying a good-sized deed-box. This he placed on the table, and, having gone deliberately through a large bunch of keys, eventually selected one and carefully fitted it into the lock while Buffham watched him hungrily. The box being opened, the two men drew their chairs up to the table and peered into its interior; which was occupied by a collection of bundles of papers, neatly tied up with red tape, each bundle being distinguished by means of a label inscribed in an old-fashioned feminine hand-writing. In addition, there were seven small, leather-bound volumes.

Buffham picked out the bundles, one after another, and read the labels. "Letters from J S to his wife," "Letters from various persons to J S," "Copies of letters from J S to various persons," "Various tradesmen's bills and accounts," and so on. Having asked his host's permission, he untied one or two of the bundles and read samples of the letters and tradesmen's bills with a feeling of stupefaction, mingled with astonished speculations as to the mental peculiarities of his host's sister.

"Yes," he said, gloomily replacing the last of them, "I dare say a careful analysis of these letters may yield some relevant information, but it will need the expert eye of the trained lawyer to detect the relevancy of some of them. There is, for instance, a bill for two pounds of pork sausages and a black pudding, which seems rather beside the mark. But you never know. Important legal points may be involved in the most unexpected matter. What are those little books? Are they the diaries that you spoke of?"

Mr Pippet nodded and handed one of them to him, which proved to be the diary for the year 1833. He turned over the leaves and scanned the entries with more interest but still with a feeling of bewilderment. After examining a few sample pages, he handed the volume back to Pippet, remarking a little wearily:

"The late Josiah didn't go into much detail. The entries are very dry and brief and seem to be concerned chiefly with the trivial happenings of his life from day to day and with money paid or received."

"Well, isn't that what diaries are usually filled with?" Pippet protested, not unreasonably. "And don't you think that those simple, commonplace entries are just the ones to give us the information that we want? My sister said that she learned quite a lot about Josiah's ways of life from those diaries."

"Did she?" said Buffham. "I am glad to hear it; because it suggests that a trained lawyer, going through those diaries with the legal issues in his mind, noting, collating and analysing the entries, will probably discover significances in the most unexpected places. Which brings us back to the point that you ought to get competent legal assistance without delay."

"Yes, I think you are right," agreed Pippet. "I've got to secure a lawyer sooner or later, so I might as well start right away. Now, to come down to brass tacks, what about this lawyer friend of yours? You say that this case of mine would be in his customary line of business; and you think he would be willing to take it on?"

Mr Buffham had no doubts whatever, but he did not think it expedient to say so. A retreating tendency on the part of the bait is apt to produce a pursuing tendency on the part of the fish.

"Naturally," said he, "I can't answer for another man's views. He is a busy man, and he might not be prepared to give time to what he might regard as a somewhat speculative case. But we can easily find out. If you like, I will call on him and put the case to him in as favourable a light as possible, and, if he doesn't seem eager to take it up, I might use a little gentle pressure. You see, I know him pretty well. Then, if I am successful, I might arrange for you to have an interview, at which, perhaps, it might be advisable for your sister to be present, as she knows more about the affair than you do. Then he could tell you what he thought of your chances and you could let him know what you are prepared to do. What do you think of that plan?"

Mr Pippet thought that it seemed to meet the case, provided that it could be carried out without delay.

"You understand," said he, "that my sister and daughter will be arriving here tomorrow, and they will be red-hot to get the business started, especially my sister."

"And quite naturally, too," said Buffham. "I sympathise with her impatience and I promise that there shall be no delay on my part. I will call at Gimbler's office tomorrow morning the first thing, before he has had time to begin his morning's work."

"It's very good of you," said Pippet, as his guest rose to take his leave, "to interest yourself in this way in the affairs of a mere stranger."

"Not at all," Buffham rejoined cheerily. "You are forgetting the romance and dramatic interest of your case. Anyone would be delighted to lend you a hand in your adventure. You may depend on hearing from me in the course of tomorrow. Good night and good luck!"

Mr Pippet, having provided his guest with a fresh cigar, accompanied him down to the entrance and watched him with a meditative eye as he walked away down the street. Apparently, the dwindling figure suggested a train of thought, for he continued to stand looking out even after it had disappeared. At length he turned with a faint sigh and thoughtfully retraced his steps to his own domain.

## CHAPTER TWO

## Mr Buffham's Legal Friend

No amount of native shrewdness can entirely compensate for deficiency of knowledge. If Mr Christopher Pippet had been intimately acquainted with English social customs, he would have known that the neighbourhood of Kennington in general, and Kennington Grove in particular, is hardly the place in which to look for the professional premises of a solicitor engaged in important Chancery practice. He did, indeed, survey the rather suburban surroundings with a certain amount of surprise, noting with intelligent interest the contrast between the ways of New York and those of London. He even ventured to comment on the circumstance as he halted at the iron gate of a small garden and read out the inscription on a well-worn brass plate affixed to the gate aforesaid; which set forth the name and professional vocation of Mr Horatio Gimbler, Solicitor and Advocate.

"Buffham didn't tell me that he was an advocate as well as a solicitor," Mr Pippet remarked, as he pushed the gate open.

"He wouldn't," replied his companion, "but left you to find out for yourself. Of course he knew you would, and then you would give him credit for having understated his friend's merits. It's just vanity."

At the street door, which was closed and bore a duplicate plate, Mr Pippet pressed an electric bell-push, with the result that there arose from within a sound like the "going off" of an alarm clock and simultaneously the upper half of a face with a pair of beady black eyes appeared for an instant above the wire blind of the adjacent window. Then, after a brief interval, the door opened and revealed an extremely alert youth of undeniably Hebraic aspect.

"Is Mr Gimbler disengaged?" Mr Pippet enquired.

"Have you got an appointment?" the youth demanded.

"Yes; eleven o'clock; and it's two minutes to the hour now. Shall I go in here?"

He turned towards a door opening out of the hall and marked "Waiting Room."

"No," the youth replied, hastily, emphatically and almost in a tone of alarm. "That'th for clienth that haven't got an appointment. What name shall I thay?"

"Mr and Miss Pippet."

"Oh, yeth, I know. Jutht thtep thith way."

He opened an inner door leading into a small inner hall, which offered to the visitors a prospect of a flight of shabbily carpeted stairs and a strong odour of fried onions. Here he approached a door marked "Private Office" and knocked softly, eliciting a responsive but inarticulate roar; whereupon he opened the door and announced: "Mr and Miss Pippet."

The opened door revealed a large man with a pair of folding pince-nez insecurely balanced on the end of a short, fat nose, apparently writing furiously. As the visitors entered, he looked round with an interrogative frown as if impatient of being interrupted. Then, appearing suddenly to realise who they were, he made a convulsive grimace, which dislodged the eyeglasses and left them dangling free on their broad black ribbon, and was succeeded by a wrinkly but affable smile. Then he rose, and, holding out a large, rather fat hand, exclaimed:

"Delighted to see you. I had no idea that it was so late. One gets so engrossed in these – er – fascinating – "

"Naturally," said Mr Pippet, "though I thought it was the documents that got engrossed. However, here we are. Let me introduce you to my sister, Miss Arminella Pippet."

Mr Gimbler bowed, and for a brief space there was a searching mutual inspection. Miss Pippet saw a physically imposing man, large in all dimensions – tall, broad, deep-chested, and still more deep in the region immediately below the chest; with a large, massive head, rather bald and very closely cropped, a large, rather fat face, marked with wrinkles suggestive of those on the edge of a pair of bellows, and singularly small pale blue eyes, which tended to become still smaller, even to total disappearance, when he smiled. Through those little blue eyes, Mr Gimbler saw a woman, shortish in stature but majestic in carriage and conveying an impression of exuberant energy and vivacity. And this impression was reinforced by the strong, mobile face with its firm mouth set above the square, pugnacious chin and below a rather formidable Roman nose, which latter gave to her a certain suggestive resemblance to a bird, a resemblance accentuated by her quick movements. But the bird suggested was not the dove. In short, Miss Arminella Pippet was a somewhat remarkable-looking lady with a most unmistakable "presence." She might have been a dame of the old French noblesse; and Mr Gimbler, looking at her through his little blue eyes and bearing in mind the peerage claim, decided that she looked the part. He also decided – comparing her with her mild-faced brother – that the grey mare was the better horse and must claim his chief attention. He was not the first who had under-valued Mr Christopher Pippet.

"I suppose," said the latter, sitting down with some care on a rather infirm cane-bottomed chair (Miss Arminella occupied the only easy chair), "Mr Buffham has given you some idea of the matter on which we have come to consult you?"

"He has done more than that," said Mr Gimbler, "and would have done more still if I had not stopped him. He is thrilled by your romantic story and wildly optimistic. If we could only get a jury of Buffhams you would walk into your inheritance without a breath of opposition."

"And what do you think of our chances with the kind of jury that we are likely to get?"

Mr Gimbler pursed up his lips and shook his massive head.

"We mustn't begin giving opinions at this stage," said he. "Remember that I have only heard the story at second hand from Mr Buffham; just a sketch of the nature of the case. Let us begin at the beginning and forget Mr Buffham. You are claiming, I believe, to be the grandson of the late Earl of Winsborough. Now, I should like to hear an outline of the grounds of your claim before we go into any details."

As he spoke, he fixed an enquiring eye on Miss Pippet, who promptly responded by opening her handbag and drawing therefrom a folded sheet of foolscap paper.

"This," said she, "is a concise statement of the nature of the claim and the known facts on which it is based. I thought it would save time if I wrote it out, as I could then leave the paper with you for reference. Will you read it or shall I?"

Mr Gimbler looked at the document, and, observing that it was covered with closely-spaced writing in a somewhat crabbed and angular hand, elected to listen to the reading in order that he might make a few notes. Accordingly Miss Pippet proceeded to read aloud from the paper with something of the air of a herald reading a royal proclamation, glancing from time to time at the lawyer to see what kind of impression it was making on him. The result of these inspections must have been a little disappointing, as Mr Gimbler listened attentively with his eyes shut, rousing only at intervals to scribble a few words on a slip of paper.

When she had come to the end of the statement – which repeated substantially, but in a more connected form, the story that her brother had told to Buffham – she laid the paper on the table and regarded the lawyer with an interrogative stare. Mr Gimbler, having opened his eyes to their normal extent, directed them to his notes.

"This," said he, "is a very singular and romantic story – romantic and strange, and yet not really incredible. But the important question is, to what extent is this interesting tradition supported by provable facts? For instance, it is stated that when Josiah Pippet used to disappear from his usual places of resort, the Earl of Winsborough made his appearance at Winsborough Castle. Now, is there any evidence that the disappearance of Josiah coincided in time with the appearance of the Earl at the Castle, and *vice versa*?"

"There is the diary," said Miss Pippet.

"Ha!" exclaimed Mr Gimbler, genuinely surprised. "The diary makes that quite plain, does it?"

"Perfectly," the lady replied. "Anyway, it is quite clear to me. Whenever Josiah was about to make one of his disappearances, he noted in his diary quite unmistakably: 'Going away tomorrow for a little spell at the old place.' Sometimes, instead of 'the old place,' he says plainly 'the Castle.' Then there is a blank space of more than half a page before he records his arrival home at the 'Fox and Grapes.'"

"H'm, yes," said Mr Gimbler, swinging his folded eyeglass on its ribbon like a pendulum. "And you think that by the expression 'the old place' or 'the Castle' he means Winsborough Castle?"

"I don't see how there can be any doubt of it. Obviously, 'the old place' must have been Winsborough Castle, where he was born."

"It would seem probable," Mr Gimbler admitted. "By the way, is there any evidence that he *was* born at the Castle?"

"Well," Miss Pippet replied a little sharply, "he said he was, and I suppose he knew."

"Naturally, naturally," the lawyer agreed. "And you can prove that he did say so?"

"My brother and I have heard our father repeat the statement over and over again. We can swear to that."

"And with regard to the Earl? Is there any evidence that, when Josiah returned home to the 'Fox and Grapes,' his Lordship disappeared from the Castle?"

"Evidence!" Miss Pippet exclaimed, slapping her handbag impatiently. "What evidence do you want? The man couldn't be in two places at once!"

"Very true," said Mr Gimbler, fixing a slightly perplexed eye on his dangling glasses; "very true. He couldn't. And with regard to the sham funeral. Naturally there wouldn't be any reference to it in the diary, but is it possible to support the current rumour by any definite facts?"

"Don't you think the fact that my father – Josiah's own son – was convinced of it is definite enough?" Miss Pippet demanded, a trifle acidly.

"It is definite enough," Gimbler admitted, "but in courts of law there is a slight prejudice against hearsay evidence. Direct, first-hand evidence, if it is possible to produce it, has a good deal more weight."

"So it may," retorted Miss Pippet, "but you can't expect us to give first-hand evidence of a funeral that took place before we were born. I suppose even a court of law has a little common sense."

"Still," her brother interposed, "Mr Gimbler has put his finger on the really vital spot. The sham funeral is the kernel of the whole business. If we *can* prove that, we shall have something solid to go on. And we can prove it – or else disprove it, as the case may be. But it need not be left in the condition of what the late President Wilson would have called a peradventure. If that funeral was a sham, there was nothing in the coffin but some lumps of lead. Now, that coffin is still in existence. It is lying in the family vault; and if we can yank it out and open it, the Winsborough Peerage Claim will be as good as settled. If we find Josiah at home to visitors, we can let the claim drop and go for a holiday. But if we find the lumps of lead, according to our programme, we shall hang on to the claim until the courts are tired of us and hand over the keys of the Castle. Mr Gimbler is quite right. That coffin is the point that we have got to concentrate on."

As Mr Pippet developed his views, the lawyer's eyeglasses, dangling from their ribbon, swung more and more violently, and their owner's eyes opened to an unprecedented width. He had never had the slightest intention of concentrating on the coffin. On the contrary, that obvious means of exploding the delusion and toppling over the house of cards had seemed to be the rock that had got to be safely circumnavigated at all costs. In his view, the coffin was the fly in the ointment; and the discovery that it was the apple of Mr Pippet's eye gave him a severe shock. And not this alone. He had assumed that the lady's invincible optimism represented the state of mind of both his clients. Now he realised that the man whom he had written down an amiable ass, and perhaps a dishonest ass at that, combined in his person two qualities most undesirable in the circumstances – hard common sense and transparent honesty.

It was a serious complication; and as he sat with his eyes fixed on the swinging eyeglasses, he endeavoured rapidly to shape a new course. At length he replied:

"Of course you are quite right, Mr Pippet. The obvious course would be to examine the coffin as a preliminary measure. But English Law does not always take the obvious course. When once a person is consigned to the tomb, the remains pass out of the control of the relatives and into that of the State; and the State views with very jealous disapproval any attempts to disturb those remains. In order to open a tomb or grave, and especially to open a coffin, it is necessary to obtain a faculty from the Home Secretary authorising an exhumation. Now, before any such faculty is granted, the Home Secretary requires the applicant to show cause for the making of such an order."

"Well," said Mr Pippet, "we can show cause. We want to know whether Josiah is in that coffin or not."

"Quite so," said Mr Gimbler. "A perfectly reasonable motive. But it would not be accepted by the Home Office. They would demand a ruling from a properly constituted court to the effect that the claim had been investigated and a prima facie case made out."

"What do you mean by a prima facie case?" Miss Pippet inquired.

"The expression means that the claim has been stated in a court of law and that sufficient evidence has been produced to establish a probability that it is a just and reasonable claim."

"You mean to say," said Mr Pippet, "that a judge and jury have got to sit and examine at great length whether the claim may possibly be a true claim before they will consent to examine a piece of evidence which will settle the question with practical certainty in the course of an hour?"

"Yes," Mr Gimbler admitted, "that, I am afraid, is the rather unreasonable position. We shall have to lay the facts, so far as they are known to us, before the court and make out as good a case as we can. Then, if the court is satisfied that we have a substantial case, it will make an order for the exhumation, which the Home Office will confirm."

"For my part," said Miss Pippet, "I don't see why we need meddle with the coffin at all. It seems a ghoulish proceeding."

"I entirely agree with you, Miss Pippet," said Mr Gimbler (and there is no possible doubt that he did). "It would be much better to deal with the whole affair in court if that were possible. Perhaps it may be possible to avoid the exhumation, after all. The court may not insist."

"It won't have to insist," said Mr Pippet. "I make it a condition that we ascertain beyond all doubt whether Josiah is or is not in that coffin. I want to make sure that I am claiming what is my just due, and I shan't be sure of that until that coffin has been opened. Isn't it possible for you to make an application to the Home Secretary without troubling the courts?"

"It would be possible to make the application," Mr Gimbler replied somewhat dryly. "But a refusal would be a foregone conclusion. Quite properly so, if you consider the conditions. The purpose of the exhumation is to establish the fact of the sham burial. But if that were established, you would be no more forward, or, at least, very little. Your claim would still have to be stated and argued in a court of law. Of course, the proof of the sham burial would be material evidence, but still, your claim would stand or fall by the decision of the court. Naturally, the Home Office, since it cannot consider evidence or give a decision, is not going to give a permit until it is informed by the proper authority that an exhumation is necessary for the purposes of Justice. Believe me, Mr Pippet, we should only prejudice our case by trying to go behind the courts; and, moreover, we should certainly fail to get a permit."

"Very well," said Mr Pippet. "You know best. Then I take it that there is not much more to say at present. We have given you the facts, such as they are, and we shall leave my sister's statement with you, and it will be up to you to consider what is to be done next."

"Yes," agreed Gimbler. "But something was said about documents – some letters and a diary. Are they available?"

"They are," replied Mr Pippet. "I've got the whole boiling of them in this box. My sister has been through them, as she mentioned to you just now."

"And you?" Mr Gimbler asked with a trace of anxiety, as he watched his client's efforts to untie the parcel. "Have you examined them thoroughly?"

"I can't truly say that I have," was the reply, as Mr Pippet deliberately opened a pocket knife and applied it to the string. "I had intended to look through them before I handed them to you, but Mr Buffham assured me that it would be a waste of labour, as you would have to study them in any case; so, as I am not what you would call a studious man, and they look a pretty stodgy collection, I have saved myself the trouble."

"I don't believe," said Miss Pippet, "that my brother cares two cents whether we succeed or not."

The lady's suspicion was not entirely unshared by her legal adviser. But he made no comment, as, at this moment, Mr Pippet, having detached the coverings of the parcel, and thereby disclosed the deed-box which he had shown to Buffham, inserted a key and unlocked it.

"There," said he, as he threw the lid open, "you can see that the things are there. Those bundles of paper are the letters and the little volumes are the diary. There is no need for you to look at them now. I guess you will like to study them at your leisure."

"Quite so," agreed Mr Gimbler. "It will be necessary for me to examine them exhaustively and systematically and make a very careful précis of their contents, with an analysis of those contents from an evidential point of view. I shall have to do that before I can give any opinion on the merits of the case, and certainly before I suggest taking any active measures. You realise that those investigations will take some time?"

"Certainly," said Mr Pippet; "and you will not find us impatient. We don't want to urge you to act precipitately."

"Not precipitately," agreed Miss Pippet. "Still, you understand that we don't want too much of the law's delay."

Mr Gimbler understood that perfectly; and, to tell the whole truth, looked with much more favour on the lady's hardly-veiled impatience than on her brother's philosophic calm.

"There will be no delay at all," he replied, "but merely a most necessary period of preparation. I need not point out to you, Madam," he continued after a moment's pause, "that we must not enter the lists unready. We must mature our plans in advance, so that when we take the field – if we decide to do so – it will be with our weapons sharpened and our armour bright."

"Certainly," said Miss Pippet. "We must be ready before we start. I realise that; only I hope it won't take too long to get ready."

"That," replied Mr Gimbler, "we shall be better able to judge when we have made a preliminary inspection of the documentary material; but I can assure you that no time will be wasted."

Here he paused to clear his throat and adjust his eyeglasses. Then he proceeded: "There is just one other little matter that I should like to be clear on. You realise that an action at law is apt to be a somewhat expensive affair. Of course, in the present case, there is a considerable set-off. If you are successful, the mere material gain in valuable property, to say nothing of the title and the great social advantages, will be enough to make the law costs appear a negligible trifle. Still, I must warn you that the outlay will be very considerable. There will be court fees, fees to counsel, costs of the necessary investigations, and, of course, my own charges, which I shall keep as low as possible. Now, the question is, are you prepared to embark on this undoubtedly costly enterprise?"

He asked the question in a tone as impassive and judicial as he could manage, but he awaited the answer with an anxiety that was difficult to conceal. It was Miss Pippet who instantly dispelled that anxiety.

"We understand all about that," said she. "We never supposed that titles and estates were to be picked up for the asking. You can take it that we shall not complain of any expense in reason. But perhaps you were thinking of our capacity to bear a heavy expense? If you were, I may tell you that my own means would be amply sufficient to meet any likely costs, even without my brother's support."

"That is so," Mr Pippet confirmed. "But, as I am the actual claimant, the costs will naturally fall on me. Could you give us any idea of our probable liabilities?"

Mr Gimbler reflected rapidly. He didn't wish to frighten his quarry, but he did very much want to take soundings of the depth of their purse. Eventually, he took his courage in both hands and made the trial cast.

"It is mere guesswork," said he, "until we know how much there may be to do. Supposing – to take an outside figure – the costs should mount to ten thousand pounds. Of course, they won't. But I mention that sum as a sort of basis to reckon from. How would that affect you?"

"Well," said Mr Pippet, "it sounds a lot of money, but it wouldn't break either of us. Only we look to you to see that the gamble is worth while before we drop too much on it."

"You may be quite confident," Gimbler replied in a voice husky with suppressed joy, "that I shall not allow you to embark on any proceedings until I have ascertained beyond a doubt that you have at least a reasonable chance of success. And that," he continued, rising as his visitors rose to depart, "is all that is humanly possible."

He stuck his glasses on his nose to shake hands and to watch Mr Pippet as he detached the key of the deed-box from his bunch. Then he opened the door and escorted his visitors through an atmosphere of fried onions to the street door, where he stood watching them reflectively as they descended the steps and made their way along the flagged path to the gate.

As Mr Gimbler closed the street door, that of the waiting-room opened softly, disclosing the figure of no less a person than Mr Buffham. And, naturally, the figure included the countenance; which was wreathed in smiles. Looking cautiously towards the kitchen stairs, Mr Buffham murmured:

"Did I exaggerate, my little Gimblet? I think not. Methought I heard a whisper of ten thousand pounds. An outside estimate, my dear sir; in fact, a wild overestimate. Hey? What O!"

Mr Gimbler did not reply. He only smiled. And when Mr Gimbler smiled – as we have mentioned – his eyes tended to disappear. They did on this occasion. Especially the left one.

# CHAPTER THREE

## Mr Pippet Gives Evidence

American visitors to London often attain to a quite remarkable familiarity with many of its features. But their accomplishments in this respect do not usually extend to an acquaintance with its intimate geography. The reason is simple enough. He who would know London, or any other great city, in the complete and intimate fashion characteristic of the genuine Town Sparrow, must habituate himself to the use of that old-fashioned conveyance known as "shanks' mare". For the humblest of creatures has some distinctive excellence; even the mere pedestrian, despised of the proud motorist (who classes him with the errant rabbit or the crawling pismire) and ignored by the law, has at least one virtue: he knows his London.

Now, the American visitor is not usually a pedestrian. As his time appears to him more valuable than his money, he tends to cut the Gordian knot of geographical difficulties by hailing a taxi; whereby he makes a swift passage at the sacrifice of everything between his starting-point and his destination.

This is what Mr Pippet did on the afternoon of the day of his conference with Mr Gimbler. The hailing was done by the hotel porter, and when the taxi was announced, Mr Pippet came forth from the hall and delivered to the driver an address in the neighbourhood of Great Saint Helen's, wherever that might be, and held open the cab door to admit the young lady who had followed him out; who thereupon slithered in with the agility born of youthful flexibility, extensive practice and no clothing to speak of.

"I am not sure, Jenny," said Mr Pippet, as he took his seat and pulled the door to, "that your aunt was not right. This is likely to be a rather gruesome business, and the place doesn't seem a very suitable one for young ladies."

Miss Jenny smiled a superior smile as she fished a gold cigarette case out of her handbag and proceeded to select a cigarette. "That's all bunk, you know, Dad," said she. "Auntie was just bursting to come herself, but she thought she had to set me an example of self-restraint. As if I wanted her examples! I am out to see all that there is to see. Isn't that what we came to Europe for?"

"I thought we came to settle this peerage business," replied Mr Pippet.

"That's part of the entertainment," she admitted, "but we may as well take anything else that happens to be going. And here we have struck a first-class mystery. I wouldn't have missed it for anything. Do you think it will be on view?" she added, holding out the cigarette case.

Mr Pippet humbly picked out a cigarette and looked at her inquiringly. "Do you mean the head?" he asked.

"Yes. That's what I want to see. You've seen it, you know."

"I don't know much about the ways of inquests in England," he replied, "but I don't fancy that the remains are shown to anyone but the jury."

"That's real mean of them," she said. "I was hoping that it would be on view, or that they would bring it in – on a charger, like John the Baptist's."

Mr Pippet smiled as he lit his cigarette. "The circumstances are not quite the same, my dear," said he; "but, as I am only a witness, you'll see as much as I shall, though, as you say, I have actually seen the thing, or, at least, a part of it; and I have no wish to see any more."

"Still," persisted Jenny, "you can say that you have really and truly seen it."

Mr Pippet admitted that he enjoyed this inestimable privilege for what it might be worth, and the conversation dropped for the moment. Miss Jenny leaned back reposefully in her corner, taking occasional "pulls" at the cigarette in its dainty amber holder, while her father regarded her with a mixture of parental pride, affection and quiet amusement. And it has to be admitted that Mr Pippet's sentiments with regard to his daughter were by no means unjustified. Miss Jenifer Pippet – to give her her full and unabridged style and title – was a girl of whom any father might have been proud. If – as Mr Gimbler had very properly decided – the majestic Arminella "looked the part" of an earl's sister (which is not invariably the case with the genuine possessors of that title), Mistress Jenifer would have sustained the character of the earl's daughter with credit even on the stage, where the demands are a good deal more exacting than in real life. In the typically "patrician" style of features, with the fine Roman nose and the level brows and firm chin, she resembled her redoubtable aunt; but she had the advantage of that lady in the matter of stature, being, like her father, well above the average height. And here it may be noted that, if the daughter reflected credit on the father, the latter was well able to hold his position on his own merits. Christopher J Pippet was fully worthy of his distinguished womenkind; a fine, upstanding gentleman with an undeniable "presence".

It was probably the possession of these personal advantages that made the way smooth for the two strangers on their arrival at the premises in which the inquest was to be held. At any rate, as soon as Mr Pippet had made known his connection with the case, the officiating police officer conducted them to a place in the front row and provided them each with a chair directly facing the table and nearly opposite the coroner's seat. At the moment, this and the jurymen's seats were empty and the large room was filled with the hum of conversation. For the sensational nature of the case had attracted a number of spectators greatly in excess of that usually found at an inquest; so much so that the accommodation was somewhat strained, and our two visitors had reason to congratulate themselves on their privileged position.

A few minutes after their arrival, a general stir among the audience and an increase in the murmur of voices seemed to indicate that something was happening. Then the nature of that something became apparent as the jurymen filed into their places and the coroner took his place at the head of the table. There was a brief interval as the jurymen settled into their places and the coroner arranged some papers before him and inspected his fountain pen. Then he looked up; and as the hum of conversation died away and silence settled down on the room, he began his opening address.

"The circumstances, gentlemen," said he, "which form the subject of this inquiry are very unusual. Ordinarily the occasion of a coroner's inquest is the discovery of the dead body of some person, known or unknown, or the death of some person from causes which have not been ascertained or certified, but whose body is available for examination. In the present case, while there is indisputable evidence of the death of some person, and certain evidence which may enable us to form some opinion as to the probable cause of death, the complete body is not available for expert examination. All that has been discovered, up to the present, is the head; whereas it is probable that the physical evidence as to the exact cause of death is to be found in the missing portion of the remains. I need not occupy your time with any account of the circumstances, all of which will transpire in the evidence. All that I need say now is that the efforts of the police to discover the identity of deceased have so far proved fruitless. We are accordingly dealing with an entirely unknown individual. The first witness whom I shall call is Thomas Crump."

At the sound of his name, Mr Crump made his way to the table, piloted thither by the coroner's officer, and took his stand, under the latter's direction, near to the coroner's chair. Having been sworn, he stated that he was an attendant in the cloakroom at Fenchurch Street Station.

"Were you on duty in the evening of Saturday the 19th of August?"

"Yes, Sir, I was."

"Do you remember receiving a certain wooden case on that evening? A case which there has been some question about since?"

"Yes. It was brought in about nine-twenty; just after the nine-fifteen from Shoeburyness had come in."

"Was there anything on the case to show where it had come from?"

"No, there were no labels on it excepting one with what I took to be the owner's name and address. I supposed that it had come by the Shoeburyness train, but that was only a guess. If it did, it couldn't have travelled in the luggage van. The guard wouldn't have had it without a label."

"Who brought the case to the cloakroom?"

"It was brought in by the gentleman whom I took to be the owner. And a rare job he must have had with it, for it weighed close on a hundredweight, as near as I could tell. He staggered in with it, carrying it by a cord that was tied round it."

"Can you give us any description of this man?"

"I didn't notice him very particularly, but I remember that he was rather tall and had a long, thin face and a big, sharp nose. He looked a bit on the thin side, but he must have been pretty strong to judge by the way he handled that case."

"Did you notice how he was dressed?"

"So far as I remember, he had on a dark suit – I fancy it was blue serge but I wouldn't be sure; but I remember that he was wearing a soft felt hat."

"Had he any moustache or was he clean shaved?"

"He had a moustache and a smallish beard, cut to a point; what they call a torpedo beard. His beard and his hair were both dark."

"About what age would you say he was?"

"He might have been about forty or perhaps a trifle more."

"And with regard to the case, can you give us any description of that?"

"It was a wooden case, about fifteen inches square and perhaps eighteen inches high. It was made of plain deal strongly put together and strengthened at the corners with iron straps. The top was fitted with hinges and held down by eight screws. The wood was a good deal stained and rubbed, as if it had seen a fair amount of use. It had a label fastened on with tacks; just a plain card with the owner's name on it — at least somebody's name — and an address. The name was Dobson, but I wouldn't swear to the address."

"Well," the coroner pursued, "you took in the case. What happened next?"

"Nothing on that night. I gave the man his ticket and he took it and said he would probably call for the case on Monday. Then he said 'Good night' and went off."

"When did you see him again?"

"That was on Monday evening, about seven o'clock. It happened to be a slack time and I had more time to attend to him. He came and handed me his ticket and asked for the case. He pointed out one which he thought was his, so I went over to it and looked at the label that had been stuck on it, but it was the wrong number. However, he said that his name was on the case — name of Dobson — and I saw that there was a private label with that name on it, so I said he had better have a look at it and see if it really was his case. So he came into the cloakroom and examined the case. And then he got into a rare state of excitement. He said it was certainly his name that was on the case and his address, but the label was not the same one that he wrote. But still he thought that the case was his case.

"Then I asked him if the contents of his case were of any particular value, and he said 'yes' they were worth several thousand pounds. Now, when he said that, I began to suspect that there was something wrong, so I suggested that we had better open the case and see if his property was inside. He jumped at the offer, so I got a screwdriver, and we took out the screws and lifted the lid. And when we lifted it, the first thing that we saw was the top of a man's head, packed in with a lot of rags. When he saw it, he seemed to be struck all of a heap. Then he slammed down the lid and asked me where he could find a policeman. I told him that he would find one outside the station, and off he went as hard as he could go."

Here the coroner held up a restraining hand as he scribbled furiously to keep up with the witness. When he had finished the paragraph, he looked up and nodded.

"Yes; he went out to look for a policeman. What happened next?"

"While we had been looking at the case, there were two gentlemen who had come to collect their luggage and who heard what was going on. When Mr Dobson − if that was his name − went out, they came over to have a look at the case; and we all waited for Mr Dobson to come back. But he didn't come back. So, after a time, one of the gentlemen went out and presently came back with a constable. I showed the constable what was in the case, and he then took possession of it."

"Yes," said the coroner, "that is all quite clear, so far. Do you think you would recognise this man, Dobson, if you were to see him again?"

"Yes," replied Crump. "I feel pretty sure I should. He was the sort of man that you would remember. And I did look at him pretty hard."

"Well," said the coroner, "I hope that you will have an opportunity of identifying him. Does any gentleman wish to ask the witness any questions? I think he has told us all that he has to tell. The other witnesses will be able to fill in the details. No questions? Then we will pass on to the next witness. William Harris."

Mr Harris came forward with rather more diffidence than had been shown by his colleague, which might have been due to his age − he was little more than a youth − or to the story that he had to tell. But, ill at ease as he obviously was, he gave his evidence in a quite clear and straightforward fashion. When he had been sworn and given the usual particulars, he stood, regarding the coroner with a look of consternation, as he waited for the dread interrogation.

"You say," the coroner began impassively, "that you are an attendant in the cloakroom at Fenchurch Street Station. How long have you been employed there?"

"Not quite three munce," the witness faltered.

"So you have not had much experience, I suppose?"

"No, Sir, not very much."

"Were you on duty on Sunday, the 20th of August?"

"Yes, Sir."

"Who was on duty with you?"

"No one, Sir. It was Mr Crump's Sunday off, and, being a slack day, I took the duty by myself."

"On that day you received a certain wooden case. Do you remember the circumstances connected with it?"

"Yes, Sir. The case was brought in about half-past ten in the morning. The man who brought it said that he would be calling for it about tea-time."

"Did this man bring the case himself?"

"Yes, Sir. He carried it by a thick cord that was tied round it, and he brought it right in and put it down not far from another case of the same kind."

"Did you examine these cases or read the labels that were on them?"

"No, Sir, I can't say that I did. I just stuck the ticket on the case that the man had brought in, but I didn't examine it. But I remember that there was another case near it that looked like the same sort of case."

"Did this man come back for the case?"

"Yes, Sir. He came about four o'clock with another man who looked like a taxi-driver. He handed me the ticket and I went with the two men and found the case. Then the man who had brought it told the other man to take it out and stow it in the taxi. Then he pulled a time-table out of his pocket and asked me to look over it with him and see how the trains ran to Loughton and Epping. So we spread out the time-table on the luggage-counter and went through the list of Sunday trains; and while we were looking at it, the taxi-man took up the case and went out of the station. When we had finished with the time-table and the man had taken one or two notes of the trains, he put the time-table back in his pocket, thanked me for helping him and went away."

"Did it never occur to you to see whether he had taken the right case?"

"No, Sir. My back was towards the taxi-man when he picked the case up. I saw him carrying it out towards the entrance, but it looked just like the right case, and it never occurred to me that he might have taken the wrong one. And the one that was left looked like the right one and it was in the right place."

"Yes," said the coroner, "it was very natural. Evidently, the exchange had been carefully planned in advance, and very skilfully planned, too. Now, with regard to these two cases: were you able to form any opinion as to the weight of either or both of them?"

"I never felt either of them," the witness replied; "but the one that the man brought in seemed rather heavy, by the way that he carried it. He had hold of it by the cord that was tied round it. The other one seemed a bit heavy, too. But when I saw the taxi-man going out with it, he had got it on his shoulder and he didn't seem to have any difficulty with it."

"And, with regard to these two men. Can you give us any description of them?"

"I hardly saw the taxi-man, and I don't remember what he was like at all, excepting that he was a big, strong-looking man. The other man was rather small, but he looked pretty strong-built, too. When we were looking at the time-tables, I noticed two things about him. One was that he seemed to have a couple of gold teeth."

"Ah!" said the coroner, "presumably gold-filled teeth. Do you remember which teeth they were?"

"They were the two middle front teeth at the top. He showed them a good deal when he talked."

"Yes; and what was the other thing that you noticed?"

"I noticed, when he put his hand on the time-table, that his fingers were stained all browny-yellow, as if he was always smoking cigarettes; and his hand was shaking, even when it was laying on the paper. I didn't notice anything else."

"Can you tell us how he was dressed?"

"He had on an ordinary tweed suit; rather a shabby suit it was. And he was wearing a cloth cap."

"Had he any moustache or beard?"

"No, Sir; he was clean-shaved – or, at least, not very clean, because he had about a couple of days' growth, and as he was a dark man, it showed pretty plainly."

"How did he strike you as to his station in life? Should you describe him as a gentleman?"

"No, Sir, I should not," the witness replied with considerable emphasis. "He struck me as quite a common sort of man, and I got the idea that he might have been a seaman or some kind of water-side character. We see a good many of that sort on our line, so we get to recognise them."

"What sort of men are you referring to?" the coroner asked with evident interest. "And where do they come from?"

"I mean sailors of all kinds from the London and the India Docks, and fishermen and longshoremen from Leigh and Benfleet and Southend and the seaside places up that way."

"Yes," said the coroner. "This is quite interesting and may be important. Fenchurch Street has always been a sailors' station. However, that is for the police rather than for us. I think that is all that we want to ask this witness, unless any of the gentlemen of the jury wish to put any questions."

He glanced interrogatively at the jury, but none of them expressed any curiosity. Accordingly, the witness was allowed to retire; which he did with undisguised relief.

The next witness was the constable who had been called in to take charge of the case, and, as his evidence amounted to little more than a statement of that fact, he was soon disposed of and dismissed. Then the coroner pronounced the name of Geoffrey Buffham, and that gentleman rose from the extreme corner of the court and worked his way to the table, casting a leer of recognition on Mr Pippet as he passed. His evidence, also, was chiefly formal; but, when he had finished his account of his search for the constable, the coroner turned to the subject of identification.

"You saw the man who had come to claim the case. Can you add any particulars to those given by the attendant?"

"I am afraid I can't tell you very much about him. The light was not very good, and, of course, until he had gone, there was nothing to make one take any special notice of him. And then it was too late. All I can say is that he was a tallish man with a rather dark beard and a prominent nose."

The coroner wrote this down without comment, and then, apparently judging Mr Buffham to be worth no more powder and shot, glanced at the jury for a moment and dismissed him. Then he pronounced the name of Christopher J Pippet, and the owner of that name rose and stepped over to the place that had been occupied by the other witnesses. The coroner looked up at the tall, dignified figure, apparently contrasting it with its rather scrubby, raffish predecessor; and when the preliminaries had been disposed of, he asked apologetically:

"It is of no particular importance, but would you tell us what the 'J' in your name stands for? It is usual to give the full name."

Mr Pippet smiled. "As I have just been sworn," said he, "I have got to be careful in my statements. My impression is that the 'J' stands for Josiah, but that is only an opinion. I have always been accustomed to use the initial only."

"Then," said the coroner, "we will accept that as your recognised personal designation. There is no need to be pedantic. Now, Mr Pippet, I don't think we need trouble you to go into details concerning the discovery of this case, but it would be useful if you could give us some further description of the man who came to claim the property. The descriptions which have been given are very sketchy and indefinite; can you amplify them in any way?"

Mr Pippet reflected. "I took a pretty careful look at him," said he, "and I have a fairly clear mental picture of the man."

"You say you took a pretty careful look at him," said the coroner. "What made you look at him carefully?"

"Well, Sir," Mr Pippet replied, "the circumstances were rather remarkable. From his conversation with the attendant it was clear that something quite irregular had been happening; and when he mentioned the value of the case, it began to look like a serious crime. Then when he rushed out pell-mell in search of a policeman, that struck me as a very strange thing to do. What was the hurry about? His own case was gone, and the one that was there wasn't going to run away. But I gathered that there was something in it that oughtn't to have been there. So when he came running out full pelt, I suspected that the cause of the hurry was behind him, not in front, and, naturally, my attention was aroused."

"You suspected that he might be making off?"

"It seemed a possibility. Anyway, I have never seen a man look more thoroughly scared."

"Then," said the coroner, "as you seem to have taken more notice of him than anyone else, perhaps you can give us a rather more complete description of him. Do you think you would recognise him if you should see him again?"

"I feel pretty sure that I should," was the reply; "but that is not the same as enabling other people to recognise him. I should describe him as a tall man, about five feet eleven, lean but muscular and broad across the shoulders. He had a long, thin face and a long, thin nose, curved on the bridge and pointed at the end. His hair and beard were nearly black, but his skin and eyes didn't seem to match them very well, for his skin was distinctly fair and his eyes were a pale blue. I got the distinct impression that his hair and beard were dyed."

"Was that merely an impression or had you any definite grounds for the suspicion?"

"At first, it was just an impression. But as he was running out he got between me and the electric light for a moment, and the light shone through his beard. Then I caught a glint of that peculiar red that you see in hair that is dyed black when the light shines through it, and that you never see in natural hair; a red with a perceptible tinge of purple in it."

"Yes," said the coroner, "it is very characteristic. But do you feel quite sure that you actually saw this colour? It is a very important point."

"I feel convinced in my own mind," replied Mr Pippet, "but, of course, I might have been mistaken. I can only say that, to the best of my belief, the hair showed that peculiar colour."

"Well," said the coroner, "that is about as much as anyone could say, under the circumstances. Did you notice anything of interest in regard to the clothing? You heard Mr Crump's evidence."

"Yes; and I don't think I can add much to it. The man was wearing a well-used dark blue serge suit, a blue cotton shirt with a collar to match, a soft felt hat and dark brown shoes. He had a wrist watch, but he seemed to have a pocket watch as well. Anyway, he had what looked like a watch-guard, made, apparently, of plaited twine."

"Is that all you can tell us about him, or is there anything else that you are able to recall?"

"I think I have told you all that I noticed. There wasn't much opportunity to examine him closely."

"No, there was not," the coroner agreed. "I can only compliment you on the excellent use that you made of your eyes in the short time that was available. And, if that is all that you have to tell us, I think that we need not trouble you any further."

He glanced at the foreman of the jury, and as that gentleman bowed to indicate that he was satisfied, Mr Pippet was allowed to return to his seat, where he received the whispered congratulations of his daughter.

"That," said the coroner, addressing the jury, "concludes the evidence relating to the discovery of the remains. We shall now proceed to the evidence afforded by the remains themselves; and we will begin with that of the medical officer to whom the head was handed for expert examination, Dr Humphrey Smith."

# CHAPTER FOUR

## The Finding of the Jury

The new witness was a man of about thirty with a clean-shaved, studious face, garnished with a pair of horn-rimmed spectacles, and a somewhat diffident, uneasy manner. Having advanced to the table and taken his seat on the chair which had been placed for him close to that occupied by the coroner, he produced from his pocket a note-book which he held unopened on his knee throughout the proceedings. In reply to the preliminary questions, he stated that his name was Humphrey Smith, that he was a bachelor of medicine, a member of the Royal College of Surgeons and a Licentiate of the Royal College of Physicians.

"You are the Police Medical Officer of this district, I believe," the coroner suggested.

"Temporarily, I hold that post," was the reply, "during the absence on sick leave of the regular medical officer."

"Quite so," said the coroner; "for the purposes of this inquiry, you are the Police Medical Officer."

The witness admitted that this was so, and the coroner proceeded: "You have had submitted to you for examination a case containing a human head. Will you give us an account of your examination and the conclusions at which you arrived?"

The witness reflected a few moments and then began his statement.

"At ten-fifteen on the morning of the twenty-second of August,
Inspector Budge called on me and asked me to come round to the
police-station to examine the contents of a case, in which he said were
certain human remains. I went with him and was shown a wooden
case, strengthened by iron straps. It had a hinged lid which was further
secured by eight screws, which, however, had been extracted. On
raising the lid, I saw what looked like the top of a man's head,
surrounded by rags and articles of clothing which had been packed
tightly round it. With the Inspector's assistance I removed the packing
material until it was possible to lift out the head, which I then took
to a table by the window where I was able to make a thorough
examination.

"The head appeared to be that of a man, although there was hardly
any visible beard or moustache and no signs of his having been
shaved."

"You say that the head *appeared* to be that of a man. Do you feel
confident that deceased *was* a man, or do you think that the head may
possibly be that of a woman?"

"I think there is no doubt that deceased was a man. The general
appearance was masculine, and the hair was quite short and arranged
like a man's hair."

"That," remarked the coroner, "is not a very safe criterion in these
days. I have seen a good many women who would have passed well
enough for men excepting for their clothes."

"Yes, that is true," the witness admitted, "but I had the present
fashion in mind when I formed my opinion; and, although there was
extremely little hair on the face, there was more than one usually finds
on the face of a woman – a young woman, at any rate."

"Then, are we to understand that this head was that of a young
person?"

"The exact age was rather difficult to determine, but I should say
that deceased was not much, if any, over thirty."

"What made it difficult to estimate the age of deceased?"

"There were two circumstances that made it difficult to judge the age. One was the physical condition of the head, and the other was the extraordinary facial character of this person."

"By the physical condition, do you mean that it had undergone considerable putrefactive changes?"

"No, not at all. It was not in the least decomposed. It had been thoroughly embalmed, or, at least, treated with preservative substance – principally formalin, I think. There was quite a distinct odour of formalin vapour."

"Then it would appear that it was in quite a good state of preservation, which ought to have helped rather than hindered your examination."

"Yes, but the effect of the formalin was to produce a certain amount of shrinkage of the tissues, which naturally resulted in some distortion of the features. But it was not easy to be sure how much of the distortion was due to the formalin and how much to the natural deformity."

"Was the shrinkage in any way due to drying of the tissues?"

"No. The tissues were not in the least dry. It appeared to me that the formalin had been mixed with glycerin; and, as glycerin does not evaporate, the head has remained perfectly moist, but without any tendency to decompose."

"How long do you consider that deceased has been dead?"

"That," replied the doctor, "is a question upon which I could form no opinion whatever. The head is so perfectly preserved that it will last in its present condition for an almost indefinite time; and, of course, what applies to the future applies equally to the past. One can estimate the time that has elapsed since death only by the changes that have occurred in the interval. But, if there are no changes, there is nothing on which to form an opinion."

"Do you mean to say that deceased might have been dead for a year?"

"Yes, or even longer than that. A year ago the head would have looked exactly as it looks now, and as it will look a year hence. The preservatives have rendered it practically unchangeable."

"That is very remarkable," said the coroner, "and it introduces a formidable difficulty into this inquiry. For we have to discover, if we can, how, when and where this person met with his death. But it would seem that the 'when' is undiscoverable. You could give no limit to the time that has elapsed since death took place?"

"No. I could make no suggestion as to the time."

The coroner wrote this down and looked at what he had written with an air of profound dissatisfaction. Then he turned to the witness and opened a new subject.

"You spoke just now of the remarkable facial peculiarities of deceased. Can you describe those peculiarities?"

"I will try. Deceased had a most extraordinary and perfectly hideous face. The peculiar appearance was due principally to the overgrown condition of the lower part, especially the lower jaw. In shape, the face was like an egg with the small end upwards; and the jaw was not only enormously broad, but the chin stuck out beyond the upper lip and the lower teeth were spread out and projected considerably in front of the upper ones. Then the nose was thick and coarse and the ears stood out from the head; but they were not like ordinary outstanding ears, which tend to be thin and membranous. They were thick and lumpy and decidedly misshapen. Altogether, the appearance of the face was quite abnormal."

"Should you regard this abnormality as a deformity, or do you think it was connected with deceased's state of health?"

"I should hardly like to give an opinion without seeing the rest of the body. There is no doubt about the deformity; but whether it was congenital or due to disease, I should not like to say. There are several rather rare diseases which tend to produce malformations of different parts of the body."

"Well," said the coroner, "medical details of that kind are a little outside the scope of this inquiry. The fact which interests us is that deceased was a very unusual-looking person, so that there ought not to be much difficulty in identifying him. To come to another question; from your examination of this head, should you say that there is any evidence of special skill or knowledge in the way in which the head has been separated from the trunk?"

"I think that there is a suggestion of some skill and knowledge. Not necessarily very much. But the separation was effected in accordance with the anatomical relations, not in the way in which it would have been done by an entirely ignorant and unskilful person. The head had been separated from the spinal column – that is, from the top of the backbone – by cutting through the ligaments that fasten the backbone to the skull; whereas a quite ignorant person would almost certainly have cut through the neck and through the joint between two of the neck vertebrae."

"You think that it would not require much skill to take the head off in the manner in which it was done?"

"No; it would be quite easy if one knew where to make the cut. But most people do not."

"You think, then, that the person who cut off his head must have had some anatomical knowledge?"

"Yes; but a very little knowledge of anatomy would suffice."

"Do you think that such knowledge as a butcher possesses would be sufficient?"

"Certainly. A butcher doesn't know much anatomy, but he knows where to find the joints."

"And now, to take another question; can you give us any information as to the cause of death?"

"No," was the very definite reply. "I examined the head most carefully with this question in view, but I could find no trace of any wound, bruise, or mark of violence, or even of rough treatment. There was no clue whatever to the cause or mode of death."

There was a brief pause while the coroner glanced through his notes. Then, looking up at the jury, he said:

"Well, gentlemen, you have heard what the doctor has to tell us. It doesn't get us on very far, but, of course, that is not the doctor's fault. He can't make evidence. Would any of you like to ask him any further questions? If not, I think we need not occupy any more of his time."

Once more he paused with his eyes on the jury; then, as no one made any sign, he thanked the witness and gave him his dismissal.

The next witness was a smart-looking uniformed inspector of the City Police, who stepped up to his post with the brisk, confident air of one familiar with the procedure. He stated that his name was William Budge, and, having rattled through the preliminaries, gave a precise and business-like account of the circumstances in which he made the acquaintance of the "remains" in the cloak-room. From this he proceeded to the examination of the case in collaboration with the medical officer. His description of the case tallied with that given by Mr Crump, but he was able to supply a few further details.

"Mr Crump referred in his evidence," said the coroner, "to a private label on this case. You examined that, of course?"

"Yes. It was a piece of card – half of a stationer's post-card – fastened to the lid of the case with four tacks. It had a name and address written on it in plain block letters with a rather fine pen. The name was J Dobson and the address was 401 Argyle Square, King's Cross, London."

"Four hundred and one!" exclaimed the coroner.

The witness smiled. "Yes, Sir. Of course, there's no such number, but I went there to make sure."

"You did not extract any other information from the label?"

"I did not make a particular examination of it. I took it off carefully with the proper precautions and handed it to the superintendent."

"You did not test it for finger-prints?"

"No, Sir. That would not be in my province."

"Exactly!" said the coroner, "and it is not really in ours." He paused for a few moments and then asked:

"Have you any idea, Inspector, where this case might have come from, or what its original contents might have been?"

"I should say," was the reply, "that it originally contained some kind of provisions and that it formed part of a ship's stores. It is very usual for firms who supply provisions to ships to send them out in cases of this kind. The lids are screwed down for security in transit, but furnished with hinges for convenience when they are in use on board.

There was no mark on the wood to indicate where the case came from. The issuer's name and address was probably on a label which has been taken off."

"Did you find anything that seemed to confirm your surmise that this case had formed part of a ship's stores?"

"Yes. When the doctor had taken the head out, I took out the clothes and rags that had been used for packing and went over them carefully. Most of them seemed to be connected with a vessel of some sort. I made out a list, which I have with me."

He produced an official-looking note-book, and, at the coroner's request, read out the list of items.

"At the top, immediately surrounding the head, was a very old, ragged blue jersey, such as fishermen wear. There was no mark of any kind on it, but there were some ends of thread that looked as if a linen tab had been cut off. Next, there was a pair of brown canvas trousers, a good deal worn and without any marks or any name on the buttons, and an old brown canvas jumper. Then there were several worn-out cotton swabs such as they use on board ship, three longish ends of inch-and-a-half Manilla rope, and, at the bottom of the case, a ragged oilskin coat. So the whole contents looked like the throw-outs collected from some ship's fo'c'sle, or from the cabin of a barge or some other small craft."

"Do you associate these cast-off things with any particular kind of vessel?"

"As far as the things themselves are concerned, I do not. But the case rather suggests a deep-water craft. A barge or a coaster can pick up her provisions at the various ports of call, and hardly needs the quantity of stores that this case suggests."

"And what about the other case – the case that was stolen? Do you connect it with the one that contained the head?"

The Inspector reflected. "There is not much information available at present," said he, "and what there is you have had in Crump's evidence. It appears that the two cases were exactly alike; and, if that is so, they might have come from the same source. Evidently, the man who brought in the case with the head in it knew all about the other case, and what was in it."

"Which, I take it, is more than you do?"

The Inspector smiled and admitted that the unknown man had the advantage of the police at present; and with that admission his evidence came to an end and he retired to his seat. There followed a pause, during which the coroner once more looked over his notes and the jury exchanged remarks in an undertone. At length, when he had run his eye over the depositions, the coroner leaned back in his chair, and, taking a general survey of the jury, began his summing-up.

"This inquiry, gentlemen," he began, "is a very remarkable one, and as unsatisfactory as it is unusual in character. It is unsatisfactory in several respects. We are inquiring into the circumstances surrounding the death of a deceased person. But we are not in possession of the body of that person but of only a part of it; and that part gives us no information on either of the three headings of our inquiry – the time, the place and the manner. We are seeking to discover: – first, when this person died; second, in what place he died; and, third, in what manner and by what means he came by his death. But, owing to the incomplete nature of the remains, the strange circumstances in which they were discovered, and the physical condition of the remains themselves, we can answer none of these questions. We do not even know who the deceased is. All that we can do is to consider the whole body of facts which are known to us and draw what reasonable conclusions we can from them.

"Let us begin by taking a glance at the succession of events in the order of their occurrence. First, on the Saturday night, comes a man with a heavy case which, according to his subsequent admission, contains property of great value. He leaves this case in the cloak-room for the weekend. Then, on the Sunday, comes another man with another case which appears to be identically similar to the first. He very adroitly manages to exchange this case for the one containing the valuable property. Then, on the Monday, comes the first man to claim his property. He sees that some substitution appears to have occurred, and, in order to make sure, opens the case. Then he discovers the head of deceased and is, naturally enough, horrified. Instantly, he rushes out of the station, ostensibly in search of a policeman, but actually, to make his escape, as becomes evident when he does not return. That is the series of events which are known to us, and which form, in effect, the whole sum of our knowledge. Let us see what conclusions we can draw from them.

"The first question that we ask ourselves is: – Why did that man not come back? The case which had been stolen contained, according to what was probably a hasty, unguarded statement, property worth several thousand pounds. Without committing ourselves to a legal opinion, we may say that he could have made a claim on the railway company for the value of that property. Yet, at the sight of that dead man's head, he rushed out and disappeared. What are we to infer from that? There are several inferences that suggest themselves. First, although it is evident that the head in the case came to him as a complete surprise, it is possible that, as soon as he saw it, he recognised it as something with which he had a guilty association. That is one possibility. Then there is the question as to what was in his own case. It was property of great value. But whose property was it? There is in the behaviour of this man a strong suggestion that the valuable contents of that case may have been stolen property, of which he was not in a position to give any account. That appears to be highly probable; but it does not greatly concern us, excepting that it suggests a criminal element in the transaction as a whole – a suggestion that is strengthened by the apparent connection between the two men.

"When we come to the second man, the criminal element is unmistakable. To say nothing of the theft which he undoubtedly committed, the fact that he was going about with the head of a dead man in a box, definitely puts upon him the responsibility for the mutilation of a human body, to say the least. The question of any further guilt depends on the view that is taken of that mutilation. And that brings us to the question as to the manner in which the deceased came by his death.

"Now, we have to recognise that we have no direct evidence on this point. The doctor's careful and expert examination failed to elicit any information as to the cause of death; which was what might have been expected from the very insufficient means at his disposal. But, if we have no direct evidence as to the actual cause of death, we have very important indirect evidence as to some of the circumstances surrounding his death. We know, for instance, that the body had been mutilated, or at least decapitated; and we know that some person was in possession of the separated head – and, probably, of the mutilated remainder of the corpse.

"But these are very material facts. What does our common sense, aided by experience, suggest in the case of a corpse which has been mutilated and a part packed in a box and planted in a railway cloak-room? What is the usual object of dismembering a corpse and of disposing of the dismembered remains in this way? In all the numerous cases which have occurred from time to time, the object has been the same: to get rid of the body of a person who has been murdered, in order to cover up the fact and the circumstances of the crime. No other reason is imaginable. There could be no object in thus making away with the body of a person who had died a natural death.

"That, however, is for you to consider in deciding on your verdict. The other known facts do not seem to be helpful. The singular and rather repulsive appearance of deceased does not concern us, although it may be important to the police. As to the curious use of a preservative, the object of that seems to be fairly obvious. Mutilated remains have been commonly discovered by the putrefactive odour which they have exhaled. If this head had not been preserved, it would have been impossible for it to have been left in the cloak-room for twenty-four hours without arousing suspicion. But, as I have said, the fact, though curious, is not material to our inquiry. The material facts are those which suggest an answer to the question, How did deceased come by his death? Those facts are in your possession; and I shall now leave you to consider your verdict."

Thereupon, while the hum of conversation once more pervaded the court-room, the jury drew together and compared notes. But their conference lasted only a very few minutes, at the end of which the foreman signified to the coroner that they had agreed on their verdict.

"Well, gentlemen," said the latter, "what is your decision?"

"We find," was the reply, "that deceased was murdered by some person or persons unknown."

"Yes," said the coroner, as he entered the verdict at the foot of the depositions, "that is what common sense suggests. I don't see that you could have arrived at any other decision. It remains only for me to thank you for your attendance and the careful attention which you have given to the evidence, and close the proceedings."

As the court rose, Mr Buffham emerged hurriedly from the corner in which he had been seated and elbowed his way towards Mr Pippet and his daughter.

"My dear sir," he exclaimed, effusively, "let me offer my most hearty congratulations on the brilliant way in which you gave your evidence. Your powers of observation positively staggered me."

The latter statement was no exaggeration. Mr Buffham had been not only staggered but slightly disconcerted by the discovery of his friend's remarkable capacity for "keeping his weather eyelid lifting." In the peculiar circumstances, it was a gift that he was disposed to view with some disfavour; and he found himself wondering, a little uncomfortably, whether Mr Pippet happened to have observed any other facts which he was not expected or desired to observe. But he did not allow these misgivings to interfere with his suave and ingratiating manner. As Mr Pippet received his congratulations without obvious emotion, he bestowed on Miss Jenny a leer which was intended to express admiring recognition and then turned with an insinuating smile to her father.

"This charming young lady," said he, "is, I presume, the daughter of whom I have heard you speak."

"You have guessed right the first time," Mr Pippet replied. "This is Mr Buffham, my dear; but you know that, as you heard him give his evidence."

Miss Jenny bowed, with a faint suggestion of stiffness. The ingratiating smile did not seem to have produced the expected effect.

The "charming young lady" was not, in fact, at all favourably impressed by Mr Buffham's personality. Nevertheless, she exchanged a few observations on the incidents of the inquest, as the audience was clearing off, and the three moved out together when the way was clear. Here, however, Mr Buffham suffered a slight disappointment. For when the taxi which Mr Pippet hailed drew up at the kerb, the hoped-for invitation was not forthcoming, and the cordial handshake and smiling farewell appeared an unsatisfactory substitute.

# CHAPTER FIVE

## The Great Platinum Robbery

Thorndyke's rather free-and-easy custom of receiving professional visitors at unconventional hours tended on certain occasions to result in slightly embarrassing situations. It did, for instance, on an evening in early October when the arrival of our old friend Mr Brodribb, was followed almost immediately by that of Mr Superintendent Miller. Both were ostensibly making a friendly call; but both, I felt sure, had their particular fish to fry. Brodribb had almost certainly come for a professional consultation, and Miller's informal chats invariably developed a professional background.

I watched with amused curiosity to see what would happen. Each man would probably give the other a chance to retire, and the question was, Which would be the first to abdicate? The event would probably be determined by the relative urgency of their respective fish frying. But the delicate balance of probabilities was upset by Polton, our invaluable laboratory assistant, who happened to be in the room when they arrived; who instantly proceeded to make the arrangements which immemorial custom had associated with each of our visitors. The two cosiest armchairs were drawn up to the fire and a small table placed by each. On one table appeared, as if by magic, the whisky decanter, siphon and cigar box which clearly appertained to Miller, and on the other, three port glasses.

"This is your chair, Sir," said Polton, shepherding the Superintendent in the way he should go. "The other is for Mr Brodribb;" and with this he vanished, and we all knew whither he had gone.

"Well," said Brodribb with slight indecision, as he subsided into his allotted chair and put his toes on the kerb, while Thorndyke and I drew up our chairs, "if I shan't be in the way, I'll just sit down and warm myself for a few minutes."

His "defeatist" tone I judged to be due to the fact that Miller, in ready response to my invitation, had mixed himself a stiff jorum, got a cigar alight and apparently settled himself comfortably for the evening. I think the old lawyer was disposed to give up the contest and retire in favour of the Superintendent. But at that moment Polton returned, bearing a decanter of port, which he deposited on Mr Brodribb's table; whereupon the balance of probabilities was restored.

"Ha!" said Brodribb, as Thorndyke filled the three glasses, "it's all very well to sentimentalise about the Last Rose of Summer, but the First Fire of Winter makes more appeal to me."

"You can hardly call it winter at the beginning of October," Miller objected.

"Can't you, by Jove!" exclaimed Brodribb. "Perhaps not by the calendar; but when I came through the Carey Street gateway just now, the wind was enough to nip the nose off a brass monkey. But I haven't got a fire yet. It's only you medico-legal sybarites who can afford such luxuries."

He sipped his wine ecstatically, spread out his toes and blinked at the fire with an air of enjoyment that suggested a particularly magnificent old Tom cat. The Superintendent made no rejoinder, and Thorndyke and I filled our pipes and waited curiously for the situation to develop.

"I suppose," said Brodribb, after an interval of silence, "you haven't got any forrarder with that Fenchurch Street mystery; I mean the box with the gentleman's head in it?"

"Gentleman, indeed!" exclaimed Miller. "He was about the ugliest beggar that I ever clapped eyes on. I don't wonder they cut his head off. He must have been a lot better-looking without it."

"Still," said Brodribb, "you've got to admit that the man was murdered."

"No doubt," rejoined Miller; "and if you had seen him, you wouldn't have been surprised. His face was an outrage on humanity."

"So it may have been," retorted Brodribb, "but ugliness is not provocation in a legal sense. You don't mean to say that you have abandoned the case?"

"We never abandon a case at The Yard," replied Miller, "but it's no use fussing about when you've nothing to go on. As a matter of fact, we expect to approach the problem from another direction. For the moment, we are letting that particular box rest while we give a little attention to the other box – the one that was stolen."

"Ha!" said Brodribb. "Yes; very necessary, I should say. But what is your idea about it? You don't think it possible that it contained the body which belonged to the head?"

Miller shook his head. "No," said he. "I think you can rule that out. If the original case had contained a headless corpse, Mr Dobson would not have been so ready to open the doubtful one in the presence of the attendant. You see, until they got it open, it wasn't certain that it was a different case."

"Then," said Brodribb, "I don't quite see the connection. You said that you were approaching the problem of the head from another direction – through the stolen box, as I understood."

"That is so," replied Miller; "and you must see that there is evidently some connection between the two cases. To begin with, the second case, which we may call the head case, was exactly similar to the first one – the stolen case – and we may take it that the similarity was purposely arranged. The head case was prepared as a counterfeit so that it could be exchanged for the other. But from that it follows that the person who prepared the head case must have known exactly what the other case was like, even to what was written on the label; and as he was at a good deal of trouble to steal the first case, we may take it that he knew what that case contained. So there you have a clear connection on the one side. As to whether the man, Dobson, recognised the head or knew anything about it, we can't be sure."

"The way in which he made himself scarce when he had seen it," said Brodribb, "rather suggests that he did."

"Not necessarily," Miller objected. "The question is, What was in the stolen case? He stated that the contents were worth several thousand pounds, but in spite of that, he made no attempt at recovery or claim for compensation. It looks as if he was not in a position to say what was in the case. But that suggests that the contents were not his lawful property; in fact, that the case contained stolen property – perhaps the loot from some robbery. Now, if that were so, he would have to clear off in any event to avoid inquiries. Naturally, then, when he came on that head, he would have realised that he was fairly in the soup. The fact that he had been in possession of stolen property wouldn't have been a bit helpful if he had been charged with complicity in a murder. I'm not surprised that he bolted."

"Is there any clue to what has become of the stolen case?" Brodribb asked.

"No," replied Miller; "but that is not the question which is interesting us. What we want to know is, not where it went, but where it came from, and what was in it."

"And that, I presume, you don't know at present," said Brodribb.

The Superintendent took a long draw at his cigar, blew out a cloud of smoke and performed the operation that he would have described as "wetting his whistle". Then he set down his glass and replied, cautiously:

"As the Doctor is listening, I mustn't use the word 'know'. But we think we've got a pretty good idea."

"Have you!" Brodribb exclaimed. "Now, I wonder what you have discovered. But I suppose it isn't in order for an outsider like me to pry into the secrets of Scotland Yard."

The Superintendent did not reply immediately, but from something in his manner, I suspected that he had come expressly to discuss the matter with us, but was "inhibited" by Brodribb's presence. At length, Thorndyke broke the silence.

"We are all very much interested, Miller, and we are all very discreet."

"M'yes," said Miller. "Three lawyers and a detective officer ought to be able to produce a fair amount of discretion between them. And I don't know that it's such a deadly secret, after all. Still, we are keeping our own counsel, so you will understand that what I may mention mustn't go any farther."

"You are perfectly safe, Miller," Thorndyke assured him. "You know Jervis and me of old, and I can tell you that Mr Brodribb is as close as an oyster."

Thus reassured, Miller (who was really bursting to give us his news) moistened his whistle afresh and began:

"You must understand that we are at present dealing with what the Doctor calls hypothesis, though we have got a solid foundation of fact. As to what was in that stolen case, we have no direct evidence but we have formed a pretty confident opinion. In fact, we think we know what that case contained. And what do you suppose it was?"

I ventured to suggest jewellery, or perhaps bullion.

"You are not so far out," said Miller. "We say that it was platinum."

"Platinum!" I exclaimed. "But there was a hundredweight of it! Why, at the present price, it must have been worth a king's ransom!"

"I don't know how much that is," said Miller, "but we reckon the value of the contents at between seventeen and eighteen thousand pounds. That is only a rough estimate, of course. We think that the witness, Crump, was mistaken about the weight, and it was only a guess, in any case. He hadn't tested the weight of the package. At any rate, we can't account for more than about half a hundredweight of platinum."

"You have some perfectly definite information, then?" said Thorndyke.

"Definite enough so far as it goes," replied Miller, "but it doesn't go far enough. We are quite clear that a parcel of platinum weighing about twenty-five kilogrammes – roughly, half a hundredweight – was stolen and has disappeared. That is actual fact. The rest is inference, or, as the Doctor would say, hypothesis. But I will give you a sketch of the affair, leaving out the details that don't matter.

"Our information is that, about the end of last June, a quantity of platinum was shipped by a Latvian firm at Riga. It was packed in small wooden cases, each containing twenty-five kilos, and consigned to various dealers in Germany, France and Italy. Well, the cases were all duly delivered at their respective destinations, and everything seemed to be in order excepting the contents of one of the Italian cases. That happened to be the last one that was delivered, and, as the ship had made a good many calls on her voyage, it wasn't delivered until the beginning of August. When it was opened, it was found to contain, instead of the platinum, an equal weight of lead.

"Obviously, there had been a robbery somewhere, but, owing to the time which had elapsed, it was difficult to trace. One thing, however, was clear; the job had been done by somebody who was in the know. That was evident from the fact that the case was in all respects exactly like the original case and all the other cases."

"Why shouldn't it have been the original case with the contents changed?" I asked.

"That hardly seems possible. It would have been difficult enough to steal the case; but to steal it, empty it, refill it and put it back, looks like an impossibility. No, we can be pretty certain that the thieves had the dummy case ready and just made a quick exchange. That must have been the method, whoever did the job; but the puzzle was to discover the time and place of the robbery. The stuff had made a long journey to the port of delivery and the robbery might have taken place anywhere along the route.

"Eventually, suspicion arose with regard to an English yacht, the *Cormorant*, which had berthed close to the *Kronstadt* – that was the name of the ship which carried the stuff – while she was taking in her cargo at Riga. It was recalled that she had occupied the next berth to the *Kronstadt* at the time when the platinum was being shipped, and someone remembered that, at that very time, the *Cormorant* was taking stores on board, including one or two big hampers. Accordingly, the Latvian police made some inquiries on the spot, and, though they didn't discover anything very sensational, the little that they did learn seemed to favour the idea that the platinum might have been taken away on the yacht. This is what it amounted to, together with what we have picked up since.

"The *Cormorant* is a sturdy little yawl-rigged vessel – she appears to be a converted fishing lugger from Shorehams – of about thirty tons. She turned up at Riga on the 21st of June and took up her berth alongside the quay where the *Kronstadt* had just berthed. She went out from time to time for a sail in the Gulf but always came back to the same berth. Her crew consisted of four men, of whom three seemed to be regular seamen of the fisherman type, while the fourth, the skipper, whose name was Bassett, was a man of a superior class. The description of Bassett agrees completely with that of the man whom we have called Dobson – the man who deposited the case that was stolen from the cloak-room; and the description of one of the crew seems to tally with that of the man who stole the case – the man whom we have called 'the head man'. Perhaps we had better call him Mr 'X' for convenience.

"Well, as I have said, at the time the platinum was shipped, the *Cormorant* was taking in stores; and her hampers and cases were on the quay at the same time as the cases of platinum and quite close to them. The platinum was unloaded from a closed van and dumped on the quay, and the *Cormorant*'s stores were unloaded from a waggon and also dumped on the quay. Then, as soon as the *Cormorant* had got her stores on board, she put out for a sail in the bay. But she was back in her berth again in about a couple of hours; and there she remained, on and off, for the next five days. It was not until the 26th of June that she left Riga for good."

"Doesn't the fact that she stayed there so long rather conflict with the idea that she had the stolen platinum on board?" I suggested.

"Well," Miller replied, "on the face of it, it does seem to. But if you bear all the circumstances in mind, I don't think it does. As soon as all the platinum was on board the *Kronstadt*, the danger of discovery was over. Remember, there was the right number of cases. There was nothing missing. It was practically certain that the robbery would not be discovered until the dummy case was opened by the consignees. Bearing that in mind, you see that it would be an excellent tactical plan to stay on at Riga as if nothing had happened; whereas it might have looked suspicious if the yacht had put to sea immediately after the shipment of the platinum.

"The next thing we hear of the yacht is that she arrived at Southend on the 17th of August."

"Have you ascertained where she had been in the interval?" I asked.

"No" he replied, "because, you see, it doesn't particularly concern us, as our theory is that she still had the platinum on board. But I must admit that, apart from the cloak-room incident, we can't get any evidence that she had. At Southend she was boarded by the Customs Officer, and, as she had just come from Rotterdam and had been cruising up the Baltic and along the German and Dutch coasts, he made a pretty rigorous search, especially for tobacco. He turned out every possible place in which a few cigars or cakes of 'hard' could have been stowed, and he even took up the trap in the cabin floor and squeezed down into the little hold. But he didn't find anything beyond the few trifles that had been declared. So his evidence is negative."

"It is rather more than negative," said I. "It amounts to positive evidence that the platinum wasn't there."

"Well, in a way, it does," Miller admitted. "It certainly doesn't help us. But there was one curious fact that we got from him. It seems that there were still four men on board the yacht; but they were not the same four men. One of them, at least, was different. The Customs man didn't see anybody corresponding to the description of Mr 'X'. On the other hand, there was a tall, clean-shaved, elderly man who didn't look like a seaman – looked more like a lawyer or a doctor and spoke like a gentleman, or, at least, an educated man, though with a slight foreign accent, and didn't seem very anxious to speak at all; seemed more disposed to keep himself to himself. But the interesting point to us is the disappearance of Mr 'X'. That seems to give us something like a complete scheme of the whole affair, including the transaction at the cloak-room."

"Were you proposing to let us hear your scheme of the robbery?" I asked.

"Well," said Miller, "I don't see why not, as I have told you so much. Of course, you will understand that it is very largely guess-work, but still, it comes together into a consistent whole. I will just give you an outline of what we believe to have been the course of events.

"We take it that this was a very carefully-planned robbery, carried out by a party of experienced criminals who must all have had a fair knowledge of sea-faring. One of them, at least – probably the skipper, Bassett – must have had some pretty exact information as to the time and place at which the platinum was shipped and the size and character of the cases that it was stowed in. They must have arrived at the selected berth with a carefully-prepared dummy case ready for use at the psychological moment. Then, when the cases of platinum arrived – and they must have known when to expect them – the dummy was smuggled up to the quay, covered up in some way, and slipped in amongst the genuine cases. Then they must have managed to cover up one of these, and they probably waited until the whole consignment, including the dummy, had been put on board and checked. There would have been the right number, you must remember.

"Well, when all the platinum appeared to have been put on board, there would have been no difficulty in taking the one that they had pinched – still covered up – on to the yacht along with their own stores. As soon as they had got it on board, they cast off and went for a sail in the bay; and during that little trip, they would be able safely to unload the case, break it up and burn it and stow the platinum in the hiding-place that they had got prepared in advance. When they came back to their berth, they had got the loot safely hidden and were ready to submit to a search, if need be. And it must have been an uncommonly cleverly devised hiding-place, for they made no difficulty about letting the Customs Officer at Southend rummage the vessel to his heart's content."

"It must, as you say, have been a mighty perfect hiding-place," I remarked, "to have eluded the Customs man. When one of those gentry becomes really inquisitive, there isn't much that escapes him. He knows all the ropes and is up to all the smugglers' dodges."

"You must bear in mind, Jervis," Thorndyke reminded me, "that he was not looking for platinum. He was looking for tobacco. Do you know, Miller, in what form the metal was shipped? Was it in ingots or bars or plates?"

"It was in plates; thin sheet, in fact, about a millimetre in thickness and thirty centimetres – roughly twelve inches – square; a most convenient form for stowing in a hiding-place, for you could roll up the plates or cut them up with shears into little pieces."

"Yes," said Thorndyke, "and the plates themselves would take up very little room. You say the Customs man squeezed down into the hold. Do you know what the ballast was like? In a fishing vessel, it usually consists of rough pigs of iron and spare ends of old chain and miscellaneous scrap, in which a few rolled-up plates of metal would not be noticed."

"Ah!" Miller replied, "the *Cormorant's* ballast wasn't like that. It was proper yacht's ballast; lead weights, properly cast to fit the timbers and set in a neat row on each side of the kelson. So the hold was perfectly clear and the Customs man was able to see all over it from end to end.

"But to return to our scheme. When they had got the platinum safely hidden, our friends decided to stay on in their berth for a few days for the sake of appearances. Then they put to sea and proceeded in a leisurely, yacht-like fashion to make their way home. But during the voyage something seems to have happened. It looks rather as if the rogues had fallen out. At any rate, Mr 'X' seems to have left the ship, and this stranger to have come on board in his place. I don't understand that stranger at all. I can't fit him into the picture. But Mr 'X' apparently had a plan for grabbing the loot for himself, and, when he went ashore, he must have left a confederate on board to keep him informed as to when the cargo was going to be landed.

"As to the landing, there wouldn't have been any difficulty about that. When the Customs man had made his search and found everything in order, the papers would be made out and the ship would be passed as 'cleared'. After that, the crew would be at liberty to take any of their goods ashore unchallenged. And the arrangements for getting the platinum landed were excellent. The yacht was brought up in Benfleet Creek, quite close to the railway. Evidently, the case was carried up to the station, and Bassett must have taken it into the carriage with him to avoid having a label stuck on it and giving a clue to the cloak-room attendant.

"Why Bassett decided to plant it in the cloak-room is not very clear. We can only suppose that he hadn't any other place to put it at the moment, and that he left it there while he was making arrangements for its disposal. But it gave Mr 'X' his chance. No doubt his pal on board made it his business to find out what became of the case, and gave Mr 'X' the tip; which Mr 'X' acted on very promptly and efficiently. And he and his pal are at this moment some seventeen thousand pounds to the good.

"That is the scheme of the affair that we suggest. Of course, it is only a rough sketch, and you will say that it is all hypothesis from beginning to end, and so it is. But it hangs together."

"Yes," I agreed, "it is a consistent story, but it is all absolutely in the air. It is just a string of assumptions without a particle of evidence at any point. You begin by assuming that the case which was stolen from the cloak-room contained the missing platinum. Then, from that, you deduce that the case came from the yacht, and therefore the man who deposited it must be Bassett, and the other man must be a member of the crew. And you don't even refer to the trivial circumstance that a box containing a man's head was left in exchange."

"I have already said," Miller rejoined a little impatiently, "that we are letting the problem of the head rest for the moment, as we have nothing to go on. But it is evidently connected in some way with the stolen case, so we are following that up. If we can connect that with the platinum robbery, and lay our hands on Bassett and Mr 'X', we shall soon know something more about that head. I don't think your criticism is quite fair, Dr Jervis. What do you say, Doctor?"

"I agree with you," said Thorndyke, "that Jervis's criticism overstates the case. Your scheme is admittedly hypothetical, and there is no direct evidence. So it may or may not be a true account of what happened. But I think the balance of probabilities is in favour of its being substantially true. You don't know anything about any of these men?"

"No; you see they are only names, and probably wrong names."

"You found no finger-prints on the address label of the 'head case'?"

"None that we could identify. Probably only those of chance strangers."

"And what has become of the yacht and the crew?"

"The yacht is still lying in Benfleet Creek. Bassett left her in charge of a local boat-builder, as there is no one on board and the crew have gone away. We got a search warrant and rummaged her thoroughly, but we didn't find anything. So we sealed up the hatches and put on special padlocks and left the keys with the local police."

"Do you know whom she belongs to?"

"She belongs to Bassett. He bought her from a man at Shoreham. And she is now supposed to be for sale; but, as the owner's whereabouts are not known, of course, she can't be sold. For practical purposes she is abandoned, but we are paying the boat-builder for keeping an eye on her, pending the reappearance of Mr Bassett. Meanwhile we are keeping a look-out for that gentleman and Mr 'X', and for the appearance on the market of any platinum of uncertain origin. And that is about all that we can do until we get some fresh information."

"I suppose it is," said Thorndyke; "and, by the way, to return to the mysterious head; what has been done with it?"

"It has been buried in an air-tight case in Tower Hamlets Cemetery, with a stone to mark the spot in case it should be wanted. But we've got a stock of photographs of it which we have been circulating in the provinces to the various police stations. Perhaps you would like me to send you a set."

"Thank you, Miller," Thorndyke replied. "I should like a set to attach to the report of the inquest, which I have filed for reference."

"On the chance that, sooner or later, the inquiry may come into your hands?"

"Yes. There is always that possibility," Thorndyke replied. And this brought the discussion to an end, at least so far as Miller was concerned.

# CHAPTER SIX

## Mr Brodribb's Dilemma

The silence which fell after Thorndyke's last rejoinder lasted for more than a minute. At length it was broken by Brodribb, who, after profound meditation, launched a sort of broadcast question, addressed to no one in particular.

"Does anyone know anything about a certain Mr Horatio Gimbler?"

"Police-court solicitor?" inquired Miller.

"That is what I assumed," replied Brodribb, "from his address, which seemed to he an unlikely one for a solicitor in general practice. Then you do, apparently, know him, at least by name."

"Yes," Miller admitted. "I have known him, more or less, for a good many years."

"Then," said Brodribb, "you can probably tell me whether you would consider him a particularly likely practitioner to have the conduct of a claim to a peerage."

"A peerage!" gasped Miller, gazing at Brodribb in astonishment. "Holy smoke! No. I – certainly – should – NOT!" He paused for a few moments to recover from his amazement and then asked: "What sort of a claim is it, and who is the claimant?"

"The claimant is an American, and, at present, I don't know much about him. I'll give you some of the particulars presently, but, first, I should like to hear what you know about Mr Gimbler."

Miller appeared to reflect rapidly, accompanying the process by the emission of voluminous clouds of smoke. At length he replied, cautiously:

"It is understood that what is said here is spoken in strict confidence."

To this reasonable stipulation we all assented with one accord and Miller continued: "This fellow, Gimbler, is a rather remarkable person. He is a good lawyer, in a sense; at any rate, he has criminal law and procedure at his finger ends. He knows all the ropes – some that he oughtn't to know quite so well. He is up to all the tricks and dodges of the professional crooks, and I should think that his acquaintance includes practically all the crooks that are on the lay. If we could only pump him, he would be a perfect mine of information. But we can't. He's as secret as the grave. The criminal class provide his living, and he makes it his business to study their interests."

"I don't see that you can complain of that," said Brodribb. "It is a lawyer's duty to consider the interests of his clients, no matter who they may be."

"That's perfectly true," replied Miller, "in respect of the individual client; but it is not the duty even of a criminal lawyer to grease the wheels of crime, so to speak. However, we are speaking of the man. Well, I have told you what we know of him, and I may add that he is about the downiest bird that I am acquainted with and as slippery as an eel. That is what we *know*."

Here Miller paused significantly with the air of a man who expects to be asked a question. Accordingly, Brodribb ventured to offer a suggestion.

"That is what you know. But I take it that you have certain opinions in addition to your actual knowledge?"

Miller nodded. "Yes," said he. "We are very much interested in Mr Gimbler. Some of us have a feeling that there may possibly be something behind his legal practice. You know, in the practice of crime there is a fine opening for a clever and crooked brain. The professional crook, himself, is usually an unmitigated donkey, who makes all sorts of blunders in planning his jobs and carrying them out;

and when you find the perfect ass doing a job that seems right outside his ordinary capabilities, you can't help wondering whether there may not be some one of a different calibre behind the scenes, pulling the strings."

"Ah!" said Brodribb. "Do I understand that you suspect this legal luminary of being the invisible operator of a sort of unlawful puppet show?"

"I would hardly use the word 'suspect'," replied Miller. "But some of us – including myself – have entertained the idea. And not, mind you, without any show of reason. There was a certain occasion on which we really thought we had got our hands on him; but we hadn't. If he was guilty – I don't say that he was, mind you – but if he was, he slipped out of the net uncommonly neatly. It was a case of forgery; at least we thought it was. But, if it was, it was so good that the experts wouldn't swear to it, and the case wasn't clear enough to take into court."

Mr Brodribb pricked up his ears. "Forgery, you say; and a good forgery at that? You don't remember the particulars, I suppose? Because the question has a rather special interest for me."

"I only remember that it was a will case. The signatures of the testator and the two witnesses were disputed, but, as all three were dead, the question had to be decided on the opinions of experts; and none of the experts were certain enough to swear that the signatures might not be genuine. So the will had to be accepted as a genuine document. I suppose I mustn't ask how the question interests you?"

"Well," said Brodribb, "we are speaking in confidence, and I don't know that the matter is one of any great secrecy. It concerns this peerage claim that I was speaking about. I have had a copy of the pleadings, and I see that the claimant relies on certain documents to prove the identity of a very doubtful person. If you would care to hear an outline of the case, I don't think there would be any harm in my giving you a few of the particulars. I really came here to talk the case over with Thorndyke."

"If the pleadings were drawn up by Mr Gimbler," said Miller, "I should like very much to hear an outline of the case. And you can take it that I shall not breathe a word to any living soul."

"The pleadings," said Brodribb, "were drawn up by counsel, but, of course, on Gimbler's instructions. The facts, or alleged facts, must have been supplied by him. However, before I come to his part in the business, there are certain other matters to consider; so it will be better if I take the case as a whole and in the natural order of events.

"Let me begin by explaining that I am the Earl of Winsborough's man of business. My father and grandfather both acted in the same capacity for former holders of the title, so, naturally, all the relevant documents on the one side are in my keeping. I am also the executor of the present Earl's will, though there is not much in that, as practically everything is left to the heir."

"You speak of the present Earl," said Thorndyke. "But, if there is a present Earl, how comes it that a claim is being made to the earldom? Is an attempt being made to oust the present holder of the title?"

"I spoke of the present Earl," replied Brodribb, "because that is the legal position, and I, as his agent, am bound to accept it. But, as a matter of fact, I do not believe that there is a present Earl of Winsborough. I have no doubt that the Earl is dead. He went away on an exploring and big-game hunting expedition to South America nearly five years ago, and has not been heard of for over four years. But, of course, in a legal sense he is still alive, and will remain alive until he is either proved or presumed to be dead. Hence these present proceedings; which began with a proposal on the part of the heir presumptive to apply to the Court for permission to presume death. The heir presumptive is a young man, a son of the Earl's first cousin, who has only recently come of age. As I had no doubt that he was the real heir presumptive – there being, in fact, no other possible claimant known to me – and very little doubt that the Earl was dead, I did not propose to contest the application; but, as the Earl's agent, I could not very well act for the applicant. Accordingly, I turned the business over to my friend, Marchmont, and intended only to watch the case in the interests of the estate. Then, suddenly, this new claimant appeared out of the blue; and his appearance has complicated the affair most infernally.

"You see the dilemma. Both claimants wish to apply for permission to presume death. But neither of them is the admitted heir presumptive, and consequently neither of them has the necessary *locus standi* to make the application."

"Couldn't they make a joint application?" Miller asked, "and fight out the claim afterwards?"

"I doubt whether that could be done," replied Brodribb, "or whether they would be prepared to act in concert. Each would probably be afraid of seeming to concede the claim to the other. The alternative plan would be for them to settle the question of heirship before applying for leave to presume death. But there is the difficulty that, until the death is presumed, the present Earl is alive in a legal sense, and, that being so, the Court might reasonably hold that the question of heirship does not arise. And, as the Earl is a bachelor and there are no near relatives, there is no one else to make the application."

"In any event," said I, "the new claimant's case would have to be dealt with by a Committee of Privileges of the House of Lords. Isn't that so?"

"I don't think it is," replied Brodribb. "This is not a case of reviving a dormant peerage. If the American's case, as stated in the pleadings, is sound, he is unquestionably the heir presumptive."

"What does his case amount to?" Thorndyke asked.

"Put in a nutshell," replied Brodribb, "it amounts to this: the American gentleman, whose name is Christopher Pippet, is the grandson of a certain Josiah Pippet who was the keeper of a tavern somewhere in London. But there is a persistent tradition in the family that the said Josiah was living a double life under an assumed name, and that he was really the Earl of Winsborough. It is stated that he was in the habit of going away from his home and his usual places of resort and leaving no address. It is further stated that during these periodical absences – which often lasted for a month or two – he was actually in residence at Winsborough Castle; that, when Josiah was absent from home, the Earl was in residence at the Castle, and when Josiah was at the tavern, the Earl was absent from the Castle."

"And did Josiah and the Earl die simultaneously and in the same place?" I inquired.

"No," said Brodribb. "The double life was brought to an end by Josiah, who is said, after the death of his wife and the marriage of his sons and daughter, to have grown weary of it. He wound up the affair by a simulated death, a mock funeral and the burial of a dummy coffin weighted with lumps of lead, after which he went to the Castle and took up his residence there for good. That is the substance of the story."

The Superintendent snorted contemptuously. "And you tell us, Sir," said he, "that this man, Gimbler, is actually going to spin that yarn in a court of law. Why, the thing's grotesque – childish. He'd be howled out of court."

"I agree," said Brodribb, "that it sounds wild enough. But it is not impossible. Few things are. It is just a question of what they can prove. According to the pleadings, there are certain passages in a diary of the late Josiah which prove incontestably that he and the Earl were one and the same person."

"That diary," said Miller, "will be worth a pretty careful examination, having regard to the circumstances that I mentioned."

"Undoubtedly," Brodribb agreed; "though it seems to me that it would he extremely difficult to interpolate passages in a diary. There is usually no space in which to put them."

"Does the claimant propose to produce the dummy coffin with the lumps of lead in it?" I asked.

"Nothing has been said on that subject up to the present," Brodribb answered. "It would certainly be highly relevant; but, of course, they couldn't produce it without an exhumation order."

"I think you can take it," said Miller, "that they will leave that coffin severely alone – if you let them."

"Probably you are right," said Brodribb. "But the difficulty that confronts us at present is that it may be impossible to proceed with the case. When it comes on for hearing, the Court may refuse to consider the application until one of the applicants has established his *locus standi* as a person competent to make it; and it may refuse to hear evidence as to the claim of either party to be the heir on the grounds that, inasmuch as the Earl has been neither proved nor presumed to be dead, he must be presumed to be alive, and that, therefore, in accordance with the legal maxim, 'Nemo est heres viventis,' neither of the applicants can be the heir."

"That," said Thorndyke, "is undoubtedly a possible contingency. But judges are eminently reasonable men, and it is not the modern practice to favour legal hair-splittings. We may assume that the Court will not raise any difficulties that are not unavoidable; and this is a case which calls for some elasticity of procedure. For the difficulty which exists today might conceivably still exist fifty years hence; and, meanwhile, the title and the estates would be left derelict. What are the proceedings that are actually in contemplation, and who is making the first move?"

"The American claimant, Pippet, is making the first move. Gimbler has briefed Rufus McGonnell, KC, as his leader with Montague Klein as junior. He is proposing to apply for permission to presume the death of the Earl. I am contesting his application and challenging his claim to be the heir presumptive. That, he thinks, will enable him to produce his evidence and argue his claim as an issue preliminary to and forming part of the main issue. But I doubt very much whether the Court will consent to hear any evidence or any arguments that are not directly relevant to the question of the probability of the Earl's death. It is a very awkward situation. Pippet's claim looks like a rather grotesque affair; and if he is depending on the entries in a diary, I shouldn't think he has the ghost of a chance. Still, it ought to be settled one way or the other for the sake of young Giles Engleheart, the real heir presumptive, as I assume."

"Why shouldn't Engleheart proceed with his application?" said I.

"Because," replied Brodribb, "the same difficulty would arise. The other claimant would challenge his competency to make the application. It is a ridiculous dilemma. There are two issues, and each of them requires the other to be settled before it can be decided. It is very difficult to know what to do."

"The only thing that you can do," said Thorndyke, "is what you seem to be doing; let things take their own course and wait upon events. Pippet is making the first move. Well, let him make it; and, if the Court won't hear him, it will be time for you to consider what you will do next. Meanwhile, it would be wise for you to assume that the Court will allow him to produce evidence of his competency to make the application. It is quite possible; and if you are supporting Mr Engleheart's claim, you ought to be ready to contest the other claim."

"Yes," said Brodribb, "that is really what I came to talk to you about; and the first question is, Do you know anything about these two counsel, McGonnell and Klein? I don't seem to remember either of them."

"You wouldn't," replied Thorndyke. "They are both almost exclusively criminal practitioners. But, in their own line, they are men of first-class capabilities. You can take it that they will give you a run for your money if they get the chance, in spite of their being rather off their usual beat. Have you decided on your own counsel?"

"I have decided to secure your services, in any event. Would you be prepared to take the brief?"

"I will take it if you wish me to," replied Thorndyke, "but I think you would be better advised to employ Anstey. For this reason. If the case comes into court, it is possible that certain questions may arise on which you might wish me to give expert evidence. I think you would do well to let me keep an eye on the technical aspects of the case and let Anstey do the actual court work."

Brodribb looked sharply at Thorndyke but made no immediate reply; and, in the ensuing silence, a low chuckle was heard to proceed from the Superintendent.

"I like the delicate way the Doctor puts it," said he, by way of explaining the chuckle. "The technical aspects of this case will call for a good deal of watching; and I need not tell you, Mr Brodribb, that, if the Doctor's eye is on them, there won't be much that will pass unobserved. In fact, I shouldn't be surprised to learn that the Doctor has got one or two of them in his eye already."

"Neither should I," said Brodribb. "Nothing surprises me where Thorndyke is concerned. At any rate I shall act on your advice, Thorndyke. One couldn't ask for a better counsel than Anstey; and it is not necessary for me to stipulate that you go over the pleadings with him and put him up to any possible dodges on the part of our friend Mr Gimbler. Remember that I am retaining you, and that you do as you please about pleading in court."

"I understand," said Thorndyke. "You will keep Anstey and me fully instructed, and I shall give the case the most careful consideration in regard to any contingencies that may arise. As Miller has hinted, there are a good many possibilities, especially if Mr Gimbler should think it necessary to throw a little extra weight into the balance of probabilities."

"Very well," said Brodribb, "then we will leave it at that. If you have the case in hand, I shall feel that I can go ahead in confidence; and I only hope that McGonnell will be able to persuade the Court to hear the evidence on his client's claim. It would be a blessed thing if we could get that question settled so that we could go straight ahead with the other question – the presumption of death. I am getting a little worried by the more or less derelict condition of the Winsborough estates and it would be a relief to see a young man fairly settled in possession."

"You are rather taking it for granted that the American's claim will fall through," I remarked.

"So I am," he admitted. "But you must allow that it does sound like a cock-and-bull story, and none too straightforward at that. However, we shall see. If I get nothing more out of it, I have had an extremely pleasant evening and a devilish good bottle of wine, and now it's about time that I took myself off and let you get to bed."

With this he rose and shook hands; and the Superintendent, taking the rather broad hint conveyed in the concluding sentence, rose too, and the pair took their departure together.

# Chapter Seven

## The Final Preparations

Most of us have wit enough to be wise after the event, and a few of us have enough to be wise before. Thorndyke was one of these few, and I, alas! was not. I am speaking in generalities, but I am thinking of a particular case – the Winsborough Peerage Claim. That case I could not bring myself to take seriously. The story appeared to me, as it had appeared to Miller, merely grotesque. Its improbabilities were so outrageous that I could not entertain it as a problem for serious consideration. And then, such as it was, it was a purely legal case, completely outside our ordinary line of practice. At least, that is how it appeared to me.

Now, Thorndyke made no such mistake. Naturally, he could not foresee developments in detail. But subsequent events showed that he had foreseen, and very carefully considered, all the possible contingencies, so that when they arose they found him prepared. And he also saw clearly that the case might turn out to be very much in our line.

As I was unaware of his views – Thorndyke being the most uncommunicative man whom I have ever known – I looked with some surprise on the obvious interest that he took in the case. So great was that interest that he actually adopted the extraordinary habit of spending weekends at Winsborough Castle. What he did there I was unable to make out. I heard rumours of his having gone over the butler's accounts and some of the old household books and papers with Brodribb, which seemed a not unreasonable proceeding, though more in Brodribb's line than ours. But most of his time he apparently spent rambling about the country with a note-book, a small camera and a set of six-inch Ordnance maps. And he evidently covered a surprising amount of ground, as I could see by the numbers of photographs that he brought home, and which he either developed himself or handed to our invaluable laboratory assistant, Polton, for development. Over those photographs, when they were printed, I pored with a feeling of stupefaction. They included churches, both inside and out, windmills, inns, churchyards, and quaint village streets; all very interesting and many of them charming. But what had they to do with the peerage case? I was completely mystified.

On one occasion I accompanied him, and a very pleasant jaunt it was. The Castle was rather a delusion, though there were some medieval ruins of a castellated building; but the mansion was a pleasant, homely brick house of the late seventeenth century in the style of Wren's country houses. But our ramblings about the house and the adjoining gardens and park yielded no information – excepting as to the mental condition of a former proprietor, as suggested by the costly and idiotic additions that he had made to the mansion.

These were, I must admit, perfectly astounding. On a low hill in the park near to the house was a stupendous brick tower – a regular Tower of Babel – from the summit of which we could look across the sea to the white cliffs of the coast of France. It stood quite alone and appeared to have no purpose beyond the view from the top, but the cost of its construction must have been enormous. But "George's Folly", to give the tower its appropriate local name, was not the most astonishing of these works. When we came down from the roof, Thorndyke produced a bunch of large keys, which he had borrowed from the butler, and with one of them opened a door in the basement. Then he switched on a portable electric lamp, by the light of which I perceived a flight of stone steps apparently descending into the bowels of the earth. Picking our way down these, we reached an archway opening into a roomy, brick-walled passage, and making our way along this for fully a hundred yards, at length reached another door which, being unlocked, gave entrance to a large room, lighted by a brick shaft that opened on the surface. A moth-eaten carpet still covered the floor and the mouldering furniture remained as it had been left, presumably, by the eccentric builder.

It was a strange and desolate-looking apartment, and the final touch of desolation was given by a multitude of bats which hung, head downwards, from the ceiling ornaments or fluttered silently in circles in the dark corners or in the dim light under the opening of the shaft.

"This is a weird place, Thorndyke," I exclaimed. "What do you think could have been the object of building it?"

"So far as I know," he replied, "there was no particular object. It was the noble lord's hobby to build towers and underground apartments. This is not the only one. The door at the other end of the room opens into another passage which leads to several other large rooms. We may as well inspect them!"

We did so. In all, there were five large rooms connected by several hundred yards of passages, and three or four small rooms, all lighted by shafts and all still containing their original furniture and fittings.

"But," I exclaimed, as we threaded our way along the interminable passages back to the tower, "this man must have been a stark lunatic."

"He was certainly highly eccentric," said Thorndyke, "though we must make some allowance for an idle rich man. But you see the significance of this. Supposing that the peerage claim were to be tried by a jury, and supposing that jury were brought here and shown these rooms and passages. Do you think Mr Pippet's story would appear to them so particularly incredible? Don't you think that they would say that a man who could busy himself in works of this kind would be capable of any folly or eccentricity?"

"I think it very likely," I admitted; "but for my own part, I must say that I cannot imagine his lordship as landlord of a London pub. Playing the fool in your own park is a slightly different occupation from drawing pints of beer for thirsty labourers. I wonder if the Kenningtonian Gimbler knows about these works of imagination."

"He does," said Thorndyke. "A description of them was included in the 'material facts' set forth in the pleadings. And he has examined them personally. He applied to Brodribb for permission to view the mansion, and, naturally, Brodribb gave it."

"I don't see why 'naturally.' He was not called on to assist the claim which he was opposing."

"He took the view – correctly, I think, – that he ought not to hinder, in any way, the ascertainment of the material facts; facts, you must remember, that he does not dispute. And, really, he can afford to deal with the American claimant in a generous and sporting spirit. Mere evidence of eccentricity on the part of the late Earl will not do more than establish a bare possibility. A positive case has to be made out. The burden of proof is on Cousin Jonathan."

"That is, if the case ever comes into court. I doubt if it will."

"Then you need doubt no longer," said he. "The case is down for hearing next week."

"The deuce it is!" I exclaimed. "Do you know what form the proceedings will take?"

"It is to be heard in the Probate Court. Ostensibly, it is an application by Christopher Pippet for permission to presume the death of Percy Engleheart, sixth Earl of Winsborough. Brodribb, acting in virtue of a power of attorney, opposes the application and challenges the *locus standi* of the applicant. Of course, we cannot say how far the case will be allowed to proceed; but I take it that it is proposed to allow Pippet to produce evidence establishing his *locus standi* as a person having such an interest in the estate as would entitle him to make the application. That is to say, he will be allowed to present the case on which he bases his claim to be the heir presumptive to the Earl. I certainly hope he will. There are all sorts of interesting possibilities in the case."

"Interesting, no doubt, in a legal sense; but I don't see where we come in."

"Perhaps we shan't come in at all," he replied with a faint smile. "But I rather suspect that we shall. The special interest of the case to me lies in the fact that Mr Pippet's counsel will be instructed by Mr Horatio Gimbler."

Something in Thorndyke's manner, as he made this last statement, seemed to suggest some special significance. But what that significance might be I was unable to guess, beyond the fact that the said Gimbler, being neither an infant nor a man of irreproachable reputation, might adopt some slightly irregular tactics. But I suspected that there was something more definite than this in my colleague's mind. However, the conversation went no farther on this occasion, and I was left to turn the problem over at my leisure.

Thorndyke's announcement had come to me as a complete surprise, for I had never believed that this fantastic case would actually find its way into the courts. But the case furnished a whole series of surprises, of which the first was administered on the day when the proceedings opened, and was connected with the personality and behaviour of the claimant. I had assumed that Mr Christopher Pippet was an American adventurer who had come over to tell this cock-and-bull story in the hope of getting possession of a valuable English estate. Probably the idea arose – not quite unreasonably – from the fact that the claimant made his appearance under the guidance of a slightly shady police-court solicitor. In my mind I had written him down an impostor, and formed a picture of a hustling, brazen vulgarian, suitable to the part and appropriate to his company. The reality was surprisingly different.

On the morning of the hearing, Brodribb appeared at our chambers accompanied by his clients, Mr Giles Engleheart and his mother, to whom he presented us in his old-fashioned, courtly manner.

"I thought it best," he explained, "that you should not meet in court as strangers. I have introduced Anstey already, and I think he is going to join us here. So we shall be able to make our descent on the Halls of Justice in a united body and thereby impress the opposition."

"I suspect," said Mrs Engleheart, "that the opposition is not so easily impressed. But my boy and I will feel some encouragement if we arrive escorted by our champions. Have we plenty of time?" she added, glancing a little anxiously at her watch.

"We have," replied Brodribb, "if Anstey doesn't keep us waiting. Ah! here he is;" and, as a quick footstep was heard on the stair, he strode over to the door and threw it open, when our leading counsel entered with an exaggerated pretence of haste, holding his watch in his hand.

"Come," he exclaimed, "this won't do. We ought to be starting."

"But," said Mrs Engleheart, "we have been waiting for you, Mr Anstey."

"Exactly," he retorted, "that is what I meant." Then, as the lady, unaccustomed to his whimsicalities, looked at him in some perplexity, he continued, briskly: "It is always desirable to be in court early on the opening day. Are we all ready? Then let us go forth and make our way to the scene of conflict. But not too much like a procession. And I want to have a few words with you, Thorndyke, *en route*."

With this, he took Thorndyke's arm and led the way out. Brodribb followed with Mrs Engleheart, and I brought up the rear with her son. As we walked at a leisurely pace – set by Anstey – across the precincts by way of the Cloisters and Pump Court, I took the opportunity to consider my companion as to his appearance and personality in general; and in all respects I was very favourably impressed, as I had been by the gentle dignity of his mother. Giles Engleheart was not only a fine, strapping, handsome young man and very unmistakably a gentleman, but – like his mother – he conveyed the impression of a kindly, generous and amiable disposition. But, unlike his mother, he seemed disposed to regard the legal proceedings as a gigantic joke.

"Well, Mr Engleheart," I said, by way of making conversation, "I think we shall make pretty short work of your American rival."

"Do you?" said he. "I don't think Mr Brodribb is so confident; and, for my part, I rather hope you won't make it too short. He ought to have a run for his money – and he may give us a run for ours. After all, you know, Sir, his statements are pretty definite, and we've no right to assume that he is a liar. And, if he isn't, his statements are probably true. And, if they are true, we've got to imagine George Augustus, fourth Earl of Winsborough, with his sleeves rolled up and a black linen apron on his tummy, pulling at the handles of the beer engine in a London pub. It's a quaint idea. I'm all agog to hear his counsel tell the story and trot out his evidence."

"For my part," said I, "I can't bring myself to view the claim as anything more than a gross and crude imposture, and I shouldn't be surprised if the case ended in a charge of perjury."

"Do you mean against Mr Pippet?" he asked.

"I don't know anything about Pippet," I replied, "but I look with considerable suspicion on his solicitor."

Engleheart laughed cheerfully. "You are like Mr Brodribb," said he. "The very mention of the name of Gimbler makes him spit – metaphorically – whereas I never hear it without thinking of Jabberwocky and the Slithy Toves."

"What is the connection?" I asked, rather foolishly.

"Don't you remember, Sir?" said he. "The Slithy Toves 'did gyre and gimble in the wabe'. Therefore they were gimblers. QED."

"Perhaps," said I, laughing at his schoolboy joke, "Mr Brodribb has noticed the connection and suspects our friend of an intention to 'gyre and gimble' in a legal sense. And perhaps he is right. Time will show. But here we are at what Anstey calls 'the scene of conflict.'"

Entering the great doorway, we followed our friends along the rather gloomy passages until Anstey pushed open a heavy swing door and stood holding it open while Mrs Engleheart and the rest of us passed through. Then he and Thorndyke and I retired to the robing-room and hastily donned our wigs and gowns.

When we returned to the court, the clock showed that there was still a quarter of an hour to spare, and, with the exception of one or two reporters, a few spectators in the gallery, and a stray barrister, we had the place to ourselves. But not for long. Even as the quarter was chiming, the heavy and noisy swing doors were pushed open and a party of strangers entered.

There was no doubt as to who they were, for, though I had not recognised the name of Gimbler, I recognised the man, having seen him on several occasions at the Central Criminal Court; a big, burly man with a large, rather fat face, and small, furtive eyes; a sly-looking fellow, I decided, and forthwith wrote him down a knave. But the other members of the party gave me quite a little surprise. There were three of them – two women and a man; and the outstanding fact which instantly impressed me was their imposing appearance. It was not only that they were all well above the average of good looks, though that was a fact worth noting; but they all had the unmistakable appearance and bearing of gentlefolk.

Of course, my surprise was quite unreasonable, being due to an entirely gratuitous preconceived idea. But still more unreasonable was the instant change in my state of mind in regard to the claim. Looking at the claimant – as I assumed him to be, seeing that there was no other man – I found myself taking a revised view of the case. Clearly, this fine, upstanding gentleman with his clear-cut, strong, reposeful face, was an entirely different creature from the raffish cosmopolitan adventurer of my imagination, who had come over to "tell the tale" and try to snatch a stray fortune.

The two parties – our own and "the opposition" – took an undissembled interest in one another, and Mr Giles conveyed his sentiments to me in an undertone.

"Good-looking crowd, Sir, aren't they? If that young lady is a fair sample of an American girl, I am going to emigrate if we lose the case."

"And if you don't lose the case?" I asked.

"Well, Sir," he replied, smilingly evading the question, "I shall be able to pay my lawyer, which will be pleasant for us both."

Here my attention was diverted by what looked like a difference between Mr Gimbler and his client. The solicitor appeared distinctly annoyed and I heard him say, almost angrily: "I do certainly object. It would be entirely out of order."

"No doubt you are right, as a lawyer," was the calm reply; "but I am not a lawyer;" and, with this, he turned away from his legal adviser, and, to that gentleman's evident dismay, began to move across in our direction. As he was obviously bearing down on us with intent, we all, excepting Mrs Engleheart, stood up, and I could hear Brodribb muttering under his breath.

Having saluted us with a comprehensive bow, the stranger addressed himself to our old friend.

"I believe you are Mr Brodribb."

"At your service, Sir," was the reply, accompanied by a bow of such extreme stiffness that I seemed to hear him creak.

"I understand," said Mr Pippet, "that I am committing a gross breach of legal etiquette. But etiquette is made for man, especially for European man, and I am venturing to take an aboriginal view of the matter. Would it appear particularly shocking if I were to ask you to do me the honour of presenting me to your clients?"

"I think," replied Brodribb, recovering himself somewhat, "that I should survive the shock, and my clients, I am sure, will be delighted to make your acquaintance."

With this he proceeded, with the air of a Gold-Stick-in-Waiting approaching a royal personage, to present the American to Mrs Engleheart.

"This is most kind of you, Mr Pippet," the lady exclaimed with a gracious smile. "Mr Brodribb is quite right. I am delighted to make your acquaintance, and so, I am sure, will my son be. May I introduce him?"

Here Giles stepped forward, and the two men shook hands heartily.

"It is very good of you, Sir, to make this friendly move," said he, "seeing that our presence here is not exactly helpful to you."

"But," said Mr Pippet, "that is just my point. All this talk of fights and battles and contests that I have been hearing from my solicitor makes me tired. I am not here to fight anybody, and neither, I take it, are you. There are certain matters of alleged fact that I am submitting for the consideration and judgement of the court. I don't know whether they are true or not. That is for the court to find out. My lawyers will argue that they are, and yours will argue that they are not. Let us leave it to them. There's no need for us to have any unfriendly feeling about it. Isn't that so, Mr Brodribb?"

"There is no reason," Brodribb replied cautiously, "why opposing litigants should not be personally friendly – without prejudice, of course. But you are not forgetting that these proceedings involve certain consequences. If the decision is in your favour, you obtain possession of a title of nobility and property of great value, which Mr Engleheart thereby loses; and *vice versa*."

"Not quite *vice versa*, Mr Brodribb," Mr Pippet corrected. "The cases are not identical. If the court decides that my respected grandfather was not the Earl of Winsborough, Mr Engleheart steps into the late Earl's shoes as soon as the death has been presumed, and I retire out of the picture. But, if it is decided that my grandfather was the Earl, then, as I have no male descendants, Mr Engleheart has only to wait for those shoes until I step out of them."

I could see that this statement made a considerable impression on both Mr Brodribb and Mrs Engleheart; and it did certainly ease the situation materially from their point of view. Brodribb, however, made no comment, and it fell to Mrs Engleheart to make the acknowledgements.

"Thank you, Mr Pippet," said she, "for letting us know the position. I won't pretend that I am not very much relieved to know that it is only a question of postponement for my son. But, whichever way the decision goes, I hope it will be a long time before a vacancy is declared in those shoes. But you haven't completed the introductions. Is that very charming girl your daughter?"

"She is, Madam," was the reply. "My only child; and, with the exception of my sister, who is with her, my only kin in the world – unless it should transpire that I have the honour to be related to you and your son."

"Well," said Mrs Engleheart, "if your kinsfolk are not very numerous, you have reason to be proud of them, as I dare say you are. Do you think they would care to know us?"

"I have their assurance that they would like very much to make your acquaintance," Mr Pippet replied; on which Mrs Engleheart rose and was requesting to be taken to them when they were seen to be moving in our direction, apparently in response to some subtle telegraphic signals on the part of Mr Pippet. As they approached, I looked them over critically and had to admit that their appearance was at least equal to their pretensions. The elder lady – like the late Queen Victoria – combined a markedly short stature with a most unmistakable "presence" aided not a little by the strong, resolute face and a somewhat out-size Roman nose; while the younger was a tall, handsome girl, noticeably like her father and her aunt both in features and in the impression of dignity and character which she conveyed. And both ladies had that unselfconscious ease of manner that is usually associated with the word "breeding".

The introductions were necessarily hurried, for the time for the opening of the proceedings was drawing nigh. The clerk had taken his seat at his desk, the reporters were in their places, the ushers had taken up their posts, a few more spectators were drifting into the seats in the public gallery and the counsel had established themselves in their respective places and were now turning over the pages of their briefs – excepting Thorndyke and myself, who had no briefs but were present merely in a watching capacity. Mr Pippet returned to the place where his solicitor sat glumly by the solicitor's table, but the two ladies remained with our party, Miss Pippet sitting by Mrs Engleheart, and the young lady (who, I gathered, bore the picturesque old English name of Jenifer) by Mr Giles.

They had hardly settled themselves when the judge entered and took his seat on the bench. Having laid some papers on his desk, he leaned back in his seat and ran his eye with undissembled interest over the parties to the proceedings.

"Now," Miss Jenifer remarked in a low tone to her companion, "we are going to hear whether we are cousins or only friends."

"Or both," added Giles.

"Of course," said she. "That was what I meant. But we mustn't talk. The play is going to begin; and that nice-looking old gentleman in that quaint wig has got his eye on us."

Thereupon she subsided into silence, and Mr McGonnell proceeded to open the case.

# CHAPTER EIGHT

## The Opening of the Case

"This, my lord," said Mr McGonnell, rising and turning an ingratiating eye on the bench, "is an application by Mr Christopher Josiah Pippet, a citizen of the United States, for permission to presume the death of Percy Engleheart, sixth Earl of Winsborough, but there are certain peculiar and unusual features in the case. The application is opposed by the representatives of the Earl, who challenge the *locus standi* of the applicant on the ground that he is, as they allege, a stranger having no legitimate interest or concern in the estate of the said Earl. The applicant, on the other hand, affirms, and is prepared to prove, that he is the direct descendant of the fourth Earl of Winsborough, and that he is, in effect, the heir presumptive to the Earldom and the settled estate.

"Accordingly, the applicant petitions to be allowed to produce evidence of his title to the estate and to obtain a decision on that issue as an issue antecedent to the application for permission to presume death."

The judge looked keenly at the counsel during the making of this statement and then he turned a slightly curious glance on Mr Pippet and from him to his solicitor.

"I must be perfectly clear," said he, "as to the scope of this further application. There appears to be a claim to a title and to the settled property associated with it. Now, I need not remind you that claims in respect of titles of honour lie within the jurisdiction of the House of Lords through a Committee of Privileges."

"We realise that, my lord," said Mr McGonnell. "But we are not seeking a final and conclusive decision in this court on the question whether the applicant, Christopher Pippet, is or is not entitled to succeed the present tenant, Earl Percy, but merely whether he has such an interest in the estate as will give him the *locus standi* necessary to entitle him to make an application for permission to presume the death of the said Earl Percy."

"That application," said the judge, "implies certain further proceedings, including, perhaps, a petition to the House of Lords."

"That is so, my lord," counsel agreed. "But we are in a difficulty, and we ask your lordship to exercise a discretion in the matter of procedure. Our difficulty is this: There is reason to believe that Earl Percy is dead; but no direct evidence of his death exists. Consequently, he is, in a legal sense, a living person; and, since no one can be the heir of a living person, it is not possible for Mr Pippet to initiate proceedings in the House of Lords. Before any such proceedings could become possible it would be necessary for the death of Earl Percy to be either proved or presumed.

"Therefore, the applicant applies for the permission of the court to presume the death. But his right to make this application is contested on the grounds that I have mentioned. Thus he is in this dilemma: He cannot prove his claim until death is presumed, and he cannot apply for permission to presume death until he has proved his claim. But this dilemma, it is submitted, is contrary to the interests of justice; and we accordingly ask your lordship to hear such evidence as shall establish the applicant's position as a person having such an interest in the estate as renders him competent to make the application."

"It is not perfectly clear," said the judge, "that the fact of his having this belief in his title to succeed does not constitute him an interested party to that extent. But we need not go into that, as the issue is not raised. What is the position of the Earl's representatives in regard to the heir presumptive?"

"Our position, my lord," said Anstey, rising as the other counsel sat down, "is that the heir presumptive is Mr Giles Engleheart, the only son of the late Charles Engleheart, Esquire, who was the Earl's first cousin. Apart from Mr Pippet's claim, there is no doubt whatever about Mr Engleheart's position. It is not contested. And I may say, if it is permissible, that we are in full agreement with what my learned friend has just said with regard to the applicant's claim. Since the question has been raised, we submit that it is desirable that the applicant be permitted to produce such evidence as may establish the existence or non-existence of a prima facie case. We agree with my learned friend that the present impasse is against the interests of justice."

"Yes," said the judge, "there ought certainly to be some escape from the dilemma which the learned counsel for the applicant has mentioned. The actual claim will, no doubt, have to be decided in another place; but there is no objection to such provisional proof as may be necessary for the purposes of the present application. I am therefore prepared to hear the evidence in support of the applicant's claim."

He looked at Mr McGonnell, who thereupon rose and proceeded to open the preliminary case, by a recital of the alleged facts in much the same terms as the sketch which I had heard from Mr Brodribb, but in somewhat greater detail; and, as I listened, with my eyes on the judge's face, to the unfolding of that incredible and ridiculous story, I was once more astonished that anyone should have the confidence to tell it seriously in a court of law. How it impressed the judge it was impossible to tell. Judges, as a class, are not easily surprised, nor are they addicted to giving facial expression to their emotions; and the present specimen was a particularly wooden-faced old gentleman. All that I could gather from my observations of his countenance was that he appeared to be listening with close attention and placid interest.

"That, my lord," said Mr McGonnell, when he came to the end of the "story" with a description of the sham funeral, "is an outline of what are alleged to be the facts of the applicant's case; and it would be useless to deny that, taken at its face value, the whole story appears wildly incredible. If it rested only on the family tradition, no one would entertain it for a moment. But it does not rest only on that tradition. It is supported by a considerable body of evidence, including certain very significant entries in a diary kept by Josiah Pippet and certain facts relating to the Earl, George Augustus, who, it is claimed, was the *alter ego* of the said Josiah. Perhaps it will be well to glance at the latter first.

"The thesis on which Mr Christopher Pippet's claim is based is that the said Earl, George Augustus, was in the habit of leaving his mansion from time to time and going to the 'Fox and Grapes' Inn, where he assumed the name and style of Josiah Pippet and lived the life and carried out the activities of an inn-keeper. Now, it will naturally be asked, Is it credible that any man in the possession of his senses would conduct himself in this manner? And the answer obviously is that it is not. But here the question arises, Was the said Earl in the possession of his senses? And the answer to that is that, apparently, he was not. At any rate, his conduct in general was so strange, so unusual and erratic, that it would be difficult to name any eccentricity of which he might not have been capable. Let us see what manner of man this was.

"In the first place, he appears to have been a man who had no fixed habits of life. He would live for months at his mansion, busying himself in certain works which we shall consider presently, and then, apparently without notice, he would disappear, leaving no clue to his whereabouts. He would stay away from home for months – in some cases for more than a year – and then would suddenly make his appearance at the mansion, unannounced and unexpected, giving no account of himself or his doings during his absence. And it is worth notice that his alleged double, Josiah Pippet, had similar peculiarities of behaviour. He also was in the habit of making mysterious disappearances and leaving no clue to his whereabouts."

"Is it ascertained," the judge asked, "that the disappearances of the two men coincided in time?"

"That is what is alleged, my lord," was the reply. "Naturally, after the many years that have elapsed, it is difficult to recover the dates as exactly as might be desired."

"No doubt," his lordship agreed; "but the point is highly material."

"Certainly, my lord," counsel admitted. "Its importance has been fully realised and the point has been carefully examined. Such evidence as has been available goes to prove that the disappearances synchronised.

"But these strange disappearances are not the only, or even the most striking evidences of the Earl's eccentricity. Still more suggestive of an unbalanced mind is the way in which he occupied himself in the intervals of those disappearances, when he was in residence at the mansion. Nothing in the traditional story which I have recited is more incredible than the history of his doings when he was at home. For then, it appears, he was in the habit of assembling an army of work-men, and, at enormous expense, employing them in carrying out works on the most gigantic scale and of the most preposterous character. In one part of his grounds, he set up an immense and lofty tower, with no ascertainable purpose except the view from the summit. From the base of this tower, a flight of steps was constructed leading down into the bowels of the earth, and communicating with a great range of subterranean passages of an aggregate length of close upon a mile. Connected with these passages were several large subterranean rooms, lighted from the surface by shafts and elaborately furnished. No reason is known for the construction of these rooms, though it appears that the Earl was accustomed, from time to time, to retire to them with a stock of provisions and pass a few days underground, hidden from the sight of men. These strange burrows and the great tower are still in existence and will be described in detail by a witness who, by the courtesy of the Earl's representatives, was enabled to make a thorough examination of them. But the slight description of them which I have given is sufficient to demonstrate that the Earl George Augustus was a man who, if not actually insane, was so strange and erratic in his behaviour that there is hardly any eccentricity of which he might not have been capable. The objection, therefore, to the traditional story, that it postulates an unbelievable degree of eccentricity in the Earl George Augustus, has no weight; since the said Earl did, in fact, give evidence of an unbelievable degree of eccentricity.

"I will say no more on the subject of this strange man's personality, though further details of his peculiarities will be given in evidence. But, before finishing with him, it will be material to note the salient facts of his life. George Augustus, fourth Earl of Winsborough, was born on the 9th of August in the year 1794 and he died unmarried in 1871, aged seventy-seven. He had no brothers. He was succeeded by his cousin Francis Engleheart, who died in 1893 and was succeeded by his only son – and only child – then twenty-six years of age, the present Earl, Percy.

"We now pass to the alleged double of the Earl George Augustus, Josiah Pippet. Of his personal character we have less direct information, but, on the other hand, we have an invaluable and unimpeachable source of evidence in a diary which he kept for many years, and up to the date of his death. From this, we, at least, gather one highly suggestive fact; that he, like the Earl, was in the habit of disappearing at intervals from his home and from his usual places of resort, of staying away for months at a time, and on two occasions for over a year, and, so far as we are able to discover, leaving no clue as to the place to which he had gone or where he was living.

"When I say that he left no clue to his whereabouts, I mean that he gave no information to his wife or family. Actually, the diary furnishes quite a considerable number of clues; and it is a very striking fact that these clues all refer to the same locality, and that the locality referred to happens to be the very one in which Winsborough Castle is situated. But not only is the locality referred to; there are actual references to the Castle itself, and in such terms as to leave no doubt that the writer was, at the time, in residence there. As the diary will be put in evidence, I need not occupy the time of the court with quotations at this stage, but will proceed to the few but important facts that are known respecting Josiah Pippet.

"The first fact that I shall mention – and a very striking and suggestive fact it is – is that, although the date of Josiah's birth is known, no entry recording it appears in any known register. Exhaustive search has been made at Somerset House and elsewhere, but, so far as can be discovered, no record whatever exists of this man's birth. He seems to have dropped from the skies.

"But, as I have said, the date of his birth is known, for it is stated with great exactness on the vault in which his coffin was deposited. Above the entrance to that vault is a marble tablet on which is carved this brief but significant inscription: 'JOSIAH PIPPET, died the 12th day of October, 1843, aged 49 years, 2 months and 3 days.'

"Now here is a very exact, though rather roundabout, statement, from which we can compute the very day of his birth. And what was that day? A simple calculation shows that it was the 9th of August, 1794 – the very same day on which George Augustus, fourth Earl of Winsborough, was born!

"If this is a coincidence, it is a most amazing one. The Earl and his alleged double were born on the same day. And not only that. The birth of the double is unrecorded. There is no evidence that it ever took place. Which is precisely what we might expect in the case of a double. The birth of the Earl duly appears in the register at Somerset House; and I submit that it is a reasonable inference that that entry records the birth, not only of George Augustus Engleheart, but also of Josiah Pippet. That those two men were, in fact, one and the same person; or, in other words, that Josiah Pippet was a purely imaginary and fictitious person.

"But the mysterious circumstances connected with the birth of these two persons – or these two aspects of the same person – are repeated in connection with their deaths. Just as only one of them is known, and can be proved, to have been born, so only one of them can be proved to have died. It is true that, in the case of Josiah, there was a funeral and a coffin which was solemnly interred. But there was a current belief that the funeral was a sham and that the coffin contained no human remains. And that belief is supported by the fact that there was no medical certificate. The death certificate was signed only by Walter Pippet, the son of the alleged deceased, as was possible in those days, before the passing of the Medical Act of 1858. There is nothing to show that the alleged deceased was attended by any medical practitioner or that there was anything to prevent the sham funeral from taking place with the collusion of the said Walter Pippet. The circumstances of the death, I repeat, like those of the birth, are fully compatible with the belief that there were not two persons at all, but only one person enacting two alternating parts. In other words, that Josiah Pippet was a mythical personage, like John Doe, created for a specific purpose.

"Nevertheless, when we come to the matter of the applicant's ancestry and descent, we must treat the said Josiah as a real person, since he is the applicant's visible ancestor. And he has undeniably the qualities of a real person, inasmuch as, in the character of Josiah Pippet, he married and had children. In the year 1822, in the church of St Helen's, Bishopsgate, he was married to Martha Bagshaw, spinster, he being then twenty-eight years of age, and, according to the register, following the occupation of a ship's steward. The exact date at which he became landlord of the 'Fox and Grapes' is not certain, but he is so described in the register where the birth of his eldest child is recorded.

"There were three children of this marriage; Walter, the eldest, born in 1824, Frederick William, born in 1826, and Susan, born in 1832. Susan married and died in 1897. Walter carried on the 'Fox and Grapes' after his father's real or fictitious death, and died unmarried in 1865. Frederick William took to a seafaring life and eventually settled, in the year 1853, at the age of twenty-seven, in the United States, in the city of Philadelphia, Pennsylvania. There he began business by opening a small shop, which grew by degrees into a large and important department store. In 1868 he married Miss Elizabeth Watson, the daughter of a well-to-do merchant of Philadelphia, by whom he had two children, a son, Christopher Josiah, the present applicant, and a daughter, Arminella. He lost his wife in 1891, and he died in 1905, leaving the bulk of his large fortune to his daughter and the residue together with the business to his son; who carried on the concern until 1921, when, having made a further considerable fortune, he sold out and retired. It was then that, for the first time, he began seriously to consider raising the claim to what he believes – justly, as I submit – to be his legitimate heritage.

"Before proceeding to call witnesses, I venture, my lord, to recapitulate briefly the points of the case which favour the belief that Josiah Pippet and the Earl George Augustus, fourth Earl of Winsborough, were one and the same person.

"First, that the said Earl was a man of such wildly eccentric habits and conduct that he might credibly have behaved in the manner alleged.

"That his habit of absenting himself from home for long periods and disappearing from his known places of resort, would have rendered the alleged personation easily possible.

"That the man called Josiah Pippet was in the same way addicted to absences and disappearances.

"That the said Josiah is reported to have claimed to be the Earl.

"That, whereas both these persons were born on the same day, there is evidence of the birth of one only.

"That, in like manner, there is evidence of the death of only one of them, the circumstances being such as to support the rumour which was current that the coffin which was interred contained no corpse.

"Those, my lord, are the facts on which the applicant's claim is based; and I submit that if they can be proved – as they will be by the testimony of the witnesses whom I shall call – they constitute a case sufficiently convincing for the purpose of this application."

Here Mr McGonnell paused and inspected his brief while the judge shifted his position in his chair and the usher pronounced the name of Christopher Josiah Pippet. Thereupon Mr Pippet moved across to the witness-box, and, having been sworn, gave his name and the usual particulars. Then his counsel proceeded to open the examination in chief.

# CHAPTER NINE

## *The Evidence of Christopher J Pippet*

---

"Can you remember, Mr Pippet," the counsel asked, "when you first became aware that you were possibly the direct descendant of the Earl of Winsborough?"

"No, Sir, I cannot," was the reply. "It must have been when I was quite a small boy."

"From whom did you receive the information?"

"From my father, Frederick William Pippet."

"Did he refer to the matter on more than one occasion?"

"Yes; on a great many occasions. It was rather a favourite subject with him."

"Did you gather that he believed in the truth of the tradition?"

"I didn't have to gather," replied the witness, with a dry smile. "He said in perfectly unmistakable terms that he regarded it as pure bunkum."

"Do you know what reasons he had for taking that view?"

"There were several reasons. In the first place, he didn't care a dime whether it was true or not. He was a prosperous American citizen, and that was good enough for him. But I think his beliefs were influenced by the character and personality of his father, Josiah Pippet. Josiah was a very peculiar man; very erratic in his behaviour, and, my father thought, not particularly reliable in his statements. Then he was an inveterate joker and much addicted to what is now called leg-pulling. I gathered that my father regarded the whole story as a leg-pull. But he did express surprise that Josiah should have kept the joke up so long and that so many people seemed to have been taken in by it."

"What people was he referring to?"

"The people who were connected with the 'Fox and Grapes' and those who frequented the place. He made a trip to England soon after the death of his brother Walter to see to the disposal of the family property. He had to go to the 'Fox and Grapes' to arrange about the sale of the good-will and effects; and there he found a general belief among the staff and the regular frequenters of the house that there was some mystery about Josiah. It was then, too, that he heard the rumour of the bogus funeral."

"Did he tell you what, exactly, it was that the staff and the other people believed?"

"A good deal of it seemed to be rather vague, though they all agreed that Josiah was not what he appeared to be – just an inn-keeper – but that he was a member of some noble house, masquerading as a publican for some unknown reasons. And they all appeared to believe that he was not really dead, but that he had arranged a sham funeral in order to bring the masquerade to an end without disclosing his real personality."

"But apart from these vague rumours, was there anything more definite?"

"Yes; there were some very definite statements, particularly those made by Walter's manager, who succeeded him. He professed to have been on terms of close intimacy with Josiah and to have received con-fidences from him which were made to no one else. Among these was the categorical statement that he, Josiah Pippet, was actually the Earl of Winsborough; that he had been born in the Castle at Winsborough and that he intended, if possible, to die there. And he, the manager, expressed himself as quite certain that Josiah was not dead, giving as his reason a number of reports which had reached him from time to time. One man, he stated, who was a frequenter of the 'Fox and Grapes', had seen Josiah coming out of the town mansion in Cavendish Square and stepping into a carriage. Another customer, a Channel pilot, had met Josiah riding along the road across the sandhills from Sandwich to Deal. He was perfectly certain that the man was Josiah Pippet, having often been served by him with liquor at the bar of the 'Fox and Grapes'. Another customer, who occasionally had business at Sandwich in Kent, happened to walk out from that town to Winsborough, and there he saw Josiah Pippet riding out of the main gate of the Castle grounds, followed by a mounted groom. He also was quite certain that the man he saw was really Josiah. And there were several other instances of persons who had seen Josiah since his alleged death which were mentioned by the manager, but my father could not remember the particulars."

"And did not all these circumstantial statements make any impression on your father?"

"No; none whatever. His opinion was that Josiah had amused himself by throwing out mysterious hints and that these had been repeated over and over again, growing with each repetition, until this story had taken definite shape."

"And as to the reports that Josiah had actually been seen in the flesh?"

"His explanation of that was that Josiah and the Earl were probably a good deal alike; and he suspected that Josiah's hints arose from that circumstance. He remarked that Josiah certainly came from that part of the country, and that he probably knew the Earl by sight."

"You do not, I presume," said the counsel, slightly disconcerted, I thought, by the witness's tone, "take quite the same view as your father."

"I am trying to keep an open mind," the witness replied, calmly, "but I am telling you what my father thought, if his opinions have any bearings on the case."

"It is not clear that they have," said the judge. "We are, I believe, endeavouring to elicit facts."

"I would submit, my lord," the counsel replied, "that they have this bearing: that the statements being those of an entirely unconvinced man, they may be assumed to be quite free from any suspicion of exaggeration. The speaker's bias was clearly against the truth of the reports and his testimony has, accordingly, an added value."

The judge acknowledged this "submission" with a grave nod but made no further comment, and the counsel resumed his examination.

"When your father used to speak to you about Josiah's story, did he give you any particulars as to what Josiah had told him?"

"He did occasionally. But most of Josiah's talk on the subject took the form of vague boastings to the effect that his real station was very different from what it appeared. But now and again he let himself go with a straight statement. For instance, on one occasion he said quite definitely that Pippet was not his real name; that he had assumed it because it seemed to be a good name for an inn-keeper. I don't know what he meant by that."

"He gave no hint as to what his real name was?"

"No. The nearest approach to a disclosure of an identity other than that of Josiah Pippet was in his parting words to my father when the latter was starting on a long voyage a few months before Josiah's death. He then said – I am quoting my father as well as I can remember his words – 'When you come back, you may not find me here. If you don't, you can look for me down at Winsborough, near Sandwich in Kent, and you will probably find me living at the Castle.' That was the last time that my father saw him."

"You have referred to the alleged bogus funeral of your grandfather, Josiah Pippet, and to a dummy coffin weighted with lead. In the accounts which you received, was any mention made of the kind of lead used – whether, for instance, it was lead pipe, or bars, or lead pig?"

"Most of the accounts referred simply to lead; but one – I forget who gave it – mentioned a roll of roofing-lead and some plumber's oddments, left after some repairs. But I am not very clear about it. I can't quote any particular account."

"Are there any other facts or statements known to you tending to prove that the man known as Josiah Pippet was in fact the Earl of Winsborough?"

"No. I think you have got them all except those contained in the diary."

"Then," said the counsel, "in that case, we will proceed to consider the entries in the diary which seem relevant." With this, he produced seven small, antique-looking, leather-bound volumes and passed them across to the witness.

"What do you say these volumes are?" he asked.

"To the best of my belief," was the reply, "they are the diary kept by my grandfather, Josiah Pippet."

"How did they come into your possession?"

"They were among the effects of my late father, Frederick William Pippet. They were obtained by him, as he informed me, when he was disposing of the effects of his deceased brother, Walter. He found them in a deed-box with a large number of letters, the whole being tied together and docketed 'Diary and letters of Josiah Pippet, deceased.' As the surviving son, he took possession of them and the letters."

"You have no doubt that these volumes are the authentic diary of Josiah Pippet?"

"No, I have not. His name is written in each volume and my father always referred to them as his father's diary, and I have no reason to doubt that that is what they are."

"Are they, in all respects, in the same condition as when they came into your possession?"

"They were up to the time that I handed them to my solicitor, and I have no doubt that they are still. They were always kept in the deed-box in which my father found them, together with the letters. I handed the whole collection in the deed-box to my solicitor for him to examine."

"Would it be correct to say that it was the study of this diary that led you seriously to entertain the possibility that Josiah Pippet was really the Earl of Winsborough?"

"It would – with the proviso that the studying was not done by me. It was my sister who used to study the diary, and she communicated her discoveries to me."

"Since you have been in England, have you made any attempts to check the accuracy of the entries in the diary?"

"I have, in the few cases in which it has been possible after all these years."

"There is an entry dated the 3rd of September, 1839: 'Home on the brig *Harmony*. Got aground on the Dyke, but off next tide.' Have you been able to check that? As to the locality, I mean."

"Yes. I find that the Dyke is the name of a shoal by the side of a navigation channel called the Old Cudd Channel, leading to Ramsgate Harbour. I find that it is used almost exclusively by vessels entering or leaving Ramsgate Harbour or Sandwich Haven. At Sandwich I was allowed to examine the old books kept by the Port authorities, and in the register of shipping using the port I found, under the date 1st September, 1839, a note that the brig *Harmony* sailed out of the Haven in ballast, bound for London."

"What significance do you attach to that entry?"

"As Sandwich is only a mile and a half from Winsborough, and is the nearest port, the fact of his embarking there is consistent with the supposition that Winsborough was the place in which he had been staying."

"There is a previous entry dated the 12th of June, 1837: 'Broached an anker of prime Dutch gin that I bought from the skipper of the *Vriendschap*.'"

"I checked that at the same time in the same register. There was an entry relating to a Dutch galliot named the *Vriendschap* which discharged a general cargo, including a quantity of gin. She arrived at Sandwich on the 10th of April and cleared outward on the 25th of the same month. At that time, the diary shows that Josiah was absent from home."

"Is there anything to show where he was at that time?"

"There is an entry made just after he arrived home. I am not sure of the date."

"Are you referring to the entry of the 6th of May, 1837: 'Home again. Feel a little strange after the life at the Castle'?"

"Yes. Taking the two entries together, it seems clear that the castle referred to was Winsborough Castle and that he was in residence there."

"I will take only one more passage from the diary – that of the 8th of October, 1842:'Back to the Fox. Exit G A and enter J P, but not for long.'What does that convey to you?"

"The meaning of it seems to me to be obvious. The initials are those of the Earl, George Augustus, and himself, Josiah Pippet. It appears plainly to indicate that George Augustus now retires from the stage and gives place to Josiah Pippet. And, as the entry was made within ten months of his alleged death, or final disappearance, the expression,'not for long,' seems to refer to that final disappearance."

On receiving this answer, counsel paused and glanced over his brief. Apparently finding no further matter for examination, he said: "I need not ask you anything about the passages from the diary which I quoted in my opening address. The diary is put in evidence and the passages speak for themselves."

With this he sat down and Anstey rose to cross-examine.

"You have told us, Mr Pippet," he began, "that you were led to entertain the belief in the dual personality of your grandfather, Josiah Pippet, by your study of certain passages in his diary."

"Not my study," was the reply. "I said that my sister studied the diary and communicated her discoveries to me."

"Yes. Now, which of these passages was it that first led you to abandon the scepticism which, I understand, you formerly felt in regard to the story of the double life and the sham funeral?"

"I cannot remember distinctly, but my impression is that my sister was strongly influenced by those passages which imply, or definitely state, that Josiah, when absent from his London home, was living at the Castle."

"But what caused you to identify 'the Castle' as Winsborough Castle? There is nothing in the diary to indicate any castle in particular. The words used are simply 'the Castle.' How did you come to decide that, of all the castles in England, the reference was to this particular castle?"

"I take it that we were influenced by what we had both heard from our father. The stories that he had been told referred explicitly to

Winsborough Castle. And the inquiries which I have made since I have been in England – "

"Pardon me," interrupted Anstey, "but those inquiries are not relevant to my question. We are speaking of your study of the diary when you were at your home in America. I suggest that you then had very little knowledge of the geography of the county of Kent."

"We had practically none."

"Then I suggest that, apart from what you had heard from your father, there was nothing to indicate that the words, 'the Castle' referred to Winsborough Castle."

"That is so. We applied what my father had told us to the entries in the diary."

"Then, since the connection was simply guess-work, is it not rather singular that the mere reference to the Castle should have made so deep an impression on you?"

"Perhaps," the witness replied, with a faint smile, "my sister may have been prepared to be impressed, and may have communicated her enthusiasm to me."

To this answer Anstey made no rejoinder, but, after a short pause and a glance at his brief, resumed:

"There is this entry of the 8th of October, 1842 'Back to the Fox. Exit G A and enter J P, but not for long.' Did that passage influence you strongly in your opinion of the truth of the story of Josiah's double life?"

The witness did not answer immediately, and it seemed to me that he looked a little worried. At length he replied:

"It is a remarkable fact, but I have no recollection of our ever having discussed that entry. It would almost seem as if my sister had overlooked it."

"Do you remember when your attention was first drawn to that entry?"

"Yes. It was at a consultation with my solicitor, Mr Gimbler, when he showed me a number of passages which he had extracted from the diary, which he considered relevant to the case, and which he wished me to try to verify if possible."

"Have you, since then, discussed this passage with your sister?"

"Yes; and she is as much surprised as I am that it did not attract her attention when she was reading the diary."

"So far as you know, did she read the entire diary?"

"I understood that she read the whole seven volumes from cover to cover."

"Has she ever made a definite statement to you to that effect?"

"Yes. A short time ago, I put the question to her explicitly and she assured me that, to the best of her belief, she had read every word of the diary."

"And you say that she had no recollection of having noticed this particular entry?"

"That is what she told me."

Here the judge interposed with a question.

"I don't understand why we are taking this hearsay testimony from the witness as to what his sister read or noticed. Is not the lady in court?"

"Yes, my lord," replied Anstey; "but I understand that it is not proposed to call Miss Pippet."

The judge turned and looked inquiringly at Mr McGonnell, who rose and explained:

"It was not considered necessary to call Miss Pippet, as she is not in possession of any facts other than those known to her brother."

With this he sat down. But, for some seconds, the judge continued to look at him fixedly as if about to ask some further question, a circumstance that seemed to occasion the learned counsel some discomfort. But, if his lordship had intended to make any further observations, he thought better of it, for he suddenly turned away, and, leaning back in his chair, glanced at Anstey, who thereupon resumed his cross-examination.

"Now, Mr Pippet," said he, taking up the last volume of the diary (the seven volumes had been passed to him at the conclusion of the examination in chief) and opening it at a place near the end, "I will ask you to look at this entry, dated the 8th of October, 1842." (Here the open book was passed across to the witness.) "You will see that there is a blank space between the last entry made before the writer went away from home and this, the first entry made after his return. Is that so?"

"It is," replied Mr Pippet.

"And does it not appear to you that this entry is in a very conspicuous position – in a position likely to catch the eye of any person glancing over the page?"

"It does," the witness agreed.

"Then I put it to you, Mr Pippet. Here is a diary which is being searched by an intelligent and attentive reader for corroboration of the story of Josiah's alleged double life. Here is an entry which seems to afford such corroboration. It is in a conspicuous position, and not only that; for, being the first entry after Josiah's return from his mysterious absence, it is in the very position in which an intelligent searcher would expect to find it. Now, I ask you, is it not an astounding and almost incredible circumstance that this entry should have been overlooked?"

"I have already said so," Mr Pippet replied, a little wearily, delivering the open diary to the usher, who handed it up to the judge. There was a short pause while Anstey turned over the leaves of his brief and the judge examined the diary; which he did with undissembled interest and at considerable length. When he had finished with it, he returned it to the usher, who brought it over to Anstey, by whom it was forthwith delivered into the hands of Thorndyke.

I watched my colleague's proceedings with grim amusement. If, in Anstey's cross-examination, certain hints were to be read between the lines, there was no such reticence on Thorndyke's part. Openly and undisguisedly, he scrutinised the entry in the diary, with the naked eye, with his pocket-lens, and finally with a queer little squat, double-barrelled microscope which he produced from a case at his side. Nor was I the only observer. The proceeding was watched by his lordship, with a sphinx-like face but a twinkling eye, by the two opposing counsel, and especially Mr Gimbler, who seemed to view it with considerable disfavour.

But my attention was diverted from Thorndyke's activities by Anstey, who now resumed his cross-examination.

"You have referred to the alleged bogus funeral of your grandfather, Josiah Pippet, and to a dummy coffin weighted with lead. Now, so far as you know, is that coffin still in existence?"

"I have no doubt that it is. I visited the cemetery, which is at a place near Stratford in the East End of London, and examined the vault from the outside. It appeared to be quite intact."

"Is the cemetery still in use?"

"No. It was closed many years ago by Act of Parliament and is now disused and deserted."

"Had you any difficulty in obtaining admission?"

The witness smiled. "I can hardly say that I was admitted," said he. "The place was locked up and there was nobody in charge; but the wall was only about six feet high. I had no difficulty in getting over."

"Then," said Anstey, "we may assume that the coffin is still there. And if it is, it contains either the body of Josiah Pippet or a roll of sheet lead and some plumber's oddments. Has it never occurred to you that it would be desirable to examine that coffin and see what it does contain?"

"It has," the witness replied emphatically. "When I came to England, my intention was to get that coffin open right away and see whether Josiah was in it or not. If I had found him there, I should have known that my father was right and that the story was all bunk; and if I had found the lead, I should have known that there was something solid to go on."

"What made you abandon that intention?"

"I was advised that, in England, it is impossible to open a coffin without a special faculty from the Home Secretary, and that no such faculty would be granted until the case had been heard in a court of law."

"Then we may take it that it was your desire to have this coffin examined as to its contents?"

"It was, and is," the witness replied, energetically. "I want to get at the truth of this business; and it seems to me, being ignorant of law, that it is against common sense to spend all this time arguing and inferring when a few turns of a screwdriver would settle the whole question in a matter of minutes."

The judge smiled approvingly. "A very sensible view," said he; "and not such particularly bad law."

"So far as you know, Mr Pippet," said Anstey, "have any measures been taken to obtain authority to open the vault and examine the coffin?"

"I am not aware of any. I understood that, until the court had given some decision on the case, any such measures would be premature."

"Are you aware that it is within the competency of this court to make an order for the exhumation of this coffin and its examination as to its contents?"

"I certainly was not," the witness answered.

Here the judge interposed with some signs of impatience.

"It seems necessary that this point should be cleared up. We are trying a case involving a number of issues, all of which are subject to one main issue. That issue is: Did Josiah Pippet die in the year 1843 and was he buried in a normal manner? Or was his alleged death a fictitious death and the funeral a sham funeral conducted with a dummy coffin weighted with lead? Now, as Mr Pippet has most reasonably remarked, it seems a strange thing that we should be listening to a mass of evidence of the most indirect kind – principally hearsay evidence at third or fourth hand – when we actually have within our grasp the means of settling this issue conclusively by evidence of the most direct and convincing character. Has the learned counsel for the applicant any instructions on this point?"

While the judge had been speaking, a hurried and anxious consultation had been taking place between Mr Gimbler and his leading counsel. The latter now rose and replied:

"It was considered, my lord, that, as these proceedings were, in a sense, preliminary to certain other proceedings possibly to be taken in another place, it might be desirable to postpone the question of the exhumation, especially as it seemed doubtful whether your lordship would be willing to make the necessary order."

"That," said the judge, "could have been ascertained by making the application; and I may say that I should certainly have complied with the request."

"Then in that case," said Mr McGonnell, "we gratefully adopt your lordship's suggestion and make the application now."

"Very well," the judge rejoined, "then the order will be made, subject to the consent of the Home Secretary, which we may assume will be given."

As he concluded, he glanced at Anstey, but, as the latter remained seated, and no re-examination followed, Mr Pippet was released from the witness-box.

Of the rest of the evidence I have but a dim recollection. The sudden entry, like a whiff of fresh air, into this fog of surmise and rumour, of a promise of real, undeniable evidence, made the testimony of the remaining witnesses appear like mere trifling. There was an architect and surveyor who described and produced plans of the old Earl's underground chambers; and there was an aged woman whose grandfather had been a potman at the "Fox and Grapes" and who gave a vague account of the strange rumours of which she had heard him speak. But it was all very shadowy and unreal. It merely left us speculating as to whether the story of the bogus funeral might or might not possibly be true. And the speculation was not worth while when we should presently be looking into the open coffin and able to settle the question definitely, yes or no.

I think everyone was relieved when the sitting came to an end and the further hearing was adjourned until the result of the exhumation should be made known.

# CHAPTER TEN

## Josiah?

The last resting-place – real or fictitious – of the late Josiah Pippet was a somewhat dismal spot. Not that it mattered. The landscape qualities of a burial-ground cannot be of much concern to the inmates. And in Josiah's day, when he came here prospecting for an eligible freehold, the aspect of the place was doubtless very different. Then it must have been a rural burial-ground adjoining some vanished hamlet (it was designated on the Ordnance map "Garwell Burial-Ground") hard by the Romford Turnpike Road. Now it was a little grimy wilderness, fronting on a narrow street, flanked by decaying stable-yards and cart-sheds, and apparently utterly neglected and forgotten of men. The only means of access was a rusty iron gate, set in the six-foot enclosing wall, and at that gate Thorndyke and I arrived a full half-hour before the appointed time, having walked thither from the nearest station – Maryland Point on the Great Eastern. But early as we were, we were not early enough from Thorndyke's point of view; for, not only did we find the rusty gate unlocked (with a brand-new key sticking out of the corroded lock), but, when we lifted the decayed latch and entered, we discovered two men in the very act of wrenching open the door of a vault.

"This," said Thorndyke, regarding the two men with a disapproving eye, "ought not to have been done until everyone was present and the unopened door had been inspected."

"Well," I said, consolingly, "it will save time."

"No doubt," he admitted. "But that is not what we are here for."

We approached the operators, one of whom appeared to be a locksmith and the other an official of some kind, to whom, at his request, we gave our names and explained our business.

"I expect," said Thorndyke, "you had your work cut out, getting that door unlocked."

"It was a bit of a job, Sir," the locksmith replied.

"Locks is like men. Gets a bit stiff in the joints after eighty years. But it wasn't as bad as I'd expected. I'd got a good strong skeleton key filed up and a tommy to turn it with; and when I'd run in a drop of paraffin and oil, she twisted round all right."

As he was speaking, I looked around me. The burial-ground was roughly square in shape, enclosed on three sides by a six-foot brick wall, while the fourth side was occupied by a range of the so-called vaults; which were not, strictly speaking, vaults at all, but sepulchral chambers above ground. There were six of them, each provided with its own door, and over each door was a stone tablet on which were inscribed brief particulars of the inmates. Josiah alone had a chamber all to himself, and, running my eye along the row of tablets and reading the dates, I noted that he appeared to be the last of the tenants.

At this moment, the sound of a motor car in the street outside caused us to step back to bring the gate within view; when, to my surprise − but not, apparently, to Thorndyke's − our old friend, Mr Superintendent Miller, was seen entering. As he approached and greeted us, I exclaimed:

"This is an unexpected pleasure, Miller. What brings you here? I didn't know that the police were interested in this case."

"They are not," he replied. "I am here on instructions from the Home Office just to see that the formalities are complied with. That is all. But it is a quaint business. What are we going to find in that coffin, Doctor?"

"That," replied Thorndyke, "is an open question, at present."

"I know," said Miller. "But I expect you have considered the probabilities. What do you say? Bones or lead?"

"Well, as a mere estimate of probabilities," replied Thorndyke, "I should say lead."

"Should you really!" I exclaimed in astonishment. "I would have wagered fifty to one on a body. The whole story of the bogus funeral sounded to me like 'sheer bunk', as Pippet would express it."

"That would certainly have been my view," said Miller, "but I expect we are both wrong. We usually are when we disagree with the Doctor. And there does seem to be a hint of something queer about that inscription. 'Josiah Pippet, died on the 12th day of October, 1843, aged 49 years, 2 months and 3 days.' If he was so blooming particular to a day, why couldn't he have just given the date of his birth and have done with it?"

While we had been talking, the official and his assistant had produced two pairs of coffin trestles, which they set up side by side opposite the open door of the vault; and they had hardly been placed in position when the sound of two cars drawing up almost at the same moment announced the arrival of the rest of the party.

"My eye!" exclaimed Miller, as the visitors filed in and the official – beadle, or whatever he was – advanced to meet them and lock the gate after them; "it's a regular congregation."

It did look a large party. First there was Mr Pippet with his sister and daughter and his solicitor and Mr McGonnell; and then followed Mrs Engleheart and her son with Mr Brodribb. But, once inside the burial-ground, the two groups tended to coalesce while mutual greetings were exchanged, and then to sort themselves out. The two elder ladies decided to wait at a distance while "the horrid business" was in progress, and the rest of us gathered round the half-open door, the two young people drawing together and seeming, as I thought, to be on uncommonly amicable terms.

"I leave the conduct of this affair in your hands, Thorndyke," said Mr Brodribb, casting a wistful glance at the two ladies, who had retired to the farther side of the enclosure. "Is there anything that you want to do before the coffin is moved?"

"I should like, as a mere formality, to inspect the interior of the vault," was the reply; "and perhaps the Superintendent, as a disinterested witness, might also take a glance at it."

As he spoke, he looked enquiringly at Mr Gimbler, and the latter, accepting the suggestion, advanced with him and Miller and threw the door wide open. There was nothing very sensational to see. The little chamber was crossed by a thick stone shelf on which rested the coffin. The latter had a very unattractive appearance, the dark, damp oak – from which every vestige of varnish had disappeared – being covered with patches of thick, green mildew and greasy-looking stains, over which was a mantle of impalpably fine grey dust. A layer of similar dust covered the shelf, the floor and every horizontal surface, but nowhere was there the faintest sign of its having been disturbed. On coffin and shelf and floor it presented a perfectly smooth, unbroken surface.

"Well, Doctor," said Miller, when he had cast a quick, searching glance round the chamber, "are you satisfied? Looks all right."

"Yes," replied Thorndyke. "But we will just take a sample or two of the dust for reference, if necessary."

As he spoke, he produced from his pockets a penknife and two of the inevitable seed-envelopes which he always carried about him. With the former he scraped up a little heap of dust on the coffin lid and shovelled it into one envelope, and then took another sample from the shelf; a proceeding which was observed with a sour smile by Mr Gimbler and with delighted amusement by the Superintendent.

"Nothing left to chance, you notice," chuckled the latter. "Thomas à Diddamus was a credulous man compared with the Doctor. Shall we have the coffin out now?"

As Thorndyke assented, the beadle and his assistant approached and drew the coffin forward on the shelf. Then they lifted the projecting end, but forthwith set it down again and stood gazing at it blankly.

"Moses!" exclaimed the locksmith. "He don't seem to have lost much weight in eighty years! This is a four-man job."

Thereupon, Miller and I stepped forward, and, as the two men lifted the foot end of the coffin, we took the weight of the other end;

and as we staggered to the trestles with our ponderous burden, Miller whispered to me:

"What's the betting now, Dr Jervis?"

"There may be a lead shell," I suggested, but without much conviction.

However, there was no use in speculating, seeing that the locksmith had already produced a screwdriver from his tool-bag and was preparing to set to work. As he began, I watched him with some interest, expecting that the screw would be rusted in immovably. But he was a skilful workman and managed the extraction with very little difficulty, though the screw, when at last he got it out and laid it on the coffin lid, was thickly encrusted with rust. Thorndyke picked it up, and, having looked it over, handed it to Miller with the whispered injunction:

"Take charge of the screws, Miller. They may have to be put in evidence."

The Superindentent made no comment, though I could see that he was a little puzzled; as also was I, for there appeared to be nothing unusual or significant in the appearance of the screw. And I think the transaction was observed – with some disfavour – by Mr Gimbler, though he took no notice, but kept a watchful and suspicious eye on Thorndyke; who, during the extraction of the other screws, occupied himself with an exhaustive examination of the exterior of the coffin, including the blackened brass nameplate (the fastening-screws of which he inspected through a lens) and the brass handles and their fastenings.

At length the last of the eight screws was extracted and pocketed by Miller – and the locksmith, inserting his screwdriver between the lid and the side, looked round as if waiting for the word. We all gathered round, making space, however, for Mr Pippet, his daughter and Mr Giles.

"Now," said Mr Pippet, "we are going to get the answer to the riddle. Up with her."

The locksmith gave a single wrench and the lid rose. He lifted it clear and laid it on the other trestles, and we all craned forward and peered into the coffin. And then, at the first glance, we had the answer. For what we saw was an untidy bundle of mouldy sacking. We could not see what the bundle contained; but it certainly did not contain the late Josiah Pippet.

The excitement now reached its climax and found expression in low-toned, inarticulate murmurs, in the midst of which Mr Pippet's calm, matter-of-fact voice was heard directing the locksmith to "get that bundle open and let's see what's inside". Accordingly, with much tugging at the unsavoury sacking, the bundle was laid open and its contents exposed to the light of day – a small roll of whitened sheet-lead and four hemispherical lumps of the same metal, apparently the remainders from a plumber's melting-pot.

For some moments there was a complete silence as nine pairs of fascinated eyes remained riveted on the objects that reposed on the bottom of the coffin. It was broken, not quite harmoniously, by the voice of Mr Gimbler.

"A roll of sheet-lead and some plumber's oddments." As he spoke, he turned, with a fat, wrinkly and rather offensive smile to Mr Giles Engleheart.

"Yes," the latter agreed, "it fits the description to a T." He held out his hand to Mr Pippet and continued: "It's heads up for you, Sir. I congratulate you on a fair win, and I wish you a long life to enjoy what you have won."

"Thank you, Giles," said Mr Pippet, shaking his hand warmly. "I am glad to have your congratulations first – even if they should turn out premature. We mustn't be too previous, you know."

He spoke in a singularly calm, unemotional tone, without a trace of triumph or even satisfaction. Indeed, I could not but be impressed (and considerably surprised) by the total absence of any sign of elation on the part either of the claimant or his daughter. It might have been simply good manners and regard for the defeated rival. But it looked uncommonly like indifference. Moreover, I could not but notice that, in the midst of the congratulations, Mr Pippet was keeping an attentive eye on Thorndyke; and, indeed, my colleague's proceedings soon began to attract more general notice.

When the leaden objects were first disclosed, he had viewed them impassively with what had almost looked like a glance of recognition. They were, in fact, as I knew, exactly what he had expected to see. But after a general, searching glance, he proceeded to a closer inspection. First, he lifted out the roll of sheet-lead, and, having looked it over, critically, laid it on the coffin-lid. Then he turned his attention to the "oddments", of which there was one appreciably larger than the other three, having apparently come from a bigger melting-pot. This mass, which looked like the half of a metallic Dutch cheese, he lifted out first, and, in spite of its great weight, he seemed to handle it without any difficulty as he turned it about to examine its various parts. When he had inspected it all over, he laid it on the coffin-lid beside the roll of sheet-lead, and then, dipping into the coffin once more, took up one of the smaller "remainders".

And it was at this moment that I became aware that "something had happened." How I knew it, I can hardly say, for Thorndyke was a perfectly impossible subject for a thought-reader. But my long association with him enabled me to detect subtle shades of expression that were perceptible to no one else. And something of the kind I had seen now. As he lifted the lump of lead, he had checked for a moment and seemed to stiffen, and a sudden intensity of attention had flashed into his eyes, to vanish in an instant, leaving his face as immobile and impassive as a mask of stone.

What could it be? I could only watch and wait for developments. As he turned the mass of lead over in his hands and pored over every inch of its surface, I caught the twinkling eye of Superintendent Miller and a low chuckle of appreciative amusement.

"Nothing taken for granted, you observe," he murmured.

But the others were less indulgent. As Thorndyke laid the last of the leaden pot-leavings on the coffin-lid, Mr McGonnell interposed, a little stiffly.

"Is there anything more, Dr Thorndyke? Because, if not, as we seem to have done what we came here to do, I suggest that we may consider the business as finished."

"That is," said Mr Pippet, "if Dr Thorndyke is satisfied. Are you satisfied, Doctor?"

"No," replied Thorndyke. "I am not satisfied with this lead. It purports to have been placed here in 1843, and part of it – the sheet-lead – was then old. It was said to have been old roofing-sheet. Now, I am not satisfied that this lead is of that age. This sheet-lead looks to me like modern milled lead."

"And how do you propose to settle that question?" McGonnell asked.

"I propose that an assay of the lead should be made to determine, if possible, its age."

McGonnell snorted. "This is Thomas Didymus, with a vengeance," he exclaimed. "But I submit that it is mere hair-splitting; and I don't believe that any assayist could give an opinion as to the age of the lead, or that the court would pay any attention to him if he did. What do you say, Gimbler?"

Mr Gimbler smiled his queer, fat, wrinkly smile, to the entire extinction of his little blue eyes, and swung his eyeglasses on their ribbon like a pendulum.

"I say," he replied, oracularly, "that the proposal is inadmissible for several reasons. First, the objection is frivolous. We came here to find out whether this coffin contained a body or some lumps of lead. We find that it contained lead. Now Dr Thorndyke doubts whether it is the original lead. He thinks it may be some other lead of a later vintage. But if it is, how came it here? What does he suggest?"

"I suggest nothing," said Thorndyke. "My function in this case is the purely scientific one of ascertaining facts."

"Still," persisted Gimbler, "there is a suggestion implied in the objection. But I let that pass. Next, I assert that an assay would not produce any evidence that the court would take seriously. The proposed proceeding is merely vexatious and obstructive. It would occasion delay and increase the costs to no useful purpose. And, finally, the order of the court does not authorise us to make an assay of the lead. It merely authorises us to open the coffin and ascertain whether it contains a body. We have done that and we find that it does not contain a body."

Here Mr Brodribb, who had been showing signs of increasing discomfort, intervened in the discussion.

"I am inclined, Thorndyke," said he, "to agree with Mr Gimbler. Your proposal to make an assay of the lead does seem to go beyond the powers conferred by the judge's order. Of course, if it is necessary, we could make a special application. But is it necessary? Do you say definitely that this lead is not of the age that it is assumed to be?"

"No," replied Thorndyke, "I do not. I merely say that I am not satisfied that it is."

"Then," said Brodribb, "I suggest that we waive the question of the assay, at least for the present. I should much prefer to do so, especially as there is no denying that your proposal does imply certain suggestions which should not be lightly made."

Thorndyke reflected for a few moments, and I waited curiously for his decision. Finally, he rejoined:

"Very well, Brodribb; I will not press the matter against your sense of the legal proprieties. We will waive the assay – at any rate, for the present."

"I think you are wise," said McGonnell. "It would have seemed an extravagant piece of scepticism and couldn't have led to any result. And now," he added, looking anxiously at his watch, "I suppose we have finished our business. I hope so. Have we got to see to the replacing of the coffin?"

"No, Sir," replied Miller. "That is my business, as official master of the ceremonies. There is nothing to detain you."

"Thank goodness for that," said McGonnell, and began, forthwith, to move towards the gate, while Mr Pippet, the two solicitors and the two young people advanced up the path to meet the two elder ladies and give them the latest news of the discoveries. Then the beadle unlocked the gate, and, as the procession moved towards it, we joined the party to exchange polite greetings and see them into their cars (in which the opposing litigants got mixed up in the most singular and amicable manner).

"Can I give you two a lift?" enquired Brodribb, as he held the door of his car open.

"No, thank you," replied Thorndyke. "We have a little business to transact with Miller."

Thereupon Brodribb wriggled, with some difficulty into his car; and we re-entered the gate, which the beadle locked after us, and rejoined the Superintendent.

# CHAPTER ELEVEN

## Plumber's Oddments and Other Matters

As Thorndyke and I returned from the gate, the Superintendent met us with a peculiarly knowing expression on his countenance.

"Well, Doctor," said he. "What about it?"

And, as this slightly ambiguous question elicited no reply beyond an indulgent smile, he continued: "When I hear a gentleman of your intellect propose to assay a lump of old lead to ascertain the exact vintage year, experience tells me that that gentleman has got something up his sleeve. Now, Doctor, let's hear what it is."

"To tell you the truth, Miller," Thorndyke replied, "I don't quite know, myself. But you are wrong about the lead. The age of a piece of lead can be judged fairly accurately by the silver content. If you find a piece of sheet-lead with a silver content of, say, ten ounces to the ton, you can be pretty sure that it was made before Pattinson's process for the desilverisation of lead was invented. Still, you are right to the extent that the question of age was not the only issue that I had in my mind. There were other reasons why the assay should be made."

"But you have abandoned the assay," objected Miller, "and very surprised I was to hear you give way so easily."

"I gave way in your favour," said Thorndyke, with a cryptic smile. "*You* are going to have the assay carried out."

"Oh, am I?" exclaimed the Superintendent. "It's as well to know these things in advance." We turned into a side path to get a little farther from the beadle and his mate, and Miller continued: "Now, look here, Doctor; I want to be clear about this business. This is a civil case, and it is no concern of mine, as a police officer. What's the game? You seem to be dumping this blooming lead on me, and then there are these screws. Why did you want me to take charge of them?" He drew out of his pocket the rusty handful and looked at them disparagingly. "I don't see anything special about them. They look to me like ordinary screws such as you could buy at any ironmonger's."

Thorndyke chuckled. "They are common-looking screws, I must admit," said he. "But don't despise them. Like many other common-looking things, they have their value. I want you to put them into an envelope and seal it with your official seal; and write on the envelope, 'Screws extracted in my presence from the coffin of Josiah Pippet,' and sign it. Will you do that?"

"Yes," replied Miller, "I don't see any objection to that, though I am hanged if I can guess what you want them for. But with regard to this lead. You want me to have it assayed on my own initiative, as a police officer. But I must have something to go on. The judge's order doesn't cover me. Now, I know quite well that you have got something perfectly definite in your mind; and, knowing you as I do, I am pretty sure that it is not a delusion. Can't you tell me what it is?"

Thorndyke reflected for a few moments. "The fact is," he said, at length, "I am in a difficulty. My position in this case is that of a counsel instructed by Brodribb." Here Miller indulged in a broad grin, but made no comment, beyond something like a wink directed towards me, and Thorndyke continued:

"You saw that Brodribb disliked the idea of the assay. He is a very acute lawyer, but he is a most scrupulously courteous old gentleman, and he was obviously unwilling to seem to throw the slightest doubt on the good faith of the other side, even Gimbler. Now, I could not act against Brodribb's wishes, and there was no need. I had given the other side their chance, and they didn't choose to take it."

"So now," said Miller, "you want, in effect, to run with the hare and hunt with the hounds. And I am the hounds. Isn't that the position?"

Thorndyke regarded the Superintendent with an appreciative smile. "Very neatly put, Miller," said he, "and I won't deny that it does seem to state the position. Nevertheless, I am going to ask you to help me, and to take on trust my assurance that, if you act on what I will call my suggestions, you will, in your official capacity, 'learn something to your advantage,' as the solicitors express it."

"Still," urged Miller, "if you don't care to let the cat out of the bag, you might at least show us her head, or even her tail, so that we may see what sort of animal is in the bag."

Once more, Thorndyke reflected for a few moments before replying. At length he said: "I fully appreciate your difficulty, Miller. You can't, as a detective officer, start an investigation in the air. But you have known me long enough to feel certain that I should not send you off in search of a mare's nest."

"I am quite clear on that point," Miller agreed, warmly. "I only want reasonable cover."

"Very well," rejoined Thorndyke; "I can give you that, if you will take my information on trust without the production of evidence."

"Let's hear the information," said Miller, cautiously.

"It is this," said Thorndyke; "and I am prepared to give you the information in writing, if you want it."

"I don't," said Miller. "I only want a definite statement."

"Then," said Thorndyke, "I will give you one. I declare, positively, that, if this is the original coffin, it has, at some time after the date of the burial, as set forth on the tomb and on the coffin, been opened and reclosed; and that the objects which we have found in it are not its original contents. But I am of the opinion that it is not the original coffin, but a new coffin substituted with the intent to commit a fraud. Will that do for you?"

"Yes," replied Miller. "That is good enough for a start; and not a bad start, either. If there has been a fraudulent substitution for the purpose of obtaining possession of valuable property, that brings the matter fairly within my province. And, what is more, it seems to bring Mr Horatio Gimbler within reach of my claws. But I have a sort of feeling that this faked coffin is not the whole of the business. How's that for a guess?"

"I will say, as the children say in the game of Hot Boiled Beans, that you are 'getting warm'. And I would rather not say any more. I want to start you on an independent investigation and keep out of it, myself, as counsel in this case. But I shall expect that, if you bring any facts to light that have a bearing on that case, you will bring them to my notice."

At this, Miller turned to me with a chuckle of delight.

"Just listen to him, Dr Jervis!" he exclaimed, waggishly. "Isn't it as good as a play? He stipulates that I shall bring the facts to his notice; when you and I know perfectly well that he has got the whole pack of cards up his sleeve at this very moment. I wouldn't use the word 'humbug' in connection with a gentleman for whom I have such a profound respect. But – well, what do you want me to do, Doctor?"

"The first thing," said Thorndyke, "is to get rid of those two men. We don't want any witnesses. As this ground is closed for burials and is not open to the public, there is no reason why you should not take possession of the keys. You will want to seal the vault and to have access to it in case any further inspection is necessary. The beadle won't make any difficulty."

He did not. On the contrary, he accepted his release gratefully and gave up the keys without a word. But, before dismissing the men, we replaced the coffin on the shelf, and, for the sake of appearances, we returned the lead to its interior and laid the lid on top.

"There is no need to screw it down," the Superintendent explained. "It may have to be re-examined, and I am going to seal up the vault."

With this he sent the two men off with a small donation for the provision of refreshments, accompanying them to the gate and watching their disappearance down the street. When they were out of sight, he signalled to the driver of his car – a big, roomy, official vehicle – and, when it had drawn up at the gate, he returned, and we began operations.

"I understand," said he, as we lifted off the coffin-lid, "that we have got to shift this stuff to some assayist's."

"I don't think we need take the sheet-lead," said Thorndyke, "though that would furnish the best evidence on the question of age."

"Then let's take the whole boiling," said Miller. "May as well do the thing thoroughly."

Accordingly, he seized the roll of lead and carried it to the gate, where he deposited it on the rear seat of the car. I followed with the biggest of the pot-leavings. The driver of the car came back with Miller, and he, Miller and Thorndyke took the other three leavings. The whole collection took up a good deal of the accommodation; but Thorndyke occupied the seat next to the driver, in order to give directions, and Miller and I packed ourselves in amongst the lead as well as we could.

"I wish the Doctor wasn't so deuced secretive," Miller remarked, as the car trundled away westward with a misleadingly leisurely air. "Of course, it doesn't really matter, as we shall know all about it presently; but I am on tenterhooks of curiosity."

"So am I, for that matter," said I; "but I am used to it. To work with Thorndyke is a fine training in restraint."

After what seemed an incredibly short journey, we drew up at a large building in Bishopsgate. Here Thorndyke alighted and disappeared into the entry; and the Superintendent's patience was subjected to a further trial. At length, our friend reappeared, accompanied by an alert-looking elderly gentleman, while three workmen in white aprons emerged from the doorway and lurked in the background. The elderly gentleman, whom I recognised as a Mr Daniels, a very eminent assayist and metallurgist, approached, and, when he had been introduced to Miller, stuck his head in at the window of the car and surveyed our collection.

"So that's the stuff you want an opinion on," said he. "Queer-looking lot. However, the first thing to do is to get it moved up to the laboratory."

He made a sign to his three myrmidons, who forthwith came forward, and, grabbing up the ponderous samples, tucked them under their arms as if they had been lumps of cork and strolled off into the building. We followed them through the weighing-rooms on the ground floor to a staircase and up to one of the great laboratories, flanked on one side by a row of tall windows, and on the other by a long range of cupel furnaces. Here, on a bench under the windows, our treasures had been dumped down, and, once more, Mr Daniels ran his eye over them.

"What's the problem with regard to this?" he asked, indicating the roll of lead.

"It is merely a question of age," replied Thorndyke. "We can leave that for the present."

"And what is this?" asked Daniels, lifting the large pot-remainder and turning it over in his hands.

"It is supposed to be lead, eighty years old," said Thorndyke.

"Well, it may be," said Daniels, laying it down and giving it a tap with a hammer and eliciting the dull sound characteristic of lead. "And what are these other lumps supposed to be?"

"They are supposed to be lead, too," replied Thorndyke.

"Well, they are not," said Daniels. "Anyone can see that." He gave one of them a tap with the hammer, and the peculiar sharp chink spoke at once of a hard, brittle metal. On this, he laid down the hammer and took the lump of metal in his hands. And then there came over him the very change that I had noticed in the case of Thorndyke, though there was now no disguise. As he lifted the mass of metal, he suddenly paused and stood quite still with his eyes fixed on Thorndyke and his mouth slightly open. Then he said: "You knew that this was not lead, Doctor."

"Yes," Thorndyke admitted.

"What do you suppose it is?"

"I don't suppose," said Thorndyke. "I have brought the Superintendent to you in order that you may ascertain what it is and give him a confidential report on the subject."

"What do *you* suppose it is?" asked Miller.

"I don't suppose either," replied Daniels with a faint grin. "I am an assayist, and it is my business to find out."

The Superintendent smiled sourly and looked at me. "These men of science don't mean to give themselves away," he remarked.

"Well," said Daniels, "what is the use of guessing, and perhaps guessing wrong, when you are going to make a test? We have our reputations to consider. Now, what do you want me to do about this stuff?"

"The Superintendent," said Thorndyke, "wants you to make a trial assay, just to let him know what the material is. You will report to him what you find; and remember, this is a confidential matter, and the Superintendent, acting for the Criminal Investigation Department, is your employer."

"And what about you?" Daniels asked.

"If the matter concerns me in any way," Thorndyke replied, "I have no doubt that the Superintendent will communicate the substance of your report to me."

"Ah!" exclaimed Daniels, with a broad smile, "and what a surprise it will be to you. Ha! ha!"

"Yes," growled Miller; "the Doctor is a regular impostor. Of course, he knows all about it, without either of us telling him. How long will this job take?"

"It will take some little time," replied Daniels, "as you will want some sort of rough estimate of quantities besides the mere qualitative test. Will five o'clock do? And shall I report to you on the phone?"

Miller considered the question. "I am not fond of telephone messages on confidential business," said he. "You never know who is at the other end, or in the middle. I think I had better run across in the car. Then we can go into the affair in more detail, and safe from eavesdroppers. If I am here at five o'clock, I can depend on getting your report?"

"Yes; I shall have everything cut and dried by then," Daniels assured him; and, the arrangements being thus concluded, we shook hands and took our departure.

As we emerged into Bishopsgate, I noticed that Miller seemed to look a little disparagingly at the big car that was drawn up at the kerb, and, instead of entering at once, he turned to Thorndyke and asked:

"What do you say, Doctor, to walking home? There are one or two matters connected with this case that I should like to talk over with you, and the car isn't very convenient; and then there is the driver. We could talk more freely if we walked."

Naturally, Thorndyke, who was an inveterate pedestrian, agreed readily; and, when Miller had informed the driver of our decision, we set forth, shortening the distance and securing more quiet by striking "across country" through the by-streets. As soon as we were clear of the main thoroughfare with its bustle and din, Miller proceeded to open the discussion.

"I suppose, Doctor, you are quite clear that there has been some faking of that coffin? You've got something solid to go on?"

"Yes," was the reply, "I have no doubt on the subject, and I am prepared to say so in the witness-box."

"That seems to settle it," said Miller. "But there are some queer features in the case. You saw the dust in the vault? But I know you did, for I spotted you taking samples of it. But it really did look as if it had not been disturbed for the best part of a century. Was there anything in that dust that looked to you suspicious, or did you take those samples just as a routine precaution?"

"I should have taken a sample in any case," replied Thorndyke. "But in this case it was not merely a routine precaution. That dust did not appear to me to agree with the conditions in which it was found. The dust that would accumulate in the course of eighty years in a vault above ground would be very miscellaneous in its origin. It would consist of particles of all sorts of materials which were light enough to float in the air, and in still air at that. They would be mostly minute fragments of fibres derived from textiles, and these would naturally be of all sorts of different colours. The result of such a miscellaneous mixture of different-coloured particles, aided by the fading effect of time, would be a dust of a completely neutral grey. But this dust was not of a completely neutral grey. It had a recognisable colour; very faint and very nearly neutral, but yet there was just a shadowy trace of red. And this subtle, almost indistinguishable, tint of red pervaded the whole mass. It was all alike. To what the colour may have been due, I cannot judge until I have examined the sample under the microscope; but the suggestion – the very strong suggestion – is that this dust was all derived from the same source; which, as I have said, is irreconcileable with the ostensible conditions."

Thorndyke's explanation seemed to furnish the Superintendent with considerable food for thought, for he made no immediate answer, but appeared to be wrapped in profound cogitation. At length, he remarked:

"You are a wonderful man, Doctor. Nothing seems to escape you, and you let nothing pass without consideration and a confirmatory test. I wish, now, that we had put you on that damned head – you know the one I mean – the human head that was found in a case at Fenchurch Street Station."

"I remember," said Thorndyke. "It was an odd affair, but I fancy that the head was only a by-product. The purpose of the man who left it was to get possession of the case containing property worth several thousand pounds. He happened to have a human head on his hands, and he, very wisely, took the opportunity to get rid of it and so kill two birds with one stone."

"That may be," said Miller; "but I am not taking that head so calmly as you are. It has been the bane of our lives at The Yard, with all the newspaper men shouting 'Unsolved Mystery' and 'Another undetected murder' and asking perpetually what the police are doing. And it really was a mysterious affair. I have been surprised to notice how little interest you have taken in that head. I should have thought it would have been a problem exactly in your line. But you medical jurists are a cold-blooded lot. You were speaking just now of this man 'having a human head on his hands' as if it were a worn-out umbrella or an old pair of boots."

Thorndyke smiled indulgently. "I am not disparaging the head, Miller," said he. "It presented quite an interesting problem. But it was not my problem. I was a mere disinterested onlooker."

"You don't usually take that sordid view," grumbled Miller. "I have generally found you ready to take an interest in a curious problem for its own sake."

To this Thorndyke made no rejoinder, and for some time we walked on in silence. Suddenly, the Superintendent stopped short and stood gazing across the road.

"By the immortal Jingo!" he exclaimed. "Talk of the Devil – "

He broke off and started to run across the road; and, following his movements with my eyes, I saw, on the opposite pavement, a newspaper boy bearing a poster on which was printed in enormous type:

### "HORRIBLE DISCOVERY. HEADLESS CORPSE BY ROADSIDE."

It was certainly curiously apropos of the subject of our conversation, and I so far shared the Superintendent's excitement that I was about to follow him when I saw that he had secured three copies of the paper and was coming back to us with them in his hand. He distributed his gifts rapidly, and then, backing into the wide entry of a draper's shop, proceeded eagerly to devour the paragraph indicated by the "scare" headlines. Following him into his retreat, I opened the paper and read:

"Some months ago the public were horrified by the discovery in the cloak-room at Fenchurch Street Station of a human head packed in a wooden case. No solution of the mystery surrounding this terrible relic was forthcoming at the inquest, nor were the police ever able to discover any clue to its origin or the identity of the murderer. The matter was allowed to lapse into oblivion, to be added to the long list of undiscovered murders. But questions relating to this tragedy have been revived by a strange and shocking discovery which was made this morning by the side of the arterial road known as the Watling Street, which passes from London through Dartford to Rochester. Between three and four miles on the Rochester side of Dartford, the road passes through a deep cutting, which was made to reduce the gradient of the hill, the sides of which are in two stages, there being, about half-way up, a shelf several feet wide. As this shelf is some thirty feet above the road, its surface is entirely invisible to anyone passing along the latter, though it is, of course, visible from above. But the hill through which the road is cut is covered with dense woodland, seldom trodden by the foot of man. Thus, for months at a time, this shelf remains unseen by any human eye.

"But this morning Fate guided the footsteps of an observer to this spot, so remote and yet so near. A local archaeologist, a Mr Elmhurst of Gravesend, happened to be making a sketch-map of the features of the wood when his wanderings took him to the edge of the cutting. Looking down the cliff-like descent, he was horrified to observe, lying on the shelf immediately below him, the headless and perfectly nude body of a man. Its huddled attitude suggested that it had rolled down the steep slope and been arrested by the shelf; and, even from the distance at which he stood, it was evident that it had been lying exposed for a considerable time.

"Mr Elmhurst did not stay to make any further observations, but, taking the shortest way to the road, hailed an approaching motorist, who very obligingly conveyed him to Gravesend, where he notified the police of his discovery. An ambulance was at once procured, and, guided by the discoverer, proceeded to the spot, whence – after a careful examination by the police – the body was conveyed to Dartford, where it now lies in the mortuary awaiting an inquest.

"The body appears to be that of a youngish man, rather short and exceptionally muscular; and the condition of the strong and well-shaped hands suggests that the deceased was a skilled workman of some kind. The inquest will be opened tomorrow."

As I reached the end of the account, I glanced at the Superintendent and remarked:

"A very creditable piece of journalism. The reporter hasn't wasted much time. What do you think of it, Miller?"

"Well, I'm very relieved," he replied. "I've been waiting for this for months. I'm fairly sick of all the talk about the unsolved mystery, and the undiscovered murder. Now we may be able to get a move on, though I must admit that it doesn't look like a very promising case. It's a long time since the man was murdered, and there doesn't seem much to go on. Still, it's better than a head in a box with no clue to the owner. What do you think of it, Doctor? I suppose you've been expecting it, too?"

"I wouldn't say 'expecting', " Thorndyke replied. "The possibility of something of this kind had occurred to me. But you must bear in mind that the head, being preserved and packed in a case, offered no suggestions as to the time or place of death. As this body was apparently not preserved, it will be possible to arrive at an approximate date of death; and, as it was found in a particular place, some idea of locality may be formed. But any conclusions as to the locality in which the murder took place will have to be very cautiously considered, having regard to the ease with which, in these days, bodies can be carried away long distances from the scene of the crime. And, again, the body is nude, so that there will be no help from the clothing towards identification; and, as it appears to have been exposed in the open for months, its own condition will make identification difficult. I agree with you, Miller. It does not look a very promising case."

The Superintendent nodded and growled an inarticulate assent. But, in spite of Thorndyke's rather cold comfort, he still seemed disposed to be optimistic; and when we parted at the Inner Temple gate, he walked away with a springy step and an almost jaunty air.

# CHAPTER TWELVE

## *Thorndyke Becomes Interested*

Miller's intense interest in the "horrible discovery" did not surprise me at all. But Thorndyke's did. For what the Superintendent had said was perfectly true. The mysterious "head in a box" had aroused in him only the most languid curiosity. Which, again to quote Miller, was entirely unlike him. It is true that he liked, if possible, to be officially appointed to investigate an interesting case. But, appointment or no appointment, from sheer professional enthusiasm, he always kept himself informed on, and followed with the closest interest, any criminal case that presented unusual or obscure features.

Now, the "head in the box" case had appeared to me eminently unusual and obscure. It had seemed to imply an atrocious crime which combined with its atrocity a remarkable degree of callous ingenuity. And the mystery surrounding it was undeniable. Excepting some vague connection with the great platinum robbery (itself an unsolved mystery), it offered not a single clue. Yet Thorndyke had seemed to dismiss it as a mere oddity. He could not have been less moved if it had been a wax-work head – which it certainly was not.

His own explanation did not seem to me to be entirely satisfactory. It was true, as he had said, that there was a total lack of data; and "a mere mystery, without a single leading fact, is not, to a medical jurist, worth powder and shot." The fact that the head was preserved and practically imperishable excluded any inferences as to time or place. It might, for any evidence to the contrary, have been the head of a person who had died in Australia twenty years ago.

So he had dismissed it into the region of the unknowable; at least, so I had understood; though I had never felt quite sure that he had not, in his queer, secret fashion, just docketted it and packed it away in some pigeon-hole of his inexhaustible memory, there to repose until such time as the "leading fact" should come into view, unrecognised by anyone but himself.

This faint suspicion now tended to revive. For though the headless body looked as hopeless a mystery as the bodyless head, there was clearly no question of dismissing it as "not worth powder and shot". That powder and shot were already being expended, I ascertained that very evening, when, returning to our chambers after a lengthy consultation, I found on the table a six-inch Ordnance map, a boxwood scale, a pair of dividers and a motor road-map.

The purpose of the latter was obvious on inspection. The Ordnance map was dated 1910 and did not show the arterial road. The motor map showed the new road – and mighty little else; but as much, no doubt, as interested the average motorist. From the road-map, the new road had been transferred in pencil to the Ordnance map, which was thus brought up to date while retaining all the original topographical features; and the locality shown left no doubt as to the nature of the investigation.

I was still looking at the maps and reflecting as above when the door opened and my colleague entered.

"I thought you were out, Thorndyke," said I.

"No," he replied; "I have been up in the laboratory, having a chat with Polton about a job that I want him to do. I see you have been inspecting what the reporters will call 'the scene of the tragedy'. "

"I see that you have," I retorted, "and have been speculating on your change of front. The 'head in the box' apparently left you cold, but you seem to be developing quite a keen interest in this problem. Why this inconsistency?"

"My dear fellow," he replied, "there is no inconsistency. The case is entirely altered. We have now a number of facts from which to start an inquiry. From the state of the body, we can form an approximate judgement as to the date about which death occurred. Perhaps the cause of death may transpire at the inquest. We know where the body was found; and even if it may have been conveyed thither from a distance, the selection of the place where it was deposited suggests some local knowledge. The spot was extremely well chosen, as events have proved."

"Yes; but it was a queer idea to dump it there. A sort of ghastly practical joke. Just think of it, Thorndyke. Think of that great procession of traffic of all kinds – cars, motor-coaches, lorries, cyclists – streaming along that road by the thousand, day after day, month after month; and all the time, within a biscuit-toss of them, that gruesome thing lying there open to the sky."

"Yes," he agreed, "there is certainly an element of the macabre in the setting of this crime, though I don't suppose it was intentional."

"Neither do I. Nor do I suppose that the horrible picturesqueness of the setting is what is attracting you. I wonder what is."

Thorndyke did not reply immediately but sat regarding me with a sort of appraising expression (which I recognised, and had come, by experience, to associate with some special exhibition of thick-headedness on my part). At length he replied:

"I don't see why you should. The problem of this headless body abounds in elements of interest. All sorts of questions arise out of it. There is that embalmed head, for instance. That seems to have an obvious connection with this body."

"Very obvious indeed," said I, with a grin; "and the connection was still closer when the head was on the body."

He smiled indulgently and continued: "Disregarding the suggested anatomical connection, there is the connection of action and motive. What, for instance, is the connection of the man who deposited the head in the cloak-room with this body? We don't know how he came by that head. The fact that he had it in his possession is an incriminating fact, but it is not evidence of murder. It is not even certain that he knew what was in the case. But whether he did or not, he is obviously involved in a complex of circumstances which includes this body.

However, it is premature to discuss the case until we have the additional facts that will probably transpire at the inquest. Meanwhile," he concluded, with an exasperating smile, "I recommend my learned friend to go carefully over all the facts in his possession, relating both to the embalmed head and the headless body. Let him consider those facts critically as to their separate value and in relation to one another. If he does this, I think he will find that some extremely interesting conclusions will emerge."

It is unnecessary to say his opinion was not justified by results. I did, indeed, chew the cud of the few, unilluminating facts that were known to me. But the only conclusion that emerged was that, in some obscure way of which I could make nothing, this headless corpse was connected with the mystery of the stolen platinum. But this, I felt sure, was not the conclusion that was in Thorndyke's mind. And at that, I had to leave it.

On the following morning, Thorndyke went forth to attend at the inquest. I was not able to go with him, nor did I particularly wish to, as I knew that I should get full information from him as to the facts elicited. He started, as I thought, unnecessarily early and he came back unexpectedly late. But this latter circumstance was presently explained by the appearance on the Ordnance map of a pencilled cross at the roadside, indicating the spot on which the body had been lying when it was first seen. Later in the evening, when giving me particulars of the inquest, he mentioned that he had visited the site of the discovery and "gone over the ground, roughly," having taken his bicycle down by train for that purpose.

"Did you pick up anything of interest at the inquest?" I asked.

"Yes," he replied, "it was quite a good inquest. The coroner was a careful man who knew his business and kept to it, and the medical witness had made a thorough examination and gave his evidence clearly and concisely. As to the facts, they were simple enough, though important. The body was, of course, a good deal the worse for exposure to the weather. As to the date of death, the doctor wisely declined to make a definite statement, but he estimated it at not less than three months ago. The body appeared to be that of a man between thirty and forty years of age, five feet six inches in height, broad-shouldered and muscular, with rather small, well-shaped hands, which showed a definite, but not considerable, thickening of the skin on the palms; from which, and from the dirty and ill-kept finger-nails, the doctor inferred that deceased was a workman of some kind, but not a labourer.

"The head had been separated from the spinal column with a knife, leaving the atlas intact, and, to this extent, the separation had been effected skilfully."

"Yes," said I. "That point was made, I remember, at the inquest on the head. It would require some skill and the knowledge as to where the joint was to be found. By the way, was the question of the head raised?"

"Yes. Naturally, a juryman wanted to question the doctor on the subject, but the witness very properly replied that his evidence dealt only with facts observed by himself, and the coroner supported him. Then the question was raised whether the head should not be produced for comparison with the body; but the doctor refused to go into the matter, and the coroner pointed out that the head had already been examined medically and that all the facts were available in the depositions of the witnesses. He did, however, read out some of the depositions from the previous inquest, and asked the doctor whether the facts set forth in them were consistent with the belief that the head and the headless body were parts of one and the same person; to which the doctor replied that the mode of separation was the same in both and that the parts which were missing in the one were present in the other, but beyond that he would give no opinion."

"Did he give any opinion as to the cause of death?" I asked.

"Oh, yes," replied Thorndyke. "There was no mystery about that. There was a knife-wound in the back, near the angle of the left scapula, penetrating deeply and transfixing the heart. It appeared to have been inflicted with a large, single-edged knife of the 'Green River' type, and obviously with great force. The witness stated, confidently, that it could not have been self-inflicted."

"That seems to be pretty obvious, too," said I. "At any rate, the man could not have cut his own head off."

"A very capable detective sergeant gave evidence," Thorndyke resumed, dismissing – to my secret amusement – the trivial and uninteresting detail of the manner in which this unfortunate creature had been done to death. "He stated that the wood had been searched for the dead man's clothing. But I suspect that it was a very perfunctory search, as he was evidently convinced that it was not there; remarking, plausibly enough, that, since the clothing must have been stripped off to prevent identification, it would not be reasonable to expect to find it in the vicinity. He was of opinion that the body had been brought from a distance in a car or van, and that, probably, two or more persons were concerned in the affair."

"It seems likely," I said, "having regard to the remoteness of the place. But it is only a guess."

"Exactly," Thorndyke agreed. "There was a good deal of guessing and not many facts; and the few facts that were really significant do not seem to have been understood."

"What are the facts that you regard as really significant?" I asked. Not that I had the slightest expectation that he would tell me. And he did not. His inevitable reply was:

"You know what the known facts are, Jervis, and you will see for yourself, if you consider them critically, which are the significant ones. But, to return to the inquest. The coroner's summing-up was excellent, having regard to the evidence that had been given. I took shorthand notes of some of it, and I will read them to you. With reference to the embalmed head he remarked:

"'It has been suggested that the head which was found at Fenchurch Street Station ought to have been brought here for comparison. But to what purpose? What kind of comparison is possible? If the head is broken off a china figure and the two parts are lost and subsequently found in different places, the question as to whether they are parts of the same figure can be settled by putting them together and seeing whether the fractured surfaces fit each other. But with a detached human head – especially after the lapse of months – this is not possible. If the preserved head had been exhumed and brought here, we could have learned nothing more from it than we can learn from the depositions of the medical witness, which I have read to you. Accordingly, we must fall back on our common sense; and I think we shall find that enough for our purpose.

"'Let us look at the facts. A headless body has been found in one place, and a bodyless head in another. The doctor has told us that they might be – though he doesn't say that they are – the head and body of one and the same person. They agree in the peculiar and unusual mode of separation. The parts which are absent in the one are present in the other. There is no part missing, and no part redundant. If that head had been cut off this body, the appearances would be exactly what they are.

" 'Now, gentlemen, if headless human bodies and bodyless human heads were quite common objects, we might have to search further. But, fortunately, they are so rare and unusual that we may almost regard these remains as unique. And if they are not parts of the same person, then there must be, somewhere, an undiscovered body belonging to the head, and, somewhere else, an undiscovered head belonging to this body. But, I submit, gentlemen, that common sense rejects such enormous improbabilities and compels us to adopt the obvious and simple explanation that the head and the body are those of one and the same person.

" 'As to the cause of death, you have heard the doctor's evidence. Deceased was killed by a knife-wound, which he could not have inflicted himself, and which was therefore inflicted by some other person. And with that I leave you to consider your verdict.'"

"An excellent summing-up," said I, "and very well argued. The verdict was Wilful Murder, of course?"

"Yes. 'By some person or persons unknown.' And the jury could hardly have come to any other conclusion. But, as you see, the case is, from the police point of view, left in the air."

"Yes," I agreed. "If Miller is taking up the case, as I assume that he is, he has got his work cut out. I don't see that this body was such a windfall as he seemed to think. Scotland Yard may catch some more trouble from the Press if something fresh does not turn up."

"Well," Thorndyke rejoined, by way of winding up the conversation, "we must hope, like medico-legal Micawbers, that something will turn up."

For the next few days, however, the case remained "in the air". But it was not alone in this respect. Presently I began to be conscious that there were other matters in the air. For instance, our invaluable assistant, Polton, suddenly developed a curious stealthy, conspiratorial manner of going about, or locking himself in the laboratory, which experience had taught me to associate with secret activities foreshadowing some important and dramatic "move" on Thorndyke's part. Then, on the forth day after the inquest, I detected my colleague in the suspicious act of pacing the pavement at the lower, and more secluded, end of King's Bench Walk, in earnest conversation with Mr Superintendent Miller. And the prima facie suspiciousness of the proceeding was confirmed by the eagerness and excitement that were evident in the face and manner of our friend, and even more by the way in which he suddenly shut up, like a snapped snuff-box, as I approached.

And, that very evening, Thorndyke exploded the mine.

"We have got an expedition on tomorrow," he announced.

"Who are we?" I asked.

"You and I, Miller and Polton. I know you have got the day free."

"Where are we going to?" I demanded.

"To Swanscombe Wood," was the reply.

"What for?"

"To collect some further facts relating to the headless body," he replied.

As a mere statement, it did not sound very sensational. But to one who knew Thorndyke as I knew him, it had certain implications that gave it a special significance. In the first place, Thorndyke tended habitually to understatement; and, in the second, he took no one into his confidence while his investigations were at the tentative stage. As Miller expressed it, "The Doctor would never show a card until he was ready to take the trick." Whence there naturally arose in my mind a strong suspicion that the "further facts" which we were to collect were already in Thorndyke's possession.

And events proved that I was not so very far wrong.

# CHAPTER THIRTEEN
## The Dene Hole

The products of Polton's labours impressed me as disappointing and hardly worthy of his mechanical ingenuity, consisting of nothing more subtle than an immense coil of rope, rove through two double blocks and forming a long and powerful tackle, a tripod formed of three very stout iron-shod seven-foot poles, and a strong basket such as builders use, furnished with strong rope slings. There was one further item, which was more worthy of its producer: a large electric lamp, fitted with adjustable lenses, and, to judge by the suspension arrangements, designed to throw a powerful beam of parallel rays vertically downwards.

But if Polton's productions were of an unexpected kind, the vehicle in which the Superintendent drove up to our entry was even more so. For, though it bore no outward distinguishing marks, it was an undeniable motor ambulance. However, if less dignified and imposing than the official car, it was a good deal more convenient. The unwieldy tripod, tackle and basket were easily disposed of in its roomy interior, still leaving ample accommodation for me and Polton and the detective sergeant whom Miller had brought as an additional assistant. The Superintendent, himself, was at the steering-wheel, and Thorndyke took the seat beside him to give directions as we approached our destination.

I asked no questions. The character of our outfit told me pretty plainly what kind of job we had in hand; and I felt a malicious satisfaction in tantalising Polton, who was, so to speak, bursting with silence and secrecy and the desire to be questioned. So, little was said – and nothing to the point – while the ambulance trundled out at the Tudor Street gate, crossed Blackfriars Bridge, threaded its way through the traffic of the South London streets, and presently came out upon the Dover Road. A few minutes later, as we mounted a steep rise, the sergeant, who, hitherto, had uttered not a word, removed his pipe from his mouth, remarked, "Shooter's Hill," and replaced it as if it were a stopper.

The ambulance bowled smoothly along the straight line of the old Roman road. Welling, Crayford and Dartford were entered and left behind. A few minutes after leaving Dartford, the road began a long ascent, and then, after a short run on the level, fell away somewhat steeply. At this point, the sergeant once more removed his pipe, nodded at the side window, and, having affirmed, stolidly, "That's the place," reinserted the stopper.

The ambulance now began to slow down, and, a minute or two later, drew in by the side of the road and halted. Then, as Thorndyke and the Superintendent alighted, we also got out, and the sergeant proceeded to occupy the driver's seat.

"You and Polton had better stay here for the present," said Thorndyke. "The Superintendent and I are going to locate the spot. When we have found it, he will remain there while I come back and help you to carry the gear."

He produced from his pocket a marching-compass and a card, on one side of which a sketch-plan had been drawn, while a number of bearings were written on the other. After a glance at the latter, he set the direction line of the compass and started off along a rough footpath, followed by the Superintendent. We watched their receding figures as they ascended the hill and approached the wood by which it was covered. At the margin of the latter, Thorndyke paused and "turned to take a last, fond look" at his starting-point and check his compass bearings. Then he faced about, and, in a few seconds, he and the Superintendent disappeared into the wood.

Waiting is usually a tedious business, and is still more so when the waiter is on the tiptoe of expectation and curiosity. Vainly, I endeavoured to repress a tendency to useless and futile speculation as to what Thorndyke was seeking (or, more probably, had already found and was now about to disclose). As for Polton, if he could have been furnished with an emotional pressure-gauge, it would certainly have burst. Even the stolid sergeant was fain to come off his perch and pace up and down by the roadside; and once he actually went so far as to take out the stopper and remark that "it seemed as if the Doctor had made some sort of discovery."

Anon our sufferings were somewhat alleviated by the arrival of a police patrol, who came free-wheeling down the hill from the direction of Dartford. As he approached us, he slowed down more and more, and eventually dismounted to make a circuit of our vehicle, with the manner of a dog sniffing at a suspicious stranger. Apparently, its appearance did not satisfy him, and he proceeded to interrogate.

"What's going on?" he asked, not uncivilly. "This looks like an ambulance but I see you have got some lifting gear inside."

Here the sergeant interposed with a brief and unlucid explanation of our business, at the same time producing his credentials; at the sight whereof the patrol officer was visibly impressed, and showed an unmistakable tendency to linger, which the sergeant by no means sought to discourage.

"Can I give any assistance?" the patrol man asked, a little wistfully.

"Well," the sergeant replied, promptly, "if you could spare the time to give an eye to this car, that would release me to lend the Superintendent a hand."

It was obvious that the patrol man would have preferred to transpose these functions, but, nevertheless, he agreed readily; and at this moment Thorndyke reappeared from the wood and came striding swiftly towards us along the footpath. As he came up, the sergeant explained the new arrangements with some anxiety as to whether they would be approved. To his evident relief, Thorndyke accepted them readily.

"We shall be none the worse for an extra hand," said he. "Now we shall be able to carry the whole kit up in one journey."

Accordingly, we proceeded to get the gear out of the ambulance and distribute the items among the party. Thorndyke and I took the tripod on our shoulders – and a deuce of a weight it was. The sergeant got the great coil of rope on to his back with the aid of a spare sling; and Polton brought up the rear with the basket, in which was stowed the lamp, while the patrol man kept a look-out with a view to heading off any inquisitive strangers who might be attracted by the queer aspect of our procession.

Appreciation of the beauties of the countryside is not favoured by the presence on one's shoulder of three massive ash poles with heavy iron fittings. The character of the ground was what chiefly occupied my attention, particularly after we had entered the wood; where I got the impression that some ingenious sylvan devil had collected all the brambles from miles around and arranged them in an interminable series of entanglements, compared with which the barbed-wire defences of a German trench were but feeble and amateurish imitations. But we tramped on, crashing through the yellow and russet leafage, Thorndyke leading with his compass in his unoccupied hand and trudging forward in silence, save for an occasional soft chuckle at my lurid comments on the landscape.

Suddenly, I heard Miller's voice informing us that "here we were," and we nearly collided with him at the edge of a small opening. Here we set down the tripod, opening it enough to enable it to stand upright.

"You didn't have to blow your whistle," said Thorndyke. "I suppose you heard us coming?"

"Heard you coming!" exclaimed Miller. "It was like a troop of blooming elephants – to say nothing of Dr Jervis's language. Hallo, Sergeant! I thought I told you to stay with the car."

The sergeant hastily explained the arrangements, adding that "the Doctor" had concurred; on which the Superintendent, having also approved, set him to work at getting the gear ready.

A glance around the little opening in which we were gathered showed me that my diagnosis of the purpose of the expedition had been correct. Near the middle of the opening, half concealed by the rank undergrowth, yawned the mouth of one of those mysterious pits known as dene holes which are scattered in such numbers over this part of Kent. Cautiously, I approached the brink and peered down into the black depths.

"Horrible, dangerous things, these dene holes are," said Miller. "Ought to be fenced in. How deep do you say this pit is, Doctor?"

"This one is just about sixty feet, but many of them are deeper. Seventy feet is about the average."

"Sixty feet!" exclaimed Polton, with a fascinated eye on the yawning hole. "And anyone coming along here in the dark might step into it without a moment's warning. Horrible! Did I understand you, Sir, to say that it was dug a very long time ago?"

"It has been there as you see it," replied Thorndyke, "for thousands of years. How many thousands we can't say. But there seems to be no doubt that these dene holes were excavated by the men of the Old Stone Age."

"Dear me!" exclaimed Polton. "Thousands of years! I should have thought that, by this time, they would have been full to the brim of the people who had tumbled into them."

While these exclamations and comments were passing, the preparations were in progress for the exploration. The tripod was set up over the hole (which was some three feet in diameter and roughly circular, like the mouth of a well), the tackle securely hooked on and the lamp suspended in position. The Superintendent switched on the light by means of a push at the end of a cord, and, grasping the tripod, leaned over the hole and peered down the well-like shaft.

"I can't make out very much," he remarked. "I seem to see what looks like a boot, and that's about all."

"It is a long way down," said Thorndyke, "and it doesn't matter much what we can see from above. We shall soon know exactly what there is down there."

As he spoke, he switched off the lamp and hooked the basket on to the tackle by means of a pair of clip-hooks, provided with a safety-catch. Then he produced a candle from his pocket and proceeded to light it.

"I don't like the idea of your going down, Doctor," said the Superintendent. "It's really our job."

"Not at all," replied Thorndyke, drawing the basket to the edge of the hole and stepping into it. "I proposed the exploration and undertook to carry it out. Besides, I want to see what the bottom of this dene hole is like."

"Don't you think, Sir," Polton interposed, earnestly, "that it would be better for me to go down? I am so much lighter and should put less strain on the tackle."

"My dear Polton," said Thorndyke, regarding his devoted henchman with an appreciative smile, "this tackle would bear a couple of tons, easily. There isn't any strain. But I will ask you to pay out the rope as steadily as you can, and keep an eye on this candle. If it goes out, you had better haul up at once without waiting for a signal, as you will know that I have dropped into foul air. Now, I am ready if you are."

He steadied himself by lightly grasping two of the tackle-ropes and I took a turn round the trunk of a birch tree with the "fall" by passing the big coil round. Then Miller and the sergeant hauled on the rope while I gathered in the slack; the tackle grew taut, the basket began to rise from the ground and swung directly over the black hole.

"Now, pay out steadily and not too fast," said Thorndyke; and as we began to ease out the rope, he slowly sank, like a stage demon, and disappeared into the bowels of the earth, while Polton, grasping the tripod and leaning over the hole, watched his descent with starting eyes and an expression of horror.

Owing to the great power of the tackle, the weight on the fall was quite trifling. I could, alone, have paid it out easily with the aid of the turn round the tree. So we were able, in turn, to leave it to satisfy our curiosity and relieve our anxiety by a glance down the shaft; which now looked even more alarming than when we had looked into the mere impenetrable blackness of the hole. For now, as we peered down the well-like shaft at our friend – already grown small in the distance – faintly illuminated by the glimmer of the candle, we were able to realise the horrible depth to which this strange memorial of a forgotten race sank into the earth.

But the unfailing glimmer of the candle-light – though it had now dwindled to a mere distant spark – reassured us; for, apart from the possibility of "choke damp," there was really no appreciable danger. Notwithstanding which, Polton was fain, from time to time, to relieve his overwrought feelings by hailing the now invisible explorer with the inquiry, "All right, Sir?" to which a strange, sepulchral, but surprisingly loud voice replied: "All right, Polton."

After an almost interminable paying-out, the diminishing remainder of rope warned us that Thorndyke must have nearly reached the bottom, and then a sudden relaxation of the tension informed us that he had already done so. Immediately afterwards, that uncanny, megaphonic voice announced the fact and directed us to switch on the light and throw down the spare sling. I at once complied with the first order and was about to carry out the other when it occurred to me that a stout rope sling might fall with unpleasant force after a drop of sixty feet. Accordingly, I coiled it loosely round the tackle-ropes, and, securing the ends with a hitch, let go; when I saw it slide smoothly down the ropes to the bottom.

"I wonder what he wants with that sling," Miller speculated, grasping the tripod and leaning over to peer down. But, as the only result was to obscure the light of the lamp and throw the shaft into shadow, he withdrew and waited for events to enlighten him. Then the voice came reverberating up the shaft, commanding us to hoist.

If the paying-out had been a long business, the hauling up was longer. There seemed to be no end to that rope; and as I hauled and hauled, I found myself wishing that Thorndyke had been a little less cautious and contented himself with a less powerful but quicker tackle. From time to time, Miller was impelled by the intensity of his curiosity to thrust his head over the hole to see what was coming up; but, as his head cut off the light of the lamp and rendered the ascending object invisible, he retired each time, defeated and muttering. At length, as the accumulating coils of rope told us that our freight must be nearing the surface, he succeeded in catching a glimpse of the object. But so far was that glimpse from allaying his curiosity that it reduced him to a frenzy of excitement.

"It looks like a body!" he exclaimed. "A man's body. But it can't be!"

It was, however. As we hauled in the last few feet of the rope and made fast to the tree, there arose out of the hole the body of a tall, well-dressed man which had been suspended from the hook of the tackle by the sling, passed round the chest under the arms. Miller helped me to haul it away from the hole, when we unfastened the sling and let the body fall on the ground.

"Well," said the Superintendent, surveying it gloomily, "this is a disappointment. We have come all this way and taken all this trouble just to salve the body of a poor devil who has stumbled into this infernal pit by accident and who is no concern of ours at all. Of course, it is not the Doctor's fault. He discovered that there was something down there and he drew the very natural conclusion, though it happened to be the wrong one. Let the damn tackle down again as fast as you can and get the Doctor up. I expect he is as sick as I am."

The lowering of the tackle was a slow and tedious business, for, as there was now no weight to pull it down, it had to be "overhauled". Fortunately, Polton had oiled the sheaves so that they turned smoothly and easily; but it was a long time before the voice from below notified us that the lower block had reached the bottom. Its reverberations had hardly died away when the order came up to hoist, and we straightway began to haul, while Polton coiled down the rope as it was gathered in. Presently I noticed a puzzled expression on the Superintendent's face, and, as I looked at him inquiringly, he exclaimed:

"This can't be the Doctor. He's a bigger man than that poor beggar, but there doesn't seem to be any weight on the rope at all."

I had noticed this, myself, and now suggested that we might take advantage of the light weight by hauling up more quickly; which we did with such a will that Miller's opinion was presently confirmed by the appearance of the basket at the mouth of the pit. As it came into view, the Superintendent gazed at it in astonishment.

"Why, it's the clothes, after all!" he exclaimed, seizing the basket and turning its contents out on to the ground, "and the right ones, too, by the look of them. A complete outfit; suit, shirt, underclothing, socks, boots – everything but the hat. He must have had a hat, and so must the other fellow. Perhaps the Doctor will bring them up with him."

Having emptied the basket, we sent it down again; and now, being able to judge the distance, we let it run down by its own weight, only checking it as it neared the bottom. After a very brief interval, the hollow voice from below directed us to haul up, and once again we began to gather in the rope and coil it down.

"This is queer," said Miller, as he took his turn at the rope. "It is no heavier than it was last time. I wonder what he is sending up now."

In his impatience to solve this new mystery, he hauled with such energy that beads of sweat began to appear on his forehead. But it is difficult to hurry a fourfold tackle, and it was a long time before the basket came into view. When, at last, it became visible a few feet down, its appearance evidently disappointed him, for he exclaimed in a tone of disgust:

"Hats. Two hats. I should have thought he might have brought them up with him and saved a journey."

"There is something in it besides the hats," said I, as the basket rose out of the mouth of the pit and I drew it aside on to the ground, while the others gathered round. I seized the two hats and lifted them out; and then I stood as if petrified, with the hats in my hands, too astounded to utter a sound.

"My God!" Miller exclaimed, huskily. "A man's head! Now what the blazes can be the meaning of this?"

He stood, staring in amazement – as, indeed, we all did – at the horrible relic that lay at the bottom of the basket. Suddenly he seized the latter and turned it upside down, when the head rolled out on the ground. Then he flung the basket into the hole and gruffly ordered us to "let go".

There was no interval this time, for, almost as the rope slackened, informing us that the basket had settled on the bottom, the hollow voice from below commanded us to haul up. And as soon as we had taken in the slack, we knew by the weight that Thorndyke was at the other end of the tackle. Accordingly, I once more took a turn round the tree to prevent the chance of a slip or jerk and the others hauled steadily and evenly. Even now, the weight seemed comparatively trifling, but what we gained from the tackle in lifting power we lost in speed. In mechanics, as in other things, you can't have it both ways. However, at long last, Polton, grasping the tripod and craning over the hole, was able to announce that "the Doctor" was nearly up; and after another couple of minutes he appeared rising slowly above ground, when Polton carefully drew the basket on to the solid earth and helped him to step out.

"Well, Doctor," said Miller, "you've given us a bit of a surprise, as you generally do. But," he added, pointing to the head, which lay with its shrunken, discoloured face turned up to the sky, "what are we to make of that? We've got a head too many."

"Too many for what?" asked Thorndyke.

"For what we were inquiring into," Miller replied testily. "See what you have done for us. We find a head in a box at Fenchurch Street Station. Then we keep a look-out for the body belonging to it, and at last it turns up. Then you bring us here and produce another head; which puts us back where we started. We've still got a spare head that we can't account for."

Thorndyke smiled grimly. "I am not under a contract," said he, "to supply facts that will fit your theory of a crime. We must take the facts as they come; and I think there can be no doubt that this head belongs to the body that was found on the shelf a few yards from here."

"Then what about the other head?" demanded Miller. "Where is the body belonging to that?"

Thorndyke shook his head. "That is another story," said he. "But the immediate problem is how these remains are to be disposed of. We can't carry them and the gear down to the ambulance without assistance."

Here the sergeant interposed with a suggestion.

"There is a big electric station a little farther down the road. If I were to run the patrol man down there, he could get on the phone to his head-quarters, and perhaps, meanwhile, they could lend us one or two men from the works. We've got a folding stretcher in the car."

"Good," said Miller. "That will do to a T, Sergeant. You cut along as fast as you can, and perhaps Mr Polton might go with you to take charge of the patrol man's bicycle."

As Polton and the sergeant retired along the now plainly visible track, Miller turned to Thorndyke with a puzzled and questioning air.

"I can't quite make this out, Doctor," said he. "You brought us here, as I understood, in the expectation of probably finding that poor devil's clothes. Had you any expectation of finding anything else?"

"I thought it probable," replied Thorndyke, "that if we found the clothes, we should probably find the head with them. But I certainly did not expect to find that body. That came as quite a surprise."

"Naturally," said Miller. "A queer coincidence that he should have happened to tumble in, just about the same time. Still, he isn't in the picture."

"There," said Thorndyke, "I think you are mistaken. I should say that he is very much in the picture. My very strong impression is that he is none other than the murderer."

"The murderer!" exclaimed Miller. "What makes you think that? Or are you just guessing?"

"I am considering the obvious probabilities," Thorndyke replied. As he spoke, he stooped over the dead man and drew up first the jacket and then the waistcoat. As the latter garment rose, there came into view, projecting up from within the waist-band of the trousers, the haft of an undeniable Green River knife. Thorndyke drew the weapon out of its leather sheath, glanced at it and silently held it out for our inspection. No expert eye was needed to read its message. The streaks of blackened rust on the blade were distinctive enough, but much more so was the shiny black deposit at the junction of the steel and the wooden handle.

"Yes," said Miller, as Thorndyke replaced the knife in its sheath, "that tells the tale pretty well. And exactly the kind of knife that the doctor described at the inquest." He cogitated profoundly for a few moments and then asked: "How do you suppose this fellow came to fall into the pit?"

"I should say," Thorndyke replied, "that the affair happened somewhat in this way: The murderer either enticed his victim into this wood, or he murdered him elsewhere and brought his body here. We shall probably never know which, and it really doesn't matter. Obviously, the murderer knew this place pretty well, as we can judge by his acquaintance with the dene hole. Having committed the murder, or deposited the body, near the edge of the wood close to the road, he stripped the corpse and carried the clothes through the wood to the hole and dropped them down. And when we bear in mind that this must, almost certainly, have been done at night, we must conclude that, not only must the murderer have been familiar with the locality, but he had probably planned the crime in advance and reconnoitred the ground.

"Having dropped the clothes down the pit, he returned to the corpse. And now he had the most difficult part of his task to do. He had to detach the head; and he had to detach it in a particuar way – and in the dark, too."

"Why did he have to?" Miller asked.

"Let us leave that question for the moment. It was part of the plan, as the case presents itself to me. Well, having detached the head, he dragged the nude and headless corpse the short distance to the edge of the cutting and pushed it over, knowing that it would roll down only as far as the shelf. Then he carried the head to the dene hole.

"Now, we may assume that he was a man of pretty strong nerves, but, by the time he had murdered this man, stripped the corpse and cut off the head – in a public place, mind you, in which discovery was possible at any moment – he must have been considerably shaken. He was walking in the dark with the dead man's head in his hands, over ground which, as Jervis can testify, is a mass of traps and entanglements. In his terror and agitation he probably hurried to get rid of his dreadful burden, and, just as he approached the hole, he must have caught his foot in a bramble and fallen, sprawling, right into the pit. That is how I picture the course of events."

"Yes," said I, "it sounds pretty convincing as to what probably did happen, though I am in the same difficulty as Miller. I don't quite see why he did it. Why, for instance, he didn't throw the body, itself, down the pit."

"We must go into that question on another occasion," said Thorndyke; "but you will notice that – but for this investigation of ours – he did actually secure a false identification of the body."

"Yes," agreed Miller, "he had us there. We had fairly fixed the body on to that Fenchurch Street head."

Once more the Superintendent fell into a train of cogitation, with a speculative eye on the body that lay on the ground at his feet. Suddenly he roused, and, turning to Thorndyke, asked:

"Have you any idea, Doctor, who these two people are?"

"I have formed an opinion," was the reply, "and I think it is probably a correct opinion. I should say that this," indicating the dead man, "is the person known as Bassett, or Dobson; the man who deposited the case of stolen platinum at the cloakroom; and this man," pointing to the head, "is the one who stole the case and left the embalmed head in exchange."

Thorndyke's answer, delivered in calm, matter-of-fact tones, fairly took my breath away. I was too astonished to make any comment. And the Superintendent was equally taken by surprise, for he, too, stood for a while gazing at my colleague without speaking. At length he said – voicing my sentiments as well as his own:

"This is a knock-out, Doctor! I wasn't aware that you knew anything about this case, or were taking any interest in it. Yet you seem to have it all cut and dried. Knowing you, I assume that this isn't just a guess. You've got something to go on?"

"In respect of the identification? Certainly. Without going into any other matters, there is the appearance of these remains. In both cases it corresponds exactly with the description given at the inquest. The man who stole the case – "

"And left the box with the human head in it," interpolated Miller. "You are ignoring that trivial detail."

"Yes," Thorndyke admitted. "We are dealing with the robbery, in which they were both concerned. Well, that man was described by the attendant as dark, clean-shaven, and having conspicuous gold fillings in both upper central incisors. If you look at that head, you can see the gold fillings plainly enough, as well as the other, less distinctive characteristics.

"In the case of this other man the correspondence is much more striking. Here is the long, thin face with the long, thin, pointed nose, curved on the bridge, and the dark, nearly black hair. The fair complexion and pale blue eye colour are not now clearly distinguishable. But there is one very impressive correspondence. You remember that the witness, Mr Pippet, was strongly of opinion that the hair and beard were dyed. Now, if you take my lens and examine the roots of the hair and beard, you will see plainly that it is light brown hair dyed black."

Miller and I took the lens in turn and made the examination; with the result that the condition was established beyond any possible doubt.

"Yes," Miller agreed, handing back the lens, "that is dyed hair, right enough, and it seems to settle the identification."

"But we needn't leave it at that," pursued Thorndyke. "The very clothing agrees perfectly. There is the blue serge suit, the brown shoes, the wrist-watch, and the additional pocket-watch with its guard of plaited twine."

He took hold of the latter and drew out of the pocket a large silver watch of the kind used by navigators as a "hack watch".

"Yes," said Miller. "It's a true bill. You are right, Doctor, as you always are. These are the two men to a moral certainty."

"Isn't it rather strange," said I, "that this man should have gone about with his dyed hair and beard and the very clothes that had been described at the inquest? He must have known that there would be a hue and cry raised after him."

"I think," said Thorndyke, "that the explanation is that this affair must have taken place within a day or two of the discovery at the station."

Miller nodded, emphatically. "I'm pretty certain you are right, Doctor," said he. "And that would account for the fact that no trace of these men was ever found. We had their descriptions circulated and the police looking for them everywhere, but nobody ever got a single glimpse of either of them. Naturally enough, as we can see now. They were lying at the bottom of this pit."

At this moment, sounds of trampling through the wood became audible and rapidly grew more distinct. At length, the sergeant and Polton emerged into the opening, followed by the patrol man and four athletic figures in blue dungaree suits, of whom two carried a folded stretcher.

"I've made all the arrangements, Sir," said the sergeant, saluting as he addressed the Superintendent. "We can take the remains and the clothing in the ambulance and hand them over to the police at Dartford; and the manager of the works has kindly lent us a car to take you and the doctors to Dartford Station."

"As to me," said Miller, "I shall go on to Dartford with the ambulance. There are two suits of clothes to be examined. I want to go through them thoroughly before I return to town. What do you say, Doctor? Are you interested in the clothes?"

"I am interested," Thorndyke replied, "but I don't think I want to take part in the examination. I daresay you will let me know if anything of importance comes to light."

"You can trust me for that," said Miller. "Then I take it that you will go on to Dartford Station."

With this, we parted; Miller remaining to superintend the removal of the remains and the gear, while Thorndyke, Polton and I retraced our way along the well-trodden track down to the road where the manager's car was waiting.

# CHAPTER FOURTEEN
## Dr Thorndyke's Evidence

The adjourned hearing in the Probate Court opened in an atmosphere which the reporters would have described as "tense". The judge had not yet learned the result of the exhumation (or he pretended that he hadn't), and when Mr Gimbler took his place in the witness-box, his lordship regarded him with very evident interest and curiosity. The examination in chief was conducted by Mr McGonnell's junior, this being the first chance that he had got of displaying his forensic skill – and a mighty small chance at that. For Gimbler's evidence amounted to no more than a recital of facts which were known to us all (excepting, perhaps, the judge), with certain inevitable inferences.

"You were present at the opening of the vault containing the coffin of Josiah Pippet, deceased?"

"I was."

"What other persons were present?"

Mr Gimbler enumerated the persons present and glanced at a list to make sure that he had omitted none.

"When the vault was opened, what was the appearance of the interior?"

"The whole interior and everything in it was covered with a thick coating of dust."

"Was there any sign indicating that that dust had ever been disturbed?"

"No. The surface of the dust was perfectly smooth and even, without any mark or trace of disturbance."

"What happened when the vault had been opened?"

"The coffin was brought out and placed upon trestles. Then the screws were extracted and the lid was removed in the presence of the persons whom I have named."

"Was the body of deceased in the coffin?"

"No. There was no body in the coffin."

"What did the coffin contain?"

"It contained a roll of sheet-lead and certain plumber's oddments; to wit, four lumps of lead of a hemispherical shape, such as are formed when molten lead sets in a plumber's melting-pot."

"Do those contents correspond with the traditional description of this coffin?"

"Yes. It was stated in evidence by Mr Christopher Pippet that the traditional story told to him by his father was to the effect that the coffin was weighted with a roll of sheet-lead and some plumber's oddments."

Having elicited this convincing statement, Mr Klein sat down; and, as Anstey made no sign of a wish to cross-examine the witness, Mr Gimbler stepped down from the witness-box with a hardly-disguised smirk, and McGonnell rose.

"That is our case, my lord," said he, and forthwith resumed his seat. There was a brief pause. Then Anstey rose and announced:

"I call witnesses, my lord," a statement that was almost immediately followed by the usher's voice, pronouncing the name,

"Dr John Thorndyke."

As my colleague stepped into the witness-box with a small portfolio under his arm, I noticed that his appearance was viewed with obvious interest by more than one person. The judge seemed to settle himself into a position of increased attention, and Mr McGonnell regarded the new witness critically, and, I thought, with slight uneasiness; while Mr Gimbler, swinging his eyeglass pendulum-wise, made a show of being unaware of the witness's existence. But I had observed that he had taken in, with one swift glance, the fact that the usher, at Anstey's request, had deposited the seven volumes of Josiah's diary on the latter's desk. Remembering the double-barrelled microscope, I viewed those volumes with sudden interest; which was heightened when Anstey picked up one of them, and, opening it, sought a particular page and handed the open volume to Thorndyke.

"This," said he, "is a volume of the diary which has been identified in evidence as the diary of Josiah Pippet. Will you kindly examine the entry dated the 8th of October, 1842?"

"Yes. It reads: 'Back to the Fox. Exit G A and enter J P, but not for long.'"

"Have you previously examined that entry?"

"Yes. I examined it at the last hearing very carefully with the naked eye and also with the Comparison Microscope invented by Albert S Osborn of New York."

"Had you any reason for making so critical an examination of this passage in the diary?"

"Yes. As this is the only passage in the diary in which the identity of the Earl, George Augustus, with Josiah Pippet is explicitly stated, it seemed necessary to make sure that it was really a genuine entry."

"Had you any further reason?"

"Yes. The position of this entry, after a blank space, made it physically possible that it might have been interpolated."

"And what opinion did you form as a result of your examination?"

"I formed the opinion that this entry is not part of the original diary, but has been interpolated at some later date."

"Can you give us your reasons for forming that opinion?"

"My principal reason is that there is a slight difference in colour between this entry and the rest of the writing on this page, either preceding it or following it. The difference is hardly perceptible to the naked eye. It is more perceptible when the writing is looked at through a magnifying lens, and it is fairly distinct when examined with the differential microscope."

"Can you explain, quite briefly, the action of the differential, or Comparison Microscope?"

"In effect, this instrument is a pair of microscopes with a single eyepiece which is common to both. The two microscopes can be brought to bear on two different letters or words on different parts of a page, and the two magnified images will appear in the field of the eyepiece side by side and can be so compared that very delicate differences of form and colour can be distinguished."

"Was your opinion based exclusively on the Comparison Microscope?"

"No. On observing this difference in colour, I applied for, and received the permission of the court to have a photograph of this page made by the official photographer. This was done, and I have here two sets of the photographs, one set being direct prints from the negative, and the other enlargements. In both, but especially in the enlargements, the difference in colour is perfectly obvious."

Here Thorndyke produced from his portfolio two sets of photographs, which he delivered to the usher, who passed one pair up to the judge and handed the remainder to Mr McGonnell and the other interested parties, including myself. The judge examined the two photographs for some moments with profound attention. Then he turned to Thorndyke and asked:

"Can you explain to us why differences of colour which are hardly distinguishable by the eye appear quite distinct in a photograph?"

"The reason, my lord," replied Thorndyke, "is that the eye and the photographic plate are affected by different rays; the eye by the luminous rays and the plate by the chemical rays. But these two kinds of rays do not vary in the same proportions in different colours. Yellow, for instance, which is very luminous, gives off only feeble chemical rays, while blue, which is less luminous, gives off very powerful chemical rays. So that a yellow device on a rather deep blue ground appears to the eye light upon dark, whereas in a photograph it appears dark upon light."

The judge nodded. "Yes," said he, "that makes the matter quite clear."

"In what way," Anstey resumed, "does this difference in colour support your opinion that this passage has been interpolated?"

"It shows that this passage was written with a different ink from the rest of the page."

"Is there any reason why Josiah Pippet should not have used a different ink in writing this particular passage?"

"Yes. In 1842, the date of this entry, there was only one kind of black ink in use, excepting the Chinese, or Indian, ink used by draughtsmen, which this is obviously not. The common writing ink was made with galls and copperas – sulphate of iron – without any of the blue colouring which is used in modern blue-black ink. This iron-gall ink may have varied slightly in colour according to whether it was freshly made or had been exposed to the air in an ink-pot. But these differences would disappear in the course of years, as the black tannate and gallate of iron changed into the reddish-brown oxide; and, there being no difference in composition, there would be no difference in the photographic reaction. In my opinion, the difference shown in the photographs indicates a difference in composition in the two inks. But a difference in composition is irreconcileable with identity in the date of this passage and the rest of the page."

"Would the difference of composition be demonstrable by a chemical test?"

"Probably, but not certainly."

"You do not question the character of the handwriting?"

"I prefer to offer no opinion on that. I detected no discrepancy that I could demonstrate."

"And now, coming from matters of opinion to demonstrable fact, what are you prepared to swear to concerning this entry in the diary?"

"That it was written with a different ink from that used in writing the rest of the page."

Having received and noted down this answer, Anstey turned over a leaf of his brief and resumed his examination.

"We will now," said he, "pass on to an entirely different subject. I believe that you have made certain investigations in the neighbourhood of Winsborough. Is that so?"

"It is."

"Perhaps, before giving us your results, it might be well if you were to tell us, in a general way, what was the object of those investigations and what led you to undertake them."

"It appeared to me," Thorndyke replied, "when I considered the story of the double life of Josiah Pippet and the Earl, George Augustus, that, although it was not impossible that it might be true, it was highly improbable. But it also seemed highly improbable that this story should have been invented by Josiah out of his inner consciousness with nothing to suggest it or give it a start. It seemed more probable that the story had its origin in some peculiar set of circumstances the nature of which might, at some later time, be entirely misunderstood. On further consideration, I found it possible to imagine a set of circumstances such as might have given rise to this kind of misunderstanding. Thereupon, I decided to go down to Winsborough and see if I could ascertain, by investigation on the spot, whether such circumstances had, in fact, existed."

"When you went to Winsborough you had certain specific objects in view?"

"Yes. I sought to ascertain whether there existed any evidence of the birth of Josiah Pippet, as a separate individual, and whether he was, in fact, born at the Castle, as alleged. Further, as a subsidiary question, I proposed to find out, if possible, whether there was, in the neighbourhood, any ancient inn of which the sign had been changed within the last eighty years."

As Thorndyke gave this last answer, the judge looked at him with a slightly puzzled expression. Then a slow smile spread over his face and he settled himself comfortably in his chair to listen with renewed attention.

"Did your investigations lead to any discoveries?" Anstey asked.

"They did," Thorndyke replied. "First, with regard to the inns. There are two inns in the village, both of considerable age. One has the sign of 'The Rose and Crown', which is probably the original sign. The other has the sign of 'The Earl of Beaconsfield'; but, as this house bears the date 1602, and was evidently built for an inn, and, as Benjamin Disraeli was created Earl of Beaconsfield only in 1876, it follows that the sign must have been altered since that date. But I could find nobody who knew what the sign had formerly been.

"I next turned my attention to the church register, and first I looked up the entry of the 9th of August, 1794. On that day there were born in this small village no less than three persons. One was George Augustus, the son of the Earl of Winsborough, born at Winsborough Castle. The second was Elizabeth Blunt, daughter of Thomas Blunt, carpenter, and the third was Josiah Bird, son of Isabella Bird, spinster, serving-maid to Mr Nathaniel Pippet of this parish; and there was a note to the effect that the said Josiah was born in the house of the said Nathaniel Pippet.

"I followed the entries in the register in search of further information concerning these persons. Three years later, on the 6th of June, 1797, there was a record of the marriage of Nathaniel Pippet, widower, and Isabella Bird, spinster. Two months later, on the 14th of August, 1797, there was recorded the death of Nathaniel Pippet of this parish, inn-keeper; and three months after this, on the 8th of November, 1797, was an entry recording the birth of Susan Pippet, the posthumous daughter of Nathaniel Pippet deceased. This child lived only four days, as her death is recorded in an entry dated the 12th of November, 1797.

"As none of these entries gave any particulars as to the residence of Nathaniel Pippet, I proceeded to explore the churchyard. There I found a tombstone the inscription on which set forth that 'Here lieth the body of Nathaniel Pippet, late keeper of the Castle Inn in this parish, who departed this life the 14th day of August, 1797.' As there was no other entry in the register, this must have been the Nathaniel Pippet referred to in the entry which I have mentioned. I took a photograph of this tombstone and I produce enlarged copies of that photograph."

As he spoke, Thorndyke opened his portfolio and took out a number of mounted enlargements which he delivered to the usher, who handed one to the judge and passed the others round to the various interested parties. Looking round the court, I was amused to note the expressions with which the different parties regarded the photograph. The judge inspected it with deep interest and an obvious effort to maintain a becoming gravity. So also with Brodribb, whose struggles to suppress his feelings produced a conspicuous heightening of his naturally florid complexion.

Mrs Engleheart viewed the photograph with polite and unsmiling indifference; the young people, Mr Giles and Miss Jenifer (who, for some reason, known only to the usher, had a single copy between them) giggled frankly; Mr Gimbler and his two counsel examined the exhibit with wooden-faced attention. The only person who made no attempt to "conceal or cloke" his amusement was Mr Christopher Pippet, who inspected the photograph through horn-rimmed spectacles and laughed joyously.

When the photograph reached me, the cause of his hilarity became apparent. It happens often enough that the designs on ancient rural tombstones are such as tend "to produce in the sinful a smile". But it was not the work of the artless village mason that was the cause of Mr Pippet's amusement. The joke was in the inscription.

The verses were certainly unconventional and tended to engender the suspicion that the jovial Nathaniel might have embodied them in certain testamentary dispositions. But, however that may have been, the inscription was profoundly significant.

Having given time for the inspection of the photographs, Anstey resumed his examination.

"What inferences do you deduce from these facts which you have discovered?" he asked. But, at this point, Mr MeGonnell rose and objected that the witness's inferences were not evidence.

"The learned counsel is technically correct," said the judge, "and I must allow his objection if he insists; though, in the case of an expert witness, where an investigation has been made *ad hoc*, it is customary to allow the witness to explain the bearing of the facts which he has elicited."

The learned counsel was, however, disposed to insist and the question was accordingly ruled out.

"Apart from any inferences," said Anstey, "what facts have your investigations disclosed?"

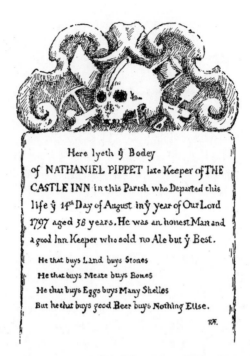

Here lyeth ÿ Bodey
of NATHANIEL PIPPET late Keeper of THE
CASTLE INN in this Parish who Departed this
life ÿ 14ᵗʰ Day of August in ÿ year of Our Lord
1797 aged 58 years. He was an honest Man and
a good Inn Keeper who sold no Ale but ÿ Best.

He that buys Land buys Stones
He that buys Meate buys Bones
He that buys Eggs buys Many Shelles
But he that buys good Beer buys Nothing Ellse.

"They have disclosed the fact," replied Thorndyke, "that on the 9th of August, 1794, the day on which the Earl, George Augustus, was born at Winsborough Castle, there was born at 'the Castle' at Winsborough an individual named Josiah whose mother subsequently married Nathaniel Pippet."

"That fact is the sum of what you discovered?"

"Yes."

"And what relation does that bear to the imaginary set of circumstances of which you have told us?"

"The circumstances that thus came to light were substantially identical with those which I had postulated theoretically."

Anstey noted down this answer and then proceeded:

"You were present at the exhumation of the coffin of Josiah Pippet with the other persons who have been mentioned?"

"I was."

"Did the appearances which you observed seem to you to agree with the conditions which were assumed to exist – that this coffin had lain undisturbed in this vault for eighty years?"

"No. In my opinion, the appearances were not reconcileable with that assumption."

"In what respect did the appearances disagree with the ostensible conditions?"

"There were three respects in which the appearances disagreed with the conditions which were assumed to exist. The disagreements were concerned with the dust in the vault, the coffin, and the contents of the coffin."

"Let us take those disagreements in order. First, as to the dust. Do you say that there were signs that it had been disturbed?"

"No. The dust that was there had not been disturbed since it was deposited. But it had not the characters of ancient dust, or of any dust which might have become deposited in a vault above ground which was situated in an open burial ground, remote from any dwelling-house."

"What are the distinguishing peculiarities of such ancient dust?"

"The dust which would be deposited in a vault over a period of eighty years would consist of very light and minute particles of matter, such as would be capable of floating in still air. There would be no mineral particles excepting excessively minute particles of the lighter minerals, and very few of these. Practically the whole of the dust would consist of tiny fragments of organic matter, of which a large part would be derived from textiles. As these fragments would be of all sorts of colours, the resulting dust would be of no colour at all; that is to say, of a perfectly neutral grey. But this dust was not of a perfectly neutral grey. It had a very faint tinge of red; and this extremely faint tinge of colour was distinguishable in the whole of the dust, not only in one part. I accordingly took two samples for examination, one from the coffin and one from the shelf on which it rested; and I have since made a microscopical examination of each of these samples separately."

"And what conclusion did you arrive at as a result of your examination?"

"I came to the conclusion that the whole of this dust had been derived from a single room. That room was covered with a carpet which had a red ground with a pattern principally of green and blue with a little black. There was also in this room a cotton drapery of some kind – either a table-cloth or curtains – dyed a darkish blue."

"Those are your conclusions. Can you give us the actual facts which you observed?"

"On examining the dust through the microscope, I observed that it consisted chiefly of woollen fibres dyed a bright red. There were also woollen fibres dyed green and blue, but smaller in number than the red, and a still smaller number of woollen fibres dyed black, together with a few cotton fibres dyed a darkish blue. In addition to the fibres there were rather numerous particles of coal and some other minerals, very small in size, but much too large to float in still air. I have here two samples of the dust mounted and arranged in small hand microscopes. On holding the microscopes up to the light, it is quite easy to see the fibres which I have described and also one or two particles of coal."

He handed the two little instruments (in which I recognised the handiwork of the ingenious and indefatigable Polton) to the usher, who passed them up to the judge. His lordship examined each of them with deep interest and then returned them to the usher, by whom they were handed, first to McGonnell and then to the other parties to the case. Eventually, they came to me; and I was surprised to see how efficiently these little instruments served their purpose. On turning them towards the window, the coloured fibres were visible with brilliant distinctness, in spite of the low magnification. And their appearance, corresponding exactly with Thorndyke's description, was absolutely convincing, as I gathered from the decidedly glum expression that began to spread over Mr McGonnell's countenance.

When the dust had been inspected, Anstey resumed his examination.

"Can you account for the presence of this dust in the vault?"

"Only in general terms. Since it was obviously not derived from anything in the vault itself, or the immediate neighbourhood of the vault, it must have been brought there from some other place."

"Can you suggest a method of procedure which would have produced the appearances which you observed?"

"A possible method, and the one which I have no doubt was employed, would be this: First, the sweepings from the room, or more probably the accumulations from the receiver of a vacuum-cleaner, would be collected and conveyed to the vault. There, the dust could be blown into the air of the upper part of the vault by means of a vacuum-cleaner with the valve reversed, or more conveniently by means of a common pair of bellows, the dust being fed into the valve-hole. If it were blown up towards the roof, it would float in the air and settle down slowly, falling eventually in a perfectly even manner on the coffin, the shelf, and the floor, producing exactly the appearance that was seen."

"You are not prepared to swear that this was the method actually employed?"

"No; but it would be a possible method, and I cannot think of any other."

"Well," said Anstey, "the method is not important. We will let it go and come to another matter.

"You referred to three discrepancies in the appearances: the dust, the coffin, and the contents of the latter. In what way did the coffin disagree with the ostensible conditions?"

"The coffin was assumed to have been lying undisturbed in the vault for eighty years. That was not the case. If this was the original coffin, it had certainly been opened and re-closed since the year 1854."

"How are you able to fix the date so exactly?"

"By the screws with which the lid was fastened down. These screws are in the possession of Detective-Superintendent Miller, who is now in court."

Here the Superintendent rose, and, producing an envelope, handed it to the usher, who passed it up to the judge. He then evicted Thorndyke from the witness-box, and, taking his place, was duly sworn, and, in reply to a question from Anstey, declared that the screws in the envelope were the screws which had been extracted in his presence from the coffin of Josiah Pippet.

The judge opened the envelope and tipped the screws out into the palm of his hand. Then he remarked – in almost the very words that I had heard the Superintendent use – that he did not see anything at all unusual about them. "To my unsophisticated eye," he concluded, "they look like the kind of screws that one could buy at any ironmonger's."

"That, my lord," said Thorndyke – who had, in his turn, evicted the Superintendent and resumed his place in the witness-box – "is exactly what they are, and that is the fact which gives them their evidential importance. This coffin was supposed to have been screwed down in the year 1843. But in that year you could *not* have bought screws like these at any ironmonger's. There were no such screws in existence. At that time, wood screws were like metal screws, excepting as to their threads. They were flat-ended, so that, in order to drive them in, it was necessary to bore a hole as deep as the screw was long. But, about 1850, an American inventor devised and patented a sharp-pointed, or gimlet-ended screw, which would find its own way through wood, regardless of the depth of the hole. Later, he came to England to dispose of his patent rights, and in 1854 he sold them to Chamberlain and Nettlefolds, who thereupon acquired the virtual monopoly of the manufacture of wood screws; for, owning to the great superiority of the sharp-pointed screw, the old, blunt-ended screw went completely out of use. I am able, by the kindness of the Master of the Worshipful Company of Ironmongers, to show a set of the old type of screws, the date of manufacture being 1845."

Here he produced a wooden tablet to which were secured six screws of various sizes with blunt, flattened ends like the screws still used by metal workers. The tablet was passed up to the judge, who inspected it curiously and compared the screws on it with those from the envelope.

"It is always easy," he moralised, "to be wise after the event; but it does really seem astonishing that mankind should have had to wait until 1854 for so obvious an improvement."

With this he returned the coffin screws to the envelope and handed the latter and the museum tablet to the usher, who proceeded to pass them round for inspection. I watched their progress with considerable interest, noting their effect on the different parties to the case. Particularly interested was I to observe the expression on Mr McGonnell's face as he compared the two exhibits. There was no question as to his recognition of their significance; and, by the flush that rose to his face, and the unmistakable expression of anger, I judged that Mr Gimbler had not taken him into his confidence and that these revelations were coming to him as a very disagreeable surprise.

When the screws had been inspected by the principal parties, Anstey resumed his examination.

"When you stated the latest date at which this coffin could have been screwed down, you used the qualification, 'If this was the original coffin.' Did you mean to express a doubt that this was the original coffin?"

"Yes. My opinion is that it is not the original coffin, but a new one to which the brass name-plate and other metal 'furniture' from the original coffin have been screwed. The plate and handles appeared to me to be the original ones, and they appeared to be fastened on with the original brass screws. The slots of those screws showed clear indications of their having been unscrewed quite recently."

"What were your reasons for believing that this was a new coffin rather than the old one, opened and re-closed?"

"There were several reasons. First, there were the screws. These were modern screws, apparently artificially rusted. At any rate, they were rusty. But if the original coffin had been opened and re-closed, it would be natural for the screws which had been extracted to be used to fasten down the lid. There would be no object in obtaining rusty screws to use in their place. Then the coffin did not look old. It was much discoloured; but the discoloration did not look like the effect of age but rather like that of staining. Further, the coffin was covered, both inside and out, with a thick coating of mildew. But there was nothing to account for this mildew. The wood was not damp, and it had the character of new wood. The mildew had the appearance of having been produced artificially by coating the surface with some substance such as size, mixed with sugar or glycerine. Moreover, on the assumption that some substitution had been made – which all the appearances indicated – it would obviously be more convenient to use a new coffin than to open and remove the contents of the old, particularly if the old one should have happened to contain a body. But that is a matter of inference. Taking only the appearances observed, I consider that they indicated that this was a new coffin."

"Then," said Anstey, "we now come to the third set of disagreements, the contents of the coffin. What have you to tell us about those?"

"The contents of the coffin," Thorndyke replied, "were, according to the traditional account, a roll of sheet-lead and some plumber's oddments, which had been left over from some repairs. Now, sheet-lead, removed in 1843, or earlier, from the roof of a house, would, even then, be old lead. It would certainly be cast sheet – cast upon a sand casting-table – and it would certainly contain a considerable proportion of silver. But the sheet of lead which was found in the coffin was the ordinary milled sheet which has, in recent times, replaced the old cast sheet. As to the amount of silver that it contained, I could form no opinion. I therefore suggested that an assay should be made to ascertain the silver content. This proposal was contested by Mr Gimbler on the ground that we had no authority to make an assay, and by Mr McGonnell on the ground that the evidence was of a kind that would not be taken seriously by the court. And Mr Brodribb objected, apparently on the ground that the proceeding would seem to throw doubt on the good faith of the applicant. Accordingly, I did not press my proposal, but I made a careful examination of the contents of the coffin, with very surprising results. In addition to the sheet-lead, the coffin contained four hemispherical lumps of metal which had apparently solidified in a plumber's melting-pot, which we may call pot-leavings. There were four of these: one large and three smaller. The large one had the appearance and all the visible and palp-able properties of lead, and I had no doubt that it was lead. The other three were evidently not lead, but had the appearance and properties of an alloy of lead and some other metal."

"Did you form any opinion as to the nature of the other metal?"

"I did, but with the reservation that the inference seemed so incredible that I was doubtful about accepting it."

"What was the opinion that you formed as to the nature of these lumps of lead alloy?"

"I was forced to the conclusion that they were composed of an alloy of lead and platinum."

"Platinum!" exclaimed the judge. "But is not platinum a very rare and precious metal?"

"It is always a precious metal," Thorndyke replied, "and since the war it has become extremely scarce and its value has gone up to an extravagant extent. At present, it is several times more valuable than gold."

"And how much platinum did you consider to be present in these lumps of alloy?" the judge asked.

"I estimated the weight of the three lumps together at about a hundredweight, and about half that weight appeared to be platinum."

"Half a hundredweight of platinum!" exclaimed the judge. "It does indeed seem incredible. Why, it is a fortune. What do you suppose the value of that amount would be?"

"At the present inflated prices," replied Thorndyke, "I should put it at anything from fifteen to seventeen thousand pounds."

"It is beyond belief," said the judge. "However, we shall see," and with this he sat back in his chair and glanced at Anstey.

"As this opinion seems to be so utterly incredible, even to yourself," said Anstey, resuming his examination, "perhaps you might explain to us how you arrived at it."

"It was principally a question of weight," Thorndyke replied.

"But," said Anstey, "have you had sufficient experience to be able to detect platinum in an alloy by the sense of weight to the hand?"

"No," Thorndyke answered, "but it was not a case of absolute weight, or I should have been still less confident. There was a term of comparison. When I picked up the big lump, it felt just as I should expect a lump of lead of that size to feel. But when I then picked up the first of the smaller ones, I received a shock; for, though it was little more than half the size of the big one, it was nearly as heavy. Now, there are not many metals that are much heavier than lead. For practical purposes, ignoring the rare metals, there are only two – gold and platinum. This did not look like gold, but it might have been; a mass of gold, for instance, with a lead casing. On the other hand, its colour – a faint, purplish grey – was exactly that of a lead-platinum alloy. So there seemed to be no escape from the conclusion that that was what it was."

While this evidence was being given, I kept my eyes on Mr Gimbler and his leading counsel. The latter listened in undisguised astonishment and little less disguised displeasure. Obviously, he had begun to smell a rat; and, as it was not his rat, he naturally resented its presence. But even Gimbler failed to maintain the aspect of wooden indifference that he had preserved hitherto. This disclosure had evidently sprung on him a complete surprise; and, as I looked at him and noted the dismay which he struggled in vain to conceal, I found myself wondering whether, by any chance, the expression of consternation on his face might have some significance other than mere surprise. But my speculations were cut short by Anstey, who was continuing his examination.

"Have you anything more to tell us about the contents of this coffin?"

"No," was the reply. "That is all the information that I have to give."

On receiving this reply, Anstey sat down and McGonnell was rising to cross-examine when the judge interposed.

"Before we pass on to other matters," said he, "we ought to be a little more clear about the nature of this metal which was found in the coffin. That is a question which is highly relevant to the issues which are before the court. But it is also relevant to certain other issues concerned with public policy. Dr Thorndyke is not prepared to say definitely that this is actually platinum; but he is evidently convinced – and on apparently sufficient, grounds – that it is. But the question cannot be left at that. It can be settled with certainty, and it should be. Do I understand that this metal, worth, possibly, many thousands of pounds, is still lying in that coffin?"

This question was addressed to Thorndyke, who accordingly replied:

"No, my lord. As my proposal of an assay was rejected, and in view of the questions of public policy to which your lordship has referred, I informed Mr Superintendent Miller that, in my opinion, an examination of the pot-leavings would yield information of great importance to the police. The Superintendent thereupon took possession of the whole of the contents of the coffin and conveyed them to the premises of Mr Daniels, the eminent assayist, and left them there for an assay to be made."

"And has an assay been made?" the judge asked.

"I believe it has, my lord, but I have no information as to the result. Mr Superintendent Miller is now in court."

Here the Superintendent rose and approached the solicitor's table carrying a small but obviously heavy box, which he laid on the table.

"I think," said the judge, "that what the Superintendent has to tell us should go in evidence."

Accordingly, Miller once more evicted Thorndyke from the witness-box, and the judge continued: "You have already been sworn, Superintendent. Will you now give the facts, so far as they are known to you, concerning the contents of this coffin?"

The Superintendent stood at "attention" and delivered himself of his evidence with a readiness born of long practice.

"In consequence of certain information communicated by Dr Thorndyke, I took possession of the contents of the coffin alleged to be that of Josiah Pippet deceased and conveyed them forthwith to the premises of Mr Daniels in Bishopsgate and delivered them to him with instructions to make a trial assay and report to me what he found. On the same evening, I received a report from him in which he informed me that he had ascertained the following facts: the roll of sheet-lead was practically pure lead almost completely free from silver, and was probably of recent manufacture. The large pot-leaving was also pure lead of the modern silver-free type. The three smaller pot-leavings were composed of a lead-platinum alloy, of which about half by weight was platinum. On receiving this report, I directed Mr Daniels to recover the whole of the platinum in a pure state and deliver it to me. He did this, and I have here, in the box on the table, the platinum which I received from him and which he assured me is practically the whole of the platinum which was contained in the pot-leavings. It amounts, roughly, to just under half a hundredweight."

As he concluded, he stepped down from the witness-box, and, approaching the table, unlocked a small padlock of the Yale type by which the hasp of the box was secured and opened the lid. Then, from the interior, he lifted out, one after another, eight little bright, silvery-looking bars, or ingots, and laid them in a row on the table. Picking up the end one, he handed it up to the judge; who weighed it in the palm of his hand, looking at it with a faint smile of amusement. When he received it back from the judge, Miller carried it round the court and allowed each of the interested parties to take it in his hand; and when it came to my turn, and the Superintendent handed it to me (with something exceedingly like a wink, and a sly glance at Thorndyke), I understood the judge's smile. There was something ridiculous in the monstrous disproportion between the size of the little bar and its weight; for, small as it was, it had the weight of a good-sized iron dumb-bell.

When Miller had returned the bars to the box and locked the padlock, he went back to the witness-box to await further questions or cross-examination; but, as neither of the counsel made any sign, the judge dismissed him and then announced the adjournment of the hearing. "I regret," he added, "that, in consequence of other and more urgent business, it will have to be adjourned for a week. The delay is unfortunate; but," here he glanced at McGonnell with a faint smile, "it will have the advantage that learned counsel will have time to consider their cross-examination of Dr Thorndyke."

Hereupon the court rose and we all prepared to take our departure. Glancing at "the other side", I observed Mr Pippet looking a little wistfully in our direction as if he would have liked to come and speak to us. But apparently his native wisdom and good sense told him that the occasion was inopportune, and, after momentary hesitation, he turned away with a somewhat troubled face and followed his legal representatives out of the court.

# Chapter Fifteen

## A Journey and a Discussion

"This adjournment," remarked the Superintendent as he attached a strong leather rug-strap to his precious box, "is a piece of luck for me – at least, I am hoping that it is. You'll have tomorrow free, I suppose, Doctor?"

"I have got plenty to do tomorrow," Thorndyke answered, "but I haven't any appointments, as I expected to be here. Why do you ask?"

"Because," replied Miller, "I have had a bit of luck of another sort. I told you that the suspected yacht was laid up in Benfleet Creek with her hatches sealed and a local boat-builder told off to keep an eye on her. Well, it seems that this man – his name is Jaff – spotted some Johnnie trying to break into her in the cool of the evening, about eleven p.m. So Mr Jaff collared the said Johnnie after a bit of a tussle, and handed him over to the local police.

"Then the police had a brain-wave – quite a good one too. They phoned down to Southend for the Customs Officers who had rummaged the yacht when she arrived from her voyage. So the Preventive men – there were two of them – hopped into the train and came over to have a look at the chappie who had been nabbed; and they both recognised him, at once, as one of the three men they had seen on board the yacht when they rummaged her. And one of them remembered his name – Bunter; and when it was mentioned, he didn't deny it, though he had given a false name, as the police had already assumed, when he said it was John Smith. Of course, there are people in the world named John Smith. Plenty of them. But the crook is apt to exaggerate the number.

"Well, when we got notice of the capture, we thought at first of having him sent up to The Yard to see if we could get a statement from him. But then I thought it would be better for me to go down and have a talk with him on the spot and just have a look at the yacht at the same time. And that's where you come in; at least, I hope you do, as you seem to be like one of those blooming spiders that I've heard about that have got eyes all over them. What do you say? I think you would find it an interesting little jaunt."

Thorndyke appeared to think so, too, for he accepted the invitation at once and included me in the acceptance, as I also had the day at my disposal. Accordingly, we settled the programme, much to the Superintendent's satisfaction, and, having arranged to meet on the following morning at Fenchurch Street Station, we escorted Miller, with his precious burden, to his car and bade him au revoir.

"I agree with Miller," said I, as, having achieved the perilous crossing of the Strand, we strolled towards the Temple Gate. "This is a bit of luck. A nice little trip to the sea-side instead of a day in that stuffy court. And it will probably be quite amusing."

"I hope it will be more than amusing," said Thorndyke. "We ought to be able to pick up some useful facts. We want them badly enough, for there are a lot of gaps that we have to fill up."

"What gaps are you referring to?" I asked.

"Well," he replied, "look at our case as it stands. It is a mere collection of disconnected facts. And yet we know that those facts must be connected, and that we have got to establish the connection. Take this platinum, for instance. It disappears from the cloak-room and is lost to view utterly. Then it reappears in the coffin; and the problem is, How did it get there, where has it been in the interval, and what is Gimbler's connection with it?"

"Aren't we rather guessing about that platinum?" I objected. "We all seem to be assuming that this platinum is the platinum that was stolen."

"And reasonably so, I think," said Thorndyke. "Consider the probabilities, Jervis. If it had been a case of an ounce, or even a pound, there might have been room for doubt. But half a hundredweight, at a time when every grain of platinum is precious and worth many times its weight of gold, and at a time when that very weight of platinum has been stolen and is still missing – well, we may be mistaken, but we are justified in accepting the overwhelming probabilities. And, after all, it is only a working hypothesis."

"Yes," I admitted, "I suppose you are right; and we shall soon know if you are on the wrong track. But you are also assuming that Gimbler has some connection with it. You haven't much to go on."

Thorndyke laughed. "You are a regular Devil's advocate, Jervis," said he. "But you are right, so far. We haven't much to go on. Still, I suppose you will agree that we have fair grounds for assuming that Gimbler has some connection with that bogus coffin."

"Yes," I was forced to admit, "I will concede that much, as the coffin appears to have been planted there to furnish evidence in support of his case. But I am not so clear as to the connection between Gimbler and that platinum. He seemed mighty surprised when you mentioned it."

"He did," Thorndyke agreed; "and there is certainly something extremely odd about the whole affair. But you see the position. Gimbler arranges for a dummy coffin to be planted, and that dummy coffin is found to contain the proceeds of a robbery. There is thus established a connection of some sort between Gimbler and this stolen property. We cannot guess the nature of the connection. It may be of the most indirect kind. Apparently, Gimbler had no suspicion of the nature of the metal in the coffin. But some kind of connection between that loot and Mr Gimbler there must be. And it is not impossible that the platinum may eventually be the means of pointing the way to some unguarded spot in Gimbler's defences; for I take it that there will be considerable difficulty in getting direct evidence of his part in the planting of the coffin."

His conclusion brought us to our doorstep, at which point the discussion lapsed. But I felt that it was only an adjournment; for something in the Superintendent's manner had suggested to me that he, also, had certain questions to propound.

And so it turned out. On our arrival on the platform at Fenchurch Street, I perceived the Superintendent doing "sentry-go" before the door of an empty first-class smoking compartment, and I suspected that he had made certain private arrangements with the guard. At any rate, we had the compartment to ourselves, and when we had passed the first few stations in safety, he proceeded to fire his first shot.

"I've been puzzling my brains, Doctor, about those pot-leavings."

"Indeed?" said Thorndyke. "What is the difficulty?"

"The difficulty is how the deuce they became pot-leavings. I have always understood that platinum was almost impossible to melt. Isn't that so?"

"Platinum is very difficult to melt," Thorndyke agreed. "It has the highest melting-point of all metals, excepting one or two of the rare metals. The melting-point is 1710 degrees Centigrade."

"And what is the melting-point of cast iron?"

"1505 degrees Centigrade," Thorndyke answered.

"Then," exclaimed Miller, "if it takes about two hundred degrees more to melt platinum than it does to melt iron, how the devil was it possible to melt the platinum in a common plumber's melting-pot which is made of cast iron? It would seem as if the pot should melt before the platinum."

"So it would, of course, if the metal had been pure," Thorndyke replied with a smile that suggested to me that he had been expecting the question, and that something of importance turned on it. "But it was not pure. It was an alloy; and alloys exhibit all kinds of queer anomalies in respect to their melting-points. However, with your permission, we will postpone the discussion of this point, as we shall have to consider it in connection with certain other matters that we have to discuss. You have not told us whether those clothes from the two dead men yielded any information."

"They gave us the means of identifying the two men, as you will have learned from the reports of the inquest; and the names were apparently their real names, or at least their usual aliases. The murderer,

Bassett, the skipper of the yacht, was a local man, as you guessed. He lived at Swanscombe, and seems to have been a Swanscombe man, which accounts, as you suggested, for his knowledge of the dene hole. The man he killed, Wicks, was living at Woolwich at the time, but he seemed to be a bird of passage. That is all that I got out of the clothes excepting the name and address of a man called Samuels, who describes himself as a gold refiner and bullion dealer, but who may be a fence. We know him by name, but we haven't anything against him, though we bear him in mind. These small bullion dealers have to be kept in view, as they have so many facilities for getting rid of stolen jewellery and plate."

"Yes," Thorndyke agreed; "and, in the special circumstances, any refiner and bullion dealer is of interest to us. It seems likely that Bassett intended to approach this man, Samuels, on the subject of the disposal of the platinum, if he hadn't already made some arrangements with him. You'll have to continue to keep Mr Samuels in view. But now tell us a little more about this present business."

"There isn't much more to tell you," said Miller. It seems that Mr Jaff, the boat-builder gent, was cruising about Benfleet Creek in his dinghy – he lives afloat, himself – when he saw our friend, Bunter, trying to prise open the yacht's fore-scuttle; whereupon, having a natural prejudice against people who break into yachts, he pulled alongside, stepped on board, and, creeping silently along the deck in his rubber mud-boots, grabbed Bunter and hauled him into his dinghy, where they seem to have had a mighty scrap until another mariner came along and lent a hand. Then they got him ashore and handed him over to the local police, as I have told you."

"What do you suppose could have been his object in trying to break into the vessel?" I asked. "There wasn't anything of value left on board, was there?"

"There was not supposed to be," said Miller, with a knowing look, "but I have an idea that there may have been. My notion is that there may have been more platinum than we thought, and that he had come to snap up what was left. What do you say, Doctor?"

Thorndyke shook his head. "I don't think so, Miller," he replied. "You have recovered practically all the platinum that was said to have been stolen. My impression is that, as our friend Mr Pippet might express it, you are barking up the wrong tree."

"Am I?" said Miller. "Then if you will point out the right tree, I'll bark up that. What do you think was his object in trying to break in?"

"My idea is," Thorndyke replied, "that he supposed that the whole of the platinum was still on board."

"But," protested Miller, "how could he? He knew that Bassett had carted the bulk of it away."

Thorndyke chuckled. "My impression is, Miller," said he, "that it was at this point that the chapter of accidents began; and it is here that the answer to the question that you raised just now comes in."

"About the melting-pot?" demanded Miller.

"Yes. I have a theory that the whole mystery of the murder and the appearance of the platinum in the coffin hinges on that question. Perhaps, as we have some time at our disposal, there would be no harm in my giving the reins to my fancy and sketching out my hypothetical scheme of the events as I believe they occurred."

"Do, by all means," Miller exclaimed, eagerly, "for, if your imaginary scheme satisfies you, it is likely to satisfy me."

"Then," said Thorndyke, "I will begin with what I believe to have been the hiding-place in which the platinum was concealed on the yacht."

"But, Good Lord, Doctor!" Miller exclaimed, "you've never seen the yacht!"

"It wasn't necessary," Thorndyke replied. "I had your description of the yacht and of the search made by the Customs Officer, and they seemed to me to indicate an excellent hiding-place. When you described how that officer crept down into the hold and found it all perfectly clear and empty with the exception of the lead ballast-weights, it occurred to me that it was quite possible that the platinum was staring him in the face all the time. Remember that he was not looking for platinum but for tobacco."

"Do you suggest that the platinum was hidden in the ballast-weights?" Miller demanded.

"That is exactly what I do suggest," replied Thorndyke; "and I will describe to you what I believe to have been the method used in concealing it. You will remember that these weights were proper yacht's ballast: lead weights cast to a correct shape to fit the timbers and sit comfortably along the kelson. Each would probably weigh about half a hundredweight, that being the usual and most convenient weight. Now, my theory is that our friends took with them a mould of the ballast-weights – an ordinary sand-flask would do, though a fireclay mould would be more convenient – so that they could cast new weights whenever they might want them. Possibly they also took some spare lead with them.

"Now, as soon as they had got possession of the platinum – which, you will remember, was in thin sheets – they cut it up into suitable sized pieces, or rolled or folded it up to a size that would go easily into the mould. They put the pieces into the mould, probably propping them up a little with some pieces of lead to keep them off the bottom, so that the platinum should not be visible on the surface. Then they melted some spare lead, or one of the ballast-weights, and poured the molten lead into the mould. When the lead set solid, there would be a quite ordinary-looking ballast-weight. Then they did the same with the rest of the platinum, producing a second ballast-weight; and the two could be laid down with the rest of the weights alongside the keel. If there was any lead left over, that would be thrown overboard together with the mould."

"Yes," said Miller, "that sounds quite convincing. Deuced ingenious, too. Uncommonly neat. That's how they were able to walk past the Customs in the way they did. But where does the chapter of accidents come in?"

"It came in at that point," said Thorndyke. "Somebody had made a trifling miscalculation. I don't say that Bassett made the mistake, though I suspect that he did. But someone did. You know, Miller, as well as I do that people who embark on a fake of any kind need to have a good deal of knowledge. And usually they haven't. Our friend

Gimbler didn't know enough about dust; and the craftsman who made the bogus coffin didn't know enough about screws. And I suspect that the downy bird who invented the ballast-weight dodge didn't know enough about platinum.

"The rock, I think, on which these gentry split was this: most people know, as you know, that platinum is one of the most infusible of metals. It cannot be melted in any ordinary furnace. Only a very special furnace, or the most powerful type of blowpipe, will melt it. Now, to a person who knew that, and no more, it would naturally seem that platinum, put into a mould and then covered up with melted lead, would simply be imbedded in lead. And, since lead is very easily fusible – it melts at the comparatively low temperature of 325 degrees Centigrade – it would naturally seem that, when it was required to recover the platinum, all that would be necessary would be to melt the lead weight and pick out the platinum."

"Yes," agreed Miller; "that seems perfectly feasible. What's the snag?"

"The snag is," replied Thorndyke, "that platinum has one most singular property. Every one knows that you can melt lead in an iron ladle or pot; and it would be quite natural to infer that, since platinum is more difficult to melt than iron, it would be equally easy to melt lead in a platinum ladle or pot. But the inference would be quite wrong. If you were to try to melt lead in a platinum pot, the bottom of the pot would drop out. In spite of its enormously high melting-point, platinum dissolves freely in melted lead."

"The deuce it does!" exclaimed Miller. "That is most extraordinary."

"It is," Thorndyke agreed; "and it is a property of the metal that would be totally unexpected by anyone who did not happen to know it. And now you will see how this curious fact affects our problem. Supposing the platinum to have been put into the mould as I have described, and the melted lead poured in on top of it; and supposing the thieves – or some of them – to be unacquainted with this property of the metal. They would expect, as I have said, that when they wanted to recover the platinum, all they would have to do would be to melt the lead weight and pick out the platinum with tongs.

"Now our friend Wicks, who made the exchange at the cloak-room, was evidently 'in the know'. He knew what was in the case that he stole; and he had come to get that case. The relic that he left in exchange was, I feel sure, merely a by-product. It may even have furnished the means or the suggestion for the exchange. Obviously, he had the thing on his hands, and it was the kind of thing that he would naturally wish to get rid of; and, if he was able to get a suitable case, as he evidently was, the exchange was a quite masterly tactical plan. But I think we may take it that it was the case – worth fifteen thousand pounds – that he had come for.

"We will assume that he knew the platinum to be concealed in the lead weights. It is practically certain that he did. He was one of the yacht's crew, or gang, and the thing must have been known to all of them. Probably he had seen the job carried out; but, at any rate, he knew what had been done. Accordingly, as soon as he had got his booty into a safe place, he proceeded to melt down the lead weights to get at the platinum.

"And then it was, I suggest, that the fatal mistake occurred. As the weights melted, he looked for the platinum to appear. Apparently, he fished for it with a ladle and then transferred the molten metal by degrees to some empty pots. But when he had ladled the whole of it into the other pots, there was still no sign of the platinum. To his eye, the pots contained nothing but melted lead.

"Now, what would he be likely to think, under the circumstances? He might have thought that Bassett had made a mistake and put the wrong weights into the case; but more probably (seeing that he had tried to rob the gang and snatch the whole of the booty for himself and the confederate who had helped him to carry off the case) he would think that he had been suspected and that 'the boss' had deliberately laid a booby-trap for him by planting a couple of the plain lead weights in the case. At any rate, he had, apparently, got nothing but a quantity of lead. What did he do with that lead? We have no means of judging. He may have thrown it away in disgust or he may have sold it to a plumber for a few pence. But, if we accept this hypothetical construction of the course of events, we can see how those lumps of lead-platinum alloy came into being."

"Yes," Miller agreed, "it all fits the facts perfectly, even to the murder of Wicks. For, of course, each of these two rascals, Wicks and Bassett, thought the other had nobbled the whole of the swag. My eye! what a lark it is!" He laughed grimly and then added: "But I begin to have an inkling of the way you dropped on that dene hole so readily. You'd been keeping an account of the case all along. I wonder if you can make any suggestion as to how that stuff got into the coffin, and who put it there."

"I am afraid not, Miller," Thorndyke replied. "You see that the hypothetical sketch that I have given you is based on known facts and fair probabilities. But the facts that we have do not carry us much farther. Still, there is one fact that we must not overlook."

"What is that?" Miller demanded, eagerly.

"You will admit, I think," said Thorndyke, "that the faking of that coffin must have been carried out on the initiative and under the direction of Gimbler. There is really no reasonable alternative."

"Unless Mr Pippet did the job himself; which doesn't seem at all likely, though he may have been a party to it. But I agree with you. Gimbler must have been the moving spirit, and probably Pippet knows nothing about it."

"That is my own view," said Thorndyke. "Pippet impresses me as a perfectly honest man, and I have no doubt that the planting of the coffin was exclusively Gimbler's scheme, carried out by certain agents. But one of these agents must have had these lumps of alloy in his possession – unconscious, of course, of their nature. But that agent must have been in touch, directly or indirectly, with Wicks. Now, it ought not to be impossible to discover who that agent was. There are several ways of approach to the problem. One of them, perhaps, is Mr Bunter. Since Wicks was not on board the yacht when Bassett took away the case of platinum, he must have had a confederate who was. Now, there were only two men left when Bassett had gone – not counting the man whom the Customs Officer saw, who seems to have been a stranger who had probably taken a passage on the yacht and is not really in the picture at all. As Bunter was one of those two, there is at least an even chance that he was Wicks's confederate; and, when you come to have a talk with him, you must bear in mind that he, also, may be assumed to be unaware of the change that the platinum would undergo when the melted lead was poured on to it."

"Yes, by Jove!" Miller agreed. "I begin to hope that we may get something really useful out of Mr Bunter, if we deal with him tactfully. But Lord! what a stroke of luck it was for me that you were able to come with me on this jaunt. If it hadn't been for what you have just told us, I might have missed the whole point of his story, even if he was prepared to tell one. I shouldn't have known any more about it than he did."

As Miller concluded this frank and generous acknowledgement, the train began to slow down and presently drew up at Benfleet Station. A sergeant of the local police was waiting on the platform, and, when we had introduced ourselves, he took us in charge and conducted us out of the station. A few steps took us to the water-side, where we halted to survey the interminable levels of Canvey Island and the winding creek, now full of water, with its amazing assemblage of houseboats and floating shacks of all kinds.

"That's the *Cormorant*," said the sergeant, pointing to a sturdy-looking, yawl-rigged yacht that was moored some distance down the creek. "I suppose you will not be wanting to go on board her?"

"Not at present," replied Miller, "and probably not at all. But we will hear what Bunter has to say."

"I'm afraid, Sir," said the sergeant, "you'll find that he hasn't very much to say. We haven't found him particularly ready to talk. But perhaps he'll let himself go a bit more with you."

We turned away from the water, and, under the sergeant's guidance, entered the little town, or village, and headed towards the police station.

# Chapter Sixteen

## The Statement of Frederick Bunter

"Well, Bunter," the Superintendent remarked, cheerfully, as the prisoner was brought into the little office and given a seat at the table, "here you are."

"Yes," Bunter agreed, gloomily, "here I am. But I don't see why they wanted to run me in. I wasn't doing no harm."

"You were trying to break into a yacht," Miller ventured to remind him. "That isn't quite according to Cocker, you know."

"I was trying to get on board," said Bunter, "and I'm not denying it. But you seem to be forgetting that I was a member of the crew of that yacht. All I wanted was to get some of my kit what I had left behind. I've told the sergeant so."

"That's right, Sir," the sergeant confirmed. "He said he had left his pocket-knife behind; and we did find a pocket-knife on board – a big knife with a corkscrew and a marlinspike in it, such as he had described. But he could have got it from us without breaking into the vessel."

"Yes," said Miller, "that's so. Still, it's a point in his favour. However, it isn't the burglary that we are interested in. If everything else was satisfactory we might let that pass, as he didn't actually break in and he has some sort of explanation. But you know, Bunter, what the real business is, and what we want to ask you about. It's that platinum job."

"What platinum job?" demanded Bunter. "I don't know nothing about any platinum."

"Now, Bunter," the Superintendent remonstrated, "don't be silly. We know all about that job, and we know that you were in it with Bassett and Wicks and the other man."

As he spoke, he drew a packet of cigarettes from his pocket, and, taking one out, pushed it across the table with a box of matches. Bunter accepted the gift with a grunt of acknowledgement but maintained his unaccommodating attitude.

"If you know all about it," said he, "there ain't no need for you to ask me no questions."

"Oh, yes, there is," said Miller. "We know enough for the purpose of the prosecution. But there are certain matters that we should like to clear up for other reasons. Still, you are not obliged to say anything if you don't want to. I suppose you have been cautioned. If you haven't, I caution you now that anything you say will be taken down in writing and may be used in evidence at the trial. But I don't want you to say anything that might make the case any worse against you. I want some particulars, as I told you, for other reasons. What you may tell us won't do your two pals any harm, as they are both dead. And I think I may say that we are not inclined to be vindictive to you, as no very great harm has been done to anybody, seeing that we have recovered the swag."

At the moment when Miller made this last statement, the prisoner was in the act of striking a match to light his cigarette. But, as the words were spoken, the action became arrested and he sat with his mouth open and the unheeded match burning – until the flame reached his finger, when he dropped it with an appropriate observation.

"Did you say," he demanded, speaking slowly and in a tone of the utmost amazement, "that you had recovered the swag?"

"I did," Miller replied, calmly, proceeding to fill his pipe.

"Do you mean the platinum?" Bunter persisted, gazing at the Superintendent with the same expression of amazed incredulity.

"I do," replied Miller. "Pass the matches when you have lit up."

Bunter lighted his cigarette perfunctorily and pushed the match-box across the table.

"How did you get hold of it?" he asked.

"We got it," Miller replied, with a twinkle of enjoyment, "from someone who had it from Wicks."

"Get out!" exclaimed Bunter. "You couldn't. Wicks never had it. You are moguing me. I don't believe you've got it at all."

"Look here, Bunter," the Superintendent said, stiffly, "I am not bound to tell you anything. But, if I do tell you anything, you can take it that it's the truth. I'm not in the habit of making false statements to prisoners, nor is any other police officer. I tell you that we have got all that platinum back, so you can take that as a fact and steer your course accordingly."

"But," persisted Bunter, "you couldn't have got it from Wicks. I tell you he never had it."

"Nonsense, Bunter," said Miller. "Didn't he pinch that case from the cloak-room at Fenchurch Street? You know he did."

"Yes, I know all about that," rejoined Bunter, "and I know that he thought the stuff was in that case. But it wasn't."

"That's what he told you," said Miller, hardly able to conceal his enjoyment of this contest of wits, and the consciousness that he had the trumps securely up his sleeve. "But it was he that was doing the moguing. He meant to keep the whole of the swag for himself."

"Now that's where you're mistaken," said Bunter. "You think I am going on what he told me. But I ain't. I *know* the stuff wasn't in that case."

"How do you know?" demanded Miller.

"That's my business, that is," was the reply.

"Well," said Miller, "I don't know that it matters so very much. We have got the stuff back, which is the important thing. But, of course, we like to fill in the details if we can.

Bunter re-lit his cigarette and reflected. No one likes a misunderstanding or cross-purposes, and Bunter evidently felt that he was being misunderstood. Furthermore, he was intensely curious as to how the platinum could possibly have been recovered. At length, he said:

"Supposing I was to tell you the whole story, would you let the prosecution drop?"

The Superintendent shook his head. "No, Bunter," he replied promptly. "I can't make any promises. The man who makes a promise which he doesn't mean to keep is a liar, which is what no police officer ought to be; and the man who keeps a promise that he oughtn't to have made, in a case like this, is guilty of bribery. The English law is dead against compounding felonies or any other crimes. But you know quite well that, if you choose to help us, you won't do yourself any harm."

Bunter took a little more time for reflection, and eventually reached a conclusion.

"Very well," he said, "I will tell you the whole blooming story, so far as it is known to me; and I look to you not to take advantage of me from what I have told you."

"I think you are wise, Bunter," said the Superintendent, obviously much relieved at the prisoner's decision. "By the way, Sergeant, what time did Bunter have his breakfast?"

"About seven o'clock, Sir," was the reply.

"Then," said Miller, "if he is going to make a longish statement, he won't be the worse for a little refreshment. What do you say, Bunter?"

Mr Bunter grinned and admitted that "he could do with a beaver".

"Very well," said Miller, "perhaps we could all do with a beaver – say, a snack of bread and cheese and a glass of beer. Can you manage that, Sergeant?"

The sergeant could, and, being provided with the wherewithal in the form of a ten-shilling note, went forth to dispatch an underling in search of the materials for the said "beaver". Meanwhile, Bunter, having been furnished with a fresh cigarette, lighted it and began his narrative.

"You must understand," said he, "that this job was run by Bassett. The rest of us carried out orders, and we didn't know much more about the job than what he told us, and he didn't tell us any more than we was bound to find out for ourselves. We didn't even know that the stuff was platinum until Wicks spotted it by its weight. All that we knew was that we were going to lift some stuff that was pretty valuable; and I doubt if the fourth man, Park, knew even that."

"How did you come to know Bassett?" the Superintendent asked.

"He came to my house – leastways my brother-in-law's house at Walworth – and said he had been recommended to me by a gentleman; but he wouldn't say who the gentleman was. Whoever he was, he must have known something about me, because he knew that I had been to sea on a sailing barge, and he knew about a little trouble that I had got into over some snide money that some fool gave me for a joke."

"Ah!" said Miller, "and how did that trouble end?"

"Charge dismissed," Bunter replied, triumphantly. "No evidence of any dishonest intent. Of course there wasn't."

"Certainly not," Miller agreed. "Of course you explained about the practical joke?"

"Rather – at least my lawyer did. He talked to the beak like a father, I can tell you."

"Yes," said Miller, "I can imagine it. These Jew advocates are uncommonly persuasive."

"He wasn't a Jew," Bunter exclaimed, indignantly. "No blooming sheenies for me. He was an English gentleman."

"Oh!" said Miller. "I thought all the police-court solicitors were Jews. What was this gentleman's name?"

"His name," Bunter replied, haughtily, "was Gimbler; and a first-class man at his business he was. Knew all the ropes like an AB."

"Yes," said Miller. "But to return to Bassett; had Wicks known him previously?"

"No. Bassett called on him, too. Got his address from a gentleman who knew him. Same gentleman, I expect, as Bassett wouldn't say who he was. But he knew that Wicks had been brought up as a waterman, and I think he knew a bit more about him – more than I did, for Wicks was a stranger to me, and he didn't let on much as to what he did for a living. So there was four of us on the yacht; Bassett, Wicks, me and a bloke named Park, but he wasn't really in the swim. He was a bawleyman out of Leigh; a simple sort of cove, but a rare good seaman. He wasn't told nothing about the job, and I fancy he thought it was some sort of smuggling racket – nothing for a honest man to mind."

"And what was the arrangement as to pay, or shares?"

"We all got monthly pay at the ordinary yachtsman's rate, and there was to be a bonus at the end of the voyage. Park was to have fifty pounds, and me and Wicks was to have two hundred each if we brought the job off and landed the swag."

Here the "beaver" arrived, and Bunter was allowed to refresh himself with a glass of beer; which he did with uncommon gusto. But the narrative proceeded without interruption, excepting such as was due to slight impairment of articulation when the narrator took an extra liberal mouthful; which we shall venture to ignore.

"I can't tell you exactly how the actual job was done at Riga, as I was down below at the time. Bassett and Wicks did the sleight of hand on the quay, but I think it was done something like this: We had been in the habit of getting our provisions on board in a big hamper, and this used to be left about on the quay so as to get the people there used to seeing it. Now, on the day when the job was done, Bassett put into the hamper the little dummy case that he had got ready with half a hundredweight of lead in it. I don't know how he got the particulars for making up the case, but I reckon he must have had a pal on the spot who gave him the tip. Anyhow, he made up the dummy case and put it in the hamper wrapped up in a waterproof sheet. Then it was took up and dumped down on the quay close to where the cases of platinum was being dumped down by the men who brought them out of the van. Then, I understand, someone gave an alarm of fire; and, while everyone was looking at the place where the fire was supposed to be, the dummy was put out on the quay and the waterproof sheet flicked off the dummy and over one of the real cases, and the dummy was shoved nearer to the other cases. Then Bassett sat down on the case that he had covered with the sheet and lit his pipe. Then they waited until all the cases, dummy and all, had been put on board the ship. Then they lifted the case, still covered with the waterproof sheet, into the hamper and brought it on board the yacht.

"As soon as it was on board, Park and me was told to cast off the shore ropes and get the yacht out of her berth and put out into the bay; which we did, though, as it was nearly a dead calm, she crept out mighty slowly. When we had got the sails set, I left Park at the helm and went below to lend a hand; and then it was that I found out how the swag was to be disposed of – and a mighty clever wheeze it was, and it worked out to a T.

"You must know that our inside ballast was a lot of lead weights, all cast to the same size – about half a hundredweight each, and forty of them, all told. Now, as soon as we was fairly under way, Bassett and Wicks lighted a big Primus stove and set a large melting-pot on it; and into the pot they put one of the lead weights from the hold. Then Bassett brought out of the lazarette a fireclay mould like the one that the weights had been cast in. It was an open mould what you just poured the lead in; and when it had set, you turned it over and the weight dropped out with the top surface rough as it had set.

"While the lead was melting, me and Bassett and Wicks opened the case and took out the platinum, which was in thin sheets about a foot square. We cut the sheets up with tinman's snips into narrow strips what would go snugly into the mould. Then Bassett put a bit of cold lead into the mould for the strips of platinum to rest on, and then we laid the strips in the mould, fitting them in carefully so as to get as many in as possible. Then, when we had got them in and the lead in the pot was melted, Bassett takes a ladle, dips it into the pot and pours it into the mould. He had made the lead a bit extra hot, so that it should not be cooled by the cold platinum. Well, when we had filled up the mould and covered up the platinum, we had to wait while it was setting; and Bassett put another ballast-weight in the pot to melt. When the lead in the mould was set, we turned it out, and there was a ordinary-looking ballast weight what you wouldn't have known from any other ballast weight.

"We did the same with the rest of the platinum, and that just made up another weight. Then we marked the numbers on them with punches – all the ballast weights were numbered and laid in their regular order, 1 to 40. These two weights was numbered 22 and 25; and when we had marked them, we laid them down in their proper places in the hold. Then we cleaned up. The lead what was left over we chucked overboard, and the fireclay mould went after it. The case what the platinum had come in we broke up and shoved the pieces in the galley fire; so now there was no trace left of this little job, and we didn't mind if the police came on board and rummaged the ship. There wasn't nothing for them to find. So we sailed back to our berth and made fast; and there we stayed for five days to give them a chance to come on board and rummage if they wanted to. But they never came. Naturally. Because nothing had been found out. So, on the sixth day, we put to sea for the voyage home.

"But we didn't come straight home. We kept up the appearances of a cruising yacht. You won't want particulars of the voyage, but there is one little incident that I must mention. It was at Rotterdam, our last port of call, in the morning when we started for home. We had got the sails loosed and was just about to cast off, when a cove appeared on the quay and hailed Bassett, who was on deck giving orders. Bassett replied as if he had expected this bloke, and reached up and took the man's luggage – a small suitcase and a brown-paper parcel with a rug-strap fastened to it – and helped the covey down the ladder. Then we cast off and put out to sea; so we could see that this stranger had arranged with Bassett for a passage to England.

"Shortly after we had started, Bassett sends me to the fore peak for one of the empty cases what our provisions had been stowed in. I took it to the cabin, but I didn't know what it was wanted for until I saw the passenger stowing it in the locker what belonged to his berth. Later, I found the brown paper from the parcel and a big bit of oiled silk which seemed a bit damp and had a nasty smell; so I chucked it overboard. I don't know whether Bassett knew what was in that parcel, but none of us ever guessed.

"Now, when we was about abreast of the Swin Middle light-ship, we met a stumpy barge what was bound, as it turned out, from London to Colchester. Bassett hailed her, and, when we was near enough, he asked the skipper if he would take a passenger. The skipper wanted further particulars, so Wicks and Park went off to the barge in the boat, taking the passenger's case with them. Apparently it was all right, for Wicks waved his hand and Park started to row back to the yacht."

"Had Wicks or Bassett told you anything about this business?" the Superintendent asked.

"No. Not a word was said at the time; but Wicks told me all about it afterwards, and I may as well tell you now. It seems that the passenger – his name was Sanders – had got Bassett's permission to make an arrangement with Wicks to smuggle the case ashore and take it to Fenchurch Street Station and leave it in the cloak-room. He gave Wicks ten pounds for the job and a pound for the barge skipper; and a rare mug he must have been to pay Wicks in advance. Well, the skipper took Wicks with him up the Colne and put him ashore, after dark, somewhere between Rowhedge and Colchester; and Wicks took a walk inland with his case and picked up a motor-bus that took him into Colchester. He stayed there a day or two, having a bit of a beano, because he wasn't due to dump the case in the cloak-room until the following Monday, so that it shouldn't be waiting there too long. But on Saturday evening he took the train to London and went straight to the house of my brother-in-law, Bert Wallis, where I was in the habit of living."

"Why did he go there?" asked Miller.

"Ah!" said Bunter, "that's another story, and I may as well tell you that now. You must know that, after Wicks found out about the platinum, he got very discontented. He reckoned that the swag might be worth anything from ten to twenty thousand pounds; and he said we'd been done in the eye. Two hundred pounds apiece, he said, wasn't anything like a fair share, seeing that we'd taken an equal share of the risk. And he was very suspicious of Bassett. He doubted whether he was a perfectly honest man."

"What a horrible suspicion!" Miller exclaimed with a grin.

"Yes," agreed Bunter. "But I believe he was right. He suspected that Bassett meant to clear off with the whole of the swag and not pay us nothing. And so did I; so we arranged that I should keep an eye on Bassett and see that he didn't get away with it.

"Now, when we had done with the Customs at Southend – of course they didn't twig nothing – we ran up into Benfleet Creek and took up moorings. Then, on Saturday, Bassett said he was going to take the stuff up to a dealer what he knew of and wouldn't be back for a day or two. So, in the evening, I helped him to carry the case, with the two doctored weights in it, up to the station and saw him into a first-class carriage and shut him in. But I didn't go back to the yacht. I'd taken the precaution to get a ticket in advance, and given Park the tip that I mightn't be back that night; so, when I left Bassett, I went to the rear of the train and got in. I travelled up to town in that train, and I followed Bassett and saw him stow the case in the cloak-room. Then, when I had seen him out of the station, I nipped straight off home to Bert Wallis's place at Walworth.

"It happened that I got there only a few minutes after Wicks had turned up. I told him what had happened, and we talked over what we should do to keep our eyes on the case of platinum. But, at the moment, Wicks was all agog to know what was in Mr Sanders' case. I pointed out to him that it was no business of his, but he said if it was worth all the money and trouble that had been spent on it, there must be something of value inside, and he was going to see what that something was, and whether it was worth while to take it to the cloak-room at all.

"Well, I got him a screwdriver and he had the screws out in a twinkling and pulled up the lid. And then he fairly hollered with surprise and I was a bit took aback, myself. You know what was inside – a man's head, packed in some of our old duds. I tell you, Wicks slammed the lid down and ran the screws in faster than he took them out. Then I asks him what he was going to do about it. 'Do!' says he.

'I'm going to plant the damn thing in the cloak-room tomorrow morning and get clear of it; and I'll send the ticket on to Sanders at Benfleet Post Office as I promised. I've been paid, and I'm going to carry out my contract like a honest man.'

"But the sight of that man's head seemed to have given him something to think about, for he was mighty thoughtful for a while. Then, all of a sudden, something seemed to strike him, for he turns to me and asks: 'What sort of case did Bassett pack them two weights in?' 'Why?' I says, 'one of the provision cases; same sort as that head is packed in.' 'Then, by gum,' says he, 'we are going to steal a march on that dishonest blighter, Bassett, if we can manage it. Do you know what marks there were on that case?' Now, it happened that I did; for I had taken the precaution to make a copy of the label. I showed it to Wicks, and he got a card like the one I had seen on Bassett's case and wrote the name and address on it from my copy and tacked it on to Sanders' case.

"'And now,' says he, 'the question is how we are going to get that case here from the station. We might take a taxi, but that wouldn't be very safe. We don't want to leave no tracks.' Then I thought of Joe Wallis, Bert Wallis's brother, what had a shop a couple of doors off and kept a motor van for carting timber about."

"What is his trade?" Miller asked.

"He is a carpenter what does work for some small builders. He served his time as a undertaker, but he give that up. Said it wasn't cheerful enough. He didn't mind the coffins, but he couldn't stick the corpses. Well, the end of it was that Wicks persuaded Joe to take on the job. I don't know what story he told him. Of course, Joe didn't know what was in either of the cases, but he is a big, strong chap, and Wicks made it worth his while. Being Sunday, he put on a leather coat and a cap like a taxi-driver, for the sake of appearances.

"Well, Wicks got rid of Sanders' case all right and posted the ticket off to Benfleet; and then, in the afternoon, he set off to do the more ticklish job of swapping Sanders' case for Bassett's. But he brought it off all right and got the right case safely to Bert's crib. Being Sunday,

Bert wasn't doing nothing, so we had the run of his workshop to do our little job in."

"What is Bert's trade?" the Superintendent asked.

"He is a plumber," replied Bunter. "That's what he is."

"Oh!" said Miller, with a sly look. "Doesn't do anything in the pewter and plaster mould line, I suppose?"

"I said he was a plumber," Bunter replied, haughtily; "and, consequentially, he'd got a workshop with a big gas ring and some melting-pots; which was just what we wanted.

"Well, we opened Bassett's case and there, sure enough, was the two lead weights. And they seemed to be the right ones, by the punch marks on them – 22 and 25. So we took the biggest melting-pot, which was half full of lead, and, when we had tipped the lump of lead out on the floor, we put the pot on the ring and lighted up; and then we shoved one of the lead weights in it.

"'Now,' said Wicks, 'we are going to make our fortunes. But we shall have some difficulty in getting rid of this stuff. We shall have to go slow.' So he sat on a chair by the gas ring and watched the weight and made all sorts of plans for getting rid of the platinum. The weight was a long time before it showed any signs of melting; but at last it began to slip down the pot, and me and Wicks leaned over the pot and watched for the bits of platinum to stick out. But we couldn't see no sign of them. We watched the weight as it slipped down farther and farther until it had crumpled up and was all melted. But still we couldn't see nothing of the platinum. Then Wicks got a iron rod and raked about in the melted lead to see if he could feel the bits of platinum. But he couldn't. Then he got a ladle and tried to fish out the bits that he couldn't see; and, I tell you, he was fair sweating with anxiety, and so was I for that matter. For nothing came up in the ladle but melted lead.

"Then I suggested that we should ladle out the whole of the lead, a little at a time, into another pot, and I got three small empty pots and set them alongside the big one; and Wicks ladled out the lead from the big one into the little ones. But still we didn't come to the platinum. And at last we come to the bottom of the pot; and then we could see that there wasn't no platinum there.

"By this time Wicks was nearly blue with rage and disappointment, and I was pretty sick, myself. However, we emptied the last drop of lead out of the big pot and started to melt the other weight. But it was the same story with that one. We ladled the lead out into the small pots, and, by way of doing the thing thoroughly, took the big pot up by its handle and drained the very last drop of lead out of it into the small pots. And there wasn't a grain of platinum to be seen anywhere.

"My eye! You ought to have seen Wicks's face when he had done with the second weight and tried it right out. His language was something awful. And no wonder. For you see it wasn't no mistake. The numbers on the weights was all right. It was a fair do. Bassett had deliberately sold us a pup. He'd got a pair of the plain lead weights, hammered the numbers out, and punched fresh numbers on them. It was a dirty trick, but I suppose he must have suspected Wicks and got this plant ready for him. At any rate, Wicks saw red, and he swore he would do Bassett in. We'd got Bassett's address at Swanscombe, because we had got to go there for the money that was owing to us when the swag should have been disposed of; and, on the Tuesday, Wicks went off to see if Bassett was at home, and, if he was, to have a few words with him. And that was the last I ever saw of Wicks. When he didn't come home, I supposed he had made himself scarce on account of the hue and cry about the head in the case. Now I know that he must have tried to do Bassett in, and Bassett must have got his whack in first. And that's all I know about the business."

"Good," said Miller. "You've made a very straightforward statement, and I can tell you that you have not done yourself any harm and what you have told us will probably be quite helpful to us. I'll write it out presently from my notes and you can read it, and, if you are satisfied with it, I'll get you to sign it. In the meantime, I want to ask you one or two questions. First of all, about this man Sanders; can you give us any description of him?"

"He was a tall man," replied Bunter; "a good six foot if he had stood up straight – which he didn't, having a stoop at the shoulders. I should put his age at about fifty. He had dark hair and beard and he wore spectacles."

"What kind of spectacles?" Thorndyke asked.

"I dunno," replied Bunter. "Spectacles is spectacles. I ain't a optician."

"Some spectacles are large," said Thorndyke, "and some are small. Some are round and some are oval, and some have a line across as if they had been cracked. Would his fit any of those descriptions?"

"Why, yes, now you come to mention it. They was big, round spectacles with a sort of crack across them. But it couldn't have been a crack because it was the same in both eyes. I'd forgotten them until you spoke."

I noticed that Miller had cast a quick look at Thorndyke and was now eagerly writing down the description. Evidently, he "smelt a fox", and so did I. For, though Thorndyke had not really put a "leading question", he had mentioned a very uncommon kind of spectacles – the old-fashioned type of bi-focal, which is hardly ever made now, having been superseded by the cemented or ground lunette. I had no doubt, nor, I think, had Miller, that he was describing a particular pair of spectacles; and this suspicion was strengthened by his next questions.

"Did you notice anything peculiar in his voice or manner of speaking?"

"Nothing extraordinary," replied Bunter. "He'd got a squeaky voice, and there's no denying it. And he didn't speak quite proper English, like you and me. Seemed to speak a bit like a Dutchman."

I surmised that Mr Bunter used the word "Dutchman" in a nautical sense, meaning any sort of foreigner who was not a "Dago"; and so, apparently, Thorndyke interpreted it, for he said:

"He spoke with a foreign accent? Was it a strong accent, or only slight?"

"Oh, it was nothing to notice. You'd hardly have taken him for a foreigner."

"Did you notice his nose?"

"You couldn't help noticing it. Lord! It was some boko. Reminded me of a parrot. And it had got a pretty strong list to starboard."

"You would say that he had a large, curved, or hook nose, which was bent towards the right. Is that so?"

"That's what I said."

"Then, Superintendent," said Thorndyke, "I think we have a working description of Mr Sanders. Shall we take a note of Mr Bert Wallis' address?"

"I don't see what you want with that," Bunter objected. "He didn't have nothing to do with the job. We used his workshop, but he didn't know what we wanted it for."

"We realise that," said Thorndyke, "and we have nothing whatever against him. But he may be able to give us some information on some other matters. By the way, speaking of that lead that you ladled out of the pot; what did you do with it?"

"Nothing. It wasn't no good to us. We just left it in the pots for Bert, in case he had any use for it."

"And Bert's address is?"

"Sixty-four Little Bolter Street, Walworth. But don't you go worrying him. He don't know nothing what he didn't ought to."

"You needn't be afraid of our giving him any trouble," said Miller. "We may not have to call on him at all, but, in any case, it will only be a matter of a few questions which he won't mind answering. And now, perhaps you'd like another fag to smoke while I am writing up your statement."

Mr Bunter accepted the "fag" readily, and even hinted that the making of statements was dry work; on which Miller directed the sergeant to provide him with a further half-pint. Meanwhile, Thorndyke and I, having no concern with the formalities of the statement, went forth to stretch our legs and take a more detailed survey of the water-side. When we returned, the statement had been transcribed and duly signed by Mr Frederick Bunter. And this brought to an end a very satisfactory day's work.

# CHAPTER SEVENTEEN

## The Unconscious Receivers

During the return journey, the Superintendent showed a natural disposition to discuss the bearings of what we had learned from Bunter and reckon up his gains in the matter of evidence.

"It was a pleasant surprise to me," said he, "to hear Bunter let himself go in the way he did. I was afraid, from what the sergeant said, that we shouldn't get much out of him."

"Yes," said I, "he was rather unexpectedly expansive. I think what started him was your insistence that Wicks had got possession of the platinum, when he knew, as he supposed, that Bassett had planted the wrong weights. He was mightily staggered when you told him that the swag had been recovered. Still, we've a good deal more to learn yet before we shall know exactly what did happen."

"That is true," agreed Miller. "We've learned a lot from Bunter, but there is a lot more that we don't know, and that Bunter doesn't know. The question is, How much do we know? What do you say, Doctor? I should like to hear you sum up what we have gained by this statement, and tell us exactly how you think we stand."

"My feeling," said Thorndyke, "is that we have advanced our knowledge considerably. We have shortened the gap between the two parts of the problem which are known to us. When we came down, our knowledge of the platinum ceased with its disappearance from the cloak-room and began again with its reappearance in the coffin. That was a big gap. But, as I have said, that gap is now to a great extent filled up. The problem that remains is to trace those lumps of alloy from Bert Wallis' workshop to the false coffin and I don't think that we shall have much difficulty in doing it. But, before we proceed to count up our gains, we had better consider what it is that we want to know.

"Now, I remind you that there are two distinct problems, which we had better keep quite separate: the platinum robbery and the substituted coffin. Bunter's statement bears on both, but we must not get them confused. Let us take the robbery first. My impression is that we now know all that we are likely to know about it. We all have probably formed certain suspicions; but suspicions are of no use unless there is some prospect of confirming them. And I do not think that there is. But, after all, is there any object in pursuing the matter? The two visible principals in the robbery are dead. As to poor Bunter, he was a mere spectator. He never knew any of the details."

"He was, at least, an accessory after the fact," said Miller.

"True. But is he worth powder and shot? Remember, this robbery was committed outside British jurisdiction. It will be an extradition case, unless you charge Bunter with complicity in the theft from the cloak-room. It will be for the Latvian police to make the first move, which they probably will not, as the property has been recovered and the principal offenders are dead."

Miller reluctantly admitted the cogency of this argument.

"Still," he insisted, "there is more in it than that. Didn't it strike you that certain parts of Bunter's statement seemed to suggest the possibility that the robbery had been planned and engineered by our friend, Gimbler?"

"It did," Thorndyke admitted. "That was what I meant when I spoke of certain suspicions that we have formed. It would be possible, from Bunter's statement, to build up quite a plausible argument to prove that Gimbler was probably the moving spirit in that robbery. But it would be a mere academic exercise; very entertaining, but quite unprofitable, since the principals are dead and Bunter knows less than we do. There are no means by which our suspicions could be put to the proof or our knowledge enlarged."

"I expect you are right," Miller agreed, gloomily; "but I should like to hear the argument, all the same."

"It will be a waste of time," said Thorndyke.

"However, our time is not very valuable just now, and there will be no harm in assembling the relevant facts. Let us take them in order.

"1. Bunter had been defended on a criminal charge by Gimbler.

"2. Bunter was introduced to Bassett by 'a gentleman', who must have, therefore, known them both.

"3. A gentleman – apparently the same gentleman – introduced Wicks to Bassett, and, therefore, knew Wicks.

"4. The said gentleman – assuming him to be the same in both cases – was, therefore, acquainted with three persons who are known to us as having been engaged in crime.

"5. One of these three persons – Bunter – was acquainted with Gimbler.

"6. The unknown 'gentleman', who was acquainted with three criminals, took an active and helpful part in the robbery, inasmuch as he introduced Bassett to persons who would be likely to agree to assist in the carrying out of a criminal enterprise.

"Those are the principal facts; and now as to their application. The appearance of this mysterious 'gentleman', acquainted with criminals, and apparently acting at least as an accessory, strongly suggests someone in the background directing, and possibly planning, this robbery. This suggestion is reinforced by the fact that someone connected with the robbery must have had a substantial amount of capital available. The yacht, even if bought quite cheap, must have cost not less than a hundred pounds; and then there were the considerable out-goings in respect of the provisioning and fitting-out for the cruise, and the payments of wages which seem to have been made, apart from the final 'bonus', which might have been paid out of the proceeds of the robbery. Of course, Bassett may have had the money; but it is not probable. Persons who get their livelihood by crime are not usually capitalists. There is a strong suggestion that the 'gentleman' was behind the robbery in a financial sense as well as furnishing the brains and management. This is all reasonable inference – though of no evidential value. But when we try to give a name to this mysterious 'gentleman', our inferences become highly speculative. However, let us speculate. Let us propose the hypothesis that the hidden hand behind this robbery was the hand of Mr Horatio Gimbler. What is there to support that hypothesis?

"First, there is the coffin. It contained the proceeds of this robbery. Gimbler was not aware of the fact; but the circumstance that it was there establishes the fact of some sort of contact between Gimbler and the persons who were concerned in the robbery. The persons whom he dealt with in the preparation of the coffin had dealings with the persons who carried out the robbery."

"There isn't much in that," I objected. "It might have been pure chance."

"So it might," he agreed, "and there is very little in it, as you say. But circumstantial evidence is made up of little things. I merely assert that some sort of connection is established.

"The next point is that, of the three criminals engaged in this robbery, the only one known to us – Bunter – was acquainted with Gimbler. But Bunter was also acquainted with the unknown gentleman. There isn't much in that, taken alone; but it points in the same direction as the other facts.

"And now let us consider how Gimbler fits the character of the hypothetical person who may have directed and financed the robbery.

"First, this hypothetical person must have had a somewhat extensive acquaintance with members of the criminal class in order to be able to select suitable persons to carry out this rather peculiar and specialised piece of work. Criminals with a practical knowledge of seamanship cannot be very common. But Gimbler has a very extensive acquaintance with the criminal class.

"The next point is that this hypothetical person must have had a modest amount of capital at his disposal, say two or three hundred pounds. We do not know much of Gimbler's circumstances, but it would be very remarkable if he were not able to produce that amount to finance a scheme which was likely to yield a profit of thousands. But, as there must be innumerable persons in the same financial position, this agreement has no significance. It is merely an agreement.

"Finally, our hypothetical person must have combined considerable ingenuity with extreme dishonesty. Here there is undoubted agreement; but, unfortunately, Gimbler is in this respect far from unique.

"That is the argument; and, as you see, though it is enough to allow of our entertaining a suspicion of Gimbler, it is not enough to establish the most flimsy prima facie case. If Gimbler was the hidden director of this crime, he was extremely well hidden, and I think he will remain hidden. Probably, Bassett was the only person who knew the whole of the facts."

"Yes," Miller agreed, glumly, "I'm afraid you are right. Unless the Latvian police raise an outcry, it will probably be best to let the matter drop. After all, the robbery failed and we have got the stuff back. Still, I feel in my bones that Gimbler engineered the job, and I should have liked to lay my hands on him. But, as you say, he kept out of sight and is out of sight still. He always does keep out of sight, damn him!"

"Not always," said Thorndyke. "You are forgetting the other case – the counterfeit coffin. That is an entirely different matter. There he is already in full view. A manifest fraud has been committed, and there are only two persons who could possibly be suspected of having committed it – Gimbler and Pippet. Actually, I suppose, no one suspects Pippet. But he is the claimant in whose interest – ostensibly – the fraud was perpetrated, and it is certain that Gimbler will try to put it on him. If it were not for Pippet, you could arrest Gimbler tomorrow and be confident of a conviction. As it is, direct evidence against Gimbler is a necessity, and it is for you, Miller, to secure that evidence. I think you will not have much difficulty, with the facts now in our possession."

"No," said Miller, "we seem to have got a pretty good lead from Bunter; but, all the same, I should like to hear your views on the evidence that we have."

"Well," said Thorndyke, "let us approach the problem from both ends. At one end we have four lumps of metal, one lead and three alloy, in the workshop of a plumber, Bert Wallis. At the other we have the same four lumps of metal in a coffin; and the problem is to bridge the interval between the two appearances.

"Now, the fact that those four lumps appeared together in the coffin is evidence that the interval was quite short. There were no intermediate wanderings during which they might have become separated. We may be sure that the passage from the workshop to the coffin was pretty direct; in effect, we may assume that the man who prepared the coffin got his lead from Bert Wallis. The next inference is very obvious, though it may be erroneous. But when we consider that a couple of doors from Bert Wallis' premises were those of a man who had served his time as an undertaker, and who was, therefore, capable of making a perfectly correct and workmanlike coffin; who had a motor van and who was Bert Wallis' brother; it is impossible to ignore the probability that the coffin was made by Joe Wallis. He had all the means of carrying out the substitution – you will remember that there was a cart-shed adjoining the wall of the burial-ground, in which a van could be conveniently hidden, and from which the coffin could be easily passed over the wall – and, if he had done the job, he would presumably have got his lead from his brother, whose premises were close by. The only weak place in the argument is that we are accusing a man, who may be a perfectly honest and reputable tradesman, of being concerned in a crime."

"I don't think you need worry yourself about that," said Miller. "You heard what I said to Bunter on the subject of pewter and plaster moulds. He knew what I meant. There had been some suspicion that Mr Bert Wallis occasionally turned his hand to the manufacture of counterfeit coin. It was never brought home to him; but the fact that Bunter – who lives with him when he is at home – had been charged with uttering counterfeit money (which I had not heard of before) gives colour to the suspicion. And Bunter, himself, as we know, is a decidedly shady customer. I don't think we need have any scruples of delicacy in giving Mr Joseph Wallis a little attention. I'll call and have a friendly talk with him."

"I shouldn't do that," said Thorndyke; "at least, not in the first place. It would be much better to make the initial attack on Bert. There, you have something definite to go on. You know that the metal was in his workshop. And, if he has not heard of the facts disclosed in the Probate Court, or has not connected them with the metal that he had, you will have a good opening for an inquiry as to what has become of certain valuable property which is known to have been in his possession. When he learns what the value of that metal was, I fancy you may look for an explosion which may give you the leading facts before he has realised the position. Besides, there is the possibility that he gave away or sold the metal without any knowledge of its origin."

"So there is," agreed Miller, leaning back to laugh with more comfort, "in fact, it is quite probable. My eye! What a lark it will be! I shall go straight on from Fenchurch Street. Couldn't I persuade you to come with me and do some of the talking?"

Thorndyke required no persuading, nor did I, for the interview promised to be highly entertaining. Accordingly, the arrangement was made and the plan of campaign settled; and, on our arrival at the terminus, after a brief halt at the buffet for a sandwich and a glass of beer, we made our way to the tube railway, by which we were conveyed to the "Elephant and Castle".

"By the way," said I, as Miller struck out towards the Walworth Road, "I suppose you have got the address?"

"Yes," was the reply, "I got it from Bunter when he signed the statement. It's in Little Bolter Street. I made a note of the number."

He brought out his note-book and glanced at it as we threaded our way through the multitude that thronged the pavement. Presently he turned to the left down a side street and walked on with his eyes on the numbers of the houses.

"This is the show," he said, at length, halting before a seedy-looking plumber's shop, the fascia of which bore the inscription, 'A Wallis.' "Shop looks as if it was open."

It was, technically, although the door was closed; but it yielded to a push, announcing the fact by the jangling of a bell, which brought a man out of the parlour at the back. Apparently, we had disturbed him at a meal, for his jaws were working as he came out, and he looked at us inquiringly without speaking. Perhaps "inquiringly" hardly expresses the kind of look that he gave us. It was a mere coincidence, but it happened that we were, all three, over six feet in height, and Miller, at least, looked a good deal like what he was.

The Superintendent opened the ball. "You are Mr Bert Wallis, I think?"

Mr Wallis nodded, chewing frantically. Finally, he bolted his mouthful and replied: "Yes, that's who I am. What about it?"

"My friend here, Dr Thorndyke, who is a lawyer, wants to make a few inquiries of you."

Mr Wallis turned to Thorndyke but made no comment, having, apparently, some slight arrears to dispose of in the matter of chewing.

"My inquiries," said Thorndyke, "have reference to certain valuable property which came into your possession some time ago."

"Valuable property in my possession," said Wallis. "It's the first I have heard of it. What property are you talking about?"

"It is a quantity of metal," replied Thorndyke. "You had it from two men named Wicks and Bunter."

Wallis stared at Thorndyke for a few seconds; and, gradually, the look of apprehension faded from his countenance and gave place to one of amusement.

His mouth extended laterally until it exhibited an undeniable grin.

"I know what you are talking about, now," he chuckled; "but you've got hold of the wrong end of the stick altogether. I'll tell you how it happened. Them two silly fools, Wicks and Bunter, thought they had got hold of some valuable stuff. I don't know what they thought it was, but they asked me to let them melt it down in my workshop. I didn't much like the idea of it, because I didn't know what stuff it was or how they had got it; but, as Bunter is my wife's brother and I knew Wicks, I didn't quite like to refuse. So I let them have the run of my workshop on a Sunday night when I was out, and they did the job. They melted down this here valuable stuff; and what do you suppose it turned out to be, after all?"

Thorndyke shook his head and waited for the answer.

"It was *lead*!" Wallis exclaimed with a triumphant giggle. "Just think of it! These two silly asses had put theirselves to no end of trouble and expense to get hold of this stuff – I don't know how they did get hold of it – and when they come to melt it down, it was just lead, worth about twopence a pound! But, my aunt! Wasn't they blooming sick! You ought to have heard the language that Wicks used!"

The recollection of this anticlimax amused him so much that he laughed aloud and had perforce to wipe his eyes with a handkerchief which might once have been clean.

"And what became of this lead?" asked Thorndyke. "Did they take it away with them?"

"No," replied Wallis. "It wasn't no good to them. They just left it in the pots."

"And is it in your workshop still?" asked Thorndyke.

"No, it ain't. I sold it to a builder for five bob, which paid for the gas that they had used and left a bit over."

"Do you know what the builder wanted it for?"

"Said he wanted some lead for to fix some iron railings in their sockets."

"Did he take the whole of it?"

"Yes; he took the whole boiling of it, and a small roll of sheet-lead as well. But the sheet wasn't included in the five bob."

"Do you mind telling us the name of this builder?" Thorndyke asked.

Wallis looked rather hard at Thorndyke, and the slightly apprehensive expression reappeared on his face.

"I don't see as his name is neither here nor there," said he. "What's all the fuss about? You was speaking of valuable property. Lead ain't valuable property."

"For legal reasons," said Thorndyke, "I wish to trace that lead and see where it went to. And there is no reason for you to be secret about it. The transaction between you and the builder was a perfectly lawful transaction; but I should like to ascertain from the builder exactly what he did with the lead."

The plumber was evidently still a little uneasy, but the question was so simple and straightforward that he could hardly refuse to answer.

"Well," he replied, grudgingly, "if you must know, the builder what I sold the lead to was my brother, Joe Wallis, what lives a couple of doors farther up the street."

"Thank you," said Thorndyke. Then, turning to Miller, he said: "That is all I wanted to know. Probably Mr Joe Wallis will be able to help us a stage further. Is there anything that you want to ask?"

"No," replied Miller; "that seems to be all plain sailing. I don't think we need trouble Mr Wallis any further."

With this, Thorndyke thanked the plumber for the assistance that he had given and we took our departure.

As soon as we were outside, the Superintendent broke out into low-voiced self-congratulations – low-voiced by reason of the fact that Mr Wallis had taken his post at the shop door to observe our further movements.

"It was just as well," said Miller, "that you were able to get the information without letting the cat out of the bag. It has saved a lot of chin-wagging. But I expect we shan't have such an easy job with our friend Joseph. Bert had nothing to conceal; but Joseph must have been in the swim to some extent. This is his house."

The premises, which bore the superscription, "J Wallis, Builder and Decorator," were divided into two parts, a carpenter's shop and an office. We entered the latter, and, as it was at the moment unoccupied, the Superintendent thumped on the counter with his stick; which brought out from some inner lair a very large youth of about eighteen, who saluted us with an amiable grin.

"Dad in?" inquired Miller, making a chance shot; which was justified by the result, as the youth replied:

"Yes. What's it about?"

"This gentleman, Dr Thorndyke, wants to see him on important legal business," Miller replied; whereupon the youth grinned again and retired. In about a minute he returned and requested us to "walk this way", indicating the direction by walking in advance. We followed him across a hall and up a flight of stairs to a door, which he opened, and, having seen us enter, once more departed.

The room was quite an interesting survival – a typical example of a Victorian tradesman's drawing-room, with the typical close, musty smell. As we entered, I noticed that Thorndyke cast his eyes down and then took a quick glance at the window. But there was no time for detailed observation, for we were almost immediately followed by a man whom I judged from his stature and a certain family resemblance to be "Dad". But the resemblance did not extend to the amiable grin. On the contrary, the newcomer viewed us with an expression compounded of a sort of foxy curiosity and a perceptible tinge of hostility.

"Which of you is Dr Thorndyke?" he inquired. My colleague introduced himself, and the inevitable question followed.

"And who are these other two gentlemen?"

"This," replied Miller, indicating me, "is Dr Jervis, also a lawyer; and" – here he produced a professional card and pushed it across an "occasional table" – "that's who I am."

Mr Wallis studied the card for a few moments, and the hostility of his expression became more pronounced. Nevertheless, he said with gruff civility: "Well, you may as well sit down," and gave us a lead by sitting down, himself, in an arm-chair.

"Now," said he, "what's this important legal business?"

"It is concerned," said Thorndyke, "with certain property which came into your hands and which you had from your brother, Albert Wallis."

"Property what I had from my brother Albert Wallis!" our friend repeated in obviously genuine surprise. "I haven't had no property from him. What do you mean?"

"I am referring to certain pieces of metal which you bought from him about three months ago."

Mr Joseph continued to stare at Thorndyke for some seconds.

"Pieces of metal!" he repeated, at length. "I haven't bought no pieces of metal from him. You've made a mistake."

"The metal that I am referring to," said Thorndyke, "consisted of a roll of sheet-lead and some remainders from melting-pots."

"Gawd!" exclaimed Joseph, contemptuously, "you don't call that property, do you? I gave him five bob for the lot, and that was more than it was worth."

"So I understood," said Thorndyke. "But we have reasons for wishing to trace that metal. We have managed to trace it to you, and we should be greatly obliged if you would tell us what has become of it, supposing it not to be still in your possession."

At this persistence on Thorndyke's part, the hostility expressed in Joseph's countenance became tinged with unmistakable uneasiness. Nevertheless, he answered truculently enough:

"I don't see what business it is of yours what I do with the material that I buy. But, if you must know, I used that sheet-lead for making a damp-course, and the other stuff for fixing some iron railings in a stone kerb."

"Then," said Miller, "somebody has got some pretty valuable iron railings."

Wallis looked at him inquiringly, and from him to Thorndyke.

"Perhaps," said the latter, "I had better explain. Some time ago, two men, one of whom was named Wicks, stole a case containing a quantity of platinum from the cloak-room at Fenchurch Street. They took it to the house of your brother Albert, who, not knowing what it was, or anything about it, allowed them to melt it down in his workshop. But, when they had melted it down, they did not recognise it. They thought it was lead, and that they had taken the wrong case. So they left the lumps in the melting-pots for your brother to do what he pleased with. But he, also, did not recognise the metal. He, also, thought that it was lead; and he sold the whole consignment to you for five shillings. And I take it that you, like the others, mistook it for lead."

Mr Wallis had suddenly become attentive and interested.

"Certainly, I took it for lead," said he. "And you say it was platinum. That's rather expensive stuff, isn't it?"

"The little lot," said Miller, "that you bought for five shillings has been valued at just under eighteen thousand pounds."

That "knocked him", as they say in the Old Kent Road. For some seconds he sat speechless, clutching the arms of his chair and staring at Miller as if he had been some dreadful apparition.

"Eighteen thousand pounds!" he exclaimed, at length, in something approaching a screech. "Eighteen − thousand − pounds! And to think − "

"Yes," said Miller, "to think of those iron railings. We shall have to see that you don't go rooting them up."

Mr Wallis made no reply. As with the dying gladiator, "his thoughts were far away," and I had little doubt whither they had strayed. I do not profess to be a thought-reader; but the expression on Joseph's face conveyed clearly to me that he had, in that moment, decided, as soon as the night fell, to make a bee-line for Josiah Pippet's vault. His reverie was interrupted by Thorndyke.

"So, Mr Wallis," said he, "you will understand our natural anxiety to find out where this metal went to."

"But I've told you," said Wallis, rousing himself from dreams of sudden opulence, "so far as I can recollect, that I used the stuff to plant some iron railings."

As we seemed to have got into a blind alley, the Superintendent abruptly changed his tone.

"Never mind about those iron railings," he said, sharply. "We want to know what you did with that stuff. Are you going to tell us?"

"I have told you," Wallis replied doggedly. "You can't expect me to remember what I did with every bit of lead that I bought."

"Very well," said Miller, "then perhaps it might help your memory if we were to do a bit of supposing. What do you say?"

"You can if you like," Joseph replied, sulkily, so long as you don't ask me to help you."

"Now, Wallis," said Miller, "you've got to bear this in mind. Those two fools didn't know this stuff when they had got it in their hands, and neither did you or Bert. But there were other people who knew what was in that case. Bassett, the man who murdered Wicks, knew, because he put the stuff in the case. And there was another man, a very artful gentleman, who kept out of sight but who knew all about it. We mustn't mention names, so we will just call him Mr Rumbler, because he rumbled what had happened.

"Now, supposing this Mr Rumbler, knowing where the stuff had been left by those two gabeys, had a bright idea for getting hold of it without showing his hand. Supposing he went to a certain undertaker whose place was close to Bert's and pitched him a yarn about wanting a dummy coffin weighted with lead. Supposing he employed him to make that coffin, knowing that he would be certain to get his lead from Bert, and plant it in a nice convenient vault in a disused burial-ground – say, somewhere out Stratford way – where he could get at it easily with a big skeleton key and a tommy to turn it with. How's that? Mind you, I am only supposing."

As Miller recited his fable, a cloud fell on Mr Wallis' countenance. The dream of sudden opulence was dissipated. The resurrection job was obviously "off". But, glum as the expression of Joseph's face became, the effect produced was not quite the one on which Miller had based his calculations.

"If you know where the coffin is," was the natural comment, "why don't you go and open it and take the stuff out?"

"Because," Miller replied, impressively, "the stuff isn't there. Somebody has had the coffin open and taken it out."

Even this did not answer. Wallis looked sulky enough, but he had not gorged the bait.

"I don't believe there is any coffin," said he.

"You've just invented it to try to get me to say something."

I detected an expression of grim amusement on Thorndyke's face. Perhaps he was contrasting – as I was – Miller's present proceedings with the lofty standard of veracity among police officers that he had presented to Bunter. But I was also aware of some signs of impatience. As a matter of fact, all these artful probings on Miller's part were getting us nowhere. Moreover, we had really ascertained nearly all that we wanted to know.

"Perhaps," said Thorndyke, "as I am not a police officer, I may venture to be a little more explicit with Mr Wallis. We are not interested in the present whereabouts of this platinum. We know where it is; but we want to know exactly how it got there. As to the coffin, we have evidence that it was made by you, Mr Wallis, and planted by you in the vault. But this coffin was made to some person's order, and we want to know with certainty who that person is. At present, our information is to the effect that it was made to the order of a Mr Gimbler, a solicitor who resides in the neighbourhood of Kennington. But Mr Gimbler has managed to keep, to some extent, out of sight and put the whole responsibility on you. Even the dust that was found in the vault was your dust. It came from this very room."

At this latter statement, Wallis started visibly, and so did Miller.

"Yes, by Jove!" the latter exclaimed, after a glance at the floor and another at the window, "here is the identical carpet that you described in court, and there are the blue cotton curtains."

"So you see, Mr Wallis," Thorndyke continued, "you have nothing to conceal respecting the coffin. The facts are known to us. The question is, Are you prepared to tell us the name of the person to whose order this coffin was made?"

"If you know his name," was the reply, "you don't want me to tell you."

"Your evidence," said Thorndyke, "would save us a good deal of trouble, and perhaps it might save you some trouble, too. Are you prepared to tell us who this person was?"

"No," was the dogged reply. "I'm not going to tell you nothing. The least said the soonest mended. I don't know nothing about any coffin, and I don't believe there ever was any coffin."

At this reply Miller's face hardened, and I think he was about to pursue the matter further; but Thorndyke calmly and civilly brought the interview to a close.

"Well, Mr Wallis," said he, "you must do as you think best. I feel that you would have been wiser to have been more open with us; but we cannot compel you to give us information which you choose to withhold."

With this, he rose, and Miller reluctantly followed suit, looking distinctly sulky. But nothing further was said until, shepherded by our host, we had descended to the office and had been thence launched into the street. Then Miller made his protest.

"I think, Doctor," said he, "that it is a pity you didn't let me play him a little longer. I believe he would have let on if we had kept rubbing into him that he had been used as a cat's-paw by Gimbler to get hold of that platinum."

"I don't think he would," said Thorndyke. "He is an obstinate man, and he evidently doesn't like the idea of turning upon his employer; and we can hardly blame him for that. But, after all, Miller, what would have been the use of going on with him? We have got a complete train of evidence. We have got Bunter's written and signed statement that he left the platinum in Bert Wallis' workshop. We have got Bert Wallis' statement, made before witnesses, that he sold the stuff to his brother Joe Wallis. We have got Joe Wallis' statement, made before witnesses, that he bought the stuff from Bert. We know that Joe is a coffin-maker, and that the stuff was found in a coffin, together with certain dust which came from a room which was identical in character with Joe Wallis' drawing-room. The agreement is complete, even without the dust."

"So it is," Miller agreed; "but it proves the wrong thing. We can fix this job on Joseph all right. But it isn't Joseph that we want. He is only the jackal; but we want the lion – Gimbler. And if Joseph won't talk, we've got no direct evidence against Gimbler."

Thorndyke shook his head. "You are magnifying the difficulties, Miller," said he. "I don't know what you, or the Public Prosecutor, may propose to do; but I can tell you what I am going to do, if you don't. I am going to lay a sworn information charging Gimbler with having conspired with Joseph Wallis to commit certain fraudulent acts, including the manufacture of false evidence, calculated and intended to defeat the ends of justice. We have enough evidence to convict him without any assistance from Wallis; but I think you will find that Joseph, when he discovers that he is involved in a fraud of which he knew nothing, will be far from willing to share the burden of that fraud with Gimbler. I think you can take it that Joseph will tell all that he knows (and perhaps a little more) when we begin to turn the screw. At any rate, I am quite satisfied with my case against Gimbler."

"Well, Doctor," said Miller in a less gloomy tone, "if you see your way to a conviction, I have nothing more to say. It's all I want."

Here the subject dropped; and the effect of the sandwiches having by this time worn off, we agreed with one accord to seek some reputable place of entertainment to make up the arrears in the matter of nourishment. As those arrears were somewhat considerable, the settling of them occupied our whole attention for a time; and it was not until our cravings had been satisfied and the stage of coffee and pipes had been reached that Miller suddenly raised a question which I had been expecting, and which I had secretly decided to raise, myself, at the first opportunity.

"By the way, Doctor," said he, "what about that head in the box? All these alarums and excursions in chase of that blooming platinum had driven it out of my head. But, now that we have done with the metal, at least for the present, supposing we have a word about the box. From the questions that you put to Bunter, it is clear to me that you have given the matter more attention than I had supposed; and it is obvious that you know something. I wonder how much you know."

"Not very much," replied Thorndyke; "but I shall probably know more when I have made a few inquiries. You are so far right that I have given the affair some attention, though not a great deal. But when I heard of the discovery in the cloak-room, and afterwards read the account of the inquest, I formed certain opinions – quite speculatively, of course, – as to what the incident probably meant; and I even formed a still more speculative opinion as to the identity of one, at least, of the persons who might be concerned in the affair. Bunter's account of the passenger with the parcel seemed to agree with my hypothesis, and his answers to my questions seemed to support my identification of the person. That is all. Of actual, definite knowledge I have none."

"And your opinions," said Miller, a trifle sourly, "I suppose you are going to keep to yourself?"

"For the present, I propose to," Thorndyke replied, suavely. "You can see, from what Bunter said, that the affair is of no importance to you. If a crime has been committed, it has not been committed within your jurisdiction. But leave the matter in my hands for a little longer. I believe that I shall be able to elucidate it; and you know that you can depend on me to keep nothing from you that ought, as a matter of public policy, to be communicated to you."

"Yes, I know that," Miller admitted, grudgingly, "and I see that the case is not what we supposed it to be. Very well, Doctor. Have it your own way, but let us have the information as soon as it is available."

Thorndyke made the required promise; and, if the Superintendent was not as satisfied as he professed to be, it was only because, like me, he was devoured with curiosity as to what the solution of the mystery might be.

# CHAPTER EIGHTEEN

## The End of the Case and Other Matters

The proceedings in the Probate Court at the third hearing of the Winsborough Peerage case were brief but somewhat dramatic. As soon as the judge had taken his seat, Mr McGonnell rose and addressed him to the following effect:

"I have, this morning, my lord, to bring to your lordship's notice certain facts which would seem to make it unnecessary to proceed with the case which has been before the court. That case was an application by Mr Christopher Pippet for permission to presume the death of Percy Engleheart, sixth Earl of Winsborough. Now, in the interval since the last hearing, information has reached the Earl's representatives that the said Earl Percy died about three years ago."

"You say 'about' three years ago," said the judge.

"The exact date, my lord, has not been ascertained, and is not, apparently, ascertainable, but it is believed that the Earl's death took place some time in March, 1918. The uncertainty, however, relates only to the time when the death occurred; of the fact that it did occur there appears to be no doubt at all. I understand that the body has been recovered and identified and is being sent to England. These facts were communicated to me by Mr Brodribb; and perhaps the Earl's representatives might more properly inform your lordship as to the exact circumstances in which the Earl's death occurred."

Here McGonnell sat down and Anstey took up the tale.

"The tidings of the Earl's death, my lord, were conveyed to us in a letter written by a certain Major Pitt at Pará and dated the 13th of last October. The facts set forth in that letter were briefly these:

"In the latter part of 1917 and the beginning of 1918, Major Pitt and the Earl were travelling together in the neighbourhood of the River Amazons, shooting, collecting and exploring. About the middle of January, 1918, the Earl announced his intention to explore the tract of country inhabited by the Munderucu Indians; and, as Major Pitt had planned a journey along the main stream of the Amazons, they separated and went their respective ways. That was the last time that Major Pitt saw the Earl alive, and for three years he had no knowledge of the Earl's whereabouts or what he was doing. The Major, himself, made a long journey and was several times laid up for long periods with severe attacks of fever. It was not until the spring of the present year that he, at last, got tidings as to what had befallen his friend. Then, taking the Munderucu country on his way back to the coast, he learned from some natives that a white man had come to the country some three years previously and had died from fever soon after his arrival, which would be about March, 1918.

"On this, Major Pitt made more particular inquiries, the result of which was to leave no doubt that the man who had died could be none other than the Earl Percy. However, the Major, realising the importance of accurate information, not only assembled the dead man's effects – a considerable part of which he was able to recover, and which he was, of course, able to identify – but he went so far as to cause the body to be disinterred. Naturally, it was, in the ordinary sense, unrecognisable; but by the stature and by certain characters, particularly the teeth, some of which had been filled with gold, he was able to identify it with certainty as the body of Earl Percy.

"But, to make assurance doubly sure, he commissioned the natives – who have great skill in preserving bodies – to preserve this corpse, in so far as there was anything to preserve, so that it could be sent to England for further examination if such examination should seem necessary or expedient. But the Major's description of the body, the clothing, the weapons, scientific instruments and other effects, together with the natives' description of the man, the time of his arrival, and all the other circumstances, leave no doubt whatever that this man was really the Earl Percy."

"In that case," said the judge, "if the fact of the Earl's death is to be accepted as proved, the application for permission to presume death necessarily lapses, automatically. And the applicant's claim to be the heir presumptive also lapses. He will now claim to be the heir; and that claim will have to be preferred in another place."

"I understand, my lord," said McGonnell, "that it is not proposed to proceed with the claim. That is what I am informed by Mr Pippet."

The judge glanced at the vacant solicitors' table and then asked:

"Was that decision reached on the advice of his solicitor?"

"No, my lord. Mr Gimbler is not in court, and, I believe, is absent from his residence. I understand that he has been unexpectedly called away from home."

The judge received this piece of information with an inscrutable face.

"It is not for me to express an opinion," he remarked, "as to whether Mr Pippet is well or ill advised to abandon his claim; but I may point out that the crucial question is still in suspense. According to the evidence which we have heard, the coffin which was examined was not the coffin of Josiah Pippet, and, consequently, the question whether the funeral was a real or a sham funeral has not been settled. It is unfortunate that that important issue should have been confused by what look like highly irregular proceedings; concerning which I may say that they will call for further investigation and that I shall consider it my duty to hand the papers in this case to the Director of Public Prosecutions."

This rather ominous observation brought the proceedings to an end; and, as we were no longer litigants, the whole party trooped out of the court to gather in the great hall for more or less friendly, unofficial discussion. Mr Pippet was the first to speak.

"His lordship," he remarked, "was extremely delicate in his language. I should call the proceedings in regard to that coffin something more than irregular."

"His lordship," McGonnell remarked, "was probably bearing in mind that all the facts are not known. He, no doubt, has his suspicions as to what has happened and who is responsible; but, until the suspicions have been verified, it is as well not to be too explicit in assigning responsibility to individuals."

Mr Pippet smiled grimly. "It is well for you to say that, Mr McGonnell," said he, "seeing that both you and I are involved in those suspicions. But I am not inclined to take this business lying down, if you are. Gimbler was acting as my agent, and I suppose I am responsible for whatever he chose to do, ostensibly in my interests. But I presume I have some remedy. Is it possible for me to prosecute him? You are my legal adviser. I put the question to you. What remedy have I for being involved in this discreditable affair?"

Mr McGonnell looked uncomfortable, as well he might, for he was in an unpleasant position in more than one respect. After a few moments' reflection, he replied:

"I have as little reason as you have to be pleased with the turn of events. If a fraud has been committed in this case, that will not enhance my professional reputation. But I must again remind you that we have not got all the facts. It does certainly appear as if that coffin had been tampered with; and if it had, the responsibility lies between you and me and Mr Gimbler. Evidently, the suspicion lies principally on Gimbler. But, having regard to the fact that a quantity of stolen property – which was certainly not his – was found in the coffin, there is a clear possibility that the coffin may have been tampered with by some persons for their own purposes and without his knowledge. We have to bear that in mind before we make any direct accusations."

"That is a very ingenious suggestion," said Mr Pippet, "but it doesn't seem to commend itself to me. I should leave it to him to prove, if he can."

McGonnell shook his head. "That is not the position at all, Mr Pippet," said he. "If you assert that Gimbler planted a sham coffin in the vault, it will be for you to prove that he did, not for him to prove that he did not. But I think that you had better take the advice of a solicitor on the subject, or, at any rate, of some lawyer other than me. You will understand that I shall naturally be reluctant to be the first to set up a hue and cry after a man who has been my colleague in this case. If he has committed a fraud, I hope that he will receive the punishment that he will have deserved; but I should rather that some hand other than mine delivered the blow."

"I understand and respect your point of view," said Pippet, "but it leaves me high and dry without any legal guidance."

Here Thorndyke interposed. "If I might venture to offer you a word of advice, Mr Pippet," said he, "it would be that you do nothing at all. If any offence against the law has been committed, you may rely on the proper authorities to take the necessary measures."

"But suppose they regard me as the offender?"

"When you are accused, it will be time to take measures of defence. At present, no one is accusing you – at least, I think I may say so. Am I right, Superintendent?" he asked, turning to Miller, who had been unostentatiously listening to the conversation.

The Superintendent was guarded in his reply. "Speaking personally," said he, "I am certainly not accusing Mr Pippet of any complicity in this fraud, if there has really been a fraud. Later, I may have to apply to him for some information as to his relations with Mr Gimbler; but that is in the future. For the present, your advice to him is the best. Just wait and see what happens."

"And meanwhile," said Thorndyke, "if it appears that Mr Gimbler has withdrawn himself from among us permanently, I am sure that Mr Brodribb will consent to take charge of your affairs so far as recovery of documents and other winding up details are concerned."

To this, Brodribb agreed readily, to Mr Pippet's evident relief.

"Then," said the latter, "as we have disposed of business matters, I am going to propose that we make up a little luncheon-party to celebrate the end of the Winsborough Peerage Case. I'd like to have the whole crowd, but I suspect that there are one or two who will cry off."

His suspicions were confirmed on particular inquiry. McGonnell had business at the Central Criminal Court; Mrs Engleheart and Miss Pippet had some secret mission the nature of which they refused to divulge, and Anstey had other legal fish to fry.

"Am I to have the pleasure of your lordship's company at lunch?" Pippet inquired, fixing a twinkling eye on Mr Giles, and obviously convinced that he was not.

Giles laughed, knowingly. "I should have been delighted," said he, "to lunch with my noble cousin, or uncle, or whatever he is, but I have an engagement with another noble cousin. I am taking Jenny to the Zoo to show her the new chimpanzee, and we shall get our lunch on the way."

Mr Pippet shook his head resignedly and turned to the faithful few, consisting of Thorndyke, Brodribb, Miller and myself, and suggested an immediate adjournment. Thorndyke and I retired to the robing-room to divest ourselves of our legal war-paint, and, on emerging, re-joined the party at the main gate, where two taxis were already waiting, and were forthwith conveyed to Mr Pippet's hotel.

Throughout these proceedings and those of the subsequent luncheon, I was aware of a rather curious feeling of pleased surprise at our host's attitude and apparent state of mind. Especially did I admire the sporting spirit in which he accepted his defeat. He was not in the least cast down; and, apart from the discreditable incidents in the conduct of the case, he appeared perfectly satisfied with the result. But the oddest thing to me was his friendly and even deferential attitude towards Thorndyke. A stranger, unacquainted with the circumstances, might have supposed my colleague to be the leading counsel who had achieved a notable victory for Mr Pippet, instead of an expert witness who had, vulgarly speaking, "put the kybosh" on Mr Pippet's case. Any pique that he might, quite naturally, have felt seemed to be swallowed up by a keen sporting interest in the manner in which he had been defeated; and I was not surprised when, as the luncheon approached the coffee and cigar stage, he began to put out feelers for more detailed information.

"This trial," said he, "has been to me an education and an entertainment. I've enjoyed every bit of it, and I'm only sorry that we missed the judge's summing-up and reasoned decision. But the real tit-bit of the entertainment was Dr Thorndyke's evidence. What delighted me was the instantaneous way in which every move in the game was spotted and countered. Those screws, now; it was all obvious enough when it was explained. But the astonishing thing was that, not only was the character of those screws observed, but the significance of that character appreciated in a moment. I want you to tell me, Doctor, how you manage to keep your eyes perpetually skinned, and your brain skinned at the same time."

Thorndyke smiled appreciatively as he thoughtfully filled his pipe.

"You are giving me more credit than is due, Mr Pippet," said he. "You are assuming that certain reactions were instantaneous which were, in fact, quite deliberate, and that certain deceptive appearances were exhibited to unprepared eyes, whereas they had been carefully considered in advance. I have no doubt that the person who prepared the evidence made a similar mistake."

"But," objected Mr Pippet, "I don't see how you could consider in advance things that you didn't know were going to happen."

"It is possible to consider in advance," Thorndyke replied, "those circumstances which may conceivably arise as well as those which will certainly arise. You seem to think that the little surprise packets which the manipulator of evidence devised for our undoing found us all unprepared. That was certainly the intention of the manipulator; but it was very far from what actually happened."

"Why call him 'the manipulator'?" Mr Pippet protested. "His name is Horatio Gimbler, and we all know it."

"Very well," said Thorndyke, "then we will throw legal caution to the winds and call him Gimbler. Now, as I said, Gimbler made his little arrangements, expecting that they would come on us with all the charm of novelty and find us unprepared to give them that exhaustive consideration which would be necessary to ascertain their real nature, but which would be impossible in the course of proceedings in court. He would assume that, whatever vague suspicions we might have, there would be neither the time nor the opportunity to test the visible facts presented. What he had overlooked was the possibility that the other players might try the moves over in advance. But this is exactly what I did. Would it interest you to have some details of my procedure?"

"It would interest me very much," Brodribb interposed, "for, as you know, I sat on the bird-lime like a lamb – if you will pardon the mixed metaphor. Perhaps I might say 'like a fool' and be nearer the mark."

"I hope you won't, Mr Brodribb," said Pippet, because the description would include the lot of us, except the Doctor. But I am sure we should all like to hear how that rascal, Gimbler, was unmasked."

"Then," said Thorndyke, "let us begin by noting what our position was. This was a claim advanced by an unknown person to a title and some extremely valuable property. The claimant was an American, but there was nothing significant in that. All Americans of English origin have, of course, English ancestors. What was significant was the fact that this stranger had elected to employ a police-court solicitor to conduct his case. Taking all the circumstances together, there was quite a fair probability that the claim was a false claim; and if that were so, we should have to be on the look-out for false evidence.

"That was my function in the case; to watch the evidence, particularly in regard to the physical characteristics of any objects produced as 'exhibits' or put in as evidence. The purely legal business was in the hands of Mr Brodribb and Mr Anstey, whereas I was a sort of Devil's Advocate, in an inverted sense, concerned, not with the legal issues, but with illegal attempts to tamper with the evidence. Now, in the criminal department of my practice, I have been in the habit, from the first, of using what I may call a synthetic method. In investigating a known or suspected crime, my custom has been to put myself in the criminal's place and ask myself what are the possible methods of committing that crime, and, of the possible methods, which would be the best; how, in fact, I should go about committing that crime, myself. Having worked out in detail the most suitable procedure, I then change over from the synthetic to the analytic method and consider all the inherent weaknesses and defects of the method, and the means by which it would be possible to detect the crime.

"That is what I did in the present case. I began by assuming that wherever the evidence was insufficient or adverse, that evidence would be falsified."

"Sounds a bit uncharitable," Mr Pippet remarked, with a smile.

"Not at all," retorted Thorndyke. "There was no accusation. It was merely a working hypothesis which I communicated to nobody. If there had been no falsification, nothing would ever have been said and nobody would ever have known that the possibility had been entertained. But supposing falsification to be attempted, what form would it take? Apart from mere oral tradition and rumour, the value of which the judge would be able to assess, there was very little evidence. Of real, demonstrable evidence there were only two items – the diary and the coffin. Let us take the diary first. In what respects was falsification of the diary possible?

"There were two possibilities. The entire diary might be a fabrication. This was extremely unlikely. There were seven volumes, extending over a great number of years. The fabrication of such a diary would be a gigantic and very difficult task. Still, it was possible; but if the diary was in fact a fabrication from beginning to end, the falsification would almost certainly have been the work of the claimant, himself. But when one considers that the latest volume of this diary was alleged to have been written eighty years ago, it is obvious that the difficulties surrounding the production of a new work which could possibly be passed off as genuine would be practically insurmountable. I need not consider those difficulties or the means by which the fraud could be detected, since the case did not arise. On inspection, it was obvious that the diary was a genuine document.

"The second possibility was the insertion of a false entry; and this was not only quite practicable but, in the known circumstances, not very improbable. The question was, therefore, supposing a false entry to be inserted, would that entry have any special characteristics for which one could be on the look-out? And the answer was that it almost certainly would.

"As to the forgery itself, it would certainly be a good forgery. For, if it had been executed by the claimant, it would have to be good enough to satisfy Mr Gimbler. That gentleman was too experienced a lawyer to attempt to pass off an indifferent forgery in a court of law. But if it were not the work of the claimant, it would have to be produced either by Gimbler, himself, or under his superintendence. In either case it would certainly be a first-class forgery; and, as the passage would probably be quite short – possibly only a few words – it would be almost impossible to detect by mere examination of the written characters. In a short passage, the forger's attention need never flag, and no effects of fatigue would become apparent. The forger could try it over and over again until he could execute it perfectly. But in such a case, even the greatest experts – such as Osborn, in America, or Mitchell or Lucas in this country – could give no more than a guarded opinion. For, however eminent an expert may be, he cannot detect differences that do not exist.

"But if the imitation of the hand-writing were too good for detection to be possible, were there any other, extrinsic, characters that we could be on the look-out for? Evidently, by the nature of the case, there must be three. First, if a passage were inserted, it would have to be inserted where insertion was possible; that is to say, in a blank space. Accordingly, we should have to keep a look-out for blank spaces. And, if those blank spaces were of any considerable size, we should look for the interpolated passage or passages either at the beginning or end of the blank space or spaces.

"The second character of an interpolated passage would be the matter contained in it. It would contain some matter of high evidential value which was not contained in any of the genuine entries; for, if it did not, there would be no object in inserting it. As to the nature of this matter; since the crucial issue in this case was whether the two persons, Josiah and the Earl, were one and the same person, an interpolated passage would almost certainly contain matter supporting the belief that they were.

"The third character would be an unavoidable difference between the ink used for the forgery and that used by the writer of the genuine entries. They could not be the same unless the writer of the diary had elected to use carbon ink; which was infinitely improbable, and, in fact, was not the case. If he used ordinary writing ink – the iron-gall ink of the period – that ink would have become changed in the course of over eighty years. The original black tannate or gallate of iron would have become converted into the faint reddish-brown of the oxide of iron. Now, the forged writing would have to imitate the colour of this old writing. But a new ink of the same colour as the old would necessarily be of a different chemical composition. Probably it would contain no iron, but would be one of the modern brown drawing-inks, treated to match the colour exactly.

"In this difference of chemical composition would lie the means of detecting and exposing the forgery. A chemical test would probably be objected to, though it could be insisted on if the forgery were definitely challenged. But, for the reasons that I gave in my evidence, a photograph would be nearly certain to demonstrate the difference in the chemical composition of the ink. And to a photograph there could be no objection.

"Thus, you see, the whole matter had been examined in advance, so that, if a forgery should be offered in evidence, we knew exactly what it would be like. And when it did appear, it corresponded perfectly with the hypothetical forgery. We heard McGonnell read out, in his opening statement, a number of quotations from the diary, all very vague and unconvincing; and then, at the end, a single short entry of an entirely different character, explicitly implying the identity of the two persons, Josiah and the Earl. Here was one of the characters of the possible forgery; and when Anstey had elicited in cross-examination that neither you nor your sister had seen it before the book went into the hands of Mr Gimbler, it became a probable forgery. Then, on inspection, it was seen to have another of the postulated characters: it was at the end of a blank space. Finally, on closer examination, it was found to have the third character: it was written in an ink which was different from that used in the rest of the diary.

"So much for the forgery. In the case of the coffin a similar method was used. I put myself in Gimbler's place and considered the best way in which to carry out the substitution."

"But," objected Mr Pippet, "Gimbler had never suggested any examination of the coffin. On the contrary, he had decided to avoid any reference to an examination until the case went to the House of Lords. I thought he was giving that coffin as wide a berth as he could."

"Exactly," said Thorndyke. "That was the impression that he managed to convey to us all. And it was that which made me suspect strongly that a substitution was intended. It looked to me like a very subtle and admirable tactical manoeuvre. For, you see, the examination could not be avoided. It was impossible to burke the coffin, and Gimbler knew it. Not only was it the one piece of definite and undeniable evidence in the case; it contained the means of settling conclusively the whole issue that was before the court. If Gimbler did not produce the coffin, himself, it would certainly be demanded by the other side or by the judge.

"But now observe the subtlety of Gimbler's tactics. The crude thing to do would have been to make the substitution and then apply for an order of the court to have the coffin examined. But, in that case, the coffin would have been approached by the other side with a certain amount of suspicion, and minutely scrutinised. But when Gimbler seemed to have been taken by surprise, and to agree reluctantly to the examination of the coffin, the suspicion that he had got it all ready and prepared for the examination would be unlikely to arise. 'The other side' would be caught off their guard."

"Yes, by Jove!" chuckled Brodribb, "and so they were. I was quite shocked and embarrassed when I saw you sniffing round that coffin and openly showing that you suspected a fraud; and McGonnell was really and genuinely indignant."

"Yes," said Pippet, "he very much resented the implied doubt as to his good faith, and I must admit that I thought the Doctor a trifle over-sceptical. But don't let me interrupt. I want to hear how you anticipated so exactly what Gimbler would do."

"As I said," Thorndyke resumed, "it was by putting myself in Gimbler's place and considering how I should go about making this substitution. There were two possible methods. One was to open the old coffin and take out the body, if there was one there; the other was to prepare a new coffin to look like an old one. The first method was much the better if it could have been properly carried out. But there were one or two serious difficulties. In the first place, there would, presumably, have been a corpse to dispose of, and the operators might have objected to handling it. But the most serious objection was the possibility of a mishap in opening the coffin. It was an old coffin, and the wood might be extensively decayed. If, in the process of opening it, the lid should have broken or some other damage should have been done, the fraud would have been hopelessly exposed. For no repair would be possible. But, in any case, an ancient coffin could not have been opened without leaving some plainly visible traces.

"The second plan had several advantages. The new coffin could be prepared at leisure and thoroughly examined, and the proceedings on the spot could be quite short. You remember that there is, adjoining the burial-ground, a stable yard with an empty cart-shed in which a van could be housed while the substitution was being made. There would be little more to do than drive into the yard, exchange the coffins and drive away again. I considered both plans in detail, and eventually decided that the second one was the one that would be more probably adopted.

"Now, suppose that it was; what would the exact procedure be, and what pitfalls lay in wait for the operators? What would they have to do, and what mistakes would they probably make in doing it? In the first place, the coffin would pretty certainly be made by a regular coffin-maker; and the chances were a hundred to one, or more, that he would use modern screws and try to produce the appearance of age by rusting them. If he did, the coffin would be definitely labelled as a fabrication beyond any possible dispute.

"Then there was the sheet-lead. What he would put in would most probably be modern, silver-free milled lead, whereas the original would almost certainly have been cast sheet. Still, he might have got some old sheet-lead; and in any case the discrepancy would not have been conclusive or very convincing to the judge. We could not have given a definite date, as in the case of the screws.

"The next pitfall would be the dust. In that vault, everything would be covered with a mantle of dust of eighty years' growth. But if once that dust were disturbed – as it necessarily would be in moving the coffin – there would be no possibility of obliterating the marks of disturbance. There would be nothing for it but to sweep the vault out clean and blow in a fresh supply of dust which would settle down in a smooth and even layer. And there one could confidently expect that a serious mistake would be made. To most persons, dust is just simply dust; a material quite devoid of individual character. Few people realise consciously that dust is merely a collection of particles detached from larger bodies, and that when those particles are magnified by the microscope, they reveal themselves as recognisable fragments of those bodies. If our friends blew dust into the vault, it would be dust that had been collected *ad hoc*, and would be demonstrably the wrong sort of dust.

"That was how I reasoned the matter out in advance; and you will see that, when I came to the vault, all that I had to do was to note whether the appearances were normal or whether they corresponded to the false appearances which were already in my mind. As soon as I saw the screws, the question was answered. It remained only to look for additional details of evidence such as the dust and anything that might be distinctive in the character of the lead."

"The platinum, I take it," said Pippet, "had not been included in your forecast?"

"No," replied Thorndyke. "That was a free gift of Providence. It came as a complete surprise; and I might easily have missed it but for the rule that I have made to let nothing pass without examination. In accordance with this routine procedure, I took up each piece of lead and inspected it to see if it showed any peculiarities by which it would be possible to date it. As soon as I lifted the first lump of platinum alloy, I realised that Providence had delivered the gay deceiver into our hands."

"Yes," said Pippet, "that was a stroke of pure luck. But it wasn't necessary. I can see that your method of playing a trial game over in advance − of ascertaining what your adversary may do, instead of waiting to see what he does do − brings you to the table with all the trumps up your sleeve, ready to be produced if the chance occurs."

He reflected awhile, stirring his coffee thoughtfully, and apparently turning something over in his mind. At length, he looked up at Thorndyke and disclosed the subject of his cogitations.

"You have told us, Doctor," said he, "that you got this vanishing-coffin stunt worked out in advance in all its details. But there is one little matter that you have not referred to, and it happens to be one which interests me a good deal. I am wondering what has become of Josiah. It may seem only a matter of sentiment; but he was my grandfather, and I feel that it is up to me to see him put back in his proper residence in accordance with his wishes and the arrangements which he made during his life. Now, did the advance scheme that you drew up include any plans for disposing of Josiah?"

"Certainly," replied Thorndyke. "Assuming a new coffin to be used, the disposal of the old one was an important part of the problem; important to those who had to carry out the proceedings, and to us who had to prove that they had been carried out. The recovery and production of the old coffin would be conclusive evidence for the prosecution."

"Well, now," said Pippet, "tell us how you proposed to dispose of Josiah and how you intend to go about getting him back."

"There were two possible methods," said Thorndyke, "of getting rid of the old coffin. First, since a van or cart must have been used to bring the new coffin to the vault, it would have been available to take the old one away. This would have been a bad method, both for the plotters and for us; for it would have left them with the coffin on their hands, and us with the task of finding out where it had been hidden.

So we will leave it until we have dealt with the more obvious and reasonable plan. I did not propose to bring the coffin away at all."

"You don't mean that you proposed to bury it?" said Pippet.

"No," replied Thorndyke. "There was no need to. You have forgotten the arrangement of the place. There were six vaults, each secured only by a large, simple lock. Now, our friends must have had a big, strong skeleton key to open Josiah's vault. With the same key they could have opened any of the other vaults; and there was a perfectly excellent and convenient hiding-place."

"Gee!" chuckled Mr Pippet. "That's a quaint idea! To think that, while we were poring over that dummy coffin, Josiah, himself, was quietly reposing next door! But I guess you are right, Doctor; and the question is, what are you going to do about it?"

Thorndyke looked at the Superintendent.

"It is your move, Miller," said he. "You have got the skeleton key, and you have the Home Office authority."

"That is all very well," Miller replied, cautiously, "but the judge's order doesn't authorise us to break into any of the other vaults."

"The judge's order," said Thorndyke, "doesn't say anything about a particular vault. It authorises and directs you to open and examine the coffin of Josiah Pippet. But you haven't done anything of the sort. You opened the wrong coffin. You have not complied with the judge's order, and it is your duty to do so without delay."

Miller grinned and glanced knowingly at Mr Pippet.

"That's the sort of hairpin the Doctor is," he said, admiringly – "Thomas à Diddamus combined with a casuist of the deepest dye. He could argue the hind leg off a donkey; and that donkey would have nothing for it but to get a wooden leg."

Here Mr Brodribb intervened with some warmth. "You are doing Dr Thorndyke an injustice, Superintendent," said he. "There is nothing casuistical in his argument. He has stated the legal position quite correctly, not only in the letter but in the spirit. The judge made an order for the examination of the coffin of Josiah Pippet for the declared purpose of ascertaining the nature of its contents. But we have not examined that coffin, and we still do not know the nature of its contents. You will remember that the judge, himself, pointed that out at this morning's proceedings."

Miller was visibly impressed by these observations from the very correct and experienced old lawyer; and I could see that he was quite willing to be impressed, for he was as keen on the examination as any of us. But he was a police officer, and, as such, Josiah Pippet was not his pigeon. Civil cases were not in his province.

Thorndyke evidently saw the difficulty, and proceeded adroitly to turn his flank.

"Besides, Miller," he said, "you seem to be overlooking the importance of this matter in relation to a possible prosecution. A police officer of your experience is lawyer enough to realise the great difference in value between positive and negative evidence. Now, at present, all that we can do is to show cause for the belief that the coffin that we found in the vault was not Josiah's coffin. But suppose that we are able to produce the actual coffin of Josiah Pippet. That would leave the defence nothing to say. And, in any case, for the sake of your own reputation and that of the CID, that coffin has got to be found; and common sense suggests that we begin the search in the most likely place."

This argument disposed effectually of Miller's difficulties.

"You are quite right, Doctor," he agreed. "We shall be expected to produce that coffin, or, at least, to prove its existence and its whereabouts; and I certainly agree with you that the vault is the most likely place in which to look for it. I hope we are both right, for, if it isn't there, we may be let in for a mighty long chase before we get hold of it."

Agreement on the principle having been reached, it remained only to settle the details. Mr Pippet, with characteristic American eagerness to "get on with it", would have started forthwith for the burial-ground; but as Miller, naturally, had not got the keys about him, and as Thorndyke had certain preparations to make, it was arranged that the parties to the expedition should meet at the latter's chambers at ten o'clock on the following morning.

# CHAPTER NINETEEN

## *Josiah?*

There was something distinctly furtive and conspiratorial in the appearance and bearing of the party of six which filed into the burial-ground under the guidance of Superintendent Miller. At least, so it seemed to me, though the impression may have been due to Polton; who carried a small suitcase with a secretive and burglarious air, persisted in walking on tiptoe, and generally surrounded himself with the atmosphere of a veritable Guy Fawkes.

As soon as we were all in, the Superintendent closed the gate and locked it from the inside, putting the key in his pocket. Then he followed us to the neighbourhood of the vaults, where we were screened from the gaze of possible onlookers.

"Well," he remarked, stating an undeniable truth, "here we are, and here are the vaults. We've got five to choose from, and the chances are that we shall open four wrong ones before we come to the right one – if there is a right one. What do you say, Doctor? Any choice?"

"On general grounds," said Thorndyke, "it would seem that one is as likely as another; but on psychological grounds, I should say that there is a slight probability in favour of the sixth vault."

"Why?" demanded Miller.

"Because," replied Thorndyke, "although, as a hiding-place, any one vault would be as good as any other, I think there would be a tendency to get as far as possible from the vault in which the dummy coffin had been planted. It is merely a guess; but, as we have nothing else to guide us, I would suggest that we begin with number six."

While this brief discussion had been taking place, Polton had been peering into the keyholes with the aid of a small electric lamp and inspecting the edges of the respective doors. He now reported the results of his observations.

"I think you are right, Sir," said he. "There seems to be a trace of grease in the inside of the lock of the last door, and there is something that looks rather like the mark of a jemmy on the jamb of the door. Perhaps Mr Miller might take a look at it."

Mr Miller, as an expert on jemmy-marks, accordingly did take a look at it, and was inclined to confirm our artificer's opinion; on which it was decided to begin operations on number six. The big skeleton key was produced from the Superintendent's pocket and handed to Polton, by whom it was tenderly anointed with oil. Then a dressing of oil was applied to the rusty wards of the lock by means of a feather poked in through the keyhole, and the key inserted. As it refused to turn, in spite of the oil, Polton produced from his case a "tommy" – a steel bar about a foot long – which he passed through the bow of the key and worked gently backwards and forwards to distribute the oil and avoid the risk of wrenching off the bow. After a few trials, the key made a complete turn, and we heard the rusty bolt grate back into the lock.

"I expect we shall have to prise the door open," said Polton, after one or two vigorous tugs at the key, using the tommy as a handle. He threw back the lid of his suitcase, which was lying on the ground at his side, and looked into it – as, also, did the Superintendent.

"Well, I'm sure, Mr Polton!" the latter exclaimed. "Are you aware that it is a misdemeanour to go abroad with housebreaking implements in your possession?"

Polton regarded him with a cunning and crinkly smile.

"May I ask, Mr Miller," he demanded, "what you would use to force open a jammed door? Would you use a corkscrew or a sardine opener?"

Miller chuckled, appreciatively. "Well," he said, as Polton selected a powerful telescopic jemmy from his outfit, "I suppose the end justifies the means."

"You can take it, Sir," said Polton, sententiously, "that people whose business it is to open doors have found out the best tools to do it with."

Having delivered himself of this profound truth, he inserted the beak of the jemmy between the door and the jamb, gave it one or two tweaks at different levels, and then, grasping the key and the tommy, pulled the complaining door wide open.

The first glance into the mouldy and dusty interior showed that Thorndyke's selection had been correct. There were two names on the stone slab above the vault, but there were three coffins; two lying in orderly fashion on the stone shelf, and a third flung untidily across them. That the latter was the coffin which we were seeking was at once suggested by the fact that the handles and name-plate were missing, though the spaces which they had occupied and the holes for the screws were conspicuously visible.

"That is Josiah's coffin right enough," said Mr Pippet, pointing to these marks. "There can't be a shadow of doubt."

"No," agreed Thorndyke, "but we mustn't leave it at that. We must put the two coffins side by side and make an exact comparison which can be described in evidence in terms of actual measurement. I noticed that the beadle had not taken away the trestles. We had better set them up and put this coffin on them. The other one can be put on the ground alongside."

We fetched the trestles, and, having set them up, the four tallest of us proceeded to hoist out the coffin.

"He's a mighty weight," Mr Pippet remarked, as he lowered his end carefully to the trestles.

"Probably there is a lead shell," said Miller. "There usually was in the better-class coffins. I'm surprised they didn't put one in the dummy to make it a bit more convincing."

While the removal was being effected, Polton, armed with the skeleton key – the jemmy was not required – had got the door of the other vault open. Thither we now proceeded, and, lifting out the empty and comparatively light dummy, carried it across and laid it on the ground beside the trestles.

"The first thing," said Thorndyke, "will be to take off the name-plate and try it on the old coffin. An actual trial will be more convincing to a judge or jury than the most careful measurements."

"Is it of any great importance," Mr Pippet asked, "to prove that the dummy was faked by using the old coffin furniture?"

"It is absolutely vital," Thorndyke replied. "How else are we to prove that this is the coffin of Josiah Pippet? There is no mark on it by which it could be identified, and we find it in a vault which is not Josiah's. Moreover, in the vault which is his, there is a coffin bearing his name-plate which is alleged to be his coffin, and which we are trying to prove is not his coffin."

"I thought you had done that pretty effectually already," said Pippet.

"We can't have too much evidence," Thorndyke rejoined; "and, in any case, we have got to produce positive evidence of the identity of this coffin. At present we are only guessing, though I have no doubt that we are guessing right. But if we can prove that the name-plate on that coffin was removed from and belonged to this one, we shall have proved the identity of this one and the fraudulent character of the other."

While Thorndyke had been arguing this rather obvious point, Polton had been engaged in carefully and methodically extracting, with a clock-maker's screwdriver, the six screws with which the nameplate was attached to the dummy coffin-lid. He now held one of them up for his employer's inspection, remarking:

"You see, Sir, that they used the original brass screws – the old, flat-ended sort; which will be better for testing purposes, as they won't go into a hole that wasn't properly bored for them."

While the screw was being passed round and examined, he proceeded with the testing operations. First, he lifted the plate from its bed, whereupon there was disclosed an oblong patch of new, unstained wood, which he regarded with a contemptuous crinkle.

"Well!" he exclaimed, "if I had been faking a coffin, I'd at least have finished the faking before I screwed on the plate and not have given the show away like this."

With this, he picked up the plate and laid it on the old coffin-lid in the vacant space, which it fitted exactly. Then, with a fine awl, he felt through one of the corner holes of the plate for the corresponding hole in the wood, and, having found it, dropped in one of the screws and ran it lightly home. Next, in the same manner, he probed the hole in the opposite corner of the plate, dropped in the screw and drove it home. Then, discarding the awl, he dropped in the other four screws, all of which ran in quite smoothly.

"There, Mr Pippet," said Thorndyke, "that establishes the identity of the coffin. The six holes in the brass plate coincide exactly with the six holes in the wood; for, as Polton points out, the screws, being blunt-ended, would not enter the wood if the holes were not precisely in the right place. So you can now take it as an established fact that this is really the coffin of your grandfather, Josiah Pippet. Does that satisfy you? Or is there anything else that you wish to have done?"

Pippet looked at him in surprise. "Why!" he exclaimed, "we've only just begun! I thought we came here to find out exactly what is in that coffin. That is what I came for. I had made up my mind before I came to England that the first thing I would do would be to find out whether Josiah was or was not in that coffin. Then I should have known whether to haul off or go ahead."

"Exactly," said Thorndyke; "but are you sure that you still want to know?"

I looked quickly at Thorndyke, and so did Mr Pippet. The question was asked in the quietest and most matter-of-fact tone; and yet I had the feeling that it carried a significance beyond either the tone or the words. And this, I think, was noticed also by our American friend, for he paused a few moments with his eyes fixed on Thorndyke before he replied:

"It doesn't matter so much now, as I've dropped the claim. But, still, if it doesn't seem irreverent, I think I should like to have a look at Josiah. I hate to leave a job unfinished."

"Very well," said Thorndyke; "it's your funeral in a literal as well as an allegorical sense. You would like to have the coffin opened?"

"I should, though I don't quite see how you are going to manage it. There don't seem to be any screws."

"The screws are plugged," Thorndyke explained, "as they usually are in well-finished coffins. They are sunk in little pits and the pits are filled up with plugs of wood, which are planed off clean so as to show an uninterrupted surface. Possibly those plugs were the deciding factor in the question as to whether the old coffin should be opened and faked, or a new one made. You can see that it would be impossible to get those plugs out and replace them without leaving very visible traces."

This statement was illustrated by Polton's proceedings. From the inexhaustible suitcase he produced a cabinet-maker's scraper, with which he set to work at the edge of the lid, scraping off the old surface, thereby bringing into view the little circular inlays which marked the position of the screws, of which there were eight. When they were all visible, he attacked them with a nose bit set in a brace, and quickly exposed the heads of the screws. But then came the tug of war. For the rust of eighty years seemed to have fixed the screws immovably; and by the time that he had managed, with the aid of a driver bit in his brace, to get them out, his crinkly countenance was streaming with perspiration.

"All right this time," said Mr Pippet, picking up one of the screws and inspecting its blunt end. "I guess I'll take these screws to keep as a memento. Ah! You were right, Doctor," he added, as Polton prised up the lid and lifted it clear. "It was the lead shell that made it so blamed ponderous."

Here Mr Brodribb, casting a slightly apprehensive glance at the leaden inner coffin, announced, as he selected a cigar from his case,

"If you are going to open the shell, Thorndyke, I think I will take a little stroll and survey the landscape. I haven't got a medical jurist's stomach."

Thorndyke smiled, unsympathetically, but, nevertheless, offered him a light; and as he moved away, exhaling fragrant clouds, Polton approached the coffin with a formidable hooked knife and a pair of tinman's shears.

"Do you want to see the whole of him, Sir?" he asked, bestowing a crinkly smile on Mr Pippet, "or do you think his head will be enough?"

"Well, Mr Polton," was the guarded reply, "perhaps his head will be enough – to begin with, anyway."

Thereupon, Polton, with a few gentle taps of a hammer, drove the point of the knife through the soft lead and began to cut a line in a U shape round the head end of the shell. When he had extended it sufficiently, he prised up the end of the tongue-shaped piece enclosed by the incision and turned it back like a flap. We stood aside respectfully to allow Mr Pippet to be the first to look upon the long-forgotten face of his ancestor; and he accordingly advanced and bent down over the dark opening. For an appreciable time he remained looking silently into the cavity, apparently overcome by the emotions natural to the occasion. But I must confess that I was somewhat startled when he gave expression to those emotions. For what he said – and he said it slowly and with the strongest emphasis – was:

"Well – I'm – damned!"

Now, when a gentleman so scrupulously correct in speech as was Mr Pippet, makes use of such an expression, it is reasonable to assume that something unusual has occurred. As he withdrew his head from the opening, mine and Thorndyke's met over it (and I am afraid mine was the harder). But in spite of the collision, I saw enough in a single glance to account for Mr Pippet's exclamation. For what met that glance was no shrivelled, mummified human face, but the end of a slender roll of canvas embedded in time-discoloured sawdust.

"Now," commented Miller, when he had made his inspection, "isn't that just like a blinking crook! They are all fools, no matter how artful they may be. And they can't imagine the possibility of anyone else being honest. Of course, Gimbler thought that the coffin story was all bunkum, so he pitched the old coffin away without troubling to open it and see what was really in it. If he had only left it alone, Mr Pippet's claim would have been as good as established."

"It would certainly have been important evidence," said I. "But, for that matter, it is still. The story of the bogus funeral is now proved beyond any possible doubt to be true. And, though the claim has lapsed for the moment, it lapsed only on a technical point. What do you say, Brodribb?" I asked as that gentleman, in the course of his perambulations, passed the vault at a respectful distance.

"What do I say to what?" he demanded, reasonably enough.

"We have opened the shell and we find that it does not contain a body."

"What does it contain?" he asked.

"Something wrapped in canvas and packed in sawdust," I replied.

"That is not a very complete account," he objected, approaching cautiously to take a peep into the interior of the shell. "It certainly does not look like a body," he admitted after a very brief inspection, "but it might be. A very small one."

"It would be a very small one indeed," said Thorndyke. "But I agree with you, Brodribb. We ought to ascertain exactly what the contents of the coffin are."

On this, Polton reinserted the hooked knife and prolonged the incision on one side to the foot of the shell and carried it across. Then he raised the long flap and turned it back, exposing the whole of the mass of sawdust and the long roll of canvas which was embedded in it. The latter, being lifted out and laid on the coffin-lid, was seen to be secured with three strands of twine or spunyarn. These Polton carefully untied – they were fastened with reef-knots – and, having thus released the canvas, unrolled it and displayed its contents; which consisted of a small roll of sheet-lead, a portion of a battered rain head and a flattened section of leaden stack-pipe.

"This is interesting," said Brodribb. "It corresponds with the description more closely than I should have expected."

"And you notice, Sir," Polton pointed out, "that the sheet-lead is proper cast sheet, as the Doctor said it would be."

"I take your word for it, Polton," said Brodribb. "And that is a further agreement; which, I may add – since we are all friends – is not without its evidential significance."

"That is the point that we were discussing," said I. "The bearing of this discovery on Mr Pippet's claim."

"I beg your pardon, Dr Jervis," Mr Pippet interposed, "but there isn't any claim. My sister and I agreed some time ago to drop the claim if we got a chance. And Dr Thorndyke gave us a very fair chance, and we are very much obliged to him."

"I am glad to hear that," said Brodribb, "because this discovery does really confuse the issues rather badly. On this new evidence it would be possible to start a long and complicated law-suit."

"That," said Mr Pippet, "is, I guess, what the Doctor meant when he asked me if I still wanted to know what was in the coffin. But a nod is as good as a wink to a blind horse; and I was that blind horse. I rather wish I had left that durned coffin alone and taken it for granted that Josiah was inside. Still, we have got the monopoly of the information. Is there any reason why we should not keep it to ourselves? What do you say, Superintendent?"

"The fact," replied Miller, "that there was no body in the coffin is of no importance to the prosecution, but I don't see how it can be burked. We shall have to produce the original coffin – or prove its existence. We needn't say that we have opened it; but the question might be asked in cross-examination, and we should have to answer it. But what is the objection to the fact being known? You have dropped the claim, and you don't intend to reopen it. Nobody will be any the worse."

"But I am afraid somebody may be," Mr Pippet rejoined. He reflected a few moments and then continued: "We are all friends, as Mr Brodribb has remarked, so I needn't mind letting you see how the land lies from my point of view. You see, I embarked on this claim under the impression that the estates were going begging. I knew nothing of any other claimant. But when my sister and I saw Mr Giles and his mother, we were a little sorry that we had started the ball. However, we had started it, and, after all, there was my girl to consider. So we went on. But very soon it became evident that our two young people were uncommonly taken with each other; and then my sister and I were still more sorry, and we began to hope that our case might fall through. While matters were in suspense, however, Giles made no formal advances, though there was no concealment of his feelings towards my girl. But in the evening of the day when the Doctor obligingly knocked the bottom right out of my case, and showed us who the genuine heir-presumptive was, Giles asked my daughter to marry him, and, naturally, she said 'yes'.

"And now you will see my point. Giles, with proper, manly pride, waited until he had something to offer besides his own very desirable person. He didn't want to come as a suitor with empty hands. When the prize was practically his, he asked Jenifer to share it with him. And I should have liked to leave it at that. And that was why I wanted that coffin opened. I had taken it as a cinch that Josiah was inside; and if he had been, that would have settled the question for good. Instead of which I have only confused the issues, as Mr Brodribb says.

"Now, see here. I want this affair kept dark if it possibly can be. I want Giles to feel that the title and estates that he asked Jenny to share with him are his own by right, and not by anyone's favour. But that would be all spoiled if he got to know about this damned lead. For then he might reasonably suspect that I had voluntarily surrendered this claim for his benefit when I could, if I had pleased, have carried it to a successful issue. Of course, I couldn't have done anything of the kind. But that is what he might think. And he mustn't. There must be no fly in his ointment; and I look to you all to keep it out."

It is needless to say that we all listened with the greatest sympathy to Mr Pippet's explanation, and we promised, so far as was possible, to suppress the fact that the coffin had been opened; which we were able to do with a clear conscience, since that fact was neither material nor even relevant to the charge of fraud against Gimbler.

"Naturally," said Mr Pippet, when he had thanked us, "you will say that I ought to have thought of all this before I asked to have the coffin opened, but I am not so long-sighted as the Doctor. If you would like to call me a fool I shan't contradict you."

"Thank you," laughed Thorndyke; "but I don't think I will avail myself of the permission. Still, I will remark that you allowed yourself to entertain a complete fallacy. You have spoken of my having knocked the bottom out of your case by my exposure of Gimbler's fraud. But that was not the position at all. The coffin which Gimbler produced as Josiah's coffin was not Josiah's coffin. Therefore it had no relevance to the issue. It proved nothing, one way or the other, as to the condition of the real coffin. The effect of my evidence was purely negative. It simply rebutted Gimbler's evidence and thus restored the *status quo ante*. The judge, if you remember, drew your attention to this fact when he reminded you that Josiah's coffin had not been examined, and that the bogus funeral had been neither proved nor disproved."

"Well," said Mr Pippet, "it has been proved now; and what I should like to know, just as a matter of curiosity, is what it really and truly means. Is it possible that the whole story was true, or was this just one of Josiah's little jokes?"

"I am afraid you will never know now," said Thorndyke.

"No," Pippet agreed. "Josiah has got us guessing. Of course, it doesn't matter now whether he was an earl or an inn-keeper, but if you have any opinion on the subject, I should like to hear it."

"Mere speculative opinions," said Thorndyke, "formed in the absence of real evidence, are not of much value. I really have nothing that one could call an opinion. All I can say is that, though the balance of probabilities for and against the truth of the story is nearly even, there seems to be a slight preponderance against, since, added to the general improbability of the story, is the very striking coincidence of Nathaniel Pippet of 'the Castle' at Winsborough. But I am afraid we shall have to return an open verdict."

"And keep it to ourselves," added Pippet. "And now the practical question arises, what are we to do with this coffin?"

"I suggest," said Thorndyke, "that Polton closes it up as neatly as possible and that we then put it, with Gimbler's masterpiece, in the vault to which it properly belongs. We may hope that it may not be necessary to disturb that vault again; in which case no one need ever know that the coffin has been opened."

This suggestion, being generally approved, was duly carried out. The two coffins were placed, side by side, on the shelf, and then Miller locked the door and dropped the key into his pocket. This done, the procession moved out of the burial ground; and the incident was formally closed when Miller slammed the outer gate and turned the key in the rusty lock.

We went back in the same order as that in which we had come. Mr Pippet and Brodribb travelled in the former's car, and the rest of us occupied the roomy police car, Polton, at his own request, occupying the seat next to the driver where he could observe the mechanical arrangements and the operator's methods.

# CHAPTER TWENTY
## Thorndyke Resolves a Mystery

Modern transport appliances have certain undeniable advantages, particularly to those who are principally concerned with rapidity of transit. But these advantages, like most of the gifts of "progress", have to be purchased by the sacrifice of certain other advantages. The Superintendent's car was, in respect of speed, incomparably superior to a horse carriage; but in the opportunity that it afforded for sustained conversation it compared very unfavourably with that obsolete type of vehicle. Thorndyke, however, not yet, perhaps, emancipated from the hansom-cab habit, chose to disregard the inevitable interruption, and, as the car trundled smoothly westward, remarked to Miller:

"The subject of coffins, with which our minds are at present occupied, suggests, by an obvious analogy, that of a head in a box. I promised, a little while ago, to pass on to you any facts that I might unearth respecting the history of that head. I have looked into the matter, and I think I now have all the material facts; and I may say that the affair turns out to be, in effect, what I had, almost from the first, supposed it to be."

"I didn't know," said Miller, "that you supposed it to be anything. I thought you were quite uninterested in the incident."

"Then," said Thorndyke, "you were mistaken. I watched the developments with the keenest interest. At first, when the head was discovered in the cloakroom, I naturally assumed, as everyone did, that it was a case of murder and mutilation. But when I read the account of the inquest I began to suspect strongly that it was something quite different, and when I saw that photograph that you were so kind as to send me, I had very little doubt of it. You remember that photograph, Jervis?"

"Indeed I do," I replied. "A most extraordinary and abnormal mug that fellow had. There seemed to me to be a suggestion of acromegaly."

"A suggestion!" Thorndyke exclaimed. "It was a perfect type. That photograph might have been used as the frontispiece of a monograph of acromegaly. Its appearance, together with the physical and anatomical facts disclosed at the inquest, seemed to me quite distinctive. I came to the conclusion that this head was no relic of a crime, but simply a museum specimen which had gone astray."

"Good Lord!" exclaimed Miller, gazing at Thorndyke in amazement. I did not share his surprise, but merely felt an urgent desire to kick myself. For the thing was so ridiculously obvious – as soon as it was stated. But that was always the way with Thorndyke. He had the uncanny gift of seeing all the obvious things that everyone else overlooked.

"But," Miller continued, after a pause, "you might have given us the tip."

"My dear Miller," Thorndyke protested, "I had no tip to give. It was merely an opinion, and it might have been a wrong opinion. However, as I said, I watched developments most attentively, for there were at least two possibilities which might be foreseen; one by no means unlikely, the other almost fantastically improbable. The first was that some person might be accused of a murder which had never been committed; the other was that some real murderer might take advantage of the extraordinary opportunity that the circumstances offered. Curiously enough, it was the wildly improbable possibility that was actually realised."

"What was the opportunity that was offered?" Miller asked.

"It was the opportunity to commit a murder with almost perfect security from detection; with a whole set of false clues ready made; with the equivalent in time of a nearly water-tight alibi."

"A murderer's chief difficulty," said Miller, "is usually in getting rid of the body. I don't see that the circumstances helped him in that."

"They helped him to the extent that he had no need to get rid of the body," Thorndyke replied. "Why does a murderer have to conceal the body? Because if it is found it will be recognised as the body of a particular person. Then the relations of the murderer to that person will be examined, with possibly fatal results. But supposing that a murderer could render the body of his victim totally unrecognisable. Then it would be the body of an unknown person; and all the persons related to it would be equally unknown. If he could go a step further and not only render the body unrecognisable but give it a false identity, he would be absolutely secure; for the body would now be related to a set of circumstances with which he had no connection.

"This is the kind of opportunity that was offered by the discovery of this head. Let us study the conditions in the light of what actually happened. On a certain day in August, Wicks deposited in the cloak-room a human head. Now, obviously, since it was brought there by Wicks, it could not be Wicks' head. Equally obviously, it must have been the head of some person who had died while Wicks was still alive. Thus the death of that person was clearly dated in one direction; and since the head had been treated with preservatives, the date of death must have been some time anterior to that of its deposition in the cloak-room. Again, obviously, there must be somewhere a headless body corresponding to this bodyless head.

"Now, Bassett evidently intended to murder Wicks, for, as we saw, the murder was clearly premeditated. See, then, what a perfect opportunity was presented to him. If he could contrive to murder Wicks, to strip and decapitate the body and deposit it in a place where it would probably remain undiscovered for some time; when it was discovered, it would, quite naturally, be assumed to be the body belonging to the embalmed head. In other words, it would be assumed to be the body of some person who could not possibly be Wicks, and who had been murdered at some time when he, Bassett, was on the high seas. No slightest breath of suspicion could possibly fall on Bassett.

"But, as so constantly happens in the case of carefully planned crimes, one little point had been overlooked, or, rather, was unknown to the intending murderer. Strangely enough, it seems also to have been overlooked by everyone else, with the result that Bassett's scheme was within a hair's-breadth of working out exactly according to plan."

"As he was at the bottom of the dene-hole," remarked Miller, "it didn't matter much to him whether it did or not."

"Very true," Thorndyke agreed. "But we are considering the plan of the crime. Now, when I read the report of the finding of the headless body, I realised that the fantastic possibility that I had hardly ventured to entertain had actually come to pass."

"You assumed that the headless body was a fake," said Miller, "and not the body belonging to the cloak-room head. Now, I wonder why you assumed that."

"I did not," replied Thorndyke. "There was no assumption. The excellent newspaper report made it perfectly clear that the body found by the Watling Street could not possibly be the body belonging to the embalmed head. That head, let me remind you, was the head of a person who suffered from acromegaly. The body of that person would have been distinguished by atrophied muscles and enormous, mis-shapen hands and feet. But our admirable reporter specially noted that the body was that of a muscular man with strong, well-shaped hands. Then he certainly was not suffering from acromegaly.

"You see what followed from this. If this body did not belong to the cloak-room head, it must belong to some other head. And that head was probably not far away. For, as no one suspected its existence, there was no need for any elaborate measures to hide it. As I happened to be aware of the existence of a number of dene-holes in the immediate neighbourhood, it occurred to me that one of them probably contained the head and the clothes. Accordingly, I examined the six-inch map of the district, on which the dene-holes are shown, and there I found that one of them was within four hundred yards of the place where the body was discovered. To that dene-hole I paid a visit after attending the inquest, having provided myself with a compass, a suitable lamp and a pair of night-glasses. I was not able to see very much, but I saw enough to justify our expedition. You know the rest of that story."

"Yes," replied Miller, "and a very interesting story it is. And now I should like to hear about these new facts that you have unearthed."

"You shall have them all," said Thorndyke, "though it is only a case of filling in details. I have told you what I decided – correctly, as it turns out – as to the nature of the mysterious head; that it was simply a pathological specimen illustrating the rare disease known as acromegaly, which had got into the wrong hands.

"Now, when one thinks of acromegaly, the name of Septimus Bernstein almost inevitably comes into one's mind. Dr Bernstein is a world-famous authority on giantism, dwarfism, acromegaly and other affections and anomalies of growth connected with disorder of the pituitary body. He is an enthusiast in his subject and gives his whole time and energy to its study. But what was still more important to me was the fact that he has a private museum devoted to the illustration of these diseases and anomalies. I have seen that museum, and a very remarkable collection it is; but, when I visited it, although it contained several gigantic and acromegalous skulls, there was no specimen of a head in its complete state.

"Naturally, then, I was disposed to suspect some connection between this stray specimen and Dr Bernstein. But this was pure hypothesis until I heard Bunter's statement. That brought my hypothesis concerning the head into the region of fact. For Bunter's description of the passenger on the yacht was a fairly exact description of Dr Bernstein; and on the strength of it I was in a position to take the necessary measures to clear the matter up.

"Accordingly I called on Bernstein. I did not, in the first place, ask him any questions. I simply informed him that a preserved human head which he had imported, apparently from Holland, had been causing the police a good deal of trouble, and that it was for him to give a full and candid explanation of all the circumstances connected with it. The alternative was for the police to charge him with being in unlawful possession of certain human remains.

"My statement seemed to give him a severe shock – he is a nervous and rather timid man – but, though greatly alarmed, he seemed, in a way, relieved to have an opportunity to explain matters. Evidently, the affair had kept him in a state of constant apprehension and expectation of some new and horrible development, and he consented almost eagerly to make a full statement as to what had really happened. This is what his story amounts to:

"He had for years been trying to get possession of the head of some person who had suffered from acromegaly; partly for the purpose of studying the pituitary body more thoroughly, and partly for the enrichment of his museum with a specimen which completely illustrated the effects of the disease. What he especially wanted to do was to remove the pituitary body without injuring the head and mount it in a specimen jar to accompany the jar containing the head, so that the abnormal condition of the pituitary and its effects on the structure of the face could be studied together."

"By the way," Miller asked, "what is the pituitary body?"

"It is a small body," Thorndyke explained, "situated at the base of the brain and lodged in a cavity in the base of the skull. Its interest – for our present purpose – lies in the fact that it is one of the so-called ductless glands and produces certain internal secretions which contain substances called hormones which are absorbed into the blood and seem to control the processes of growth. If the pituitary – or, at least, its anterior part – becomes overgrown, it appears that it produces an excess of secretion, with the result that either the whole body becomes overgrown and the sufferer develops into a giant, or certain parts only of the body, particularly the face and the extremities, become gigantic while the rest of the body remains of its normal size. That is a very rough account of it, just enough to make the matter intelligible."

"I think I have taken in the idea," said Miller, "and I'm glad you explained it. Now, I am able to feel a bit more sympathetic towards Dr Bernstein. He isn't such an unmitigated cannibal as I thought he was. But let us hear the rest of the story."

"Well," Thorndyke resumed, "a short time ago, Bernstein heard from a Dutch doctor of a set of specimens the very description of which made his mouth water. It appeared that an unclaimed body had been delivered for dissection at a medical school in a certain town in Holland. Bernstein asked to be excused from giving the name of the town, and I did not press him. But, of course, if it is essential, he is prepared to disclose the further particulars. On examining this body, it was found to present the typical characters of acromegaly; whereupon the pathologist decided to annex the head and extremities for the hospital museum and return the remainder in the coffin. At the time when the information reached Bernstein, the specimens had not been put in the museum but were in the curator's laboratory in course of preparation.

"Thereupon, Bernstein started off, hot-foot, to see if he could persuade the pathologist to let him have the head. And his mission was obviously successful. What methods of persuasion he used, and what was the nature of the deal, he preferred not to say; and I did not insist, as it is no particular concern of ours. It would seem as if it must have been slightly irregular. However, he obtained the head, and, having got it, embarked on the series of foolish proceedings about which Bunter told us. A bolder and more self-confident man would probably have had no serious difficulty. He would have travelled by an ordinary passenger ship and simply declared the head at the Customs as a pathological specimen. The Customs people might have communicated with the police, and there might have been some inquiries. But if there had been no secrecy there would have been no trouble."

"No," Miller agreed. "Secrecy was the stupidest thing possible under the circumstances. Why the deuce didn't he notify us, when the thing was found in the cloak-room? It would have saved us a world of trouble."

"Of course that is what he ought to have done," said Thorndyke; "but the discovery took him unawares, and, when he suddenly found himself involved in a murder mystery, he got in a panic and made things worse by trying to keep out of sight. He is in a mighty twitter now, I can assure you."

"I expect he is," said Miller; "and the question is, What is to be done? It's a queer case, in a legal sense. Have you any suggestion to make?"

"Well," said Thorndyke, "I think you should first consider what the legal position really is. You will admit that no crime has been committed."

"Apparently not," Miller agreed; "at any rate, not in British jurisdiction."

"Furthermore," pursued Thorndyke, "it is not clear to me that any offence against the law has been committed. Admittedly, Bernstein evaded the Customs; but, as a human head is not a customable commodity, there was no offence against the Revenue. And so with the rest of his proceedings; they were very improper, but they do not appear to amount to any definite legal offence."

"So I take it," said Miller, "that you think we might as well let the matter drop. I don't quite like that, after all the fuss and outcry there has been."

"I was hardly suggesting that," said Thorndyke. "I certainly think that, for the credit of the Force, the mystery ought to be cleared up in a more or less public manner. But, since you invite me to make a suggestion, I will make one. Perhaps it may surprise you a little. But what I think would be the best way to bring the case to a satisfactory conclusion would be for you to disinter the specimen – which I believe was buried temporarily, in the case in which it was found, in the Tower Hamlets Cemetery – have it examined and reported on by some authorised persons, verify Bernstein's statements so far as may be necessary, and, if you find everything correct, hand the specimen back to Bernstein."

"My eye!" exclaimed Miller, "that's a pretty large order! But how could we? The head is not lawfully his property. No one is entitled to the possession of human remains."

"I am not sure that I can agree to that," Thorndyke dissented; "not, at any rate, without certain reservations. The legal status of anatomical and pathological specimens in museums is rather obscure; and perhaps it has been wisely kept obscure. It is not covered by the Anatomy Act, which merely legalises the temporary possession of a human body for the purpose of dissection. As you say, no one can establish a title to the possession of a human body, or part of one, as an ordinary chattel. But you know as well as I do, Miller, that sensible people turn a blind eye to this question on suitable occasions. Take the case of the Hunterian Museum of the Royal College of Surgeons. There, the anatomical and pathological collections are filled with human remains, all of which must have been acquired by methods which are not strictly legal. There are even the remains of entire individuals, some of whom are actually known by name. Now, if they were challenged, what title to the possession of those remains could the Council of the College establish? In practice, they are not challenged. Reasonable people tacitly assume a title.

"And that is what you would do, yourself. Supposing that some one were to steal the skeleton of the late Corporal Byrne, or O'Brian, the Irish Giant, which is in that museum, and supposing you were able to recover it; what would you do? Why, of course, you would hand it back to the museum, title or no title."

"Yes," Miller admitted, "that is so. But Bernstein's case is not quite the same. His is a private museum, and he wants this head as a personal chattel."

"The principle is the same," Thorndyke rejoined. "Bernstein is a proper person to possess this head; he wants it for a legitimate purpose – for the advancement of medical knowledge, which is for the benefit of all. I insist, Miller, that, as a matter of public policy, this specimen ought to be given back to Bernstein."

Miller looked at me with an undissembled grin. "The Doctor can be mighty persuasive on occasion," he remarked.

"Still," I urged, "it is a perfectly reasonable proposition. You are concerned, primarily, with crime, but ultimately with the public welfare. Now, there hasn't been any crime, or any criminal intent; and it is against the public welfare to put obstacles in the way of legitimate and useful medical research."

"Well," Miller rejoined, "the decision doesn't rest with me. I must see what the Commissioner has to say. I will give him the facts, and you can depend on me to tell him what you say and to put your case as strongly as I can. He is not out to make unnecessary trouble any more than I am. So we must leave it at that. I will let you know what he says. If he falls in with your view, he will probably want your assistance in fixing up the details of the exhumation and the inspection of the specimen. You may as well give me Bernstein's address."

Thorndyke wrote the name and address down on one of his own cards and handed it to the Superintendent. And this brought the business to an end. The latter part of the conversation had been carried on in the stationary car, which had been drawn up in King's Bench Walk opposite our chambers. We now shook hands with Miller and got out; and, as the car turned away towards Crown Office Row, we entered the wide doorway and ascended the stairs to our own domain.

# Chapter Twenty One
## Jervis Completes the Story

The time has come for us to gather up the threads of this somewhat discursive history. They are but ends, and short ones at that; for, in effect, my tale is told. But even as the weaver's work is judged by the quality of the selvedge, so the historian's is apt to be judged by its freedom from loose ends and uncompleted episodes.

But since the mere bald narration of the few outstanding incidents would be but a dull affair, I shall venture (on the principle that the greater includes the less) to present an account of them all under cover of that which most definitely marked the completion of our labours; the establishment of the young Earl and his Countess in firm possession of the ancestral domain. For, however thrilling may have been the alarums and excursions that befell by the way, they were but by-products and side issues of the Winsborough Peerage Case. With the settlement of that case we could fairly say that our work was done; and, if disposed to tags or aphorisms, could take our choice between *Nunc dimittis* and *Finis coronat opus*.

It was a brilliant morning in that most joyous season of the year when late spring is merging into early summer; and the place was the spot upon the earth's surface where that season develops its most perfect loveliness – the south-east corner of Kent; or, to be more precise, the great lawn at the rear of the unpretentious mansion "known as and being" Winsborough Castle. Thither Thorndyke and my wife and I, together with Brodribb (who came also in his official capacity), had been invited to the house-warming on the return of the young Earl and Countess from their prolonged honeymoon. But we had not come as mere visitors, or even friends. The warmhearted Jenifer had formally adopted us as members of the family, and as no one could ask for more delightful relatives, we had accepted the position gratefully.

As we strolled together across the sunlit lawn, I glanced from time to time at the young couple with that sober pleasure which a middle-aged man feels in contemplating the too-rare spectacle of a pair of entirely satisfactory human beings. They were both far beyond the average in good looks; of splendid physique, gay and sprightly in temperament and gifted with the faultless manners that spring from natural kindliness and generosity coupled with quick intelligence. Looking at them, one could not but reflect pensively on the might-have-been; and think what a pleasant place the world would be if it could be peopled with their like.

"I wonder," said Jenny, "what has become of Pap and Uncle John." ("Uncle John" was Thorndyke.)

"I don't," said Giles, "because I know. I saw them sneaking off together towards the churchyard. My impression is that they are trying to make a complete and exhaustive collection of ancestral Pippets."

Jenny laughed delightedly. "Inquisitive old things!" she exclaimed. "But I don't see why they need fuss themselves. There are no particular points about the ancestral Pippets. They never did anything worth speaking of excepting that they sold good beer – and, incidentally, they produced me."

"Not incidentally," Giles objected. "It was their crowning achievement. And I don't know what more you would have. I call it a deuced good effort."

The girl glanced at me with sparkling eyes. "Conceited young feller, isn't he, Uncle Kit? He will persist in thinking that his goose is a swan."

"He knows that she is," retorted Giles. "But, I say, Jenny. You'll have to keep an eye on Dad. What do you think he has done?"

She looked at him in mock alarm. "Break it gently," she pleaded.

"To my certain knowledge," said Giles, "he has taken over the lease of the 'Earl of Beaconsfield' and he is having the sign changed back to the 'Castle Arms'. What do you make of that?"

"My prophetic soul!" she exclaimed. "I see it all. He's going to have 'by C Pippet' written underneath the sign. If we don't mind our eyes, we shall have him behind the bar before we can say 'knife'. 'What's bred in the bone,' you know."

Giles laughed in his delightful school-boy fashion.

"My word, yes!" he agreed. "We shall have to take a strong hand. We are not going to spend our lives under the Upas shadow of the 'Fox and Grapes'. But I must hook off. Mr Brodribb has got the bailiff chappie here – Mr Solly – and they are going to rub my nose on all the things that they say a landowner ought to understand. Brodribb insists that there is no eye like the master's eye, and I expect he is right, though I fancy I know an eye that is better still; to wit, the eye that adorns the countenance of the master's Pa-in-law. What are you going to do?"

"I," replied Jenny, "am going to extract a statement from Uncle Kit on the subject of the various happenings since we had Mr Brodribb's summary. I want to know how it all ended."

"Good!" said Giles; "and when you have wormed all the facts out of him, you can pass them on to me. Now I'm off."

With a flourish of his hat and a mock-ceremonial bow, he turned and strode away across the turf towards the old brick porch, the very type and embodiment of healthy, virile youth. Jenny followed him with her eyes until he disappeared into the porch; then she opened her cross-examination.

"Now, Uncle K, you've got to tell me all you know about everything."

"Yes," I agreed, "that seems to offer some scope for conversation. Would you like to begin anywhere in particular?"

"I want, first of all, to know just exactly what has happened to poor Mr Gimbler."

"Poor Mr Gimbler!" I exclaimed. "You needn't waste your sympathy on a rascal like that."

"I know," said she. "Of course he is a rascal. But he did manage things so bee-yutifully."

Her tone jarred upon me slightly, and I think she must have observed something in my expression, for she continued:

"You think I am taking a purely selfish view of the case, and I must admit that, as events have turned out, I am the greatest gainer by what Giles calls 'Mr Gimbler's gimblings'. But I assure you, Uncle Kit, that Mr Gimbler did the very best for us all. Pap loves him. He says he is going to give him a pension when he comes out of chokee – if that is where he is. I suppose it is."

"Yes," I replied. "Chokee is his present address."

"I was afraid it was," said she. "The benefactor of humanity is languishing in a dungeon, and you don't care a hoot. You seem even to feel a callous satisfaction in his misfortunes. But see here, now, Uncle K, I want you to understand the benefits that he has showered on us. And, first of all, you've got to understand my father's position. You have got to realise that he never wanted the earldom at all. Pap is a thorough-bred American. He had no use for titles of nobility; and he was very clear that he didn't want to stand in the way of anyone else who had.

"But Auntie Arminella and I didn't take that view at all. We were as keen as mustard on an English title and a beautiful English estate, and Auntie started to stir my father up. He didn't take much stirring up. As soon as he realised that I wanted 'this toy', as he called it, and had ascertained, as he thought, that the title and estates were lying derelict and unclaimed, he decided to go for them all out. And when Pap makes a decision, he usually gets a move on, right away.

"Now, the first shock that he got was when he discovered that there was another claimant. Then he met Giles and his mother, and he fell in love with them both at first sight, as Auntie and I did. He didn't know how poor Giles was – he was actually working in a stock-broker's office, if you will believe me – but he realised that the decision of the court meant a lot more to Giles than it did to him, and he would have liked to back out of the claim."

"Why didn't he?" I asked.

"He couldn't. When once the claim had been raised, it had got to be settled. Giles didn't want the earldom as a gift, and Mr Brodribb wouldn't have let the case drop, with the chance of its being re-opened in the future. So it had to go on. And now see what Mr Gimbler did for us. Supposing he hadn't changed the coffins; and supposing the real one had been found to be stuffed with lead. It might have been. That would have gone a long way towards establishing my father's claim. Supposing the decision had gone in his favour. Then he would have been the Earl of Winsborough. And he would have hated it. Supposing I had married Giles – and I guess I should have had to ask him, myself, as he was a poor man and as proud as Lucifer – what would Pap's position have been? He would have defeated his own plans. He would have got the title for himself, and he would have kept his daughter and her husband out of it during his lifetime. But now, thanks to Mr Gimbler, we have all got what we wanted. Pap has escaped the title, and he has the satisfaction of seeing his girl Countess of Winsborough."

I smiled at her quaint and somewhat wrongheaded way of looking at the case. But I refrained from pointing out that "Mr Gimbler's gimblings" might easily have produced the undesired results but for Thorndyke's intervention. It was a dangerous topic, with my secret knowledge of what was in the real coffin. So I held my peace; or rather, led the conversation away from possible shoals and quicksands.

"By the way," I said, "if Giles had no money, who was going to pay his costs if he had lost the case?"

"I don't know," she replied. "We suspect dear old Brodribb. He told Giles and his mother that 'there were funds available,' but he wouldn't say what they were. Of course, it is all right now. But you haven't told me what happened to Mr Gimbler."

"You will be relieved to hear that he was let off quite lightly. Three years. It might easily have been seven, or even fourteen. Probably it would have been if we had included the forgery in the charges against him."

"I suppose it really was a forgery?"

"Yes, it was undoubtedly. For your father's satisfaction, we tested it chemically – but not until after the conviction. The ink was a modern synthetic drawing-ink. But it was a wonderfully skilful forgery."

"Pity," Jenny commented. "He is a really clever and ingenious man. Why couldn't he have run straight? But now tell me about the other people. There was an undertaker man, who made the coffin. What happened to him?"

"Joseph Wallis was his name. He also had better luck than he deserved, for he got only three months. It was originally proposed to charge him and Gimbler together with conspiracy. But there is this awkward peculiarity about an indictment for conspiracy in which only two persons are involved; if one of them is acquitted, the other is acquitted automatically. For a conspiracy is like a quarrel; it can't be a single-handed job. A man can't conspire with himself. So if, of two alleged conspirators, one is found innocent, it follows that there was no conspiracy, and the other man must be innocent, too.

"Now, Joseph pleaded that he had no knowledge of the purpose for which the coffin was required; thought it was a practical joke or a wager. And this plea was supported by Gimbler, who, in a statement to the police, declared that he never told Joseph what the coffin was really wanted for. Which seems likely enough. So the conspiracy charge against Joseph was dropped; and, of course, it had also to be dropped in respect of Gimbler."

"I am glad," said Jenny, "that the Slithy Tove, as Giles calls him, was man enough to clear his confederate."

"Yes, it is something in his favour; though we must bear in mind that the Tove was a criminal lawyer – in more senses than one – and knew all about the law of conspiracy. Is there anything else that you want to know?"

"There was a man named Bunter; but I don't think he was much concern of ours, was he?"

"He was an invaluable link in the chain of evidence," I replied, "though he seems rather outside the picture. However, I can report favourably on his case, for he got off altogether. Nobody wanted his blood. The police accepted his explanation of his attempt to break into the yacht, *Cormorant*, for, though it was probably untrue, it was quite plausible. There remained only his complicity in the platinum robbery. But that had been committed outside British jurisdiction; and, as the platinum had been recovered and restored to its lawful owners, and as the principal robbers were dead, no one was inclined to move in the matter. Accordingly, Mr Frederick Bunter was released and went on his way rejoicing, with only one or two slight stains on his otherwise spotless character. And I think that completes the list, unless you can think of anything more."

"No," she answered, "I think that finishes up the history of the Winsborough Peerage Case. A queer story it is, looking back on it, with its ups and downs, its hopes and anxieties, to say nothing of one or two ugly passages."

"Yes," I agreed, "there have been some anxious moments. But all's well that ends well."

"Very true," said she. "And it has ended very well indeed; for me and for Giles, for our parents and for Arminella. We have all got what we wanted most, we are all happy and contented, and we are all tremendously pleased with one another. It couldn't have ended better. And to think that we owe it all to poor Mr Gimbler!"

I smiled, but I didn't contradict her. It was a harmless delusion. Perhaps it was not a delusion at all. At any rate, one might fairly say of Mr Horatio Gimbler that he builded better than he knew.

# R Austin Freeman

## The D'Arblay Mystery
### A Dr Thorndyke Mystery

When a man is found floating beneath the skin of a green-skimmed pond one morning, Dr Thorndyke becomes embroiled in an astonishing case. This wickedly entertaining detective fiction reveals that the victim was murdered through a lethal injection and someone out there is trying a cover-up.

## Felo De Se
### A Dr Thorndyke Mystery

John Gillam was a gambler. John Gillam faced financial ruin and was the victim of a sinister blackmail attempt. John Gillam is now dead. In this exceptional mystery, Dr Thorndyke is brought in to untangle the secrecy surrounding the death of John Gillam, a man not known for insanity and thoughts of suicide.

# R Austin Freeman

## Flighty Phyllis

Chronicling the adventures and misadventures of Phyllis Dudley, Richard Austin Freeman brings to life a charming character always getting into scrapes. From impersonating a man to discovering mysterious trapdoors, *Flighty Phyllis* is an entertaining glimpse at the times and trials of a wayward woman.

## Helen Vardon's Confession
### A Dr Thorndyke Mystery

Through the open door of a library, Helen Vardon hears an argument that changes her life forever. Helen's father and a man called Otway argue over missing funds in a trust one night. Otway proposes a marriage between him and Helen in exchange for his co-operation and silence. What transpires is a captivating tale of blackmail, fraud and death. Dr Thorndyke is left to piece together the clues in this enticing mystery.

# R Austin Freeman

## Mr Pottermack's Oversight

Mr Pottermack is a law-abiding, settled homebody who has nothing to hide until the appearance of the shadowy Lewison, a gambler and blackmailer with an incredible story. It appears that Pottermack is in fact a runaway prisoner, convicted of fraud, and Lewison is about to spill the beans unless he receives a large bribe in return for his silence. But Pottermack protests his innocence, and resolves to shut Lewison up once and for all. Will he do it? And if he does, will he get away with it?

## The Mystery of Angelina Frood
### A Dr Thorndyke Mystery

A beautiful young woman is in shock. She calls John Strangeways, a medical lawyer who must piece together the strange disparate facts of her case and, in turn, becomes fearful for his life. Only Dr Thorndyke, a master of detection, may be able to solve the baffling mystery of Angelina Frood.

'Bright, ingenious and amusing' - *The Times Literary Supplement*

1538095R0

Printed in Great Britain by
Amazon.co.uk, Ltd.,
Marston Gate.